Praise for
Wonders Will Never Cease

"I have friends who love smart, deep fantasy novels, and can never find enough. Robert Irwin's novel *The Arabian Nightmare* was one of my favourite books of the early 1980s and one of the finest fantasies of the last century. His newest novel, *Wonders Will Never Cease*, is as erudite and well-constructed a historical fiction as *The Arabian Nightmare*, but is set in a medieval England that never quite was, and uses stories and fictions to illuminate and to make us gasp with awe. It's also often genuinely funny and quite beautifully written."

—Neil Gaiman in *Authors at Christmas*

"Robert Irwin's latest novel has much in common with *Game of Thrones*. Both are based on the gory struggle of the Wars of the Roses, both inject large amounts of magic and the occult into their narratives, and both are hugely enjoyable, fast-moving and filled with dark humour. . . . As one character observes: 'The real world is a poor thing compared to the stories that are told about it.'"

—*Prospect Magazine*

"The novel is a sort of marriage between A. S. Byatt and Terry Pratchett: one you can enjoy greatly on the first reading, but which will be even better second time round, as it's so densely packed with learning and allusions. . . . Bravo."

—Tibor Fischer, *Guardian*

"Extraordinary . . . After closing this book, its spell still lingers. Irwin has brilliantly refashioned medieval history as a myth for our time."

—Andrew Crumey, *Literary Review*

"He intertwines his central plot with myths and digressions worthy of Homer to transform what could easily be a dull report into something more mythical and magical. With disturbing tales, gruesome details of torture, a talking head and a museum of skulls, this novel will keep you in the Halloween spirit."

—*Buzz Magazine*

"One might conclude from these descriptions that Robert Irwin believes history and fiction to be indistinguishable. But this rather pedestrian interpretation fades away beside the enthralling delights of narrative, life itself to Scheharazade. This is a novel crammed with wonders."

—*Times Literary Supplement*

"A dazzling compendium of a golden age of storytelling . . . *Wonders Will Never Cease* completely lives up to its promise, expertly and meaningfully blending myths and reality in a way that the author hasn't done quite as spectacularly since *The Arabian Nightmare*."

—*Digital Fix/Geek Life*

"The miracle of *Wonders Will Never Cease* is the wedding of all this vivid but essentially verifiable material with what one might tentatively identify as the stories that told the tales to those who lived them: the fables, legends, flesh-out sententiae, songs, all couched as though time were a shuttlecock."

—*Strange Horizons*

"Meticulously and exquisitely researched, in astonishing detail, the book is soaked through with myths, legends and folklore. . . . The prose is beautifully lyrical and completely captures the reader as they wind through the many threads within. Highly recommended."

—*Historical Novel Society Review*

"'It's a book about stories and the way we react to them. It's about changes in the world, about religion, about knowing what is real and what isn't. It's about something in the distance that we can't explain, something glimpsed out of the corner of our eyes. . . . It is a most entertaining read. It is a wonderful book."
—clothesinbooks.blogspot

"Robert Irwin's most recent novel, *Wonders Will Never Cease*, is in many ways a return to the form of his first, *The Arabian Nightmare*. . . . As in *The Arabian Nightmare*, the boundaries between the imaginary and the 'real' become very porous, and the reader is ultimately left with no defence against the fact that the contents of the book are all a story, but such a manifold and self-devouring story as to make one question the 'reality' of the reader as well."

—*Hermetic Library*

WONDERS *Will* NEVER CEASE

WONDERS *Will* NEVER CEASE

A Novel

ROBERT IRWIN

Arcade Publishing • New York

First North American Edition 2017

First published in the United Kingdom in 2016 by Dedalus Limited

This is a work of fiction. Names, places, characters, and incidents are either the products of the author's imagination or are used fictitiously.

Arcade Publishing books may be purchased in bulk at special discounts for sales promotion, corporate gifts, fund-raising, or educational purposes. Special editions can also be created to specifications. For details, contact the Special Sales Department, Arcade Publishing, 307 West 36th Street, 11th Floor, New York, NY 10018 or arcade@skyhorsepublishing.com.

Arcade Publishing® is a registered trademark of Skyhorse Publishing, Inc.®, a Delaware corporation.

Visit our website at www.arcadepub.com.

10 9 8 7 6 5 4 3 2 1

Library of Congress Cataloging-in-Publication Data

Names: Irwin, Robert, author.
Title: Wonders will never cease : a novel / Robert Irwin.
Description: First North American edition. | New York, NY : Arcade Publishing, 2017.
Identifiers: LCCN 2017018012 (print) | LCCN 2017024100 (ebook) | ISBN 9781628728644 (eBook) | ISBN 9781628728637 (print : alk. paper)
Subjects: | GSAFD: Fantasy fiction.
Classification: LCC PR6059.R96 (ebook) | LCC PR6059.R96 W66 2017 (print) | DDC 823/.914--dc23
LC record available at https://lccn.loc.gov/2017018012

Cover design by Erin Seaward-Hiatt
Cover illustration: iStockphoto

Printed in the United States of America

'*The aim of the wise is to make wonders cease.*'
Albertus Magnus, De Coelo et Mundo

'*A thing that has not been understood inevitably reappears;
like an unlaid ghost, it cannot rest until the mystery has been
solved and the spell broken.*'
Sigmund Freud,
'Analysis of a Five-Year-Old Boy: Little Hans'

Contents

List of Characters ix

CHAPTER ONE   Towton .1
CHAPTER TWO   Crowland 17
CHAPTER THREE   Gerfalcon 30
CHAPTER FOUR   Coronation 45
CHAPTER FIVE   Alnwick 60
CHAPTER SIX   Corbenic. 85
CHAPTER SEVEN   Wedding 112
CHAPTER EIGHT   Tiltyard. 131
CHAPTER NINE   White Tower. 171
CHAPTER TEN   Joust. .197
CHAPTER ELEVEN   Manhunt. 222
CHAPTER TWELVE   Sea Battle 248
CHAPTER THIRTEEN   Exile .257
CHAPTER FOURTEEN   Barnet. 272
CHAPTER FIFTEEN   Coterels 291
CHAPTER SIXTEEN   Compostella 302
CHAPTER SEVENTEEN   *Locus Amoenus* 317
CHAPTER EIGHTEEN   Ludlow 339

About the Author 353

List of Characters

(All those listed here really existed.)

The House of Lancaster:

Henry VI: Born in 1421, he was the only son of Henry V. He came to the throne as a minor in 1422.

Margaret of Anjou: Henry VI's Queen.

Edward of Lancaster, Prince of Wales: The son of Henry and Margaret.

The House of York:

Richard Duke of York: Claimant to the throne. He was slain at the Battle of Wakefield, shortly before the narrative of *Wonders Will Never Cease* begins.

Edward Duke of York: Son of Richard of York. Born 1422. Claimant to the throne and crowned in 1461 as Edward IV.

Elizabeth Woodville, from 1464 Edward's Queen. See below, 'Woodvilles'.

Edward, Prince of Wales: Son of Edward IV and Elizabeth, later briefly Edward V, April-June 1483.

Richard Duke of York: The younger brother of Edward V.

Richard, Edward IV's younger brother. Later Duke of Gloucester. Later Richard III.

George: Edward's youngest brother. Later Duke of Clarence. Executed 1478.

The Woodvilles:

Richard Woodville, Earl Rivers: Born c.1410.

Jacquetta de St Pol: Daughter of the Count of St Pol. Formerly married to John Duke of Bedford, Regent of Henry VI. After being widowed, she married Richard Woodville.

Anthony Woodville, Lord Scales: Born c.1422. The oldest son of Richard and Jacquetta and heir to the Earldom of Rivers. Jouster and scholar.

Elizabeth Woodville: Born c.1440. Daughter of Richard and Jacquetta. First married to Sir John Grey of Groby. After his death in battle, she married Edward IV. See above 'York'.

Other Lords:

Richard Neville, Earl of Warwick: Called 'The Kingmaker'. Born 1428.

George Neville: Archbishop of York and Chancellor of England in the early years of Edward IV's reign.

Henry Beaufort, Duke of Somerset: A leading Lancastrian.

James Butler, Earl of Wiltshire: A Lancastrian Lord.

William, Lord Hastings: Born c.1431. A leading Yorkist supporter and Edward IV's High Chamberlain.

John Tiptoft, Earl of Worcester: A Yorkist. Constable of England and a leading scholar.

Lord John Howard: Edward IV's Admiral.

Thomas Grey, Marquess Dorset: The elder son of Elizabeth Woodville and John Grey.

Ralph Grey: The younger son of Elizabeth and John Grey.

The Bastard Fauconberg: Otherwise known as Thomas Neville, Earl of Kent. A Yorkist.

Antoine: Known as 'the Bastard of Burgundy', or the 'Great Bastard', the illegitimate son of Philip III, Duke of Burgundy. A famous jouster.

The Gentry:

Sir Andrew Trollope: A prominent Lancastrian.

Sir Thomas Malory of Newbold Revel: A disorderly knight and marvellous writer.

John Paston: A landowner and letter writer.

Sundry:

John Littlington: Benedictine Abbot of Crowland.

The anonymous Crowland Chronicler: One of a series of contributors to the Crowland Chronicle, compiled from 655 to 1486.

George Ripley: Augustinian canon and alchemist in the service of Edward IV.

Scoggin, Edward IV's Fool: Alleged author of 'a book of merie jests'.

William Caxton: Mercer, merchant and the man who introduced printing to England.

Louys de Bretaylles, a French knight: Owner of a manuscript, Les Dits Moraux des Philosophes.

The Coterels: A London criminal family.

WONDERS *Will* NEVER CEASE

CHAPTER ONE

Towton

Anthony Woodville, the Lord Scales, is one of those who sustain the King of England's cause against that contumacious rebel, York. It is Palm Sunday, the beginning of Holy Week, and the dawn before battle. Consequently Anthony kneels to receive the wafer that is dipped in the wine that is Christ's blood. Mass is being celebrated in the largest of the pavilions which is that of the Duke of Somerset. The pavilion's canvas billows inward before the fierce wind. *'Hoc est corpus meum.'* The Duke's chaplain, as he intones these words, is weeping for the multitude that must be slain today, but Anthony has no tears to shed, for he is young and knows that he will live forever and, though young, he is already an expert in despatching men to meet their Maker. He gazes on the sacramental chalice and ponders the paschal miracle. He and his fellows have feasted on the body of Christ. *'Ita, missa est,'* declares the chaplain. Go, it is the dismissal.

His father Richard Woodville, Earl Rivers is in the arming tent before him. While their armour is being brought out from the barrels of sand, a squire plies them both with jugs of wine. Neither man has ever fought a battle sober. Once outside the tent, they stroke their horses farewell before the beasts are led away by the grooms. Though the grooms wished to know why King Henry was not with his army, but instead lingered in York, they received no direct reply from their masters, except Rivers telling them, 'Somerset will know how to deal with the rebels. We have the numbers and the high ground and we serve the anointed King. Victory is certain and we shall give no quarter.'

Anthony nods and hefts his poleaxe. Besides the poleaxe, a shortsword hangs from his hip. The meadow where the fighting is to take place, close by the village of Towton, soon to be known as the Bloody Meadow, had only a few years earlier been cropland, but now, like so much of England, has become waste. All over the kingdom the waste can be seen coming down from the hills. The Lancastrian vanguard is commanded by the Earl of Northumberland and Sir Andrew Trollope. The Woodville father and son are part of the second line under the command of Somerset. They stand a little distance away from the Duke's banner, which displays the arms of England quartered with those of France within a blue-and-white chequered border. Earl Rivers's own banner shows a pitcher and magpie. From where the Woodvilles stand there is little to be seen and the snow which has just started to fall is blowing in their faces, but the word has been passed through the ranks that Edward of York's archers are starting their advance across Towton meadow and they are heading towards the crest of the rise that is commanded by the Lancastrians. Perhaps the second line will see no fighting, for the Yorkists will find it hard to advance up the slope. In any case the Woodvilles are waiting until the last moment before lacing their helmets.

He waits and says nothing to his father. There is no word yet for what Anthony feels. He thirsts for violence, danger, quests and new and unheard of things. He hates the waiting under a leaden sky and then, after the fighting shall be done, he fears for a tomorrow that will be followed by many other days that will perfectly resemble that tomorrow. Daily life is more frightening to him than a sword thrust. If only armies could just rush against one another like stags in a forest. Alas, there has to be so much done first, in the way of mustering, travelling, feeding and arming. Life is too slow.

Then they hear of a commotion in the front line of

men-at-arms. The blue lion rampant of the banner of North-umberland is seen moving forward. Somerset's line is under orders to follow. The devil has set the weather against the Lancastrian archers, for their arrows have been falling short while the Yorkist arrows travel swiftly on the wind. There is no help for it but to descend from their point of vantage and engage with the enemy directly. On the meadow Anthony finds himself in a series of tight melées. For a while the beasts of England—wyverns, unicorns, boars, lions, griffins, yales and dragons—seem to be in combat over their heads, as the men-at-arms struggle to keep the banners aloft in the great press, but soon the banners are down. Though Anthony is able at times to use his poleaxe to steady himself, there is no possibility of wielding it in such a scrum. He and his men, as they press against the enemy, tread through the bloody slush, churn up the mud and trample on the bodies of friend and foe. By now, despite the snow-laden bitter wind, Anthony feels himself to be encased in a furnace and, unless he can find a space in which to unlace his helmet, he will surely pass out.

Providentially it seems, the press around him thins and he can unlace his helmet, but, having done so, he hears the screaming and wailing carried on the wind. Now that he can at last gaze over the field, he sees that all around him his fellows are in retreat. He lets his helmet fall and runs with them. A breathless squire shouts to him that Somerset and Wiltshire have found their horses and are already fled. Rivers is nowhere to be seen. Anthony follows the great mass of the Lancastrian foot who are hastening to the right down a steep slope which descends to the Cock River. It is difficult to keep his footing. The trap is closing in on them and the killing time has begun. Already many have perished trying to wade through the fast-flowing water, so many that Anthony runs on a bridge of bodies, but he is safe across the river and he exults.

Then it seems to him that he has been asleep. He feels well. The howling wind has died down and there is no shouting and screaming, but he hears a gentle voice intoning 'Follow the light. Follow the light.' White-robed figures get him to rise and they usher him up through a brightly lit tunnel until he comes out before a castle in a forest. Snow is still falling and Anthony should find lodging for the night. He knocks at the gate of the castle. There is a long wait before the gate is opened and, then after his wounds have been inspected, he is allowed to enter, but when he seeks to proceed on into the great hall to make his plea for hospitality, he cannot. Though he is angry and insulted to find his way barred, even so he stands at the door, waiting and looking in, for he knows that something is about to happen. It is bright within, for the light of scores of torches is reflected off walls that have been painted silver and gold. At the far end he can see a figure with a face that has been painted white. He is propped up by cushions on a pallet. This man, who must be very sick, wears a golden crown made of paper set at a precarious angle.

Anthony has only just enough time to register this before the procession begins to cross the middle of the hall from right to left. It is led by a maiden of extraordinary beauty with a bloody cloth round her neck and she carries a broken sword. She is followed by a man who bears a lance whose tip is stained blood red, then six maidens bearing candelabras, and after them a priest who is bent under the weight of a thing which is covered in a mantle of red samite. The last in the procession is a huntsman who supports a white gerfalcon on his wrist. Not a word is uttered by the celebrants or by those who look on. The colours of everything that Anthony looks on are of extraordinary purity: the red robe of the 'King', the green dresses of the maidens, the purple cassock of the priest and the blue jerkin of the huntsman. It is like a child's image of a sacred mystery. The calm that Anthony feels is more powerful than any passion that he has ever experienced.

Since the ceremony is now over, Anthony turns away, and, as he does so, he sees that Sir Andrew Trollope has been standing just behind him. He has sustained a nasty wound in the fighting, though it does not seem to trouble him any more. There are other knights beside Sir Andrew, but Anthony recognises none of them, nor their blazons. Though he is very glad to find a familiar face in this place of mystery, Andrew seems not so pleased.

'Friend, I am sorry to see you. What do you do here?' he asks.

Anthony, feeling at peace, does not know how to reply to this. What is he doing here?

Then Andrew points back to the crowned man lolling on the pallet.

'He is pretending to be our King,' he says. 'See how he writhes as if he suffers from a terrible wound.'

Anthony is still at a loss for words. If he did speak, he senses that it would be like trying to talk underwater. Suddenly Andrew seems impatient to be away.

'I am summoned to a feast,' he says. 'Friend, will you not join me? Come dine with me for fellowship's sake.' He smiles and tries to pluck at Anthony's sleeve, but at his touch, Anthony, strangely terrified, faints.

When he comes round, he wakes to a body of pain. He lies with his eyes shut while he locates that pain, which is mostly above his left hip and at the back of his head. Stripped of his armour and padding, he is naked and cold. Then he opens his eyes and finds himself on the stone floor of a small dark chamber and a scrawny balding priest in a brown robe is bending over him and plucking at the lead figurine of a little man that is attached to a chain round Anthony's neck. When the priest sees that Anthony's eyes are open he draws back in surprise. Anthony gazes dispassionately at him. Then he asks, 'Where am I?'

'My lord, this is the Chapel of Aberford. You have been dead for two days, I think. This is the third. Some women, six women, carried your corpse here on a bier, asking that you might be buried beside the Chapel. They told me that yours

was the corpse of Lord Scales, as could be seen from your surcoat and they left money for your burial. Indeed, you should
have been buried already, only the ground was too hard for
the gravediggers and besides they had plenty of work elsewhere. There is your shroud.'

The white cloth lies close beside Anthony. The priest, recollecting himself, throws the shroud over Anthony's lower
parts. Then he grows excited, 'But you are a new Lazarus!
How is it to die? What did you see on the other side? Is there a
purgatory, or is there, as some men say, only heaven and hell?
Are there animals in the afterlife? What shapes do men have
after they are dead? Is it true that the saved can look down on
the damned?...'

The priest has many more questions, but Anthony cuts
him off, 'I was never dead. I was in a castle in the middle of a
forest. Which castles are near this place?'

'There are many castles in this shire. Though I do not know
of a castle in a forest, I never travel far from this holy place.'

The priest helps Anthony to a bed and for the next three
days he rests. Though he has asked the priest about the whereabouts of Lord Rivers, Sir Andrew Trollope, King Henry and
others, the piously narrow-minded priest knows nothing of
the affairs of the great men of state. But he is well-versed in
the Bible and returns again and again to the subject of Lazarus
and how he had lain sick unto death in Bethany and when
Jesus was told of this he delayed his coming to that town.
He waited until Lazarus was dead and the worms of sin and
decay held carnival in the poor man's body. Only on the fourth
day did Jesus enter Bethany and, though Lazarus's body was
already stinking, Jesus commanded him to come forth from
the dead, saying, 'Whosoever lives and believes in me shall
never die'.

Anthony wants to know why Jesus waited four days before
coming to the rescue of Lazarus. He is told that Jesus had
determined on a miracle, a sacred wonder, so that believers

might be encouraged and unbelievers damned. The priest continues, 'For those who were there to witness it, it was a miracle; for those of us who come after, it is a story of a special sort which we call a parable.'

'What is a parable?'

'A parable is a story which refers to something other than what the story seems to be about. Every incident or adventure related in the Bible has four meanings...'

But Anthony sinks back into delirium without learning what the four levels of meaning might be. He thinks that he hears himself ask the priest, 'Why just Lazarus? Why did Jesus not raise all the dead in Bethany? Or all the dead in the world since the beginning of creation?' But, if there is an answer to this, he cannot hear it, and in any case what he was really asking was 'Why me?'

On the fourth day Yorkist men-at-arms come to seize Anthony. They have heard rumours that a Lancastrian rebel lord was being sheltered in the chapel.

'We will take you outside. You may say your prayers first, for you are a dead man, Lord Scales,' the sergeant tells Anthony, before he begins to read out the bill of attainder:

'At Towton, in the shire of York, accompanied with Frenchmen and Scots, the King's enemies, the following lords falsely and traitorously against their faith and liegeance, there raised war against King Edward, their rightwise, true and natural liege lord, purposing there and then to have destroyed him, and deposed him of his royal estate, crown and dignity, and then and there to that intent, falsely and traitorously moved battle against his said estate, shedding therein blood of a great number of his subjects. In which battle it pleased almighty God to give unto him, of the mystery of his might and grace, the victory of his enemies and rebels, and to avoid the effect of their false and traitorous purpose. Whereupon the following traitors are condemned to death...'

At this point the sergeant pauses and he runs his finger and his eyes down the long list of those who are so condemned. Reading is difficult for him and he tries again. His lips move as he struggles with one name after another. Then, 'You say you are the Lord Scales?'

'I am Lord Scales.'

'Your name is not here.' The sergeant hesitates before going from the chapel to confer with some of his comrades who are mustered outside.

When the sergeant returns, he is smiling, 'All is well. You were thought to be slain on the field, but, if by God's mercy you were to be found alive, then our orders are to bring you before King Edward and your father, the High Constable of England, Lord Rivers.'

This makes no sense. As Anthony closes his eyes, he hears the priest exclaim, 'Now you have bested Lazarus, for this is the second time that you have risen from the grave!'

A little later, Anthony is helped onto a cart which will carry him to York. Though it is undignified, there is no help for it since he is very weak from his wounds. The roads are rutted and the way is painful. The wound in his side reopens and has to be dressed once more. Anthony is often feverish, but in his lucid intervals he learns of the extent of Edward's victory and of the battle's aftermath. It is thought that there were 200,000 men at the Battle of Palm Sunday and a great proportion of this number were slain. But were there ever so many men in England? Welles, Morley and John Neville were among those dead on the battlefield and, though gentlemen, they were pitched into mass graves with the commoners. Northumberland has died of his wounds in York. King Henry, Queen Margaret and the Duke of Somerset are fled to Scotland. Wiltshire is also fled. The cause of Lancaster is judged to be at an end. But Anthony's escort has no detailed knowledge of Lord Rivers and his place in the new order.

As they travel, he asks the sergeant to let him see the bill of attainder. Not only is his name not on it, but neither is that of

the military adviser to the Duke of Somerset, Sir Andrew Trollope. Anthony knew Andrew from of old. Andrew had started
out as a man-at-arms and risen from the ranks under the command of Earl Rivers in the French war. Later, he had fought
at Wakefield and had been knighted after St Albans. If only
Anthony can find him, he can learn the name of the castle.

He asks the sergeant if he has had word of where Sir Andrew
is now and learns that Andrew was another of those slain on
the battlefield. Andrew had continued to fight until both his
arms were severed. Anthony should be sad, but instead he is
angry with the spectral dream figure which had so deceived
him and invited him to what he now knows would have been
an insubstantial feast. Then, recollecting himself, he feels
angry with himself at having been so easily deceived. Dreams
are for people who have failed to find enough excitement in
their waking lives. The mysterious procession he witnessed in
the unnamed castle had no meaning.

Though the feverish spells diminish, he still has occasional
visions in bright heraldic colours of arms rising from the
water, of a passage up a mountain through a forest that is on
fire, of a table laden with rotting food, and he awakes from
these visions full of foreboding. The way is slow, but Anthony
is not impatient to reach his destination, for he dreads seeing
his father once again. This should be a joyous occasion, but
he knows that it will be no such thing and he tries to rehearse
the argument that they must have.

Once in York, he is helped out of the cart. A crutch has
been found for him and he is supported into the cathedral
close where he finds his father sitting under a blossoming
hawthorn tree. His father rises and they embrace. His father
looks hard at him and runs his hand over Anthony's face and
torso as if to reassure himself that this is his son and he is still
alive. Then his father sinks down back to the ground and the
recriminations begin.

'I lost sight of you on the field,' says Anthony. He cannot

stop himself. 'Where did you go? Had you already gone to sell your sword to the Duke of York?'

His father slumps back down, resumes his resting place against the tree and gestures that Anthony should join him on the ground, but he will not and instead, though it is painful for him to be propping himself upright, stands looking down on his father.

'The sun of York has brought us better weather. You must learn to call Edward King... And it was not like that,' says his father. 'Seeing that Northumberland was in trouble, I went to his assistance, or tried to, but was unable to cut my way through to his banner and when I realised that I could not, I then saw that all around me were retreating and I did what they did, but I was captured before I could reach the horse park. After such a battle I knew that the cause of Lancaster was forever lost, so, when I was brought before Edward, I submitted to him and begged for pardon and that great prince showed me mercy and even favour and so it is that I remain High Constable of England. If I have sold my sword, I have bought your head with it, Anthony. Edward has spared your life also and you may find preferment with him. I thought that I had already lost you. To lose –'

But Anthony is impatient, 'Then I should be forsworn as you are forsworn. Forsworn and damned.'

'You should smile and thank your father for your life. Now tell me how you think you are forsworn.'

By now they were shouting at one another. Attracted perhaps by the shouting, a man comes and stands close enough to listen to the argument. He wears a jerkin crudely stitched together from sackcloth and his legs are sheathed in scuffed brown leather. His narrow bony face is clouded with anxiety and he makes a supplicatory gesture, as if he is about to ask Anthony and his father to calm down, or at least lower their voices. But perhaps he is merely about to beg for money. They decide to ignore him.

'It is not what I think, but what I know. We both knelt and swore before God fealty to King Henry. It is a fearful thing to break an oath given before God.'

But his father has anticipated this.

'Yes, it is so,' he agrees. 'An oath before God indeed! Then how must it be with King Henry who on the day of his coronation swore before God's power to cause Law and Justice in Mercy to be executed in all his judgements and to keep peace in the kingdom? This he has not done.

Do you remember how young Rutland was slaughtered? And do you remember how the Earl of Devonshire's men surrounded the house of the lawyer, Nicholas Radford and entreated him to come down from his chamber, promising him that he should endure no bodily harm. So Radford descended. His rooms were looted and he was told that he must go to talk with the Duke and Radford said that he would ride there straightaway, whereupon he was told that all his horses were taken away. Then Radford said to the Duke's son, who was their leader, "Sir, your men have robbed my chamber, and they have my horses that I may not ride with you to my Lord your father. Wherefore I pray you let me ride, for I am old and cannot walk." But he was told that he must walk and when he was just a slingshot from his house, nine men fell upon the old man and cut his throat...'

Now the man in sackcloth butts in, 'A certain gentleman was getting drunk in a tavern and his companions decided to play a prank upon him. So one of them slipped out and turned the saddle on his horse the other way about. Then, when they all met in the tavern the following evening, they asked him how he had got home the previous night. 'You do well to ask,' he replied. 'When I got out I found that some evil-minded person had cut my horse's head off and I had to guide the horse home with my finger stuck up its windpipe... Ah hah hah hah! You must laugh, yet, gentle sirs, you both look so grim and glum.'

He pauses to pull an exaggeratedly gloomy face before

continuing, 'Scoggin is the name! It is sure that all that befell Radford was long ago and old Scoggin thinks that now it is the Maytime, it is time for us all to be jolly.'

Earl Rivers waves his hand as if he would swat a fly.

'Go away. We are busy and have no time for beggars.'

'But, my lord, forgive Scoggin, for you are mistaken. Scoggin is no beggar. He is here to entertain you with a hundred merry jests and capers. He does not beg for money, for everyone knows that a fool and his money are easily parted. Instead he seeks for livery and maintenance, for he presents himself here to be your household fool. Ta ra!'

Rivers ignores Scoggin and continues, 'Was Radford's end not pitiful? Where then was the King's justice? And think on how the Duke of Suffolk was betrayed on his way to Calais and his head cut off with half a dozen strokes from a rusty sword and that head left on the sand at Dover. How many crimes and atrocities must I list? Under Henry, misgovernance, unrest, inward war and trouble, foolish counsels, shedding and effusion of innocent blood, abuse of laws, partiality, riot, extortion, murder, rape and vicious living have been the guiders and leaders of the noble realm of England. Moreover, he has lost us our kingdom in France. A King cannot seat himself on a throne and think to himself "Now that I am King, I can do whatever I want", for a coronation is in truth a contract that is binding on both parties.'

Scoggin cannot contain himself, 'Once a King always a King: once a knight is enough! Ah ha ha ha!'

He is ignored. Rivers continues, 'Henry owed his subjects good lordship and this he has failed to provide. Moreover, he has broken the Act of Accord that was ratified by the lords and parliament last year. According to that Act, Edward's father Richard and Edward after him were declared to be Henry's heirs and successors to the crown when Henry should die or abdicate. Now, Henry broke his oath and did not conform to the Act of Accord and indeed he had Richard of York slain and his severed head wearing a paper crown, impaled on the Micklegate Bar at York. So no oaths taken to such a perjured King can be binding.'

'Perjured or not, Henry is still King. He has not died or abdicated.'

'Oh, but he has abdicated. He has abandoned his kingdom, for by his flight to the Scots, who are England's enemies, Henry must be deemed to have abdicated his rule.'

Before Anthony can interrupt, his father hurries on, 'The rule of the house of Lancaster was from the first based on violence not blood-right. All the line of Lancaster must be deemed usurpers, as more than half a century ago, Henry IV rose against King Richard II and had him murdered. When King Richard died, his heir should have been Edmund Mortimer, the grandson of the second son of Edward III and since then it is from the line of Mortimer that York, his cousin, derives his true right to the throne. In this world a man who is ignorant of genealogy is lost. Genealogy and heraldry are the only two sciences worth knowing.'

'This is wise. Scoggin wishes that he was so clever,' says the would-be jester, stroking his chin. Then he continues, 'Sirs, though I am nobody who comes from nowhere, yet through your good lordship I can become somebody. Though I have no past, you can give me a future.' And to Anthony, he says, 'You have a most pretty face. Surely it betokens kindness?'

Richard had been speaking urgently, for he knows that he is speaking for the life of his son. But now he pauses, distracted by Scoggin's interruption and momentarily at a loss for further arguments.

Then Anthony rushes in, 'It is a great shame to depose such a holy man, for Henry is a sainted King whose prayers have sustained and protected the kingdom.'

'Ha ha!'

Richard's laugh is mirthless. Anthony realises that he has never heard his father laugh at anything humorous. After the rhetorical laugh, Richard continues, 'So we have known government by a sainted innocent, have we? How many miracles has our saint performed? The truth is that Henry is capricious, cruel, cowardly and mad. Because of Henry Bolingbroke's usurpation, God has made the kingdom desolate and cursed his grandson with madness, just as he cursed Nebuchadnezzar, who was "made to eat grass as oxen" and "his hairs were grown like eagles' feathers, and his nails were like birds' claws". As for sainted Henry, his wits are gone and he can scarcely remember how to walk. He drools and, when he speaks, he speaks like a child...'

The image of a man propped up on a pallet and wearing a crown awry rose up in Anthony's mind. His father continued in full spate, 'Whereas Edward... Edward is the man who God has made King. At six feet and three inches, he is every inch a King, vigorous, courageous, resolute and generous. Edward does not skulk in a chapel, but he leads in battle.'

Now Scoggin has the impertinence to shake his finger in Earl Rivers's face.

'Edward is up and Henry is down. That is the way of the wheel of fortune, for it turns and turns. Watch and let Scoggin's shiny head be Edward and Scoggin's dirty feet be Henry.'

Then the grotesque creature begins a series of cartwheels that are designed to show that he who is on top shall one day be down and he who is beneath shall one day be above. Then he pauses to catch his breath before continuing, 'It is the same with Scoggin. You see how poorly he is apparelled. He does not have a cap and bells, nor his garb of motley, nor his pig's bladder. All the wherewithal of foolery are lacking to him, but one day it shall be different, his feet shall be above his head and he shall be acclaimed the King of Buffoons and it shall be Scoggin who presides over the Council of Fools.'

And the fool does a few more cartwheels to bring home his point.

But his father turns away and addresses Anthony, 'Those

who are wise will follow the man who is born to lead. There is no reward for stupidity, unless it be the gallows or the headsman's block. Are you hearing me, Anthony? Could you not stop shifting about for a single moment?'

Now Scoggin, who brightens at the word 'stupidity', jumps in with a new interruption, 'Scoggin was not always thus. He has spent seven years as a hermit telling his beads and hoping for visions, at the end of which he had a vision of an angel who spoke to him, saying, "God has listened to your prayers and is minded to reward you for your piety. He offers you a choice between beauty and stupidity. Which will you have?" '

But Rivers has no interest in what might have been Scoggin's choice, 'Be off with you or I shall have you seized and whipped.'

'Scoggin shall go. But over the years Scoggin has noticed that those he thinks ill of always come to a bad end. We will meet again in different circumstances and up shall be down and down shall be up.' And with that prophecy the would-be fool starts to shuffle off. But suddenly he turns and points a finger at Anthony and says, 'No man knows for sure whether he serves God or the Devil!'

Anthony wonders if this observation can possibly have been meant as a joke, as he watches Scoggin shuffle away.

Anthony who has come back from the dead has seen no cause for laughter. He watches the scrounging maledictory beggar depart before resuming the argument.

'I have heard you, but I am thinking that only three weeks ago you were happy enough to follow the man that you now denounce as a perjured imbecile. You were preaching no quarter to those who have now become your fellows. Have you forgotten that the Yorkists have slaughtered our friends? You are become the servant of those who killed Northumberland, Welles and Trollope, who were our companions. All that you have said is very clever, but that does not mean that you are right. If you were so minded, you could easily make a better case for Henry and a worse one for Edward—and, if the tide of war turns again, perhaps you will. Of course, you are cleverer than me and you will always be able to batter me down with your words, but you cannot make me believe you.'

'Will you not sit down? My neck hurts from gazing up at you. This century had barely started when I was born and I am now an old man. I am too old to face exile in France or, worse, seek refuge in the desolate wilds of Scotland. As a youth I served in France with the Duke of Suffolk and with Richard of York. They have both lost their heads, but I am still here, sitting in the sun and ready and able to serve the kingdom. If you will not pay homage to the new King, you too will be beheaded and I will be forced to watch. No man should have to witness the death of his child. Not only that, but if you should run off to Lancaster, then I will be incriminated and my head will be cut off. It is true that I am cleverer than you and it is because of this and because I am your father and because you must be sensible of the obedience that a son owes his father that you will obey me and make your peace with Edward.'

So it is that Anthony drops to the ground and joins his father under the hawthorn.

'You are young and it will soon be summer,' says his father comfortably. 'Now we must reunite you with your wife.'

CHAPTER TWO

Crowland

Homage has been paid to King Edward and Anthony has bound himself to attend the coronation that will soon be held in London. Now he rides out of York heading south to Doncaster and from there to Lincoln and on into Norfolk. The estates of the Barony of Scales are scattered round Bishop's Lynn. The county and the Scales estates within the county have become rich from the wool trade. A woman's beauty can receive an extra sheen from money and so it was with Elizabeth de Scales, sole daughter and heiress of Thomas Lord Scales, widow of Henry Bourchier, and now Anthony's wife. When Anthony had set out from the Manor of Middleton on his way to muster with the Duke of Somerset before the great battle, Elizabeth, or Beth rather, had still been dressing in black in deep mourning for Bourchier and she had denied Anthony her bed.

'It is too soon,' she had said. 'I need to grieve and pray that his soul is at peace.'

Heavy spring showers make the journey south difficult as well as painful. Happily his horse, a courser he has named Black Saladin, is sure-footed. Anthony travels through a ravaged land. Everywhere he notes abandoned farmsteads, cold harbours and forests that encroach again on land that had been theirs a century or more ago. He knows that there had once been more people in England. But then came the plagues and these were followed by the blood-letting at the battles of St Albans, then Blore Heath, Ludford, Northampton, Wakefield,

Mortimer's Cross and Palm Sunday. When will this curse be lifted from the kingdom? Perhaps those battles are the prelude to the End of the World.

It is possible that the hurling times are over and that Anthony will see no more battles in his lifetime. But his father has been shaped by and made cynical by past disasters. Above all, his father broods obsessively over his humiliation at Calais earlier in this year. Earl Rivers had been sent by Henry's Council to Sandwich where he was to organise the mustering of a fleet to assist the Duke of Somerset against the rebels in Calais who were commanded by Warwick and Edward of March, the son and heir of York. But before much of Earl Rivers' work was done, a Yorkist captain launched a surprise attack on Sandwich and not only sank some of the Lancastrian ships but captured Earl Rivers and Anthony and carried them off to Calais. There they were brought before Edward of March and the Earl of Warwick. When his father started to protest, Warwick had shouted him down and told him that he was 'the son of a squire and so not fit to talk to lords who were of the King's blood' and he added that Rivers was 'a knave who was not born of a noble lineage, but who had seduced his way to marrying into it'. Anthony continued to watch as Warwick berated his father as if he were a naughty schoolboy. Though the Woodvilles were released soon enough after this, since at that time Warwick and York still pretended loyalty to King Henry, Warwick's abuse continued to fester in River's mind.

Now that both Warwick and his father serve King Edward and sit in his Privy Council, Anthony wonders how things will turn out. He knows that his father thirsts for revenge and has a penchant for plots with long fuses. Anthony thinks that, if Warwick had been clever, he should have killed them both while he had the chance. Yet Anthony cannot die. And he will not allow himself to become an accomplice in his father's intrigues. Nor will he pay attention to his mother, Jacquetta's relaying of fairy whisperings. He thinks that he will shape his own story far away from the court.

He stops and rests at monasteries when he can. The talk at mealtimes is customarily about holy matters. The Priory of Holbeach is no more than a day's journey from Norfolk. There he has to attend a sermon in which the Prior dwells particularly on the virtue of chastity.

'Samson was undone by his lust for Delilah. Lancelot would have been judged a perfect knight had it not been for his adultery with Guinevere, after which his sin sent him running mad in the forest. Lust makes fools of all men. Love is a kind of madness that chains men to women. Bright eyes, golden hair and young flesh give enchantment, yet all end up in the grave as food for worms. It is written in Proverbs: "For the lips of a strange woman drop as an honeycomb, and her mouth is smoother than oil: but her end is bitter as wormwood, sharp as a two-edged sword. Her feet go down to death; her steps take hold on hell." May God never forgive him who wishes to honour and serve these passionate and impassioned whores who are worse than I can tell you. And consider these words from Corinthians: "Flesh and blood cannot inherit the kingdom of God; neither doth corruption inherit incorruption."'

The following day as Anthony rides on, he broods on the Prior's words, yet though he should meditate on the decay of mortal flesh and the steps that lead to hell, the image of Lady Scales rises up before him and he recalls her high-arched eyebrows, her arrogant face and the fleshy curves encased in a gleaming black dress—a promise not of Hell but of Paradise. As he considers her assumed piety and the difficulties she has made, his suspicions return. She is not really in mourning for her late husband, he thinks. The truth is that she has been lusting after handsome James Butler, the Earl of Wiltshire and 'the fairest knight of this land'. When they were at Eltham, he has watched how Beth gazed at Butler who was demonstrating some fancy piece of swordplay. Half the noblewomen in

England, including Anthony's own sister, have been dreaming of bedding him. Butler was slim and he had long, dark curly hair, piercing eyes and a strong chin. Though he was dubbed 'the fairest knight in all the land', he has also been called the 'flying earl' and men, most of them, liked him little and said of him that he fought 'mainly with his heels', since he had fled from the Battle of St Albans disguised as a monk, and he then had run away from Mortimer's Cross before the battle had even begun, dressed this time as a serving man. Still it was enviable to have been blessed with such looks.

By the time Anthony reaches Norfolk, he has resolved to put an end to his wife's playing at chaste mourning and to take her by storm, even if he should find her kneeling in the chapel where she pretends to pray for her dead husband. He spurs Black Saladin on.

It is night by the time he arrives at the Manor of Middleton. Once there, he brushes the servants aside and he runs up the stairs as urgently as if he were scaling a fortress and he flings open the door of the bedroom. The four-poster bed is surrounded by candles. By their light he can see that she is seated upright and terrified and beside her, also seated upright, is James Butler, who grins.

Anthony turns away shuddering. He had not guessed that there could be such horror in the world... for now he has seen his wife in bed with a dead man. At Towton, James Butler, 'the flying earl', had fled the field, but this time not fast enough and Yorkist horsemen caught up with him at Cockermouth and brought him to Newcastle, where, at the King's command, he was beheaded. The earl's head was then sent south and presently, so Anthony had heard, the head is displayed impaled on the gate of London Bridge. Though the thing he had seen in Beth's bed still had its head on its shoulders, James Butler, if it was he and not some simulacrum, could no longer be described as 'the fairest in the land', for his face was hideously gashed about and plastered with blood.

Anthony hurls himself downstairs and runs out to his courser and leaps into the saddle. His wife, barefoot and in her shift, comes running after him. She is crying out to him to take her with him, but he will not face her and he digs his spurs into Black Saladin's flanks and rides at a wallop, as if his wife were the spectre that was pursuing him. A little before dawn, he arrives at Crowland Abbey. The Abbey is a kind of closely guarded castle; the monks are its garrison against the wickedness of the world outside, and perhaps he should be safe here from the monstrous thing that he has seen in Elizabeth's bed. This Benedictine Abbey is particularly well-provisioned against any siege by demons, and indeed its monks pray and meditate in great comfort. Anthony is found lodgings in the most luxurious of the guest rooms in the Abbey's hostelry.

Having slept for many hours, towards the end of the day he asks to make confession. His confessor advises him to tell the Abbot about the apparitions.

'He will love hearing of this.'

As they make their way from the vespers service to the refectory for dinner, Anthony starts to talk about his visions of dead men. Abbot John Littlington smiles broadly, but puts a finger to his lips. They dine without speaking on roast bream and salted Cambridge eels with barley bread and Gascon wine. As they eat, a young monk standing at a lectern in front of the table reads the chapter in the life of St Guthlac in which the saint's participation in the Wild Hunt is described. After dinner the Abbot and some of the senior monks, including the Prior, the guest-master, the almoner, the librarian, the infirmarian, the cellarer and the Chronicler, process to the chapterhouse. Its hall is hung with tapestries, one of which shows the three dead and the three living Kings, a second the siege of Jerusalem and a third the instruments of the Passion. The monks are eager to hear from Anthony of the great battle in the north and the politics arising from the gathering of the Yorkist lords around Edward, but Anthony has little to say on these matters. Instead he hurries on to tell them how he has encountered two men who are dead but yet seemed as if they were alive.

'Now reverend sirs,' Anthony asks, 'Am I mad or am I cursed?'

Though he hopes that they will advise him on how to avoid any future visitations of the dead, in this he is disappointed.

The Abbot is a big man, vigorous in his movements and opinions. He is also a little drunk and he boisterously thumps the table so hard that it shakes.

'Certainly not mad!' he insists. 'The world is full of wonders and is not as the commonalty conceive of it. Did you hear what happened at Coggeshall only a few years ago? All the parishioners of Coggeshall witnessed it, for they were coming out from Sunday service. They saw before them an anchor attached to a rope and, though the ship was above and hidden in the clouds, they could hear the sailors trying to haul the rope up, but to no avail. At length one of the sailors came down the rope, hand under hand, whereupon he was seized by the church-goers who wanted to know what he did. Alas, he could not breathe in the moisture of our denser air and expired almost immediately.'

Anthony senses that the other monks had heard it all before. The infirmarian does not trouble to conceal his disdain.

The Abbot claps his hands.

'God has created marvellous things for us to marvel at! Rejoice and be astonished! Who has not heard of the green men and women who live in caves and under the ferns and who cannot speak English? And what do you say about the rain of frogs and toads that fell upon Tilbury only last year? Wise men know that one thing shades into another and there are no hard frontiers between the living and the dead, the animal and the vegetable, those who dwell in the sky and those who dwell on earth, for it is all a perfect continuum. Consider

the wondrous vegetable lamb of Tartary, which grows everywhere in the meadowlands inhabited by the Mongols. The
lamb, which has its roots in the earth, feeds on the grass
around it and then when it had eaten all the grass which the
lamb's stem allows it to reach it starves to death. But its seeds
give birth to other vegetable lambs. Our earth has trapdoors
that are hidden and strange things go in and out of them. Why
only last week here in Crowland we all saw a troupe of naked
men and women standing on the branches of a tree less than
a bowshot from the entrance to the Abbey! As we read in
the Dialogus Miraculorum of Caesarius of Heisterbach, God
sends us miracles as signposts to guide us to the greatest Miracle which is Himself.'

The Abbot spreads out his hands as if inviting Anthony to
come to the God of wonders, and Anthony replies, 'These are
marvels indeed. But I have seen Sir Andrew Trollope and the
Earl of Wiltshire, who were men I was familiar with but who
are now dead. How can this be?'

But the Abbot is at home in such matters and he replies,
'It would not be easy to believe that the corpses of the dead
should sally (I know not by what agency) from their graves,
and should wander about to the terror and destruction of the
living, and again return to the tomb, which of its own accord
spontaneously opened to receive them. Did not frequent
examples occur in our own times which suffice to establish
this fact, the truth of which there is abundant testimony?'

The Abbot's voice drops as he continues, 'Dead men walking are common enough and I could tell you many tales about
them. I will tell you just one. It is this. An evil man on the run
from the law fled from York and settled in a distant village and
married there. But he soon became suspicious of his wife and
so he hid in the rafters of their bedroom from where he was
able to observe her infidelity. But in so doing he was careless
and fell to the floor and his fall proved mortal for he died of
it a few days later. The man received a Christian burial even

though he, being the handiwork of Satan, did not deserve it and afterwards he was not suffered to remain in his grave but was pursued by a pack of dogs with horrible barkings, so that the people of the village were compelled to bolt their doors from sunset to sunrise for fear of encountering this horrible monster. Those who did stray from their homes were invariably killed.'

'In the end the villagers took spades to the man's grave and were surprised how little earth they had to clear before they found the corpse, swollen to an enormous corpulence and the face turgid and thick with blood and the monster's shroud mostly ripped to pieces. Anger gave courage to the young men beside the grave and they hacked at the corpse with the edges of their spades, whereupon so much blood poured out from it that they might have been attacking a sack full of leeches that had fed on many persons. Then, when they dragged the body to its pyre, they found that it would not burn until they had cut its heart out and then finally it did burn. Events such as these are warnings, calling us to a virtuous life. My lord, what you have seen is not so very unusual or important. Still I admit that I do envy you for your encounter with the creatures of the afterlife.'

His tale concluded the Abbot asked the Chronicler of Crowland to conduct Anthony to the scriptorium so that Anthony might dictate what he had seen at the Battle of Palm Sunday, as well as give an account of his ghostly visitations. (The Abbot was particularly interested and pleased to hear how the dead are conducted up along a tunnel of light to be greeted by men in white robes.)

Alone with the Chronicler Anthony asks, 'Am I mad or is the Abbot mad?'

'Our Abbot is a great man,' says the Chronicler sulkily before he sets to writing. He dutifully and briefly records what Anthony is prepared to tell him about the ghosts. But really he is more interested in what Anthony can tell him about his meetings with King Henry and King Edward, as well as the Battle of Palm Sunday.

'Do I have it right?' the Chronicler wants to know. 'I have never been in a fight.' He sounded wistful. Anthony tries to describe the battle, but in truth, so long as his visor was down, he had seen so little of the fighting—just the confusion and the crowds of armoured men pressing against one another. The Chronicler showed him what he had written already: 'The blood of the slain mixed with the snow, which covered the land at that time, and when the snow melted it flowed into furrows and ditches over an area of two or three miles in a most gruesome fashion'. Yes, that was how it had been and was it not strange that those carefully inked words should conjure it up so exactly? Anthony is impressed.

The Chronicler persists in questioning him about politics and warfare. Finally he puts his pen down and sighs.

'You and your peers make history whereas I merely record it. The names of Scales and Rivers are already famous and talked about, whereas my own name will be forgotten within a generation. Even now there are few enough people who know my name.'

(This must be true. Even though Anthony had been properly introduced to the Chronicler, he has already forgotten his name.)

Anthony turns over a few of the earlier pages of the chronicle. Most of it is the stuff of parish talk and a record of the remarkably few things that had happened to the Abbey and, above all, repeated praise of the deeds and wisdom of Abbot John Littlington. Indeed, the Abbot features more prominently in the chronicle than do King Henry or the Duke of York. Apart from Anthony's deposition, the most recent entry deals with the Abbot's inspection of a two-headed calf in a nearby village.

At this point the Abbot comes staggering in, 'My lord, it will soon be compline. Will you walk with me?'

As they walk towards the abbey church, the Abbot turns to Anthony, 'You say that you saw the Earl of Wiltshire, though dead, in the bed that you customarily share with your wife?'

Anthony nods and then the Abbot continues, 'According to St Augustine, "Passionate love for one's own wife is adultery." If you have had a vision of the Earl of Wiltshire in such a place, then it was to put a curb on your own lust for your wife. But what a wonder! I wish that I had been there to see it.'

Anthony is thankful that this was not the case. The Abbot has been no help at all. A little later, Anthony is listening to the evil-averting prayer of compline.

'*Scuto circumdabit te veritas ejus; non timebis a timore nocturno, a sagitta volante in die, a negotio perambulente in tenebris ab incursu et daemonio meridiano.*'

'His truth shall be thy shield and buckler. Thou shalt not be afraid for the terror by night; nor for the arrow that flieth by day. Nor for the pestilence that walketh in darkness; nor for the destruction that wasteth at noonday.'

Though there are no apparitions in the night, Anthony's sleep is fitful at best. First, he makes plans to escape the tedium of England and the wearisome factions that struggle for power at the English court. He wants to see the vegetable lamb of Tartary with his own eyes. He conjures up his future journey to distant lands where there are underground cities and smoking lakes and where men in conical hats walk amidst mountains built of bricks, while long-snouted creatures with teeth struggle out of the swamps. There is nothing for him in England, where everything is so old and familiar: old roads, old customs, old castles, old lineages, old feuds, old laws, old churches, old books and an old religion. Living in England is like camping in a graveyard.

But no sooner has his mind touched on the graveyard than it turns to less pleasant things. The fear comes upon him that some ghostly demon may smuggle itself into the monastery and make its way into his chamber. In fact, no demon visits him, but in his mind's eye again and again he imagines Lady Elizabeth de Scales raising the hem of her black satin skirt... And only now does it come to him as a thought that is vague and confused yet horridly powerful that the monster may already be in the room, already on the bed, for is he himself not the monster? And was not the Abbot's story a warning to those who are prey to demonic lust and jealousy? Though night is frightful, he fears the coming dawn more, for in the morning he will ride out and he knows that then he must return to Scales Hall to confront his wife and, if it must be, also the spectre that was her companion in bed.

The following morning he has an appointment with the infirmarian who is to inspect how well his wound is healing. The infirmary is in the form of a long aisle with bays running off it with beds in them. All the beds are empty and Anthony lies on one of them and, while the infirmarian runs his fingers over his scars, Anthony thinks about his visions and he fears that the seeing of such things may be a symptom of some weakness in himself. To his mind, a visionary is a sick man, no better than a cripple. At length he repeats the question he had asked of the Chronicler, 'Am I mad, or is the Abbot mad?'

The infirmarian replies, 'Neither of you is mad. Only the Abbot has an excessively sanguine temperament, arising from the richness of his red blood. You can see the redness in his face. This humour makes him eager for all things new and strange. Whereas, in your case, the melancholy humour has come upon you in the form of an excess of black bile which distempers your imaginative faculty. Just by looking at you, I can tell that your turds are black. But this may pass if you will follow my advice and it is this. You must seek to be only in the company of people who are young. So shun the old, the sick and the crippled. Only wear bright colours. Hawking, dancing and feasting are good for you and so is bedding young women. If you can afford it, take a jester into your service. Learn to laugh and smile, for ghosts can never appear before a man who is laughing. If you find yourself thinking deep thoughts, shake your head clear of them and instead take your horse and hounds out to exercise. Keep away from ruins, chantry chapels, processions of mourners and cemeteries. For it is written in Matthew, "God is not the God of the dead, but of the living."

Anthony thanks the infirmarian for his wise counsel. Just as he is leaving the infirmarian shouts after him, 'One more thing, my lord. From henceforth you should avoid the company of monks!'

Anthony walks over to the Abbey's shop to purchase food for his journey. He is mounted and ready to depart when the Abbot comes staggering out, as he says, to bid farewell and give his journey a blessing. But his chief purpose is to urge Anthony to seek to return to the castle of marvels. Though the Abbot has no notion of where it is or what it is called, he believes that it has been written about in certain French books, but he has no French.

Though Anthony listens politely, he does not care for books in any language, since he thinks that he prefers life to reading.

He rides out from Crowland, heading back for Scales Hall and what he foresees must be a strange and difficult meeting, but he has only ridden a short distance when he encounters a royal courier. The courier is mightily relieved, for having been at Middleton Manor and not found Lord Scales there, he had been riding around asking after his whereabouts and he had only just got word that Anthony had spent the night at Crowland and the courier feared that he had already missed him at the Abbey. He carries two letters, one of which is from the King and the other from Beth. Anthony must read the King's message first. He is forthwith summoned to London to attend the coronation and the Pentecostal hunt which shall precede it.

The second letter is less easy to read for the writing is hasty, the pen strokes jagged and the content hard to understand:

'Husband, I greet you well and beg for God's blessing and protection on us for which we are in dire need, as I fear that I am accursed and punished for I know not what, for I never did any wrong that I should be visited by such a gory creature, against which prayers and lighted candles were no protection and he would clamber into bed with me saying that I knew him well and this had long been my desire and besides he waited for you, saying "I am his scarecrow" and then, when you entered the chamber and ran out again to your horse, the dreadful thing who once was James Butler shrugged its shoulders and said "It is no matter, for I will find him elsewhere" and, saying this, the head fell sideways and then he was gone. I know not whether this was a messenger from the horrors of Hell or something that an ill-wisher has called up through sorcery, but I beg you husband do not come near me until the horror has been exorcised and I am free of fear, for if you return to the Manor, so will it and I know not what to do and so write to me and tell me what to do. By your wife.'

Then in a scribbled postscript, 'A messenger from the King has just now arrived here and I entrust this letter to him in the hope that he may find you somewhere on your road.'

CHAPTER THREE

Gerfalcon

Since Edward will only make his state entry into London two days before his coronation, he resides meanwhile in the Black Prince's Palace at Kennington and it is from there that the Pentecostal hunt has been organised. Though it is still dark when Anthony and his squire ride out across Vauxhall Marshes, attendants with torches have been posted to mark the safe road through the wetland and, as Anthony rides on, he is joined by other courtiers travelling to the meet. William Lord Hastings and Humphrey Stafford now ride beside him and they exchange insincere politenesses in low voices. This is a strange sort of hunt, for all the while they will pretend to be racing after a stag the true quest is for the King's favour.

Breakfast is served at the meet just beyond the gardens of the Palace. Edward moves among the throng slapping men on the back and hugging women tightly to him. He is so young—only nineteen—and so tall and confident. It is evident that he too has something other than stag hunting on his mind, for he is looking for men he can trust to govern with and perhaps also appraising the bedworthiness of the women who are here.

Edward grips Anthony by the shoulders and gazes into his eyes, before saying, 'God give you welcome. I am heartily glad that you are with us today.'

And now Anthony knows that Edward does not trust him.

A little later, he hears Edward muttering to Stafford, 'That is the strange lord who was killed on the field at Towton, but who came back to life again.'

Few of the nobles assembled for the hunt are much older than Edward. Hastings, Herbert, Somerset, Stafford, and Anthony himself, they are all young. The King's younger brother, George will ride with them and he is only twelve. So many of the old lords have perished in battle or on the block that the prospects for advancement of these young men are excellent and perhaps, since the old had refused to make way for them, it is good that they are gone. The young lords and ladies who have ridden out to join their King are like butterflies in their bright robes. They are all rich and healthy and have the world before them. As they take their stirrup cups, Anthony and his rivals can dream of heroic feats to come, ordeals to be surmounted and fair women to be encountered. Anthony briefly thinks of the advice of the infirmarian.

Greyhounds and mastiffs run whimpering between the legs of the horses.

The lymerers report that a warrantable hart with a stack of antlers of fourteen tines has been sighted. This can be no surprise, for on the previous day several harts were let out from the royal deer park and driven in the direction of Kennington. The shouting of the beaters can be heard in the distance.

The horn having been blown three times, the hunt commences. Though the sun is not yet up, it is light enough. Anthony can see strands of mist rising and thinning between the alders and willows and there is still dew on the leaves of the trees. At first the pace is slow, since the hounds are underfoot and there is marshland and narrow water channels to be splashed across. The colours of this world, that is still young, are sharply edged and unfaded. Spring rains have washed the sky clear, and the yellow kingcups and the marsh violets are like bright heraldic figures on a field vert under an azure sky. As the hunters ride on to higher ground where the vegetation is thicker and more varied, the pace accelerates and the brave company race across the meadows and through the trees. Life and speed have seized them and

rush them forward. Youth! Youth! Surely they will all live
forever.

The lymerers and other underlings on foot are left behind
and soon also the ladies, who ride sidesaddle, begin to fall
back. But the pace of the hunt begins to falter for the hart
is swift and cunning and it doubles back towards the wetter
ground and perhaps it has thrown off the hounds by running
up a watercourse. So the spoor is lost and the riders find themselves looking over to the Thames in the distance and beyond
the river the spires and battlements of London and they hear
the double blast of the horn that signals that the quarry has
indeed been lost. The sound of the same horn directs them to
the picnic.

The hunters' lunch in a pleasant lodge of green boughs
that has been erected in the middle of a copse. While the
hunters are eating, the lymerers will go to work to track
another hart. Meanwhile the hunters are served baked
meats in pastry coffins, the pastry being glazed with saffron and egg yolks and this is followed by sugared cakes.
Edward is noisily holding forth to a cluster of courtiers, of
whom Hastings and Herbert stand closest to him. Hunting and hawking are vital for the future of the Kingdom,
Edward says, and there must be more jousting. The shadowed years of Henry's reign—years of prayer, of chanted
hymns, of mourning, and the reading of useless books—are
over. Things shall be as they once were. The lists shall be
remade and the deer parks restocked, for true nobility is
fashioned in the open air and on horseback. Also there must
be laughter at court, for Edward has decreed it.

Though the King's youngest brother, Richard has not been
allowed to take part in the hunt, he has been allowed to join
the hunters at their lunch. Now Anthony sees that a group of
men has gathered round the boy who appears to be lecturing
or preaching to them. Curious, Anthony walks over and joins
the audience.

'No, I swear to you by my faith,' says the boy, 'I am heartily glad to have no part in your hunt, for today is a holy day, the fiftieth day after Easter, the day when the Holy Spirit descended on the disciples and their friends and they spoke in tongues and young men had visions and old men dreamed dreams and it is a sin to hunt on a Sunday or any holy day and those who do so are doomed to join the Wild Hunt.'

The pious little boy looks round at his listeners, 'Shall I tell you the story of the Wild Hunt? Very well then. Heedless of all warnings, a certain marquis went out to hunt on a Sunday. When he was told this was a sin, he replied "Who cares for bells, monks and prohibitions? Holla ho." When a marvellous stag was sighted, the marquis spurred his horse on and as he did so, he was joined by two strange horsemen, one dressed all in white and the other dressed all in black. The marquis told them he was glad of their company and they rode on apace. They chased the stag across moor and field until finally the stag bolted into a hermitage where a holy man dwelt. The horseman in white told the marquis that he should desist, dismount and go in to pray with the holy man, but the man in black just laughed at this. The marquis, balked of his prey, stood on his stirrups and cursed God. Then he raised his horn to his lips and blew upon it, but no sound came out. Instead he heard a voice from a cloud which said, "The measure of your cup is full. Be chased forever through the wood!" At which point the hounds of Hell issued from the bowels of the earth and pursued the damned marquis and they pursue him still.'

With that Richard stumbles away in search of another pie. His audience are glad to see him go, for they are all agreed that this was not the right time or place for such a story.

Hastings had come to stand beside Anthony.

'Somebody should murder that boy as a favour to us all,' he mutters. 'The impudence of that child daring to lecture his elders and betters. And I hate stories with morals. If I am with a woman or I am listening to a story, I want to be entertained.

I do not want to be told how to be good, since I get enough of that in church.'

Anthony nods. He also thinks that he does not like to know how a story must end as soon as it has begun. From the first it was obvious that the marquis would ride to his doom and where was the story in that?

At last, a new spoor having been found, that of a fallow deer, the hunt rides out again. This time the hunters strain to follow the belling of the hounds that are ahead in the distance. Once again the pace quickens and the hunters revel in their speed as they ride to the kill. The sun is low in the sky by the time the hounds overtake their quarry. The Master of the Hunt blows the prise. The killing that follows is a bloody business. The hounds tear at the carcase and lap up the blood and the huntsmen stand back a little while to let the dogs take their reward before driving them off. Then the deer, which is still just alive, is dragged over to a nearby glade where the Master of the Hunt hacks the head off, before cutting the sides away from the chine and commencing the quartering and dressing of the carcase.

Edward and his personal retinue have already set off back to the palace where there are preparations to be made. Most of the company who have remained to watch the death agonies of the beast are smiling. It is certain that a man is never more alive than when he is watching the violent death of another creature, for then he may feel himself at one with the bloody reality of nature. Anthony thinks back to a few days earlier when he had ridden over to London Bridge just to see if Wiltshire's head was indeed impaled at its gate. It was, though scarcely recognisable, for crows had pecked out the eyes, the flesh was gone and a kind of brown fungus grew upon the skull. In cruelly contemplating the death of another, perhaps Anthony can reflect on his own end.

A lymerer reaches into the deer's insides and pulls out the

giblets that are traditionally left at the place of the kill as the 'fee of the raven'.

Anthony, looking on the passion of the deer, is asking himself how would it be to die? But then shouldn't the question be how had it been to die?

At that moment, there is a breeze through the glade and a flutter of white on one of the trees. The whole company looks up to see a white gerfalcon landed on a branch that sags under its weight. It would be hardly more unusual to come across a unicorn in these woods and for a few moments the huntsmen are silent and marvel at the sight. Then the lymerer who has the giblets in his hand suggests to the Master of the Hunt that they offer the raven's fee to the gerfalcon as a lure. Though the Master of the Hunt demurs, saying that it might be bad luck to offer what belonged to the raven to another bird, nevertheless the lymerer holds out the meat and, as he does so, there is a fierce beating of wings and the gerfalcon swoops down. Yet it ignores the lymerer's lure and flies directly at Anthony who throws up his arm to protect his face and the bird drops onto the gauntlet that Anthony has held up. A cold shiver passes through him. He slowly lowers the arm on which the bird now heavily and peaceably rests.

Once more, there is silence. It is as if the whole company is under some enchantment. Then slowly the questioning and debating begin. What can a gerfalcon be doing in these woods? They breed and hunt in the far north, in Lapland and Iceland and just occasionally they have been seen in the farthest reaches of Scotland. Then what shall be done with the bird? It cannot become Anthony's property for he is a mere lord, whereas, according to the lore of falconry, it is a gerfalcon for a King, a falcon gentle for a prince, a falcon of the rock for a duke, a falcon peregrine for an earl… all the way down to a kestrel for a knave. So then it is agreed that Anthony should present the bird to the King. One of the huntsmen produces some leather strips which will serve as jesses to keep the ger-falcon on the wrist and then Anthony, so encumbered, has to be helped to mount before being escorted back through the gathering dark to the Black Prince's Palace.

The High Feast of Pentecost begins with a homily from the court chaplain, 'How passionate you all were in quest of the deer today. How much more passionate you should be in your hunt for salvation? You chase after the things of this world that dance ahead of you like will-o'-the-wisps and you ride among phantoms, hastening without knowing it to your deaths and the end of your hunt, when you have reached it, is likely to be a bloody business. You clutch at things that rot, corrupt, rust and crumble away. How will the hunt for what is perishable ever content you? While your eyes are on your quarry you cannot see that you are hastening into the yawn-ing jaws of Eternity. This evening is the evening of Pentecost. Now call to mind how the first Pentecost was a day of mar-vels, for when it was come and the disciples were all in one place, then 'suddenly there came a sound from heaven as of a rushing mighty wind, and it filled all the house where they were sitting. And there appeared unto them cloven tongues as of fire, and it sat upon each of them…'

Edward signals that they have heard enough. But his scowl soon passes. The hunt has been a success and the remarkable finding of the gerfalcon is a blessing that has crowned the day.

Anthony has presented the gerfalcon to Edward and now the hulking bird occupies a perch of honour just behind the King's shoulder and from that place it gazes fiercely at the din-ers. Anthony is less well situated, for his table is far from that of the King. At the royal table under an elaborate baldachin Edward sits with his mistress Lady Elizabeth Lucy. Richard Neville, the Earl of Warwick is also sat at that table, together with Hastings, Herbert, Wenlock and their wives.

All who dine here tonight have been presented with badges of their allegiance, silver collars of suns and roses. The food—roasted swans, smoked badger ham, galantine pies, roasted salmon, Lombard custard, tansy cakes—is brought forth in a rush. The servants carrying the meats on brass trays are directed to the tables by the steward, who wears a blue hood and a long blue robe. Almost everything is highly spiced and in Anthony's mouth those spices—saffron, cardamom, ambergris, nutmeg, cinnamon, ginger—speak to him of the seductive heat and opulence of eastern parts.

Earl Rivers, who had refused to rise so early for the hunt is at another table together with his wife, Jacquetta. Anthony finds no friends seated at his table. He is seated between Giles Cromwell and Ismania Rougemont-Grey. The talk around him is of famous huntsmen of past centuries: Nimrod, Herne, Tristan, Saint Eustace, Saint Julian and William Twiti who was Edward II's Master of the Hunt. Anthony does not participate in this conversation. He is hoping that perhaps the King will look more favourably on him since he has presented him with the gerfalcon. Then Ismania abruptly demands to know his lineage.

'I am the oldest son of Earl Rivers. He is the High Constable of England and, as Constable, he...'

But Ismania is not interested in his father, 'Then Jacquetta de St Pol, the Dowager Duchess of Bedford, must be your mother. I have heard that there is something strange about her ancestry, though I do not recollect what it is.'

So Anthony tells her the story of Melusine, at the end of which Ismania exclaims, 'So you are descended from a lizard!' And she continues, 'What a strange thing for a family to boast about, as if one were to claim descent from a dog or a monkey! But perhaps we are all descended from animals. Does not the King truly resemble a lion? Whereas Hastings over there looks more like an ordinary cat. Which animal do you think I most resemble?'

Because he has drunk so much of the hippocras, a wine that is spiced with ginger, cinnamon, cardamom and pepper, Anthony is a little dizzy and he promptly replies, 'A horse.'

Whereupon the conversation is suddenly at an end. He is about to add 'a very handsome horse', when he becomes aware that there is a sudden hush in the hall.

A man has brushed past the attendants at the door and he advances on the King. His face is very dark and he is dressed from head to foot in white; from the hat trimmed in white ermine to the white leather boots. Only his falconer's gauntlet is thick with dried blood.

Without ceremony he says, 'I have come for the falcon.'

And he walks round Edward's table and proceeds to hood the gerfalcon and then unties the jesses on the perch. The company at the royal table are silent, fascinated and perhaps a little afraid. With the gerfalcon on his wrist the strange intruder marches towards the door. He is almost there when Edward calls out, 'Stop! Who are you? Give me your name.'

Though the man stops, he does not trouble to turn round, but his booming voice can be clearly heard. It is as if he speaks not with his tongue but from within his innards as if from a large empty jar.

'I am Hellequin.'

Edward looks puzzled.

'What business do you have with my falcon?'

'The bird was sent to Lord Scales as a sign, but now I am taking it back to its true master.'

And with that Hellequin is gone. The room erupts with applause and much thumping on the tables. The diners are delighted with the strange and original tableau that the King has arranged for them, yet Edward looks dismayed. The Lords Rivers and Fauconberg rise from their tables and go to confer in low voices with Edward. Then Anthony is summoned before the royal table.

Edward whispers without preamble,

'I thought I recognised that man, though I was so young when I last saw him, but your father here and Fauconberg both confirm my guess. That Hellequin was my father's Master of the Hunt. But yet he has been dead these twelve years.' And, turning to Rivers, Edward continues, 'Your son has brought an accursed thing into my palace. Hellequin was his name and this is a hellish business, which we must dress up as best we may.' Then Edward whispers angrily to Anthony, 'Come Scales and stand beside me while I speak to our company and smile as I smile.'

And Edward drains his goblet and puts on a smile before rising to speak and the diners once again fall silent.

'We have heard from our good chaplain that Pentecost is a day of marvels and so it is and it will be again from this year on.' He puts his arm round Anthony's shoulder, before continuing, 'This evening it is Lord Scale's adventure and it shall be his quest to reclaim that bird for me. And now I recall that it was at such a Pentecostal feast as this in the days of Arthur that the Grail was last seen in England. It entered Arthur's hall with a cracking and crying of thunder and every knight was struck dumb when he saw it veiled and lit by the grace of the Holy Ghost and then it was suddenly gone and never seen again in our lands. But on each Pentecost that is to come from now on there shall be a challenge and a quest as it was in the days of Arthur and as it was in those days there shall be a brotherhood of arms and chivalry. Our adventures and deeds of arms shall be written down for later generations to marvel at. In Arthur's day there was the Brotherhood of the Round Table, but in these modern times the Order of the Garter shall be refashioned to serve the same purpose. I believe that it is fully thirty years since there was last a joust at Smithfield and the art of managing a lance and a destrier have been all but forgotten, so that now we only read about these things in books. This must change and I will make them change. Things in England have not been right since the rebellion of Mordred, but I propose with your loyal help to establish a new Camelot. England, which is most prosperous when at war, shall be great again and reclaim the lands that are rightfully

English in France and Ireland. And... I have said enough and now I will have another drink.'

Edward sits down abruptly and dismisses Anthony who returns to his table.

Towards noon on the following day Anthony sits on the ground at the edge of Sergeant Raker's tiltyard that is just to the south of Charing Cross. This morning he has practised briefly against the quintain, a wooden figure in the shape of a Turk bearing a sword, which, if the jouster's lance hits it at the wrong angle, will revolve to whack the jouster on the back. Then, after Black Saladin has been led away, Anthony has spent hours plunging his sword again and again into a large heap of wet clay and then drawing it out. So now he is weary and aches all over and the sun is high. He has thrown off his sweat-drenched shirt. A shadow falls over him and he looks up to find William Lord Hastings standing in front of him. Hastings is accompanied by a young man in the robe of an Augustinian canon.

The young man crouches down to be on a level with Anthony and plucks at the figurine that hangs from a chain round Anthony's neck, and, when he speaks, it is with a strong northern accent, so that Anthony struggles to follow what he is saying.

'Lead. I thought that it would be lead', the young man says. 'Lustreless prime matter, under Saturn the ruler of the dead. This metal offers limitation, restraint, protection. But you probably know that. I am so very glad to have met you. You will do very well.'

Then abruptly the man stands erect again and Anthony staggers to his feet and he and Hastings engage in a kind of mock embrace, Hastings being careful not to get any of Anthony's sweat on his doublet.

'My dear Lord Scales, your father told us that we would find you here,' says Hastings. 'I am come from the King. But we cannot talk here, for there are too many curious ears.'

Many of the knights in the tiltyard have paused in their training and look on, curious to know what could have brought the King's Lord High Chamberlain to this rundown establishment. Anthony leads Hastings and his companion up the ramshackle stairs to an inner gallery from where they may look down on the other knights riding against the quintain, hefting lances, fencing with batons, doing press-ups and other exercises.

Hastings resumes, 'My dear Lord Scales, I am come from the King. I am sorry that what I have to say will not please you. I am truly sorry. It is this. The quest that everyone now supposes that you will be on, it must not succeed. The King does not want the accursed bird back and he fears lest his future feasts may be attended by dead men who want to lay claim to what they say is theirs. So the King commands you that next Pentecost you will attend the feast and there you will have to confess your failure. I am heartily sorry for this. We must see if we can find some other way for you to prove yourself. That is all my message and I now have business elsewhere. But you must be aware that there are questions concerning you. The King asks what have you to do with the dead man who was once a Master of the Hunt? Also there are rumours that the ghost of the Earl of Wiltshire has been seen at Scales Hall.'

Hastings smiles reassuringly, before concluding, 'But I give these rumours little credence for I have no belief in ghosts.'

Though Anthony says nothing, he is not surprised by the King's message. He had expected something like this. And besides he had no wish to seek out a gerfalcon in some realm of the dead. Still he is saddened that he does not enjoy Edward's favour.

Now Hastings gestures to the Augustinian canon, 'This is George Ripley. He has become the royal alchemist, since Edward met him on the field of Towton. We all have to listen to what he says.'

Hastings raises his eyebrows, before continuing, 'After a

battle, apart from the common looters crawling over the field to see what they can steal from the slain, there are usually also a few alchemists who move among the corpses and pop out their eyeballs to bottle them for their elixirs. So of course Ripley was there with his bottles. I ask myself what does the King need an alchemist for? It is all stinks, explosions, snake oil and glass bottles containing dead babies... Euurrgh!'

And Hastings shakes himself like a dog, before smiling at Ripley to show that he is not serious and that he does not mean to be offensive and Ripley smiles back, for he is not offended.

'Anyway I leave you with him. He insisted on coming with me. I have no idea why, but he knows about these things.'

These things?

Anthony and Ripley nod to one another and then they watch Hastings moving among the knights below embracing some and laughing with others. Everyone loves Hastings. He is young, smiles easily and is almost always polite. Once he is gone, the master of the tiltyard, a certain Sergeant Raker resumes his bellowing at the young men who are in training. Ripley looks on fascinated. At length he turns reluctantly to Anthony.

'I am interested in seeing how men fight, since I have little knowledge of this activity. The clash of opposites is always interesting. I like to see how enemies are drawn together in their urge to kill one another. It is true that I wanted to see how men train to fight, but I really came here because I wanted to meet Jacquetta de St Pol's son. And now that I see you, I see that you are downcast. But you need not be so. Hastings is mistaken and your quest does not have to be seen to fail.'

'But we have just heard that the King will be angry if I present him with a bird from the Kingdom of the Dead.'

'Oh, there is no need to go to the Kingdom of the Dead. We shall send to the Queen of Lapland and purchase a gerfalcon from her. There is plenty of time for that and the drunken feasters next Pentecost will never be able to tell the difference and it will make a good impression, for it will seem that the days of Arthur have indeed returned—days when royal paladins went on successful quests and returned with trophies and exciting stories to tell. I will arrange the procurement of the bird. It is your task to decide what exciting adventures you shall have had. So it is that the goal of your quest will be to determine what has been your quest.'

'But... but the King will never agree to this!'

'He will, if I advise it and I will also get Hastings to change his mind.'

'So Edward does what his alchemists tell him to do?' Anthony cannot keep the sarcasm out of his voice. Ripley smiles.

'Ah, forgive me. You share the common folk's simple and mistaken view of alchemy. It is true that I have a laboratory equipped with furnaces, alembics and pelican flasks. The King has been very generous and I find metals and volatile fluids good to think with. Making gold from lead would be merely vulgar. There is enough gold in the Kingdom as it is. No, my primary task is to distil base ambition and intrigue into high policy. Also I seek a cordial which will cure the ferment in the north where Margaret's army is making trouble. Also I publish prophecies which, because I have published them, come to be fulfilled. As I say, metals are good to think with and the court is a kitchen of elements. Gold of course represents the King. Mercury is a messenger, like Hastings. Lead is low born. Sulphur is dangerously volatile. And so on. I work with symbolic forms. Hastings is one of the managers of outward politics, while I descry the inwardness of political things. But this is not the place or time for a lesson in elementary alchemy. And I see that you want to ask me something.'

'Yes, you said that you came here because you wanted to see Jacquetta de St Pol's son?'

'Indeed. She interests me. The dragon lady, Melusine

features largely in my writings. I suppose you know that people are saying that it was your mother that had you brought back from the dead.'

'But it seems that others of the dead have followed me back into the land of the living.'

'Yes, that makes difficulties.' Ripley pauses for such a long time that Anthony wonders if their strange conversation is at an end.

At length Ripley speaks again, 'There is a saying that when Hell is full, the dead shall walk amongst us.'

'But Hellequin looked as alive as you or me and so did Wiltshire, except for his bloody wounds. Wiltshire looked so alive that, even though I knew for certain that he had been beheaded after Palm Sunday, I went to London Bridge to see his head on a spike and there it was, a grisly thing with the eyes gone and all covered with brown lichen. So I know that he really is dead, but…'

But now Ripley is excited, 'Brown lichen! Why, that is skull moss! How did I miss this? I shall go straightaway to the King to ask for the head before it is too late.'

And he turns to go, but Anthony grabs at his robes to stop him from leaving, 'What do you want the skull for? And I have other questions…'

Ripley smiles joyously back at him, but he will not stay.

'You must unhand me. I must hurry and have the head! How lovely life is! Skull moss! All this and heaven too! And besides I have many things to prepare for the coronation. But come to my laboratory tomorrow and I shall answer all your questions and show you marvels. I swear that in the future you shall relate many strange adventures to the King. And whatever happens, always remember that it is love that moves the sun and the other stars. Now let me go.'

And Anthony does.

CHAPTER FOUR

Coronation

Centuries ago Guy de Lusignan, Count of Poitou, went hunting in a forest. He became separated from his companions and while still lost, he came to a river on the banks of which he encountered a barefoot woman with long nut-brown hair and the look of an elf about her. She offered to show him the way out of the forest. Her name was Melusine, but she would not say what her ancestry was, nor would she answer any further questions. Once they were out of the forest, he proposed marriage to her. She agreed, but on one condition—that he promise not to enter her chamber when she birthed or bathed. She gave him three children, but he was curious about what he had been made to promise. You are curious too. You do not want him to break his promise, for you know that something bad will happen if he does so and you do not like bad things happening in stories, but yet you do want him to break his promise, for if he does not there will be no story and what would be the point of that? Stop reading this story! But no, you must carry on reading this story! Do not look through the keyhole, but, oh yes, do look through the keyhole! Guy's life had to be a story and so, while she was bathing, he spied upon her through a keyhole and he saw that she was washing her reptilian legs. When she discovered what he had done, she was angry but forgave him, but then months later, when quarrelling at a banquet, he publicly called her a dragon, at which point she gave a terrible shriek and indeed became a dragon with wings and scaly legs and, having flown out of one of the windows of the banqueting hall, she lashed out with her tail and demolished one of the towers of the Castle of Lusignan before flying off. Her husband and children never saw her again.

Anthony has grown up with this story, for it is the story of Jacquetta de St Pol's grandmother thirteen times removed. He is with his mother when a harbinger arrives. The Abbot of Crowland, having been invited to the coronation, is now only a few hours away from London. In his company are many of the lords and gentry of Norfolk also on their way to the coronation, as well as Lady Elizabeth de Scales. Earl Rivers and Anthony promptly saddle up and ride out in the direction of Bishopsgate which will be where the Abbot and his company must enter the city.

When they have ridden just a little way from the Woodville townhouse, they overtake a cart on which a man and a woman are being paraded in chains. Then Earl Rivers rides back to enquire of their guards who the couple are and what was their offence.

'They are adherents of the Brothers and Sisters of the Blessed Vespers,' his father reports to Anthony. 'They will be burnt at the stake on Friday.'

'What are the Brothers and Sisters of the Blessed Vespers?' Anthony had never heard of such a group before.

'They profess an evil heresy. They are almost as bad as Lollards, though not quite so evil. The adherents of the Blessed Vespers are dedicated to coupling in churches.'

'What do they do that for?'

'It is not one thing. As far as I can understand it, some do it in hope that such a blasphemous act will put them beyond any hope of redemption in the afterlife and thus thereafter they may worship God without any expectation of reward and that is the purest form of worship there is, for they envisage themselves still offering up prayers and thanks to God from the flaming pits of Hell. Some, on the other hand, believe that having sex in a church confers a blessing both on the act and on any children that may be born as a result. Then it is well known that demons and ghosts cannot interrupt couplings in churches and there are yet others who go to church to fornicate in the summer months because it is cooler there. There is no one body of doctrine among these awful heretics.'

The way to Bishopsgate is slow for the streets are already crowded with people here to see Edward's state entry into London and then his crowning. Already there are carpets and cloths hanging out of the windows. Scaffolding is going up in Westcheap. Richard and Anthony Woodville have to wait almost two hours before they see the approach of the Abbot's company to the city's gate.

The Abbot John Littlington and most of his company dismount when they see the Woodvilles waiting for them and Anthony and Beth embrace, before they all proceed on into the city. Anthony, who sees that Beth is no longer in widow's weeds, mutters to her that he will take her to Woodville townhouse, for there his mother's power should ensure that Beth may be safe from unwelcome visitants. The Abbot looks worried when he sees their embrace and Anthony fears that they are about to receive a homily about the virtue of continence in marriage, but the Abbot contents himself with reciting, as if to no one in particular, a verse from Matthew:

'For there are some eunuchs, which were so born from their mother's womb; and there are some eunuchs, which were made eunuchs of men; and there be eunuchs, which have made themselves eunuchs for the kingdom of heaven's sake. He that is able to receive it, let him receive it.'

As they continue to walk together in the direction of Cornhill, Anthony's next fear is that the Abbot will ask him if he has seen any more ghosts and then will start to cross-question him about Hellequin. But the Abbot, who has brought his Chronicler with him, has other things on his mind. The two of them have been working on a universal chronology based upon the Bible, but supplemented by certain writings of the Greeks and Egyptians. The matter is certainly complex and ancient calendars are hard to understand. Even so, the Abbot has established that the world is almost 4,000 years old.

'Think of it, 4,000 years! The mind grows dizzy contemplating such a vast stretch of time! Imagine, 4,000 years before our mothers conceived us! I feel the horror in my stomach when I think of a world without me and I feel sick and close to vomiting when I contemplate my not having existed for so many centuries and I marvel that there have been so many generations of men and women who have trod this earth and who never even dreamed that one day I would be born.'

The Abbot has also calculated that the Great Flood happened roughly 3,500 years ago.

'We read in Genesis that before the Flood there were giants on this earth. The first race of giants was known as the Nephilim, "the fallen ones". They were said to be the sons of God and they mated with human women in Canaan. "There were giants in the earth in those days; and also after that, when the sons of God came in unto the daughters of men, and they bore children unto them..." We ordinary humans were like grasshoppers in their sight.'

Oh to be so learned! But the Abbot's discourse is halted halfway along Westcheap, for by now the scaffolding work has been completed and the street is completely blocked by a stage. Suddenly there is shouting behind them, 'Make way! Make way for the King's fool!'

It is an ancient tradition that before the King of England can be crowned, the coronation of the King of Fools must first take place and it is this ceremony that now prevents their advance. Anthony's party find themselves part of a great throng of beggars, cripples, tumblers, pickpockets, bawdy baskets and Abraham men, as well as some ordinary people. Anthony turns to look on the progress of the King's fool through the crowd and to his dismay sees that it is Scoggin.

The man is hardly recognisable, for he has had his hair cut and he now wears a padded jerkin of brocaded silk decorated with white and blue lozenges, and besides he is smiling, not whining, but it is Scoggin. He does not see Anthony as he makes his way to the stage, where his throne, a chamber pot set upon a rickety stool, is ready for him. There he is joined by Mother Folly, a man in a woman's dress who is to be his consort. Attendant lords of misrule stand respectfully behind the throne. One of these calls out that, if anyone dares question Will Scoggin's right to be crowned King of Fools, then he must sustain his challenge by force of arms and of course there is such a challenge in which two lords of misrule, mounted on hobby horses, joust and belabour one another with pillows. His champion having won, Scoggin is then anointed with the white and yolk of an egg, before he is crowned with the three-horned cap and bells. Then he must make a speech. In order to do so, he steps forward from the throne, turns his back on his audience, lowers his trousers and proceeds to issue forth a rhythmic series of farts. The crowd goes wild with cheering.

Then Scoggin, having resumed his throne, proceeds to mimic the speech and pious postures of the deposed Henry of Lancaster and sets to alternately reading from a Psalter and using its pages to wipe his bum. Revolted, Anthony turns away and is about to lead Beth by some other route to the Woodville townhouse, when Scoggin sees and recognises him and his father.

'What? Going so soon my lords? I thank God I am a London man, for now in the countryside, the woods are so vile. They have a rotten fishy smell.'

And, pointing at Anthony, 'Here is a Scaly fish indeed! Ha! Ha! But all is in jest, my lord, and no harm is meant.'

Now everybody is looking at them. The Abbot and his Chronicler have already departed for Westminster. As the Woodvilles elbow their way back through the crowd, Scoggin shouts after them, 'How do rivers run? Why, Rivers always runs away! Ah ha ha!'

As they enter the family house, Richard says, 'I wonder if that zany may not be better acquainted with a river in the days to come.'

Jacquetta de St Pol waits for them upstairs in the solar. She sits by the fireplace and Beth goes to kneel to kiss her hand. Though they have met on the day of the wedding, hitherto Anthony's wife and his mother have had no conversation of any length. Now that he sees them together again, Anthony sees how alike they are. Beth is arrogant, wealthy and nobly born. Jacquetta is all of these things and in all respects to a greater degree. As Margaret of Anjou's friend and confidante, she had wielded great influence until the fortunes of Lancaster foundered at the Battle of Palm Sunday, but she knows that she will soon be powerful once more. As widow of John Duke of Bedford, she has inherited great estates in England and France. As daughter of Pierre of Luxemburg, she is of the noblest lineage—one that goes back to Guy of Lusignan and Melusine. There may even be a sense that Jacquetta outranks Beth physically, for, being plump, her curves are larger than those of her daughter-in-law.

Though Jacquetta makes most men afraid, it is not her pride, her rank or wealth that they fear. It is that she has looked upon things that men have not dreamt of and now she tries to explain to Beth how it is that the living and the dead can consort with one another.

Because of the recent slaughterings, the Kingdom of the Dead is full and overflowing. Time is needed to build more halls for the slain warriors to train and feast in. Then, since Anthony has died but returned from death, the veil between the living and dead has thinned and wherever he is it is especially thin and the dead seek him out because they hold him to be one of them and they want him as their companion to eat with them. The gerfalcon was a sign of that, perhaps a lure, though messages from the other side rarely make sense. Only Jacquetta's amulet which Anthony has hanging from his neck keeps him among the living. Beth must realise that it is all very strange on the other side. Some that are dead want vengeance for their bloody wounds, though they do not know how to achieve this, but most are very confused and have no definite aim. It is all so different over there. We cannot imagine how different and frightening it is. Perhaps Wiltshire is malicious and obstinate and he will not accept that he cannot bed women as he used to, but the greater number of the newly dead are lost creatures and for the most part they do not want to frighten anyone. Pitiful creatures, they shuffle behind us. They only seek the warmth and comfort of the living and the familiar.

Jacquetta believes herself to be an expert on the world of the dead and talks for over an hour on the subject. (Her other favourite topic is Tir Nan Og, the fairy realm to the west where no one ever ages or dies and the grass is always green. She has spent years seeking a way into it.) In the past Anthony had regarded her accounts of the world of the dead as mad. Recent encounters have changed his mind. Is it even possible that she has the power to turn her fantasies into reality? Suddenly Jacquetta looks hard at Beth and says, 'I want a grandchild! I must have one! Anthony has told me how Wiltshire sought out your bed and I have read the letter you wrote afterwards. You two will have to face off Wiltshire and any of his gory friends should they appear around your bed. You will just have to be brave and shameless in the nights to come.'

Beth's eyes widen, but nothing else shows on her face.

Jacquetta is impatient, 'Anthony, you must bed her as soon as possible.'

He nods. He dare not say no.

The following morning, which is that of the 28th of June, Earl Rivers leaves the house early, for as High Constable of England he has much to oversee and in a few hours' time he will ride in procession with Edward and the senior peers from St Paul's to Westminster Abbey. But Anthony, Beth, Jacquetta and other members of the Woodville household make their way directly to the Abbey. Outside Anthony re-encounters the Abbot and his Chronicler. The Chronicler has been brought down from Crowland so that he may set down a record of the royal ceremony and he talks to himself as he seeks to commit all the rituals to memory. As for the Abbot, he has had an exciting new idea. The earth, as all educated people know, is a rotating sphere, but it would not roll evenly if almost all the landmass, all of Europe, Asia and most of Africa, were in the northern hemisphere and there was nothing weightier than water in the southern hemisphere, for then our planet would be top-heavy. After much thought, the Abbot has decided that Mount Purgatory must be located in the south and he thinks that he will petition the King to send an expedition to find it. Though the Abbot has many proofs for the placing of Purgatory in the southern seas, happily there is no time for Anthony to hear them before the coronation ritual begins. They all sit together and Beth's thigh presses against Anthony's leg. Edward's entry under a canopy of silk borne on four lances is preceded by that of the Kings of arms and the junior heralds, all in brightly blazoned costumes. King Edward wears a robe of cloth of gold and purple and he is followed by the great lords who all wear cloaks of scarlet furred with miniver. Standing before the throne Edward takes the coronation oath and then once he is seated he is anointed with Thomas Becket's coronation oil, before having the crown of Edward the Confessor lowered onto his head and being handed the orb and sword of justice. Beth's skin is white as marble.

The Chronicler is excited by the ceremony. Anthony is also excited, though not by the coronation. He is thinking that flesh is the stuff of a real man's life, for he eats flesh, rides flesh and rubs up against flesh. This ostentatious and extravagant flummery that is now being paraded before him is tedious. He judges Edward's coronation oath to be as worthless as the one that he previously swore to the effect that he would ever be Henry's loyal subject. There was more life and truth in Scoggin's parody than in all today's time-worn pageantry. Anthony longs for the rituals to be over and, with Beth pressed close beside him in the Abbey, he is thinking of another holy place, for he has fixed upon the Church of St Bartholomew for their coupling on the following night, which will be that of the feast of St Peter and St Paul and he imagines the sexual act taking place under the winged eye of God. The coronation rituals being concluded, they rise to leave, but by now Anthony can hardly walk, for the pain between his legs is so great.

The coronation feast is held in the Great Hall of Westminster. Before it starts, Earl Rivers reads out the list of new appointments. The King's brothers are given dukedoms, so that George becomes Duke of Clarence and Richard is named Duke of Gloucester. Warwick is made Lieutenant of the North. Fauconberg is named Earl of Kent and Keeper of the King's Falcons. The list goes on, but there is nothing for Anthony. Then Sir John Dymoke, the King's Champion, rides into the hall and issues the traditional challenge to anyone who may dare to question the rightful rule of the King. He is followed by the serving men who are also on horseback and who ride around the tables, dishing out food from great brass platters. The King, but only the King, dines on lampreys, for that is the royal prerogative. His steward passes him his drinking horn at frequent intervals. The common ruck of the nobility are served with capons, beef pie and St John's rice.

Though Beth sits with Anthony, the place is too noisy for conversation and with the servants riding around and the clatter of dishes, the dinner makes Anthony think of a melée in a tournament. Then Scoggin, the malignant zany, is seen weaving his way among the tables and mounted men. Anthony and Elizabeth rise to leave, but not fast enough.

'Lord Scales, I see that you never laugh at my merry pranks.'

Scoggin has to shout and his face is red with the effort. 'Indeed I do not think that you ever laugh. Your face is grave and I wonder if not all of you is also of the grave? Ah ha ha!'

Now Anthony and Beth are in a hurry to get out of the hall. But at its threshold they pause in mingled terror and astonishment. For outside they behold thunder and lightning and golden serpents that spit fire as they travel along the ground and then there is a shower of scarlet rain. It is Ripley, smiling broadly, who presides over this pandemonium. He tells Anthony how since the Earl of Warwick has presented him with a quantity of gunpowder, he has been experimenting by mixing it with sodium, copper, sulphur, phosphorus and other ingredients.

'God has sent me to turn England once more into a land of marvels!' Ripley declares grandiloquently.

Anthony resolves to pay the alchemist a visit in the near future.

The following evening Anthony and Beth present themselves at the Priory Church of St Bartholomew the Great, just outside the city walls by Smithfield. Anthony wears a red tunic and cloak, black stockings and a white belt, the colours signifying respectively warlike courage, awareness of mortality and purity. Beth is in a doublet and hose and has a broad-brimmed hat in the Burgundian style pressed low over her brow. Anthony is renting the church for the night and he has told the verger that, since he will be knighted on the morrow, he wishes to spend the intervening hours in pious vigil with his page in attendance. If the verger has any suspicions he keeps them to himself, for he has been well paid.

Once inside Beth is in a rush to strip and then, naked, she stands in front of the altarpiece in the Lady Chapel with her feet together and her arms outstretched in parody of the crucified Christ behind her.

'Dear husband, how like you this?'

Anthony had imagined his taking of a woman as something

like the siege of a strongly defended town, but it is nothing like that, for Beth is the experienced one and she undresses him and leads him to the altar where Anthony enters her as she lies on top of a red cloak. Outside a dog howls. At least, Anthony hopes that it is a dog. Towards morning, at Anthony's insistence, they kneel and offer a prayer in thanksgiving, before dressing and hurrying out of the church. Anthony had thought that Beth would balk at the idea of coupling in a church, but he now understands that she regards Christian piety as something that is only appropriate for the lower orders.

The house of the Augustinian canons is located just within the city wall, up beyond Broad Street, but Ripley has been given lodgings inside the palace and that is where Anthony finds him when, two days later, he pays him a visit. Ripley is busy shelving books and whistling as he does so. The laboratory is a cheerful place. Sun streams through the window and catches on glass flasks and silver instruments. A padded wooden chair has been placed close by the furnace. Shelves are crowded with stoppered jars, albarellos, alembics, retorts and sieves. Two lecterns bear open books, displaying brightly painted designs. On a table there is an owl in a cage, an enormous hourglass and a gashed skull. It is all quite pleasant, only there is a faint smell of sulphur.

Ripley is pleased to see him.

'It is as if you have just walked into my head, for my brain is shaped just like this room. You can imagine that the window over there is my solitary eye through which I look out on the world and my head is crowded, as this room is crowded, with books as well as with the earths, metals and volatile fluids that I use to think with.'

Then pointing at the skull, Ripley continues, 'That is Wiltshire's head. I got the moss off it and now have it sealed in a jar.'

A lecture follows:

'Skull moss is brown and it grows in the rot of the skull.

It is the chief ingredient in unguentum armarium, which is to say the weapon salve for the magnetic cure of wounds. The best, most potent skull moss comes from a man who has been murdered, executed or died in battle, since the vital force of a man who has died violently lingers on longer than that of one who has died of natural causes. The physician applies the compound, of which the other ingredients are honey and pork fat, to the weapon which has caused the wound and he then presses the weapon against the wound which will infallibly heal quickly and cleanly. We call this method of treatment hoplochrisma. If the original weapon cannot be obtained, then one of the same shape will do. You may have need of skull moss one of these days,' Ripley concludes.

Then he draws Anthony's attention to one of the books displayed on a lectern, *The Compound of Alchemy*, which is open on a complex design which is called Ripley's wheel. At the centre of a series of concentric circles, all of which carry inscriptions, Anthony reads the words 'Here is the red man to his white wife. Married to the spirit of life—Here to purgatory they must go—thereto be purged of pain and woe—Here they have passed their pains all—And made resplendent as is crystal—Here to paradise they go having won—Brighter made than is the sun'.

'I write in code, lest others in reading may understand,' says Ripley cryptically.

Then he turns the pages to show pictures of a red man and a black man dismembering a trussed dragon, the sun and the moon jousting at the wedding of mercury and sulphur, and finally a man and a woman copulating in an enormous glass flask. This last is known as the Perfect Solution. Love draws the necessary ingredients together, just as it moves the sun and the stars.

'The Abbot was here yesterday, for he wanted to see how I make gold,' says Ripley. 'I have to pretend that that is what

I do. Otherwise folk would wonder what I really did. The Abbot told me that he expects great things from you, for, having risen Christ-like from the grave, you are the virgin knight who one day will be vouchsafed an unveiled vision of the Holy Grail.'

'Then the Abbot is mistaken,' replies Anthony, 'for I am no virgin.'

Ripley is not troubled by this.

'That is no matter,' he says. 'I will have it put about that you are indeed a virgin knight and that, though you share a bed with your wife, you do so in perfect continence and you sleep with a sword between you and her. In this way you put your virtue to a nightly test. Now I think about it, I will also have it rumoured that you always wear a hair shirt under your other garments. Also you scourge yourself before retiring at night. I shall see to it that you shall have a great future. You are to become a hero. You only have to let yourself be guided by me.'

'But none of this is the truth!' Anthony protests.

'No,' agrees Ripley. 'But it improves upon the truth. I wonder if Arthur really did pull a sword from a stone. Is it possible to do such a thing? Or did Merlin put it about that the sword had been so extracted? Since the world of the ordinary is shaded in such dull colours, we must... we must paint it brighter. Now that Edward is on the throne, the people expect great things and it is my task, our task, to see that they are not disappointed. So far you have had little to say for yourself, for there is indeed, as yet, little about you. This shall change and we must give you a story that people will want to listen to.'

Anthony shakes his head, 'Thank you, but I shall make my own way in the world.'

'No, you need me, as you will hear. First I have a question for you and then some news you will not like. The question is who rules England?'

'Edward. Henry's rule is finished.'

'You fool. Edward sits on the throne, but anyone can see that Warwick rules the Kingdom. He has the men, the ships, the great estates, the money and the energy. When he wants Edward to do something, he tells him what to do and Edward obeys. People call Warwick the "Kingmaker". It is only a matter of time before he makes himself King, since Edward is only keeping the throne warm for him. Now for what you will not like. Warwick has instructed Edward to dismiss your father from the office of High Constable and send him away from Westminster. He will be replaced in that office by the Earl of Worcester, John Tiptoft, who has just returned from his studies in Italy. Tiptoft is of the old nobility and that is in his favour. As for you, you will be sent north to assist in the sieges of those border fortresses still held by the Lancastrians. You will be closely watched for there you will be under Warwick's command and Warwick has already warned the King that you and your father are not to be trusted.'

'How do you know all this?'

'I have my intelligencers. Smile, my lord. Smile. It is good to have enemies. A man can be judged by the quality of his enemies and Warwick is a redoubtable enemy, an enemy to treasure. He hates your father and Lord Hastings. Warwick claims that they give the King evil counsel, to his own dishonour and the destruction of the Holy Church and of all his people. You, your father and others now at court are new men, jumped-up men, frivolous, cynical and greedy, who, trading on their wits and handsome faces, hope to push the old nobility aside. Do not pull that face! I am only telling you what Warwick believes. Warwick is for the old blood who have provided the Kings of England with generations of service and achievement. Wise counsellors should only be drawn from the ranks of the old nobility, for they have the best interests of the kingdom at heart. I should tell you that your father and you yourself are his chosen enemies, since Warwick also hates sorcery and he hates Jacquetta de St Pol. The odd thing is that he does not believe in sorcery and yet he does fear it, and he maintains that English politics is being poisoned by sorcery, or at least the pretence of sorcery—amulets, poisons, lures of enchantment, alchemical compounds, curses of sterility, demonic prophecies. There are many who think like him. He is to be admired and I confess I do admire his belief in himself and his ruthlessness. Accidents can happen during sieges. You should be very careful since he now wishes he had killed you and your father at Calais.'

Ripley smiles and continues. 'But be of good cheer, my lord. I am on your side. Let us hope that you have some luck in the north. Certain things bring luck, such as seeing two crows together, stroking the hump of a hunchback, pictures of elephants and having sex in a church—though, now I think of it, I suppose that having sex anywhere could be thought to be lucky. Now go with God, for in His will is our peace.'

CHAPTER FIVE

Alnwick

On their way back to Norfolk, Anthony and Beth dedicate more nights to vigils in churches. Once in Norfolk Anthony is busy on the lengthy business of assembling musters for the coming campaign. His parting from Beth is melancholy and then the soldiers' march to the north is slow, tedious and hard, but without peril or any other notable event. England sleeps under a mantle of snow.

Northumberland is Percy territory and the Percy Dukes of Northumberland have always been supporters of Lancaster. Now forces loyal to Margaret of Anjou and the Lancastrian cause hold the Border castles of Bamburgh, Dunstanburgh and Alnwick. Anthony and his men have been assigned to the siege of Alnwick in which campaign he is the deputy of the Earl of Warwick's uncle, Thomas Neville, the Bastard of Fauconberg. Fauconberg is a grizzled old campaigner who has little need of Anthony's assistance or advice and no liking for him. Ralph Grey oversees the siege at Dunstanburgh until the new High Constable, John Tiptoft, Earl of Worcester arrives to take command, while Lord Montagu and the Bastard Ogle are outside Bamburgh. The Earl of Warwick, who has overall charge of the northern campaign, has his headquarters three miles from Alnwick at Warkworth and he rides out daily from there to see what progress the sieges are making, which is very little.

Their meeting outside the walls of Alnwick had been an awkward one. Warwick frowned at Anthony before his face cleared.

'My Lord Scales, we meet again!' and Warwick spread his palms out in supplication. 'Our first meeting was not a happy one (at Calais, was it not?), but let bygones be bygones. Time changes everything. Now that we fight for the same King, I am happy to bid you a most hearty welcome, for we need all the good men we can get. I am sure that we shall be friends. Come let us embrace.'

They exchanged a formal kiss of peace and Warwick continued, 'That churchman in London, George Ripley speaks highly of you. I confess that I find him a strange man, somewhat given to unwarrantable fantasies, but I respect his intelligence. He does the most remarkable things with gunpowder.'

Warwick was all bluffness and energy and Anthony, despite himself admired this. Now Warwick had to see to how the investing of Alnwick was being conducted. Having inspected the three trebuchets that are in daily operation against the walls of Alnwick, Warwick strokes his stubbled jaw. He could not conceal his contempt, 'All this might have done very well at the siege of Jericho or perhaps that of Troy, but, by God, we are now in the fifteenth century! Our sieges move too slowly. We must give them a push. Chivalry is a thing to be mocked at if it does not dispose of the latest machinery of war.'

He has had six great iron bombards brought up by ships from Newcastle, together with more manageable culverins, roughly hewn stone balls and casks of gunpowder and he supervises their unloading. Once the bombards are on land, he goes over to them and strokes them as if they were dogs, or even perhaps women. He has a name for each of them and he is particularly fond of Katy Bombartel and he kisses her barrel.

'These pieces are my lucky charms,' he says and then he plunges his fist into one of the casks to bring out a handful of gunpowder. 'I see in this handful of dust the future of our kingdom!'

Then turning to Anthony, he says, 'Ripley has greatly improved the composition of our powder. So now it is four fifths saltpetre, one tenth charcoal and one tenth sulphur and thus its force is greatly increased... Now I think of it, Ripley told me that you wear a hair shirt. Tell me, how do you get to sleep in a hair shirt?'

But Warwick, who was by then already in the saddle, did not stay for an answer and it was evident that he has no intention of sleeping in a hair shirt. Everybody is in awe of him. He has already done so many great things. Then he was off at a gallop. Fauconberg and Anthony agree that, for fear of the damp getting to the powder, they will wait for a dry day before deploying the new artillery, but mostly it rains. Alnwick's castle is strongly garrisoned by the French and Scots under the command of the Duke of Somerset. The castle has a strong curtain-wall and powerful wall-towers, together with an impregnable barbican. Stone warriors stand on the battlements and in the grey winter mists it is often difficult to distinguish these statues from the living Scotsmen who move silently behind them. Apart from the punishment of those of his men who have attempted to desert, Anthony has almost no responsibilities and he frets at the inaction. In the mornings he rides Black Saladin at a gallop along the beaches. It is so cold that the edge of the sea is sometimes frozen. On sandbanks a little way out the seals, resembling recumbent women in shrouds, sing to him and his horse as if they were mourning this exile in the north.

Later each day, Anthony exercises with the long-sword against John Paston or one or other of the enthusiastic young men. Now he begins to master skills that he knew nothing of when he trained in the tiltyard below Charing Cross. He is learning when to use the true edge of the sword and when the false. He now steps into the cut in order to deliver the full weight of the sword and, if he can, he will go over the enemy's hilt rather than under it. Much more important, it is not enough, it is never enough merely to parry one's opponent's cut or thrust, for the way in which one parries the attack should at the same time be the way one counterattacks. His steps are as if he is showing off a dance. He masters the iron gate defence, the squinting guard, the murder stroke, the thunderclap stroke and the downward diagonal of the thrust of wrath. He can swiftly shift his blade to the left hand and then use it to trap his opponent's blade against the side of his body. It is all like a very fast moving game of chess in which he successively inhabits each of his pieces as they move. God help all averagely competent swordsmen, should they ever come up against Anthony Lord Scales. In talk and boast of reputation, character or wit there can always be doubt and debate, but in the display of sword technique, it is never a matter of opinion—only the brute fact of victory for one and defeat for the other. For the first time Anthony knows his worth and takes pride in it.

But otherwise there is little to do. Letters are slow to arrive. The first to do so comes from his father:

'Son, I recommend me to you. Your mother and I now rest at our manor at Grafton and your sister Elizabeth is also here, for since her husband's death in the fighting at St Albans and the forfeiture of his estates, his mother Lady Ferrers contends for the three remaining estates that are rightfully Elizabeth's, these estates having been settled upon her by her late husband, but Lady Ferrers' men have driven Elizabeth and her sons out of her properties. I do not know how this may be amended, nor the loss of my former high office, but your mother swears that all shall be well, for she has caused two more lead figurines to be cast. For my part, I believe that Elizabeth should make suit to Lord Hastings to gain the King's favour and the return of her manors. We must seek out a new husband for Elizabeth and a father for her children, though without her estates, I fear that she will be no great catch. The planting and the sowing have begun here, though we still fear the frosts, and after the high winds, the roof of the barn must be repaired. There is little other news, except that we hear that some weeks ago the jester Scoggin was set upon by stout fellows armed with cudgels and he lost some teeth before he was thrown into the Thames. In this manner he may learn that some rivers indeed run deep and are dangerous. Also I have heard rumours that the King will soon be found a bride in Burgundy, for this is what Warwick prefers. I pray that you are well and safe and that we may soon see you again. These are hurling times. I pray that you will send me a letter about how you do and what tidings you have, for we have had no word from you until now.'

The next letter comes from the Chronicler of Crowland who begs that Anthony will send him intelligence of the campaign-ing in the north. In a long and rambling letter the Chronicler reveals that the Abbot has discovered a serious discrepancy in their calculations for the universal chronology. It now seems that there are too many centuries to fit their estimation of the age of the earth. However, after much thought and the consultation of old chronicles, the Abbot has succeeded in conclusively demonstrating that most of the centuries between 600 Anno Domini and 900 Anno Domini have been invented by a tenth-century Chronicler working for the German Emperor Otto III. These centuries were conjured up by him so that, when the year 1000 began, Otto could be hailed as the apocalyptic Emperor of the Millennium. It has struck the Abbot and the Chronicler of Crowland that it was most suspicious how very little happens in those phantom centuries and, once they have been done away with, the Abbot's chronology works perfectly.

Anthony, reading this, is doubtful, but when he tries to think of anything that happened in those three centuries, he cannot. He writes back to Crowland about the sieges and the fear that an army of French and Scots that is assembling in Scotland may move south to relieve the Border castles. But he is curious to know why the Chronicler troubles himself to write about battles, sieges and executions. Should he not confine himself to the record of holy matters?

Ripley's letter to Anthony is very brief. He is praying for him. As soon as Anthony can, he must send him an account of the adventures that he fancies he has had, so that the seeds of his reputation as a knight errant and perfect paladin may be sown. And he is always to remember that it is love that moves the sun and the other stars.

Many weeks pass before the monotony of the siege is decisively broken up by the arrival of John Tiptoft in the North. He is a noisy man and his speech is like a pack of dogs barking, 'On our way up here we were set upon by forty or more brigands, but we beat them off and our fight with them cheered me greatly and I will tell you why. I respected them for the attempt! They were poorly armed with bows and arrows and staffs, whereas I had trained soldiers in my retinue. When I travelled through France on my way back from the Holy Land, I saw that in France when a man has no work and no patrimony, he sits down and begs or starves. But in England a man without employment will take to the road with a cudgel or a knife and will steal to live. We hang more sturdy rogues in a year than France does in seven! I tell you, so long as England has such stout fellows ready for a fight, we have nothing to fear from our enemies.'

A pale yellow sun has emerged from the clouds and from all over the camp thin white vapours arise from the ramshackle erections of skins and sticks. Tiptoft struts among the rotting fabrics and skips over ropes. He is bald, his nose is hooked and his eyes glitter in a skull that is darkly tanned. He wears a vermillion doublet slashed in yellow and he is followed by a dwarf and by a squire who bears a parakeet upon his wrist. As soon as Tiptoft decently can, he shakes off Fauconberg and goes to sit with Anthony in his tent.

Anthony had expected to dislike the man who has replaced

his father as High Constable. But he finds Tiptoft's liveliness and intensity charming. The Earl talks at a rapid rate about his studies in Padua and Verona, his pilgrimage to Jerusalem, his work as Constable and his additional responsibilities as President of the Court of Chivalry and he finishes off by commending the good looks of the Woodville clan—of Anthony, his father, his mother and his sister. Then he takes hold of Anthony's chin and turns his face so that he may study it more closely.

'I love beauty and am not ashamed to confess it, but though I had much rather be beautiful than love beauty, yet one must make the best of what one has and is. I would be a sodomite if I could, only the Bible forbids it. So I am not.'

Then looking round the tent, Tiptoft asks, 'Where do you keep your books?'

Anthony shrugs and confesses that he has brought none with him. In fact, he reads as little as possible, for he much prefers brightly coloured pictures and heraldic emblems to those little black squiggles that crawl across manuscript pages like malformed insects.

Tiptoft is not happy with Anthony's reply and says, 'People prate about how wonderful life is, but I swear to you that reading is better. Search how you may you will never find happy endings in life. It is only there in books. Our Christian faith is based upon a book and our salvation depends upon a book which is the Bible. Books give us saints and heroes to emulate. Our lives are such paltry things that we must at least have the possibility of a dream of something grander. I see clearly that this world is a prison in which we are closely confined and, short of death, it is only books that can deliver us from this prison. For myself, I swear that books do most to mitigate the desperate melancholy and the weariness and the thoughts of self-harm that are my constant burdens. You must read many books and read them fast. There are so many books and you have so little time.'

Temporarily exhausted, Tiptoft falls silent.

Thinking to amuse him, Anthony tells Tiptoft about the Abbot of Crowland's strange ideas about the southern continent and the lost centuries, but surprisingly Tiptoft does not find them strange at all.

'The Abbot is right,' he says. 'It is just so in Dante's *Inferno*;

'E se' or sotto l'emisperio giunto
Ch'è contraposto a quell che la gran secca
Coverchia, e sotto 'l cui colmo consunto
Fu l'uom che nacque e visse sanza pecca...'

Then, shocked to see that Anthony knows no Italian, Tiptoft translates:

'And you are now come beneath the hemisphere opposite to that which canopies the great dry land and underneath whose zenith the Man was slain who was born and lived without sin.'

And Tiptoft explains that, having travelled through the circles of Hell, Virgil and Dante have come out in the southern hemisphere at a point directly opposite to the hill on which Jesus was crucified. In the next part of the *Divina Commedia*, *Purgatorio*, Dante will behold the great mountain of Purgatory rising high in the southern hemisphere in sunlit solitude in a region where ships have never penetrated.

As for the notion that three centuries have been invented, though this is new to Tiptoft, he is not hostile to it.

'Of course, there is the problem of the ninth-century Emperor Charlemagne,' he says. 'We know a lot about Charlemagne, but I have long thought that we know too much about him. He fights too many battles, he builds too many churches and he commissions far too many manuscripts. He is wise, brave, learned, generous—he has all the perfections. Moreover his paladins, Roland and Oliver, perform impossibly heroic feats against incredible odds. His empire is too big. I have long thought that Charlemagne and his knights might be mythical figures... just like King Arthur.'

'How is that? You hold that the history of Arthur is only a legend?'

'The story of Arthur is the founding legend of our nation and one Englishmen take pride in, for it is a very good story, but it is only a story and what really happened must have been much duller, for I always find life to be duller than the stories I read in books.'

'But it cannot be true that Arthur is a creature of our imaginations.' Anthony is shocked. 'For one thing the bones of Arthur and Guinevere have been disinterred and reburied by the monks at Glastonbury. I have prayed at their tomb. Then the round table is displayed at Winchester and I have seen that too with the places of the knights written on its circumference and we have armorial rolls showing the blazons of all Arthur's knights. It is common knowledge that Guildford was once known as Camelot. Moreover, we have histories of Britain written by William of Malmesbury, a monk, and Geoffrey of Monmouth, a bishop—and there are others. Such holy men would not have invented the deeds of Arthur.'

But Tiptoft is unimpressed by this supposed evidence, 'Most of our history is invented and it is better that way. History is nothing but the lies we tell about our ancestors. If a German monk can make up three centuries, I do not see why our British clergy should not be up to faking half a century or so. For myself, I no longer read romances about Arthur and his knights, for I find them too fantastical. At the moment I am reading the Emperor Claudius's *Tyrrenika*, his excessively lengthy history of the Etruscans, but I do not believe most of what he tells me about the Etruscan Kings and their wars. Much of that must be made up. Still I enjoy reading falsehoods about the past, so long as they seem plausible, which the stories about Arthur are not.'

'But if Arthur and his fellowship of the Round Table never existed, then we have no exemplars to match ourselves against and the attempt to resurrect Camelot is a mere folly.'

'Yes, Edward must never be allowed to suspect the truth, for folly has its uses. I marvel at the story of Arthur and am a little afraid, since I regard the conjuring up of people who never existed as a special kind of witchcraft. But I guess that you may know more about witchcraft than I do... You never heard me say that...'

Then, to change the topic, Tiptoft asks about Anthony's family and Anthony starts to explain that Elizabeth's manors in Leicestershire have been seized by Lady Ferrers's men.

'I did not know that your wife had properties in Leicestershire.'

'No, I mean my sister who is also Elizabeth.'

Suddenly Tiptoft is in a fury, 'By the five wounds of Christ! This is the curse of the English aristocracy. We lords and ladies are so brainless that we cannot think of any names for our children except Elizabeth, Anne, Katherine, Henry, Richard, Edward and John. And then again Henry, Elizabeth, John, Katherine, Richard, Edward and Anne. So we are in a constant muddle as to who is who. The lower orders have more sense and imagination, for they take names like Hodge, Poyns, Garth, Alfred, Marigold and Beverley. By God, I am heartily tired of my own name, John, and I believe that I shall have myself called Actaeon, Zoroaster, or perhaps Fabrice.'

With that, John Tiptoft stomps out of the tent. Anthony guesses that the truth is that Tiptoft is angry with himself for having touched on witchcraft. At the last moment, before Tiptoft is about to ride off, he recovers himself enough to invite Anthony to visit him at Dunstanburgh. Perhaps they may enjoy a bout of swordplay.

The castle of Dolorous Gard was first known by that name because it was a place of sinister enchantment. Here Lancelot fought two bands of ten knights under its walls and defeated them. Thus Lancelot captured the castle and there in its chapel he saw a great metal slab and, when he lifted it, he discovered a tomb with his own name carved upon it. So he knew for the first time who he was and he knew that when he died his body would lie in this castle. Next he found a chest concealed in a pillar and the chest was full of horrible voices, but when he opened this chest all the devils flew out in a great whirlwind and the enchantment of the Dolorous Gard was broken and the castle became Sir Lancelot's possession.

When Sir Lancelot entertained King Arthur and Queen Guinevere with good cheer in this castle, he renamed it Joyous Gard. Later, Sir Lancelot brought Sir Tristram and La Beale Isoud to his castle and lodged them in it as if they were a King and a Queen, though theirs was a story that ended unhappily. Years later, after Sir Tristram and La Beale Isoud were dead, and when Queen Guinevere was convicted of adultery and brought forth in her smock to be burnt to death, then Sir Lancelot came to the place which was to be the place of her execution and, having fought with many knights and slain several, among whose number were Sir Gawain's brothers Sir Gareth and Sir Gaheris, Sir Lancelot rescued the queen. Wit you well the queen was glad that she was escaped from death. And then she thanked God and Sir Lancelot: and so he rode his way with the queen, as the French book says, unto Joyous Gard, and there he kept her as a noble knight should do. Then King Arthur at the request of Sir Gawain concluded to make war against Sir Lancelot and laid siege to his castle called Joyous Gard, for Gawain would have vengeance for his brothers. But Sir Lancelot withdrew himself to his strong castle with all manner of victuals and as many noble men as he might suffice within the town and the castle.

At length, when fifteen weeks of the siege had passed, a bishop that was sent from the pope made peace between the warring parties and, according to the terms that were made in Carlisle, Queen Guinevere surrendered herself to the King and Sir Lancelot consented to depart from the King's lands and dwell in foreign parts. And when the noble Sir Lancelot took his horse to ride out of Carlisle, there was sobbing and weeping for the pure sorrow of his departing; and he took his way unto Joyous Gard. And thus departed Sir Lancelot from the court forever. And then, having set out from Joyous Gard and crossed over the waters, ever after in sad remembrance he called that castle once more the Dolorous Gard. After the last battle between King Arthur and Sir Mordred at which the two of them were slain, Sir Lancelot returned to England and spent a long time grieving for Arthur's death, before Sir Lancelot fell sick and died. His body was carried to Dolorous Gard, which today is known as Bamburgh and you may see his tomb there.

This was the story of Bamburgh which Anthony had from Sir Thomas Malory of Newbold Revel. Warwick has sent Anthony over to Bamburgh to report on the siege there which is under the command of the Bastard Ogle. Malory, who is one of Ogle's deputies, has been deputed to deal with Anthony's queries. Malory is a thickset man with a scarred face and close-cropped hair and he speaks in a slow growl. He keeps looking at Anthony in an odd way as if he suspects him of something.

His replies to Anthony's queries are brief, even perfunctory. He hates Bamburgh and says it should still bear the name Dolorous Gard. Then it turns out that he, like Tiptoft is an enthusiast for books. He says that books were a great solace to him when he was in prison and what he really wants to talk about are *Sir Gawain and the Green Knight*, *The Wedding of Sir Gawain and Dame Ragnell*, *Peredur*, *The White Book of Rhydderch*, *The Red Book of Hergest*, *Merlin*, *The Life of Joseph of Arimathea* and Chaucer's *Book of the Lion* and suchlike romances.

Once the inspection of the trenches, bombards and tents is over, Malory promptly turns to the Matter of Britain. They walk along the beach a while and then, sitting beside a rock pool, Malory speaks of Arthur, Merlin, Nimue, Lancelot, Percival, the Dolorous Stroke, the Loathly Lady, the Perilous Seat, Stonehenge, the Island of Sarras, the beheading game and such like matters. It is as if Malory swims in a sea of stories.

Anthony cannot refrain from boasting about his descent from a dragon and tells Malory the story of Melusine. Malory, in turn, tells the story of a local dragon, the Laidly Worm, which is the story of a girl who was turned by the curse of her stepmother into a dragon and threw her off a crag into the sea. Her breath grew strong and her hair grew long and twisted about her. This horrid creature would come out from the sea to raid and devour livestock. Eventually a knight appeared who was determined to slay her, but when he confronted the dragon, she offered to give him a magic belt if he would kiss her three times. Suppressing his fear and revulsion, he did so and the enchantment was broken, or rather the enchantment was transferred, for while the girl resumed her normal shape, the stepmother was transformed into a venomous toad that still hops along the beach by Bamburgh Castle.

'What is the meaning of this strange tale?' Anthony wants to know.

Malory's reply, which is slow in coming, is also strange, 'I suppose that, like so many stories, it is a fable about the fear and danger in the relations between any man and a woman. Every kiss must be a conquest of repulsion.'

Anthony shakes his head to clear it.

'But there once were real dragons in this land?'

'Assuredly there were still dragons in Arthur's day. But perhaps they have all been killed. England's forests and moors have always been battlegrounds in which beasts prey upon other beasts in a struggle for survival. It may be that the dragons were not strong enough or fast enough to survive, for men are more dangerous than dragons and I believe that the last dragons were slain by men—just as in a few years' time some man will kill the last wolf in England. Nevertheless, I have heard that there are still dragons in Africa where they haunt rivers and devour men.'

As they walk back to Bamburgh, Anthony relates Tiptoft's belief that Arthur never existed.

Malory laughs at this. For the moment he has forgotten whatever is troubling him. Then he says, 'The Earl of Worcester would deny that Jesus ever existed, if it were not for his fear of the punishments of Hell. But how can that clever man prove the non-existence of Arthur? If Arthur never existed, what evidence can there possibly be for his never having existed? Can the Earl of Worcester point to the place where Arthur never was, name the people he never knew and produce the shoes he never wore? His doubting is a kind of madness. His sojourn abroad has led him to hate England and English things. I have heard that he also denies that Saint George ever existed, but yet he reveres hundreds of Italian saints and prates endlessly about their miracles. He is not a true Englishman. It has been well said of him that *un Inglese italianato é diavolo incarnato*.'

Anthony guesses at the meaning of this last expression. By now they were back at the camp below the walls of the castle.

'You should be on your way back to Alnwick,' says Malory who seems suddenly impatient to see Anthony go.

Malory waits until Anthony is mounted and ready to ride off before running out with a book. It is *The Avowing of Arthur*.

'Take this,' says Malory. 'This book will change your life.'

Anthony doubts it. There is too much sadness in the stories of Arthur and his court, too many treasons, too many deaths and too many castles that deserve the name Dolorous Gard. And besides Anthony is not fond of reading and, when he does read, it is very slowly.

He has only ridden a little way before he is intercepted by a troop of horsemen. They salute him courteously and explain that they are under the Earl of Warwick's orders to escort him to Tiptoft at Dunstanburgh.

Tiptoft receives him in a pavilion that is more luxurious than any they have at Alnwick. The parakeet sits chained to its perch at the entrance. A Turkey carpet is on the ground and a baldachin overhangs the bed. The travelling library is kept in trunks at the far end of the pavilion where it is over-seen by a Carraran marble sculpture of the crucified Christ. No sooner has Anthony entered the pavilion than Chernomor steps across the entrance and there stands guard. Tiptoft rap-idly barks something at the dwarf in what Anthony guesses is Latin. His guess must be correct.

'Chernomor speaks only Russian and a little Latin,' says Tiptoft. 'If you try to leave without my permission, he will rip your arms off.'

While Anthony is struggling to understand what is going on, Tiptoft's squire enters with *The Avowing of Arthur* which he has extracted from Anthony's saddlebag. The squire pre-sents it to Tiptoft, who negligently flicks through its pages until he finds what he wants. It is a letter that has been pasted into the middle of the book. Tiptoft rips it out and scans it. Even in his panic Anthony marvels how swiftly Tiptoft reads and without moving his lips!

Tiptoft shows the document to Anthony and says, 'It is as I expected. This letter, which seems to come from the Duke of Somerset, is addressed to you. In it he praises you for reconsidering where your loyalties lie and promises that you shall be well rewarded by the King—I mean Henry of Lancas-ter. Then he provides details on how you and those you can trust may safely cross over and join the garrison in Alnwick. Tomorrow night, when you give the signal, you will be met by a sally party and they will see you safely in through the castle's postern gate. It is all just as the Earl of Warwick said it would be. He recommended that you be brought to me, since as President of the Court of Chivalry, I have the power and duty to dispense summary justice.'

'But I know nothing of this!' protests Anthony.

Tiptoft does not seem to hear. Now he instructs his squire to light a candle and then he moves it so close to Anthony that his face can feel its heat. Tiptoft's own face is just behind the candle so that its flame is reflected in his pupils, which in its light are like those of a lizard, and he gazes deep into Anthony's eyes for a long time. At last he says, 'It would be a shame to mar such a beautiful face and sad to see a handsome head severed from the shoulders to which it belongs.'

Abruptly he whisks the candle away from Anthony and holds the letter up to the flame until it is entirely burnt.

'I cannot believe that such a beautiful face can possibly harbour treasonable thoughts. I will have to tell Warwick that I have found no incriminating evidence on you.' He shrugs. 'He ought to be relieved that we have no traitors in our midst. *The Avowing of Arthur* is worth reading though.'

Then he hands the torch back to his squire and continues, 'I hear that you exercise with the sword every morning below the walls of Alnwick. Will you fence with me?'

Straightaway Tiptoft has blunted swords fetched and they go out to cut and lunge at one another. Weeks of practising with the sword outside Alnwick have made Anthony confident. Moreover, being taller, he has the longer reach and indeed within a few strokes he comes close to disarming Tiptoft, but he, once he has taken the measure of his opponent, swiftly recovers and thereafter Anthony is unable to land a blow, as Tiptoft, all the time slowly stepping round to the left, uses his sword to create something which comes to resemble a sphere of invincibility. Anthony, who has met nothing like it before, is baffled.

Once they are out of breath and sweating, they break off and return to the tent.

'I am fairly beaten,' says Anthony, 'though it felt like sorcery.'

'You are not far off the mark,' replies Tiptoft. 'I will tell you how it is done. First, you should know how much I hate it here. So much wildness in nature is very ugly. I wish that we could leave this northern region to the benighted followers of Henry of Lancaster, together with the Scots and similar wild beasts. Things are better ordered in Italy.'

And now Tiptoft speaks at length about his studies in Padua and Ferrara, where he sought to polish up his Latin style. He also attended lectures by John Argyropoulos in Florence before going on to Rome where he made an oration in Latin whose eloquence, he is not ashamed to admit, moved the Pope to tears of joy. Tiptoft also oversaw and contributed a translation of *Laus Calvitii* (In Praise of Baldness) by Synesius the Cyrene. Wild animals are hairy, whereas bald animals are more intelligent. All the great philosophers of the ancient world were bald. The sphere is a perfect form since it echoes in microcosm the shape of the heavens. Prostitutes have long hair. *Quod erat demonstrandum.*

Listening to all this, Anthony is annoyed, for what Tiptoft is talking about has no bearing on sword fighting, and besides Anthony's own hair is quite long. But now Tiptoft, having touched on the divine properties of spheres and circles, moves on to talk of his study in Rome of the related topics of sword fighting and demon raising and, picking up his sword once more, he leads Anthony out of the tent and down to the water's edge, where the sand will help him to demonstrate what he is talking about.

'The sword is a tool for investigating the way the world works.'

Then Tiptoft takes careful steps backwards and forwards as he uses his blunted sword to draw what he describes as a 'magic circle' in the sand. Its circumference delineates the reach of his sword arm together with that of his hypothetical opponent. Fencing is like geometry and as such it can be demonstrated by mathematical principles. The swordsman who follows the teachings of the Italian school of humanist geometers will seek to move as a ball does, for it is impossible to strike a ball with a direct blow, as it defends itself with its motion. Within the larger circle Tiptoft uses his sword to draw a smaller one to mark out the distance between the antagonists' leading feet. Every part of these circles are proportionate to the human body. Tiptoft goes on to draw chords (straight lines joining two points on a curve) which serve to mark out, not only the various thrusts and lunges that are available to the swordsman, but also the defensive side-steps and traverses. The lunges should be avoided save in cases of extremity for, though swift, they are perilous and the swordsman should strive to hold himself erect as if he were suspended by an invisible thread from the apex of the heavens. The chords of defence will form an eight-pointed star. The steps and traverses are always made to the left, assuming that one is a right-handed fighter. The swordsman uses this complex geometrical figure in order to rehearse and perfect his footwork and to gauge the distance that he must keep from his enemy's weapon and, after much practice, he may be able to internalise these circles and chords, so that he carries them with him always in his head. This system is called 'The Distress' because of the damage it causes to the victim. However a single false step will mean death for the man who thought that he had mastered the magic circle.

'While I was in Ferrara I had read in the sorcerer's manual known as *Picatrix* that man is the measure of all things,' says Tiptoft, 'For his head resembles the heavens in their roundness and his two eyes are like the sun and the moon, while his nostrils are the two winds in miniature and his ears signify the orient and the occident. From my reading of *Picatrix* I was led by easy steps to study the more ancient art of constructing occult pentacles, since it is from this which the magic circles of the swordsman derive. A man who is possessed of the right names and sigils can draw up a pentacle that will defend him from all sorts of spiritual assault. Standing within it, the conjuror can safely call demons to appear before him. So I made myself master of the Pentacle of the Clavicle with its four defending angels, Vehiel, Gashiel, Vaol and Shoel. Then it came to me that I might use this pentacle to summon up demons to spar with me, for I had spent so much time over my books in Ferrara that I was somewhat out of practice as a fighter.'

'It is my belief that demons have no form of their own and therefore they summon up for their use the semblances of dead men. Consequently demons are usually mistaken for ghosts, though the truth is there are no such things as ghosts, but only demonic impostors who pretend to bring messages from the other world and messages from Hell are never worthy of credence.'

Tiptoft sighed as he remembered his first duel in Rome with one of these 'ghosts'.

'It was a warm summer night and the air was soft and carried the scent of quinces and oleander. On my way to my duel I had passed barefoot friars celebrating vespers in a ruined temple and I could still hear their singing as I began my conjuration. I had chosen to draw my pentacle on gravel in a spot close to the Baths of Diocletian, for this place was secluded by cypress trees and oleander. Within the Pentacle of the Clavicle I marked out the traverses of the swordsman and I placed candles at the points where the chords touched the circumference of the greater circle. Only a few moments passed before a figure emerged from the trees. My antagonist pretended to be an Englishman called Robert Elphick who had been killed in a brawl in a Roman taverna a few years earlier.'

'Intimidation is an important part of duelling and pseudo-Elphick hoped to scare me as he rushed upon me with his gashed and bloody head and his banshee howls. But I laughed and howled back at him, for I knew myself to be secure within my pentacle. We fenced for over an hour during which the apparition sustained many cuts and punctures, while I remained invulnerable as long as I kept stepping along the traverses of the smaller circle. At last I dismissed my deathly partner with a few words of exorcism. I was very content to be so well exercised and entertained and the boredom from which I mostly suffer had abated for that night at least. In the weeks that followed I made frequent use of the Pentacle of the Clavicle and I delighted in always having a sparring partner at my beck and call. Sometimes it was Elphick, but there were other riff-raff from the cemeteries of Rome who occasionally made their appearance. I was so happy then. God, I wish I were back in Rome, for I much prefer the company of demons to northerners…'

As he speaks, Tiptoft moves along the lines in the sand and strikes postures. Hitherto the two of them had been alone on the bleak seashore, but now Anthony points to a dark figure who has emerged from the grey mist further up the sands. He is carrying a sword and seems to be hurrying towards them, though he struggles against a fierce wind which has suddenly blown up. Tiptoft hastily kicks at the gravel in order to scuff out the pentacle and then he leads Anthony back to his pavilion.

Once inside the tent Tiptoft gabbles as he tells Anthony that he must learn to read on horseback, so that no time for learning is wasted. Also Anthony must learn Italian so that he may read Dante. And Tiptoft is enthusiastic about the new science of punctuation. The introduction of slash marks to bracket groups of words and the use of the point and double point to indicate breathing pauses will make it so much easier to read rapidly and understand what one has read. Indentation in manuscripts is the other great thing. We can see that the world is changing.

'I am heart and soul for what is young and new!' declares Tiptoft.

Anthony does not pay much attention to what is being said, for he is thinking about Tiptoft's encounter with dead men in Rome. Surely it is fiction. But why? What is the point of such a fantastic tale? Is it told to cause fear?

Now Tiptoft gestures to the trunks full of books and boasts that they represent only a small selection of his library. He longs to be back in London with the rest of his books and his instruments. Of his instruments, he is particularly fond of the Duke of Exeter's Daughter, so called because it was devised by Thomas Holland, the Duke of Exeter, in the last century. That man was surely a genius and Tiptoft goes into considerable detail concerning the instrument's iron frame and wooden rollers and ratchets. He also speaks briefly of the pilliwinks which he uses for crushing hands.

'I use these devices as another would play upon a musical instrument. Now fast and now slow. I find that it takes some sensitivity to get the right sounds out of the creature on the rack and I am ever careful to listen out for false notes. I tell my prisoners not to be dismayed, for, if rightly thought about, the whole world is a prison and I am the usher who will show them the way out. What hope for us is there in the world, short of death?'

'Christ saves.' Though Anthony's response is one of conventional piety, Tiptoft pauses to think about it.

'But does he? Can he? I am fearful and have doubts. When I was on pilgrimage to the Holy Sepulchre in Jerusalem, I saw a man crucified by the Turks. It was a slave's death. Nails through the hands and feet... that is not such a great thing. It is not enough pain. Can mankind really have been saved by the Incarnation and the Sacrifice? I do not think that we can have been redeemed by the Crucifixion, if I can make my prisoners suffer more than Christ suffered. And I can. There is a sickly thing... I am vowed to the service of the God that has failed.'

Now Tiptoft is most unhappy. He flaps his hands as if to bat away the evil thought. Then, he looks hard at Anthony,

'But I have heard that, after the Battle of Palm Sunday, you were freed from your mortal body and earthly pain for three days. Then on the third day you rose again like Christ. What was it like to be dead?'

Anthony is about to reply that it was very peaceful in the nameless castle, but abruptly he changes his mind and he speaks slowly, as if reluctant to describe what he has seen, 'I saw the spirits of the dead driven about in a fearful hurricane and others battered by a perpetual rain and yet others forced to push great boulders in front of them. I saw men and women clawed at by winged demons. There were people trapped in red-hot sepulchres and there were some who had been turned into trees that writhed about...'

'Enough! I have heard enough. Hell is just as I have read about in books... Lord Scales, will you pray with me?'

They kneel together in silent prayer before the crucifix and Tiptoft's face streams with tears.

Then he wordlessly hands Anthony some books that he must read. But Tiptoft has lost the desire for any further conversation, except that he asks after the health of Anthony's mother and, hearing that it is good, hopes that it will remain so. People have to be careful about their health and their mothers. As Anthony, once mounted, looks back, he sees a man with a sword waiting outside Tiptoft's pavilion.

On his arrival back at Alnwick Anthony finds a letter waiting for him. It is from the Chronicler of Crowland. Anthony had written to him asking him why he was so obsessed with recording battles. Now he gets his reply. The Chronicler sees his job as being to detect God's will as it is revealed in the outcome of battles. Battles are like ordeals by fire or by water, in which the guilty are found out and the virtuous vindicated. God speaks to us and shapes our history through battles.

Anthony, reading this, doubts that God's purpose is revealed through battles, since the first battle of St Albans was a victory for York and so was Blore Heath, but York was defeated at Ludford. But then York won at Northampton, only to be defeated at Wakefield. Then the Yorkist cause is triumphant at Mortimer's Cross and Towton. Why cannot God make his mind up as to which cause he is supporting? As it is, the divinely-decreed destiny of the kingdom is a zigzag.

The Chronicler also reports that the Abbot has found a new problem to wrestle with, for he has now interested himself in Nimrod, the world's first tyrant, and Nimrod's project to build a tower which would reach the heavens. Once again the Abbot has used his mathematical skills to demonstrate that, even without divine intervention, the Tower of Babel was doomed to fail, since in order to reach the sphere of moon, 178,672 miles above the Earth, 374,731,250,000,000,000 bricks would have been needed for the Tower's construction and this would have overbalanced the Earth, since the Tower would be heavier than Purgatory in the southern hemisphere.

The following day Anthony wrote to Ripley:

'I give you salutation and ask for your blessing. Yesterday I had a strange adventure...

I was walking along the coast north of Alnwick when I saw her. From a distance and in the fading light I took the huddled black shape for a seal, but the rocky outcrop over the sea was far too high for a seal to have clambered onto and, when I got closer, I saw that it was a woman dressed in black. When she looked back and saw me approaching, she gestured that I should join her and sit with her and look down on the sea from the rock. I did so. Now that I was close, I could see that she had bright green eyes and red hair which she kept brushing away from her eyes. She began speaking without any preamble, "When I was young, I dwelt with the sea people under the curve of the wave. We used to sport in the great breaking rollers and move to and from the shore according to the pulse of the sea. The sound of water drawing back over shingle was like my breathing. Sometimes we used to lie in the shallows and watch the land people and wonder how they did. Though I believe we had our origins in the deep sea, we grew up close to the shore where we rode the breaking waves. I was happy with the sea people, but there came the day when they said I had grown too big and that I must join the land people and they pushed and pulled me ashore. So I walked onto dry land and learnt its ways. Several times I returned to the sea and at first the sea people would talk and play with me, but eventually they shunned me and I found myself swimming alone in a dark green sea that was so dark that it was almost black—as it is now. When we are grown to adulthood we forget this sort of thing. Now come stand with me and I will show you something."

We both rose and she pointed to dark shapes some distance away in the sea.

"Seals," I said, for that is what I thought they were.

"No, those are the sea people. Would it not be pleasant to join them?"

She moved closer to me and embraced me. I thought that this was affectionate, but her embrace was strong and in the next moment she hurled herself and me with her into the sea. Underwater she clung to me and we fought one another as the undertow carried us away from the rock. It was only when I had got one of my hands free and stabbed it in the direction of her face and got my finger in her eye that her grip slackened and I freed myself from the embrace of the she-demon. I rose to the surface, but the tide was so strong that I was carried half a mile along the coastline before I could step out onto a spit of land.'

Ripley, having received this, writes back that it was good to be reminded of the sea people, but what he really needs is the story of the gerfalcon and what strange and marvellous feats Anthony had performed before he rescued it from the

guardianship of the dead. The actual bird, which was purchased in Lapland, has arrived and is kept in a safe and secret
place outside London, until Anthony shall be back in the
south and ready to present it to the King. Though Anthony is
as slow a writer as he is a reader, he thinks that he will have no
great difficulty in concocting a strange adventure, for he has
spent his childhood listening to his mother Jacquetta's flood
of stories concerning errant knights, enchanted princesses,
sinister heretics, mysteriously deserted castles, warlocks, elves
and speaking statues. He has grown up more familiar with a
magical world than he is with the real one.

Made-up stories about royal battles and errant knights
customarily have exciting endings in which, after much danger, there is either great triumph or horrid despair. However,
there is no exciting ending to the sieges in the north. Bamburgh and Dunstanburgh are starved into submission and
the Duke of Somerset surrenders to the King's mercy, while
Alnwick is abandoned by its defenders. So this part of the war
is ended and at last Anthony is suffered to return to the south.
Now he urgently needs to find some adventure that may end
with his recapture of a gerfalcon.

Chapter Six

Corbenic

After our taking of the castle of Alnwick, I was sent south
with the first detachment of discharged troops. Early on the
second morning and some way north of Newcastle I became
impatient with the slow progress of the marching men and
I pressed my horse to a canter and rode ahead, planning to
wait for them further up the road, but as I rode on, a thick
fog descended and I thought it better to advance no further.
So I dismounted and waited for them to join me. I waited a
long time but I neither heard nor saw anything of my troop.
The shapes of ancient mossy trees were dimly visible in the
dense fog and I only heard the occasional sound of melting
snow falling from the branches. I had then no recourse but to
follow the path I was on and travel in the direction which I
judged to be south. I longed to be out of these bleak northern
lands where once monstrous worms roamed and perhaps, for
all I knew, they still did. Surely my route would eventually
take me to a habitation where I would get better guidance. Yet
the path was long and grew ever narrower as I rode on. I was
almost asleep in the saddle when my horse halted and I saw
that our way was blocked and overgrown with briers. Seeing
this, I dismounted and set to hacking at the briers, though I
was sick with dread, for now it was clear to me that this path
would never lead me to any human settlement.

But then, as I wielded my sword in the undergrowth, I
heard voices lamenting. Though I was fearful, I was also curious to know the cause of this grief. Having cut my way through

the worst of the bushes, I led my horse forward by the bridle
and shortly I came to a castle. The place was familiar to me,
though I could not give it a name. Its curtain wall was partly
collapsed and the outer gate swung back and forth in the rising
wind. When I reached the inner gate, that of the keep, I blew
upon my horn, but no one answered. I dismounted and pushed
the door open and entered upon a scene of dereliction. There I
was surprised to see four men squatting beside a bonfire in the
middle of the great hall and I realised that it was their weeping
and groaning that I had heard as I approached the castle. They
looked grimly up at me and fell silent. Then I saw at the far
end of the hall a crowned King seated on a throne on a dais.
I thought that his eyes, which glittered in the dim light, gazed
angrily at me. However, he did not move and it was one of the
men beside the fire who rose and shuffled towards me.

I told him how I was on my way back from the northern
sieges and had become lost. I requested lodging for the night
and stabling for my horse and finally I asked the name of this
place.

'Now you ask a question!' the man replied. He was
bearded and he wore a white surcoat on which a red cross
was displayed. He continued, 'But all that you may ask shall
be answered.'

The men who stayed beside the fire also wore the red-cross
surcoat. Another of these now rose and went out to attend to
my horse.

'We see that you are very cold, so now come join us by
our fire.'

As I did so, I noted that they were warming themselves by
burning worn tapestries and broken bits of furniture. I started
to declare my name and rank, but immediately they silenced
me.

'We know who you are. Anthony Woodville, you were
present in this castle on the Palm Sunday on which the last
procession of the Holy Grail took place. Then we had hoped

that you would ask a question. What is the Grail? What purpose does the Grail serve? What caused the three dolorous wounds from which the Maimed King suffered? Any question would have sufficed, but nothing could happen unless a question was asked.'

At this, I looked across to the King on his throne and saw that he still gazed furiously upon me. Indeed his eyes, which caught the reflection from the fire, seemed to burn with hatred.

One of the men beside the fire continued, 'You did not ask a question and since you did not ask one, there was no story and, since there was and is no story, the procession of the Grail is no more. You, who were our last hope, have returned too late. What purpose did the Grail serve? It served itself. Know that the Grail was a hidden thing which needed to be sought after and known, but men knew it not and, after the passing of Arthur, it was no longer sought for. Consequently it is forever withdrawn from the world and its glory is departed. We who have guarded it have waited too long and so now the Matter of Britain is finished.'

'Who are you?'

'We were members of the Order of the Knights Templar. It is an order of great antiquity and it was a grandmaster of our order who received from Joseph of Arimathea the chalice in which Christ's blood had been collected. Our knights brought the chalice back from overseas and have guarded it here ever since. Later, some hundred and fifty years ago in the reign of King Edward II, our order was denounced for heresy and so vehemently defamed that we could not purge ourselves. Consequently our order was suppressed and our preceptories and manors were confiscated. Yet some of the order went into hiding and, though we died long ago, we have remained in the service of the Maimed King and we have all drunk from the Grail and it was this which has sustained us. But we do not know what our end shall be now that the Grail has been withdrawn and our King is dead.'

'But your King is not dead! I see him over there staring at me.'

I was angry at what I judged to be their deceit or delusion. One of the Templars sought to detain me, but I brushed his hand away and marched towards the enthroned King. The Templar shambled behind me and feebly pleaded with me not to disturb their late lord. It was only when I reached the foot of the dais that I saw that the King was indeed dead. Propped up on his throne, he was a mummified thing and, though the eyes still glittered, I could now see that the sockets had been filled with quicksilver. Moreover, his body was imperfectly preserved for the wounds that he had sustained when alive continued to rot and I reeled back from the stench of putre-faction.

When I turned away I saw that Hellequin had entered the hall. He bore the gerfalcon on one arm and carried two dead partridges. He recognised me.

'So, Lord Scales, you have come—but too late.'

One of the Templars by the fire cried out,

'Hellequin, these are fine plump birds you have brought us. We shall feast royally tonight!'

'But you are dead!' I protested.

'And so are the birds,' the Templar replied. 'Like calls to like. You were once dead too and that is why you have found our castle.'

Then Hellequin told the Templars that it was the last such meal that they would enjoy, for he would shortly give me the gerfalcon to take to King Edward. The Maimed King was dead, the Grail departed and, with the passing of the Grail, its attendant maidens and the bleeding lance were also departed. So it was time therefore to yield up the bird, for there would never again be a procession at which it must be shown.

The Templars were dismayed at his speech.

'Without our bird, how shall we eat?' And the four of them set up a great wailing and feebly flapped their hands at

Hellequin. He made no reply, but merely passed the gerfalcon to me and then gestured that I should leave. The Templars came shuffling and wailing after me.

'What will we eat if he takes our falcon?'

'He is stealing our dinners!'

But they could not catch me up as I ran out to find my horse. However, since I carried the gerfalcon on my wrist, I was slow to mount Black Saladin and by the time I was in the saddle the Templars had formed a line that blocked the outer gate. I rode directly at them and, when we reached the gateway, Black Saladin reared and struck at two of the Templars with his hooves and so I rode free from the dolorous place and back into the forest.

Once I judged that I had covered enough distance to be safe from those half-men who called themselves Templars, I dismounted in a clearing and laid myself down to sleep on the soggy ground. I was so very tired that it was no matter where I slept. Much later I was awoken by the sound of church bells. It was morning and Black Saladin and the gerfalcon stood as sentinels over me. The sound of those bells guided me to a village where I was able to get directions to Newcastle and there I rejoined my troop.

That is the tale of the winning of the gerfalcon that Anthony composes as soon as he has arrived back in London. The truth is that during the long ride down from the north he had been beset by fears that he would be overtaken on the road by a posse of Warwick's men armed with freshly forged evidence of treason. Now Anthony's writing of the tale in the Woodville townhouse passes the time while he waits for his father to come up from Grafton and join him. Once his father arrives, Anthony loses no time in telling him about the encounters with Warwick, Malory and Tiptoft and the attempt to ensnare him with a charge of treason.

His father listens carefully and when Anthony has finished, he says, 'I am most sorry for this. You were not Warwick's real target, since he was seeking to strike at me through you. He fears that I may be returned to the King's favour and he is right to be so afraid. I have had several secret meetings with Edward outside London where I have been allowed to present the case for a marriage alliance and treaty with Burgundy. At least I hope those meetings were secret, but Warwick has allies and informants everywhere. Therefore I have been most careful in all my dealings and always travel with an armed escort. Now you must be similarly careful. Do not ride out alone. Be suspicious of unsolicited gifts. Be careful of what you eat and drink. Shun strangers who say they want to be your friend. Send no letters that are not sealed. Keep your doors bolted. Your days and nights will be full of peril and I am most sad to have brought this upon you, my son.'

Anthony is not in the least interested in international politics. Nevertheless he asks his father, 'Why are you urging the King to ally with Burgundy?'

'Why? Because Warwick is pressing Edward to conclude a treaty with Louis of France and marry a French princess. But if Edward instead chooses the Burgundian alliance, it will be a sign that Warwick's influence at court is waning. Rage and despair will overwhelm him. He might even kill himself. If he does not, then I shall find some other means to ensure his disgrace and death. As God is my witness, I swear that Warwick will repent the day that he abused and dishonoured us at Calais. I will see him grovel before he dies.'

After a long silence, Anthony summons up the courage to say what he really wants to say, 'Why not forget what happened at Calais? I have. Leave Warwick to his King-making and live at ease. We have wives, money, rank and health. What should the whisperings, the malice, the vying for influence, the hunt for patronage, and the ups and downs at court matter to us? We have all we need at Grafton and Bishop's Lynn.'

But his father replies, 'I am who I am and I will do what I will do.'

Further argument is useless and to change the subject Anthony asks about Malory. Anthony had come to the conclusion that all Malory's enthusiasm for Arthur, Lancelot and Camelot was all a verbose subterfuge that prepared the way for passing on to Anthony *The Avowing of Arthur* and the forged letter concealed within it. But his father says that Malory is indeed much esteemed for his knowledge of Arthurian matters and is said to be writing a great book on the Matter of Britain.

'He is an evil man and doubtless it will be an evil book,' is his father's verdict.

When Anthony presses him further, his father continues, 'Malory is a hard man. He has been in and out of prison many times and I only wonder that he has kept his head upon his shoulders, since at sundry times he has been found guilty of robbery, abduction, rape, extortion, rustling, poaching, and most recently the felonious sheltering of horse thieves, for which last he ended up in Newgate Gaol, but from there he was ransomed by Warwick's kinsman, Fauconberg. Malory is one of Warwick's retainers and an embarrassment to him—doubly so, since Malory is known to be at heart still loyal to Henry of Lancaster. Yet Warwick tolerates this, since he finds it useful to have a go-between who can carry messages to and from the Lancastrians. But one day Malory will go too far and it may be that his crimes and his treason will serve also to bring down his overmighty master...'

And, since his father then resumes his ranting against the Earl of Warwick, Anthony leaves as soon as he politely can. He has no intention of hiring bodyguards and spending his days in fear.

The following morning Anthony presents his narrative of the reclaiming of the gerfalcon to Ripley who skims it rapidly before looking up and smiling. His teeth are so white that they shine like stars.

'Well done, Lord Scales! Well done indeed! You are as

skilled with the pen as you are with the lance. This could hardly be bettered.'

Then he frowns.

'But perhaps it could be bettered.' Ripley hesitates before continuing, 'For I have no sense that you were in any danger in the castle. Yet a story will run better if there is a feeling of jeopardy and the listener cannot be sure whether the hero will finish the tale alive... Also the fervour of your devotion to God is not apparent... I should not say this as I am a priest, but I find that a story is more interesting if there is a beautiful woman in it and the hero is carnally tempted.'

The brilliant smile again.

'You are too modest, but I shall be bold on your behalf. Leave this with me and I will refashion your story in such a manner that it will serve you and your King better. Come to me tomorrow evening at around the time of compline and you will see what I have for you.'

The following evening Anthony returns to Ripley's laboratory and this is what he reads:

After our taking of the castle of Alnwick, I was sent south with the first detachment of discharged troops. Early on the second morning and some way north of Newcastle I became impatient with the slow progress of the marching men and I pressed my horse to a canter and rode ahead, planning to wait for them further up the road, but as I rode on a thick fog descended and I thought it better to advance no further. So I dismounted and waited for them to join me. I waited a long time but I neither heard nor saw anything of my troop. I had then no recourse but to follow the path I was on and travel in the direction which I judged to be south. Surely my route would eventually take me to a habitation where I would get better guidance.

I was in a dark wood in which the right way was obscure. Though fear then filled my blood, I gained so much good from my adventure that I will now relate what happened next.

Eventually I came to a steep hillside and, as I spurred on down the hill, I was amazed and afraid to encounter a gaunt, lean-flanked wolf. I had not thought that there were still wolves in these parts. My horse reared and I struggled to control it. It was not possible to force my horse any closer to the beast. Then, as we turned, I saw another horseman on the brow of the hill. He looked down at me as if I was the person he had been waiting for. I spurred my horse to join him and called out, 'Help! Have pity on me, whether you be man or ghost.'

And he replied, 'I am no man, though I once was one.'

And now that I had ridden close to him, I knew that I had seen him before and his next words confirmed this, 'I was born in Knaresborough. Hellequin is my name. I was known throughout Yorkshire as the chief falconer of Richard Duke of York.'

Then I pointed to the slavering wolf which crouched and waited at the foot of the hill and asked, 'Will you help me kill that beast?'

But he replied, 'That wolf has come from the mouth of Hell and there will be no getting past this creature until the last King of England shall lead me and his other huntsmen in pursuit of it. But come ride with me and we shall take another way.'

And saying this, he led me back down the other side of the hill and along a valley until we came to a fair-seeming castle. As we approached, I heard shouting and the blowing of trumpets from the battlements.

'This is the joyous castle of Corbenic where all hearts are blessed,' said Hellequin.

Once we were inside the castle and I had handed over my horse to a groom, Hellequin led me into a narrow courtyard with benches along its sides. I was to wait here while he fetched the steward who would find me lodgings in the castle. After Hellequin had gone, I saw that there was one other person seated on a bench at the far end of the courtyard. Since he was moaning piteously, I approached and, as I got closer, I perceived that this man was a leper and that there was a bowl of water at his feet.

'Ah, here you are at last!' he said. 'The steward said that someone would be here very shortly to wash my feet, but you have been an age getting here. Well, set to it man. I want my feet washed, as was promised.'

He was ill-tempered and horrible looking, for part of his nose had been eaten away and there were only a few wisps of hair on his head, so that his face somewhat resembled a skull. I was minded to reply that the servant who was to perform this task had not yet arrived and that I would go and see if he was coming soon, but I saw that the leper was in an agony of impatience and distress and so I knelt and placed one of the man's feet in the water and began to wash it. I was shaking with revulsion, for the foot was filthy and deformed. Some of the toes were missing, the arch under the foot was gone and, once I had cleared the mud off, I saw that the upper part of the foot was covered in open ulcers. Having washed one foot, I then took hold of the other, though my hands shook so badly that I could hardly manage this task. The leper crooned with pleasure as he looked down on me.

At last the task was done and I stood up and drew away shuddering. But no sooner had I done so than I reflected that it was not right to nourish such a contemptuous attitude to one of God's creatures and one, moreover, who had been so badly afflicted. So I knelt once more at the leper's feet and, taking the bowl in both hands, I drank from its water in great gulps and I found that it had an oddly sweet flavour. The leper looked down on me curiously. Then I arose and told him that I would go and find others to attend to his further needs.

As I came out of the courtyard, I met the steward who was hurrying to find me. I told him that, since I had washed the leper's feet, there was no need for him to find anyone else to perform this disagreeable task.

'What leper?' he said. 'There are no lepers in this joyous castle.'

And he drew me into the courtyard and I saw that indeed there was no leper there, nor was there a bowl of water.

'That was surely an angel,' said the steward. 'And that was the first of the two trials that you must face while you are here. Only if you also succeed in the second trial will we give you the gerfalcon that was taken from your King. Now I will show you the room in which you are to sleep.'

The room was comfortable and furnished with a few books. I sat on the bed and read from a psalter until I was summoned to dinner. The senior officers of the castle and their wives were all seated at one long table. There were two empty places. One at the head of the table was for the master of this castle. Though he was unwell and would not dine with us this night, I was told that I would be presented to him tomorrow. The other chair was mine and I found myself placed opposite the lady of the castle, very pale with raven-dark hair, and Hellequin was seated beside me. He had no need of food and he only sat with us to keep us company. Indeed, he did most of the talking, as he reminisced about his late master, Richard of York, and what a generous patron and outstanding huntsman this great Duke had been. Though in truth Hellequin rarely had occasion to serve the Duke on hunts, for Richard was so often away fighting in France and Ireland, or deliberating with the other great lords in Westminster. Hellequin swore that Richard had died a martyr for the cause of good government and his death at the Battle of Wakefield made him the greatest King England never had.

The lady was quieter. She seemed displeased by Hellequin's words and, ignoring him, she questioned me about my lineage and achievements and I told her how I had fought for Lancaster at the Battle of Palm Sunday and had been left for dead. But then, when I recovered, I had seen the error of my ways and embraced the cause of the true King, who is Edward. I spoke also about the hardships I and my men had endured during the sieges of the northern castles and I talked about my struggle to master every aspect of swordsmanship and make myself worthy to be the champion of all England. She seemed very interested in everything I had to say and, when the meal was over, she offered to light me to my chamber and make sure that I was comfortable.

Once there she looked round the room and then hurried out of the door without saying good night. I thought this odd. The night was cold and when I got into bed I was still wearing my surcoat, the one which my sister Elizabeth had embroidered with the Woodville blazon: a wreath vert, gules and argent. I was about to blow out my guttering candle, when I saw that the door was being stealthily opened. In another moment I would have tumbled out of bed and grabbed for my sword, but then I saw that it was the lady of the castle who had returned.

'I noticed that your candle was low and thought that you should have a new one,' she said.

Then she sat upon the bed and reached across to press down upon the blanket, so that I was trapped under it.

'Now you are my prisoner,' she said laughing.

'Then I must surrender and there is no one I would rather surrender to.'

But she replied, 'It is I who wish to surrender to you.' And she pressed down upon the blanket between my thighs. 'Perhaps your candle will burn more brightly now. Take me, for my body aches for you and I must be yours.'

I was horrified, for I had meant nothing very much by my gallant offer of surrender and, may God forgive me, I was now tempted. It was as if I had strayed into an orchard in which all the sinful fruits were low hanging. Nevertheless I replied, 'Lady, though this is a fair offer, I cannot take it, for your husband is my host and it would be against my honour to betray his hospitality.'

'Your concern with honour does you credit and I love you the more for it. But my husband will not mind. Rather he will be pleased, for since he was horribly wounded, he has been unable to take me to bed. He cannot satisfy me any more and he knows of my strong needs. So he will be pleased that they have been met by such a man as you.'

I just shook my head at this and she, sweetly sighing, released me from my comfortable prison. Still she sat for a while on the bed, talking of many strange things which I may relate on some future occasion. For now I will only pass on these words of hers.

'You are not as other men, for you are a man of destiny, born to be a hero. Adventures will come running up to you like hungry dogs.'

At length she finished talking and, after she had given me a good night kiss, she departed. When she had gone, I lay awake a long time wondering what kind of thing the second ordeal might be.

I was awoken in the morning by a servant bringing in breakfast on a tray. Later, I girded on my sword and went down into the yard of the castle to exercise and practice certain strokes with my sword. After a while the master of the castle's armoury brought out two blunted swords and offered to train with me, and so we lunged and parried for over an hour. Then I saw that my exercising was being observed by a man propped up on a litter borne by four sturdy porters and I knew that this must be my host, the master of the castle, the Maimed King. The armourer and I put down our swords, while the King instructed his porters to lower his litter to the ground.

Then he crooked his finger to summon me over. He had long hair and a greying beard. Pain had driven deep grooves down his face and I thought that he much resembled Christ as I had seen Him portrayed in images of the Crucifixion.

He lay back on the litter and was silent for a while and

doubtless he was pondering what he should say. Finally, 'You are welcome to my castle. My lady speaks well of you and she urges me to take you into my service. If you would be willing to pledge yourself to me and renounce your former lord, you would find me a good and generous master.'

I replied that I had taken an oath of loyalty to King Edward and, though I had become lost in these northern forests, I ought to seek out my troops as soon as my horse was rested and then I should lead the men back to Norfolk.

He nodded, as if he had been expecting a reply like this. Then he said, 'I see that you do not understand what is on offer. I can make you master of this castle and much else besides—not only lands and money. My wife is very beautiful, is she not? Now look at me. I am so sorely afflicted that you can see I will never be able to father a child. I would like to make you and any child of yours that the lady may bear my heirs, for as I look at you and as I hear about your worth, I feel that you could be like a son to me.'

I replied that I owed service to King Edward and that I would never be forsworn.

Then he said, 'Well done! I now see that earthly things mean little to you. You were right to turn down my offer of my lands and everything in it, including my wife, for in refusing me, you have passed the second test of the castle. But know that I am guardian of the Holy Grail which is kept in this castle and I shall shortly conduct you into its presence. After I am gone, you shall be its guardian. The only thing that is necessary in order to experience this glorious vision is that you should be pure in heart and owe no service to any earthly lord.'

But I was still obstinate and said that I would remain King Edward's man.

And at this point, Hellequin appeared. He was very cheerful.

'Hurrah! Now you really have passed the second ordeal.'

And he signalled to the Maimed King that he should go. The King, who was very angry, rose from the litter and, fending off the porters' attempts to assist him, scuttled away. He was bent double and I thought that in his dark robes he somewhat resembled a black beetle.

Hellequin continued, 'Since you have passed the second test, the gerfalcon, which is kept mewed in a neighbouring castle, will be fetched and the lady of the castle will present you with it tomorrow and then you may be on your way south.'

Saluting me gravely, he then departed and, after a while, the armourer and I resumed our fencing.

At dinner that night, Hellequin talked about falconry and especially about hunting with gerfalcons. He also spoke about his hopes for Richard of York's son, now that the boy was a man and had become King. The lady of the castle sat quietly watching me, feasting on me with her eyes. As soon as the meal was over, I hurried up to my room, for I was very tired and I ached all over from having spent so long exercising with the sword. I threw myself fully dressed on top of the blanket and was close to sleep, when, alas, I heard the door creak and then, when I opened my eyes, I saw that the lady was bending over me.

'It is not courteous of you to refuse me,' she said. 'At least let me kiss you,' and she kissed me softly on the mouth. Then, 'If you are a man, then let me see that you are so. Let me at least gaze upon your body.'

And she set to tugging at my surcoat to pull it off. I was too tired to resist her and besides I thought that I would let her look upon what was beneath it. When she had pulled it off, she was dismayed and her hand went to her mouth. Since I am dedicated to chastity, I wear a hair shirt and, because I wash it only once every forty days, it is usually verminous. Those tiny white crab-like creatures which toiled up and down my shirt were the defenders of my chastity that night. The lady had to steel herself to give me a second kiss before she fled the room.

The following morning I rose early and donned my armour, for I was eager to collect the gerfalcon and depart. But, as I came out into the courtyard, I encountered Hellequin who seemed distressed. He told me that the gerfalcon had been brought over from the neighbouring mews and given to the lady of the castle who was to present it to me. But she, being afraid of such a fierce bird, could not hold it properly and it flew off to a high elm where its jesses became entangled with a branch, so that it could not fly any further, but hung upside down from the tree. Hellequin then led me and my horse, Black Saladin, to the tree, where I saw the bird trapped, hanging upside down like Absalom and beside the tree stood the lady who seemed to be in a grievous state. Then Hellequin walked away and sat on the grass at some distance as if what was to happen was no business of his. The lady was tearful and spread out her hands helplessly.

'The King will be angry with me,' she said. 'If I have let the falcon escape after it has been promised to you, then I fear that he will be so wrathful that he may slay me.'

But I told her that her fears were groundless and that, since as a boy I had climbed many trees, I would find no difficulty in climbing this one and rescuing the bird. I only needed her assistance in unarming me. So she set to removing my sword, helmet, breastplate and other pieces until I was stripped down to my hair shirt. Then I set to climbing the tree and when I was level with the bird I wrenched off the branch on which the bird was caught and threw it and the bird down and, though the bird tried to fly off again, it was still so entangled with the branch that it could not.

I had almost completed my descent when I saw that two men armed *cap-à-pie* stood close by the tree and they waved their swords as signal of their intent to kill me and then they beat those swords on their shields and shouted 'Lancaster! Lancaster!' I was in desperate straits, for my own sword and armour had been removed by the lady to some distance away where she stood looking on and laughing with pleasure at my discomfiture and the Maimed King had come up beside her to hold her hand.

I shouted to the two knights that it would be shameful to make a treasonable attack on an unarmed man and they should at least let me have my sword so that the combat should be fairer. And one of them replied, saying, 'No, no, we think that you are far too good a swordsman for us to risk that. I swear that if you come down and kneel before us, we will allow you enough time to make your peace with God before we behead you.'

I now knew who one of the knights was, as I recognised the voice of James Butler, the late and unlamented Earl of Wiltshire. But, since I did not consider his offer a fair one, I climbed higher up the tree and, breaking off as thick a branch as I could manage, I then whistled for Black Saladin, which being well-trained, came and stood beneath the tree, so that I was able to leap into my saddle and then I rode my horse directly at Butler and he, being true to his nature, turned and fled. I did not trouble to pursue him, for there was the second man to deal with.

When I brought my horse round to face him, I recognised him also, for the face under the sallet was that of my former comrade in arms, Sir Andrew Trollope, one of those who had died at the Battle of Palm Sunday. I was a little sad that it was him that I would have to fight with, though this was scarcely a time for grieving. Because I did not want Sir Andrew to strike at Black Saladin with his sword, I dismounted and pushed my horse to move away. Sir Andrew stood hefting his sword and waiting to see what I would do next. He was confident that I could do no damage to him with my stick, but what I did then surprised him very much, for I hurried over to the gerfalcon, freed it from the encumbering branch and then threw the bird at Sir Andrew's face. He screamed horribly and then, when the bird flew up to rest upon one of the lowest branches of the elm, I saw that it had clawed at the unhappy knight's eyes. He kept screaming in his blindness and he turned and turned, pointing his sword in front of him, but he had no chance, for I crept up on him and brought my stick down hard on his wrist, knocking the sword from his grasp, and then I used the stick again to rain blows upon his sallet until he fell unconscious to the ground.

The lady of the castle had been excited by the combat. As I stood over Sir Andrew, I saw that she was flushed and she looked on me with parted lips. Something in my spirit moved. In some strange way I had found her evil intent as seductive as her laughter and I thought that I knew what I must do with her.

But first I sat down, propped up against the tree, for I was breathless and then Hellequin walked over to congratulate me. He was genuinely pleased for I am sure that he had no love for old Lancastrians.

'Well done!' he said. 'You passed the third ordeal.'

'But I was told that there would only be two ordeals,' I replied.

'I know. We lied.' Then seeing that I was discontented with this, he continued, 'In real life you, like everyone else on this earth, will always be facing ordeals, one coming fast after another, and even after you draw your dying breath you will still have the Final Judgement to face. Ordeals are a necessary part of life, everybody has to face them and it is only in stories that there are just three ordeals after which the champion may retire to live happily ever after. As for you, I am sure that you face ordeals by night as well as by day.'

Having admonished me in this fashion, he lured the ger-falcon from its branch and walked off with it in the direction of the castle. When I had got some of my breath back, I staggered over to the Maimed King, told him that my plans had changed and asked him for one more night of hospitality.

'Yes, you have to stay another night. You must. You are forbidden to leave today.'

Yet though he was so emphatic about this, I saw that he was also sad that I would stay another night in the castle. Then I took the lady aside and whispered to her, 'If you will come to my chamber tonight, I promise that you will find me naked.' And she blushed to hear me say this.

At dinner the Maimed King took his place at the head of the table. He said that he wanted to talk about history, which he regarded as a sort of science that revealed moral laws. Yet it is my belief that his foul intent was to put us all off our food. For he spoke first about how King Richard II died in Pontefract Castle over a hundred and sixty years ago. It is said that he was starved to death. Without food and water it takes perhaps as much as two weeks to die and during that period the starved man is in anguish, for he suffers from headaches, stomach pains and cramps. He longs to cry, but there is no moisture for his tears and then finally his heart gives out. After all this, Richard's body was brought out from Pontefract and paraded and displayed at various places on the road to London, as if his corpse was some freak to be marvelled at.

Now, said the Maimed King, we were to compare that awful fate to the earlier death of Edward II in Berkeley Castle. His jailers kept him in a cell above a chamber full of the corpses of rotting animals, in the hope that their stink would infect him with some fatal disease, yet he remained healthy. So eventually three men seized him and they forced a red-hot poker up his arse. Though it is said that his screams could be heard for miles around, at least his death was relatively quick. Then the Maimed King went on to speak of the horrid deaths of Kings as reported in the Bible, as well as slaughtered monarchs in foreign parts. He particularly lingered over the murder of Evil-Merodach, Nebuchadnezzar's successor as King of Babylon. The lady said nothing, but kept her eyes fixed on me. We all drank heavily, the lady as much as anyone else.

I stumbled up to my room and, removing my hair shirt and brushing a few lice off my chest, I got under the blanket. I had

not long to wait, before she entered smiling. She kissed me
before pulling off the blanket and then she screamed, for she
now saw that my chest was crisscrossed with hideous welts
that were the product of my regular penitential scourgings. I
rolled onto my front so that she could see that my back was in
an even worse state. Then I got out of bed and picked up the
whip which I kept close by on the floor. I handed her the whip
and knelt before her.

'Now you see how I am dedicated to chastity,' I said. 'But
I have lusted after your generous body and, may God forgive
me, came close to surrendering to your sweet charms. If of
your grace you care for me at all, I beg you to whip the evil
out.'

Though her eyes were moist, she nodded and gripped
the whip and walked behind me and set to flogging me. Her
strokes were fierce and I thought that it might be that she was
angry at having her own lusts frustrated in this unexpected
fashion. When the scourging was over because of her exhaus-
tion, she knelt beside me and fingered the leaden image of a
little man that hung from my neck, wanting to know what it
was and I told her that it was an amulet that my mother had
fashioned to keep me safe in battle.

Then I had a question.

'It is most curious. I have spent two days and two nights in
your castle and yet I still do not know your name. Is it secret,
or will you tell it to me?

'My name was Theophania,' she replied. 'But henceforth
I choose to be known as Dame Discipline de la Chevalerie.
You have done well to resist my charms these three nights and
I shall trouble you no more in this fashion. Now I shall leave
you.'

But I gripped her by the arm to detain her and asked, 'One
more question, what purpose does the gerfalcon serve? Why
was it sent to me in Kennington and why was it taken away
again after I had presented it to King Edward?'

Her smile was glorious and she replied, 'Now at last you have asked the question and, with the asking of the question, our adventure can be completed. Know then that bird served only as a lure and a messenger to bring you back to us. And now sleep well, for tomorrow I must conduct you to your greatest test.'

And I lay back sleepless and in pain on my bloody bed.

The following morning after breakfast I met Dame Discipline de la Chevalerie outside the castle's chapel.

'Good morning, Sir Anthony. Hellequin waits to hand on the gerfalcon to you. But one thing is yet to be faced. You are handsome, brave and chaste. Yet there is still a flaw in you. You are slow to ask questions and you ask too few of them. Even so, you have asked the right question and now you are to be granted an unveiled showing of the Holy Grail. Steel yourself, for it is a fearsome thing.'

Steel myself? How? Who can prepare himself for an encounter with the Divine? What kind of armour can serve in an encounter with God? But I nodded and then she unlocked the outer door of the chapel and we walked into a little space that was as brightly lit as if it had been under direct sunlight. Then, when she unlocked the second door, she turned away and shielded her eyes, but I did not and I saw that the Grail was brighter than five thousand suns and whole worlds burned within it. I saw the inside of my skull all lit up and the Eye of God hovering within it and then I saw no more, for my plight was like that of Sir Andrew Trollope, since I had become blind.

I followed the voice of Dame Discipline de la Chevalerie out of the chapel. Her voice was soothing, though I was in no state to understand what she was saying. Then Hellequin came up and told me that I could no longer remain in the castle. I was helped into the saddle and two men were assigned to me. One of them led my horse while the other walked beside, and after a while, I understood that this second man

carried the gerfalcon. My companions said very little and I
was not disposed to talk either, for I was wondering how I
should make my way in the world since I had become a blind
man. In an instant I who was strong had become a weak-
ling and an object of pity. I should withdraw from court and
hand over my sword and armour to someone who could use
them. I should become dependent on small boys to lead me
about. My legs should be covered in bruises from walking
into things. I should listen to priests reading things to me in
singsong voices. I should spill my food as I tried to eat. Never
again should I gaze on the beauty of women. Though I was
blind, the inside of my head was lit up with the light of the
Grail which burned like a sun. I thought blindness was a fearful price to pay for having gazed upon it. I could feel the tears
streaming down my face.

The day was nearly over before I was delivered to a hermitage called No Man's Chapel where I was told that my eyes
were to be healed. The hermit, whose name was Piers, pushed
me down onto my knees and joined me in prayer before he
applied a salve to my eyes and told me not to rub them. Then
he ordered me to sleep. It was easy to obey. I thought that I
was swimming in a golden sea before I drowned and lost consciousness. The following morning when I opened my eyes I
saw light and dark shapes, though nothing clearly. Seeing I
was awake, Piers applied more salve to my eyes and told me
to keep them shut for an hour. Though the light of the Grail
still shone on my closed eyelids, that light was now silvery like
the light of the moon.

'You who were blind to God's power and mercy have been
gently punished.'

Then it may be that because he saw that I was restless and
impatient that Piers started to tell me about his life.

'I was once a knight and a courtier as you are and I saw
service with John of Bedford in France. I was wild and passionate, as perhaps all young men should be. It was in the

city of Rouen that I fell desperately in love with a married Frenchwoman. Though I, in a fever of desire, followed her everywhere, she would not so much as look at me. Then one Sunday I was riding through the streets when I saw her enter a church. May God forgive me, I resolved to follow her. So I spurred my horse on and rode up the steps and entered the church on my mount.'

There was a certain pride in Piers' voice as he described riding into church. He continued, 'I do not know what I meant to do next, but in any case the whole congregation turned on me and drove me and my horse out before I could even speak to the lady. Though it was a great scandal and the Archbishop complained to the Duke of Bedford, still I was an Englishman and this city was ours to do with more or less as we wished. So I was merely reprimanded.'

'But then it seems the lady conferred with her husband, before she invited me to an assignation. We met in a secluded place where I was confident of attaining the object of my desire, but all of a sudden she uncovered her bosom to reveal a breast that was being eaten away by a cancer and, when I saw that the breast was covered with red and brown pustules, I shrank from her.

'See Englishman,' she cried. 'Is this diseased and dying body what you desired so much? It would be better for your soul if you loved Jesus and not me.'

And with that I was dismissed. Then I sought permission from the Duke to return to England, where I sold my armour, weapons and estate and used the money to build this chapel some distance away from any other habitation.'

When I was allowed to open my eyes again, I saw a little more clearly, though things were blurred and their edges wavered as if I was looking at the world under water. The hermitage did not resemble a chapel at all. Standing outside in the pale sunshine, I could see that the hermitage was a pleasant-seeming little cottage with timbered walls and a neatly thatched roof. Piers had an extravagant beard and, though I seemed to see bees in the beard, I put this down to my still faulty vision. That morning I helped in the garden as well as I was able.

In the afternoon, he applied the salve once more and once more I sat with my eyes closed while he talked, 'Here in my hermitage, since I am withdrawn from the great events—the crown wearings, parliamentary assemblies, battles and plague epidemics—I have had the sense that I understand more clearly how history is made, and so, many years ago, I decided that I would become a historian, but I would not chronicle the past, for there were many learned scholars already engaged in that task. Instead I would become and indeed have become an historian of the future.'

This time I interrupted him, 'An historian of the future? How is that possible? How can you make a record of things that have not happened yet?'

'It seems to me that it is no more difficult to research the future than the past, for how do we know about the past? Only through things that are here in the present—ruins, relics and manuscripts. In the same manner, I believe that we can deduce the future from things that are here in the present. So I ask myself what must the future be like, given that things are here as they are now? The world around us—the stars, the growth of trees and plants, the faces of men and women, the shifting watercourses—all tell us the way the world is going.'

I was obstinate, 'You cannot make records of things that have not happened.'

'Oh, yet I know what will happen to you and what your end will be,' he said, but after that he would not argue with me and he just sat beside me muttering to himself. At last it was time for me to open my eyes again and this time I saw things clearly. Indeed I thought that I saw more clearly than before, since things appeared sharper edged and more solid. Now Piers was able to show me properly round his garden, with its carefully tended rows of vegetables, its orchard and its beehives. The bees in the beard had not been an hallucination. From time to time he amused himself by strapping the queen bee in a cage under his chin and by this means he was able to attract a great swarm of bees to his beard.

The following morning he took me into the garden again and made a sweeping gesture with his arms to encompass it all.

'Don't go to London. Join me here and tend the rows of beans, collect fruit, listen to the bees and join me in fishing from the river. It is quiet here. Step out of history.'

But I was young and not ready to retire from life. Just before I was about to ride off I leant down from my saddle and said to Piers, 'I think that, on your honour as a knight, you should have embraced the lady with the cancerous breast and given her comfort in any way you could.'

'I know,' he said sadly.

Then I rode back into history.

I found my men who had made very slow progress for they were still a little way short of Newcastle. They had missed me and feared that I had been killed by robbers. But I was astounded to hear that they were sure that I had only been gone for part of a day and a night. This was certainly wrong and I wondered if it was possible that my place had been taken by a phantom horseman who had impersonated me. I had no further adventures. My troop disbanded on the edge of Norfolk and I rode on to London.

Ripley looks anxiously at Anthony as he reads all this. Though Anthony keeps control of his face, he is angry at many things. He is most annoyed that Ripley has kept hardly anything of his own story. He does not like the hint that he has been afraid of the wolf. He does not want to wash a leper's feet, still less drink the water afterwards. He does not want to wear a hair shirt covered with lice. He would much rather have made love to the lady of the castle, instead of kneeling before her and begging to be flogged. He does not like Piers to lecture him like a schoolboy and Piers' confidence that he knew how Anthony would die seemed oddly like a threat. He thinks that Ripley's story is cruel, for in it he was much abused and suffered unreasonably. Also it was hard on his old friend Andrew Trollope that he should have his eyes clawed out. And, in any case, can he really trust Ripley, a man of whom Warwick has spoken well? Yet none of this shows on Anthony's face.

Instead he says, 'This is a remarkable story, but it is so remarkable that no one will believe it.'

'Why should they not?' replies Ripley. 'There is a church in Evesham which guards as a holy relic the hole in the ground in which the cross of the Crucifixion was placed and in Carlisle they venerate the bones of St Francis as they were when he was a boy of thirteen. If people can believe such things, then surely they can believe our story about the finding of the gerfalcon?'

Then, seeing that Anthony looks dubious, Ripley tries another tack.

'No, most people will not swallow this tale whole, but they will believe that some of it may be true, and remember that this is only the first of many stories that we shall circulate about you. It is a matter of drip, drip, drip.'

'I shall deny what you claim ever happened to me.'

'Then people will only think that you are being very modest. So much the better.'

'I am amazed that you have invented such a strange story,' says Anthony.

'My dear lord, I did not invent it all,' Ripley replies. 'I steal other men's stories... Now I have work to do and I am sure that you should go away and resume your exercising with the sword and lance. And remember this. The lady of the castle was right. You are the hero of your story. I, on the other hand, am in the shadows of that story.' And he continues wistfully,

'Knights and lords can become heroes, but no one has ever heard of an heroic alchemist and no alchemist has ever gazed upon the Grail. Please remain my friend, for all shall be well, all things shall be well, and all manner of things shall be well.'

CHAPTER SEVEN

Wedding

Centuries ago a young King went hunting in a forest. He became separated from his companions and while still lost, he came to a river on the bank of which he encountered a beautiful woman with blonde hair and the look of an elf about her. She offered to show him the way out of the forest...

Anthony remembers that, when they were little, he and his older sister Elizabeth used to listen to fairy stories told to them by their mother. According to her, fairy stories are stories which fairies tell about themselves and it was Jacquetta's fairy blood, by virtue of her descent from Melusine, which licensed her to tell such stories. Her eyes rolled and she summoned up her stories as if she were calling on angels or demons to present themselves. Indeed she believes that every story has its own spirit and they are urgent in seeking storytellers who can tell them accurately and well. She mostly told stories about beautiful maidens who married Kings or Princes. According to Jacquetta, both Elizabeth and Anthony had been born ugly, but she reassured them that she had got her cat, Bastet, to lick the ugliness out of them and, since they were both now quite beautiful, they would surely feature in their own fairy tales when they were older.

Anthony reflects that, if his life is turning into any kind of tale, then it is a strange one. Ever since the Battle of Palm Sunday, nothing has been normal and he toys with the notion that he was indeed killed at that battle and, instead of returning to life, he now inhabits an afterlife which presents him with a diabolic and flawed simulacrum of living reality. Again and again he finds his way taking him down hitherto unvisited paths. Familiar objects, once he closely examines them, dissolve into things that are strange and threatening. Surely it cannot continue like this? He wishes that he could return to the easy certainties of his boyhood.

Anthony is glad to return to Scales Hall. Though his wife embraces him passionately, her first words are full of mockery, for, of course, Beth has recognised the rumours Ripley has been putting about regarding Anthony's asceticism, his resistance to erotic temptation and the vision of the Grail for the fantasies that they all are. She feels under the tabard just to make sure that there is no hair shirt and she whispers in his ear inquiring whether he would like her to give him a good flogging.

He finds that a parcel of books has been sent by Tiptoft to await his arrival, including one he had requested on the construction of circles of protection. Since frequent 'vigils' in the nearby church would be looked upon by the locals as suspicious, he proposes to Beth that they spend the night together within a magic circle under the protection of its four angels. Beth knows nothing of magic. Nevertheless she agrees, for she likes danger and adventure, or at least she thinks she does. Moreover, she is bored with travelling to distant churches and coupling on cold stone floors. They shall see what the night shall bring them.

It is past midnight when Anthony begins his conjuration in the solar. But first he has servants create a temporary bed consisting of a thick layer of rushes covered by a blanket and cushions. Then he uses sticks of charcoal to mark out the circle of protection with the names of the guardian angels Talvi, Casmaran, Ardarel and Farlas inscribed inside and he places lighted candles at those four points, though he does not trouble to mark out the traverses which a swordsman might make. Then he leads Beth into the circle and they undress. But no sooner have they done so, than the bloodied Earl of Wiltshire appears in the doorway. Though dead and gashed about he is still curiously handsome.

Beth screams and Anthony shouts, 'Go away! In the name of God, I conjure you to go.'

Wiltshire does not reply, but looks behind him. Other figures are filing through the door. There is Sir Andrew Trollope and Anthony's sister's late husband, Sir John Grey, and there are a few others he recognises, men who failed to survive the Battle of Palm Sunday, but there are many more that he could not remember seeing before and it may be that some fell in earlier battles. There are also a few women in the crowd. Beth is hurrying to get dressed again, but she is in such a panic that her tunic and under-tunic are in a horrible tangle. By now the solar is full and the circle is surrounded, but it seems that there are others outside the solar who are trying to force their way in. Those at the front, just outside the circle of protection, keep moving their legs as if they were still advancing, though they are unable to break into the protected space.

Wiltshire is the first to speak, 'We mean you no harm. We come in good fellowship.'

'You are one of us,' says another, addressing Anthony.

'You are very beautiful,' says a third to Beth. 'We like looking at you.'

'Your wife is beautiful, is she not?' says Wiltshire to Anthony.

Now there is a regular clamour of voices.

'We only want to watch.'

'She has beautiful thighs.'

'And lips like rubies.'

'You lucky dog.'

'We like watching. It is good to look on the love of a man for a woman.'

Several of the creatures at the front have begun to masturbate, or at least to simulate that act.

'It is very cold out here. Let us into the circle.'

A trio of women, all very beautiful, though one shows a bloody gash across her breasts, force their way forwards. They call out to Anthony,

'Let us in Lord Scales. Let us join your wife on the blanket, for we would love you too. We can all be jolly together.'

But the men, on the contrary, are now urging Anthony to come out from the circle and join them in their feast.

By now the press is such that naked corpses are scaling the walls and crawling upside down on the ceiling. The floorboards under Anthony and Beth are creaking and bulging as someone or something pushes at them from below. So it continues for over an hour, before the voices begin to turn nasty, 'Dear lady, surely you know that your husband is not a living human. He is one of us. That is why we are here.'

'Nothing can come from his seed—nothing good at least.'

'It is a damnable thing for a woman to surrender herself to a corpse. The end of it is eternal perdition.'

'He really is one of us and once he has had his way with you, he will break the circle and let us have our turn, will you not, my lord? You promised us. Share and share alike.'

Anthony seeing that Beth is gazing raptly at the mob of corpses, tries to draw her round to face him.

'Pull away,' he begs her. 'Pull away. Do not look at them.'

Then he tries to cover her eyes, but she pushes his hands away. He is losing her. He crawls under the blanket and calls to her, 'Beth, as you love me, join me here.'

She does not answer, but the dead reply, 'She is ours.'

The creatures outside the circle have reverted to flattering her and praising her beautiful flesh. At the same time others threaten and abuse Anthony. So he puts his head under the blanket and claps his hands over his ears, but he still hears the voices.

'There can be no escape. We dead are always watching,

watching and judging even when you cannot see us. We shall always be in your thoughts.'

'We are your thoughts. We live inside your head. Inside or outside of the circle, we are in your head.'

'Hell is too crowded. So we have come to live with you.'

Anthony takes to singing and babbling loudly in order to drown out the threats and insinuations. Towards dawn, the numbers of the watchful dead diminish somewhat. At the last they are attended on only by Wiltshire and a couple of his comrades, but then as the nearby church's bells begin to peal, summoning the village to Sunday worship, the three of them stumble away and the sound of their wailing in the distance is soon drowned by the noise of the bells. Anthony, more tired than he has ever been in his life, now falls asleep to their tolling.

He is awoken by something damp on his face. He opens his eyes and sees that it is spittle from Beth's mouth. She is crouched and drooling over him and there is a vacant look in her eyes as if she does not know what she is looking at. Those eyes now never blink.

In the days that follow all manner of remedies are tried, starting with bloodletting and cupping, followed by purges, then an exorcism carried out by the parish priest, and this is followed by sweatings in hot baths, a diet of eggs and wine, and readings from the lives of the saints. Beth suffers it all without speaking or blinking.

Anthony writes a careful account of the horrid ordeal and sends it to Ripley and he asks him for advice on how Beth can be cured. He is infuriated when Ripley, in reply, has no suggestions to make with regard to Beth's malady. But among other improvements to the narrative of the ordeal, Ripley suggests that there should be a goat-headed devil in charge of the corpses and that those outside the circle should produce an angelic child, the son of one of the household servants, and then they should threaten to slit the child's throat as a sacrifice to the goat-headed devil, unless Anthony steps outside the circle. But Anthony, Elizabeth and the little child will be rescued when the four angels whose names are inscribed in the circle manifest themselves. It seems that Ripley has difficulty in separating reality and fantasy.

Finally, Anthony reluctantly escorts Beth to a convent outside York where she will be confined and carefully tended. Her soul has travelled elsewhere. The ride back to Scales Hall is a melancholy business. The nuns will write if there is any sign of a recovery.

Anthony does not return to London until shortly before Pentecost. When he presents himself at court, he finds that some men look on him strangely and that the ladies, in particular, are careful to keep their distance from him and it is some time before he realises that this must be because Ripley's account of the unwashed and verminous hair shirt has after all attained some credence. God knows what else people believe.

The presentation of the gerfalcon takes place at the entrance to the Palace of Westminster at noon on the day of Pentecost. The bird had been brought up from its place of concealment in a mews in Woking on the previous day. Anthony advances with the massive hooded bird on his glove and carefully hands it over to the keeping of the King's head falconer. Edward formally thanks him for undertaking this difficult quest and bringing it to a successful conclusion. Only Edward, Anthony, Hastings and Ripley know that this business is a charade, though others may have their suspicions. Edward, standing beside his falconer, has difficulty in concealing his irritation at having been persuaded by Ripley to go along with this imposture. As far as Edward is concerned, Anthony is still the young man who was killed fighting for Henry of Lancaster at Towton and then came back to life. So Anthony is a freak of nature, like Tiptoft's dwarf, Chernomor.

The crowd who look on are mostly puzzled. Anthony has been carefully vague about how he tracked down the bird and won it back and he hopes his vagueness will be taken for modesty. His story is that long searching led him to a castle in a remote part of northern England. There he had to undergo a series of tests before the lord of the castle would allow him to take away the bird. Meanwhile Ripley's intelligencers have been spreading the more detailed and fantastical story of Anthony's encounter with a maimed King, his fight with dead men, his resistance to the temptation of Dame Discipline de la Chevalerie and his vision of the Grail, but, as Anthony had expected, few people believe this and, when Anthony is asked if he has seen the Grail, he firmly denies it.

The Earl of Warwick is the leader of those who mock this ceremony.

'The dead do not walk,' he loudly declares.

But Jacquetta is standing close by and she points a bony finger at him, 'A man who does not believe in ghosts is on the way to godlessness,' she says, 'Since from there it is but a short step to not believing in God's power to work miracles and from there then another short step to not believing in God Himself.'

Warwick seems bewildered. It had not occurred to him (or to Anthony) that it was actually possible not to believe in God. Looking at him, Anthony realises that, while Warwick hates and despises him and his father, Warwick is actually afraid of Jacquetta.

Then Edward demands that, before proceeding into the Abbey for mass, the assembled lords and knights should take an oath, 'Never to do outrageously, nor murder, and always to flee treason; also by no means to be cruel, but to give mercy unto him that asks for mercy. Also that no man takes battles in a wrongful quarrel for no law.' This is the revival of an ancient custom, for Arthur had his knights swear just such an oath. After the oath and mass, the courtiers proceed to the Palace for the Pentecostal feast. At the door of Westminster Hall pages stand and hold out bowls for the washing of hands.

The seat on Edward's left is vacant, a sign that England still has no queen. Henry Beaufort Duke of Somerset sits on Edward's right, for he is in high favour since he has been won over from the Lancastrian cause. Grace is said, food brought in to drums and pipes and everyone is about to sit down, but then it is seen that Edward is still standing and he now declares that he will not sit nor eat until he hears of an unusual adventure or of some wrong that must be righted. No sooner has he announced this than the door is flung open and a woman comes rushing in. Her hair is loose and she is barefoot. Three children, also barefoot, follow her. She throws herself at Edward's feet and begs for his grace and justice. Her name is Alice Lytton and she is a widow, for her husband was killed at the Battle of Palm Sunday when he fought for King Henry, and being a widow of a man who fought for the wrong side, she has no means to defend herself against the depredations of her neighbours and they have forcibly occupied her house, the Manor of High Selling, and left her and her children homeless and penniless. Edward smiles and raises her to her feet. He declares that he will make sure that justice will be done and that swiftly and he summons over John Tiptoft, who as President of the Court of Chivalry will deal with the matter. It can be seen that the sun of royal justice shines equally over those loyal to the house of York and over former partisans of Lancaster and their dependents. Anthony guesses that this perfunctory little play has been arranged by Hastings in consultation with Ripley.

Now they may sit down, but Warwick is annoyed at being displaced from the King's side by Somerset. And there is more. At the far end of the table Warwick mutters angrily about all this mock Arthurian mummery, 'I know little about Arthur, but from what I know I say that, since he was cuckolded by Lancelot and lost the allegiance of half his knights, before being fatally wounded by Mordred, he was a King who failed. All this play at being paladins and knights errant is just for the amusement of women. I say that we can worry about the giants and the dragons that may beset our land after we have dealt with Henry and that harridan, Margaret. Indeed where is Henry lurking? We sit here drinking ourselves senseless, discussing ancient chivalry, when we should be talking money, munitions, foreign alliances, mercenaries and subsidies. This pageant is all a monstrous folly.'

'Of course it is folly,' replies a smiling Hastings. 'But we cannot always be worrying about commissions of array, bombards, entails and bills of lading. There must also be feasting, dancing and pageants, or what is the point of being alive? This evening there are fireworks and dancing yet to come—and here is Scoggin to make us merry!'

Warwick growls. He is under some strain, for he sees it as his task to detach the French and Scots from their support of the House of Lancaster and that will not be easy.

Scoggin has indeed presented himself before Warwick's table. Anthony notes that, since he last saw him, the jester walks with a limp, has lost some teeth and seems to have difficulty getting his jokes out. He will not be doing cartwheels anymore.

'How many calves' tails does it take to reach from the earth to the sky?' he wants to know.

The diners profess their bafflement.

'Just the one, so long as it is long enough!' is the answer. Then, 'What beast is it that has her tail between her eyes?'

Again Scoggin has to provide the correct answer, which is 'A cat when she licks her arse!'

With this and other jolly quips the diners are royally entertained, except that Warwick and Rivers, though divided on so many other issues, look on the jester stonily.

'I hate jokes,' says Earl Rivers. 'Jokes feed on ugliness, stupidity and misfortune. I would much rather encounter a footpad than a clown.'

The firework display is mounted by Ripley in the courtyard.

Edward looks on as the heavens open with crimson rain and emerald serpents run along the ground, but he is as dissatisfied with the evening as is Warwick, though for different reasons.

'All this is very well,' Edward says. 'But I want a real adventure. I want magic. I want to see something marvellous.'

'Your Grace must come to Grafton,' says Jacquetta. 'And I swear to you that you will behold something truly marvellous.'

And her husband adds that the hunting in Northamptonshire is exceptionally good. Edward nods distractedly. Jacquetta is still beautiful and her gaze on him is fierce. Finally Edward says that he may come to Northamptonshire some time soon for the hunting.

The day after the Pentecostal Feast Anthony travels with his parents for a brief stay at Grafton. It will be the first time in four years that he has seen his sister Elizabeth who, since her husband's death, has moved back to be with her parents. The Woodville Manor of Grafton, on the road from London to Northampton, has been built on the ruins of an old monastery. It is evening when they reach it. They find Elizabeth waiting for them in the great parlour. She, Earl Rivers and Anthony sit at a trestle table at one end of the room. Though Elizabeth asks a few questions about Anthony's experiences in the north, it soon becomes clear that talk about fighting and munitions bores her and she really wants to discuss money and properties with her father. Jacquetta sits apart from them on a high carved chair in the shadows of one of the far corners, contentedly muttering to herself as she plays with her set of lead dolls and has them speak to each other in rhyme. When she was younger she assisted her husband John of Bedford in the management of his vast estates in England and France and, then until a few years ago, she was the trusted confidante and adviser of Margaret of Anjou. Yet, despite all this, there has always been something childlike about Jacquetta, for she still believes in the reality of the fairy folk that she was told about when she was little, even though, according to her, full-blooded fairies went into exile long ago and the place they now inhabit is hard even for her to reach. It needs a special sort of squinting and letting one's eyes focus beyond what is in front of them. When, soon after Rivers married Jacquetta, he asked whether she really believed in fairies, she replied that they had a very poor reputation for telling the truth.

Elizabeth must find a new husband who will be a father to her two boys, Thomas and Richard, to secure the property that is rightly hers as a result of her husband's death. The dower shares and property valuations at issue are complex and Anthony cannot get interested in these matters, but as he watches Elizabeth he notes how the excitement of all this talk of money and property makes her blush and seem more beautiful than ever. This somewhat resembles the charm of a small child who demands more sweets. Jacquetta has often spoken of Elizabeth's glamour and described it as a kind of witchery. Her dower manors—Newbottle and Brington in Northamptonshire and Woodham Ferrers in Essex—should provide ample income for her and her sons. But Lady Ferrers has recently wed Sir John Bourchier and it appears that the two of them are plotting to entail what should have been Thomas' inheritance from his father. Her father advises Elizabeth that she must seek protection at court from someone more powerful than himself and he proposes that she should write to Lord Hastings offering half the value of her dower estates in exchange for an indenture of covenant and a favourable settlement. Clearly this will be expensive but needs must when the Devil drives. Her father will dictate the letter that Elizabeth must write to Hastings.

Jacquetta, who has always been rich, does not see money as so important and she finds all this talk about dowers and entails as boring as Anthony does. She would rather talk about love and romance, but for now she sits at a small octagonal table and continues to move the small lead figurines about on a chequered tray that somewhat resembles a chess board. One by one these manikins are brought before a slightly larger figure who is crowned and they are tilted to bow before him. Watching this, Anthony guesses that these little people stand for fairies in Jacquetta's imagination and that they are being made to pay obeisance to Oberon, the King of the Fairies.

At length her father and Elizabeth have finished their talk of money and properties. Then it is time for Jacquetta to tell one of her ghost stories. This really happened, she says, to one of the reeves in the service of her previous husband, John of Bedford.

This man's wife had just given birth to a stillborn son. So then the reeve decided to go on pilgrimage to Santiago de Compostella to pray to St James that his wife might have better fortune next time and they might be blessed with a son and heir. While he was on the road he was overtaken by a great procession of people riding horses, oxen, sheep and other animals. But then he saw in the middle of the procession a tiny child wriggling along the ground in a stocking. He asked the little creature what it did there and it replied, 'It is not right for you to adjure me, for you were my father and I am your miscarried son, buried without a name and without baptism.'

So then the father wrapped his shirt around the child and baptised and named him. Then the infant rejoined the procession, this time joyfully toddling on his two legs. The man kept the stocking. Back in England there was a party to celebrate the reeve's return from pilgrimage. Then the reeve produced the stocking and demanded an explanation. The midwives admitted that they had wrapped the infant in the stocking and buried him without baptising him or giving him a name.

It is of course a moral tale. That is the way with ghost stories. Since sheriffs, magistrates and beadles do not suffice, ghosts must walk our streets and enter our houses to issue warnings and enforce law and morality. A ghost, any ghost, should be the friend of a virtuous man, and one should take comfort from ghost stories, yet Anthony finds the image of a child in a stocking slithering along the road to be a sinister one. He finds it difficult to sleep that night.

A few days later, Anthony has to make his farewells before he rides off to Scales Hall. He finds the women in the parlour where Jacquetta is braiding Elizabeth's hair. He waits until this is over and listens to them speculating about what sort of man might serve as Elizabeth's second husband. This chatter is all quite ordinary, but then suddenly Jacquetta, standing before Elizabeth intones the words, 'As the raven desires the cadavers of dead men, so should he desire you.' It is almost as if a curse has been uttered and it brings the women's chatter to an end.

In the months that follow Anthony only receives a few letters from his father. Mostly his father writes about his manoeuvres to secure Elizabeth's dower property and his meetings in London with Lord Hastings on that subject. A couple of lords with estates in Northamptonshire have visited Grafton ostensibly to discuss matters relating to the keeping of the peace in the county, but Rivers suspects that their real motive was to inspect his daughter and consider her as a possible wife, though he has heard nothing more from either of them. The winter has been mild and the harvest is expected to be better this year, though of course it is far too early to tell. The King, who has been staying at Stony Stratford, has also visited the Manor of Grafton a few times at the end of a day's hunting in the area and on one occasion has invited Rivers to join him on the hunt. Edward seemed to enjoy talking to Jacquetta. The northern fortresses that Warwick, Tiptoft, Anthony and others spent so long besieging are once more in the hands of the Lancastrians. The Earl of Warwick is in France where he is negotiating for a marriage alliance with Bona of Savoy. The wedding, once it takes place, will tie England to France in an alliance against Burgundy. The chief advantage of this marriage is that it will cut off French support for the armies of

Henry of Lancaster and Margaret of Anjou. (Simply because Warwick is for a French alliance, Rivers is of course set upon one with Burgundy.) Somerset, who so recently sat at Edward's side at table, has betrayed his trust and once more commands the Lancastrian forces.

These are distant matters and Anthony only worries that he may be summoned to lead levies from Norfolk to pursue Somerset or to besiege once more the northern fortresses. He tries to keep busy in Beth's absence. Then on May 10th 1464 while Anthony is about on the estate supervising the replacement of thatching on some of the cottages, he receives a letter that changes everything. It is covered by an unusual number of seals. Moreover the messenger who delivers it has an escort of four mounted men-at-arms. Anthony's first thought is that Warwick has accused him of treason and has had new evidence forged to that effect and his hands tremble as he reaches for the letter, but then he sees that the seals are those of his father. His father's letter, which is very brief, contains no details, but from it Anthony learns that his sister and the King were secretly married near Grafton on May 1st.

Anthony's first thought is that his father must be joking, but he immediately recalls that his father is not fond of jokes. Then Anthony is angry that all this has been kept secret from him, Elizabeth's brother, but as he studies the letter more carefully he realises that his father only learnt of this after the ceremony had been performed and the marriage consummated. The whole business must be kept secret for some months more, for Edward fears that Warwick, once he returns from France, will try to find some means to challenge the validity of the ceremony and overturn the marriage. The ground must be prepared before Edward can reveal to Parliament that he has a wife and only after that can Elizabeth be crowned Queen. All this news is so unexpected and so strange that Anthony once again wonders if he has been resurrected in another world in which the normal considerations of probability do not apply.

It is of course Ripley who prepares the ground and it is Ripley's version of events that eventually will circulate throughout England. How much of it is true, it is impossible to say. It is said that Edward became lost while hunting in the forest of Wychwood, near Grafton, and, while still lost, he encountered a beautiful young woman with blonde hair and the look of faery about her. Flanked by her two small sons, she stood under an oak tree. When she recognised the King, she ran forwards to grab at the bridle of his horse and began to pour out the story of the dispossession of the estates that were rightly hers. Edward leant over his saddlehorn to hear her long and complex saga all about money and lands, though he paid little attention to the details of this story, for he was thinking that she, who looked so beautiful standing in the dappled sunlight and dressed in russet and green, was like a spirit of the woods. Finally he dismounted and sat with her under the oak, and once he had assured her that her wrongs could easily be set at right, they talked at length of other matters, until Edward's officers of the hunt found him and he was obliged to leave her. But he arranged to meet her again under that same tree the following day and he asked that she should come without her children.

Now Edward put the hunting of wild animals out of his mind. The following day he rode out alone to the assignation at the oak tree. This time Elizabeth wore a cloak of vermillion velvet over a yellow dress. For a little while they talked about the estates in Essex and Northamptonshire that should by rights be Elizabeth's and, as they talked, she allowed him to hold her hand. Finally they kissed and she allowed him to stroke her breasts. But that was as much as she would allow him. Then he respectfully proposed that she should become his mistress. If she became the royal mistress, she would enjoy an honourable status at court and would be richly rewarded. She replied, 'Though I am not highborn enough to be your Queen, yet I am too modest to be your concubine.'

Elizabeth's virtue only increased Edward's ardour and, after a third meeting, he resolved to marry her. She should be his Queen. He told no one about their meetings except his mother, Cecily of York, who was angry and told him that, 'Though there is nothing about Elizabeth to be disliked, nevertheless she is doubly unsuitable, for she has been married already, which is a great blemish to the majesty of a prince. Moreover she is your subject and of quite humble birth, rather than some noble progeny out of this realm.'

'That she is a widow and already has children bodes well for the succession of the realm,' Edward replied and continued, 'By God and his blessed lady, I am a bachelor who has also fathered children, and so each of us has proof that neither of us is likely to be barren. That her kin were formerly supporters of Lancaster may help heal the divisions of our nation. That she is English is a great advantage, for it is the loyalty and love of my own countrymen that I most desire. One of my brothers must marry a foreign princess, if our politics requires it. I shall marry whom I like.'

'Warwick will not care for this,' said Cecily quietly.

'I am sure that Warwick does not dislike me so much that he will begrudge me marrying for love, nor is it so unreasonable that I should choose my own wife rather than be governed by his eye. It is not as if I am his ward and he is my guardian. I am King and free to marry whom I choose. As for foreign marriage alliances, they are often more trouble than they are worth. We should be content with what we have.'

Elizabeth had decided to tell no one about her meetings with the King except her mother, but it seemed that Jacquetta knew all about the romance already and it was she who was to arrange the secret ceremony. Having set out from Stony Stratford late on the evening of April 30th, Edward arrived at Grafton very late. Beltane fires burning in the village lit his way to the Manor. Rivers, who still knew nothing of this high affair, was away on business in London. It was past midnight when Edward and Elizabeth were married in the Manor's private chapel. The priest who officiated was accompanied by a boy who helped him in the singing. Otherwise the only people who attended the service were Jacquetta and two of her gentlewomen. Straightaway afterwards Edward took Elizabeth to bed. The following morning they rode out into Wychwood and, as they did so, they passed many young men and women walking out from the forest. As was the custom, these folk had gone out first thing in the morning a-maying to pick flowers and greenery while the dew was still upon them. It was a joyous morning. Elizabeth and Edward kissed farewell under the oak tree before he rode back alone to Stony Stratford.

Ripley's version suggested how good it was that it was an English match and harped on the theme that it was love that held our blessed kingdom together. But it was months later and not until the holding of the parliament at Reading that this story became public. Meanwhile there were more battles and beheadings and the numbers of the restless dead increased. In the wake of a Lancastrian defeat at Hexham, Tiptoft arrived too late to preside over the execution of the Duke of Somerset, but he supervised the beheadings of five lesser lords two days later and then had fourteen more Lancastrians executed at York. Though the days of mercy and pardon for the defeated were now over, Tiptoft had not yet won for himself the title of the 'Butcher of England'. Henry was thought to be in hiding in the Lake District, while Margaret had fled back to her native Anjou.

Once more Anthony receives a request from the Chronicler of Crowland for more information about these battles and other matters of high politics. Appended to the Chronicler's enquiries are short notes from the Abbot who has belatedly become aware of the rumours that were circulating about Anthony. With respect to the washing of a leper's feet, this is not recommended, unless that is, the leper has been first cleansed according to the prescription of Leviticus: 'Then shall the priest command to take for him that is to be cleansed two birds alive and clean and cedar wood, and scarlet, and hyssop. And the priest shall command that one of the birds be killed in an earthen vessel over running water: As for the living bird, he shall take it, and the cedar wood, and the scarlet, and the hyssop, and shall dip them and the living bird in the blood of the bird that was killed over the running water: And he shall sprinkle upon him that is to be cleansed from the leprosy seven times, and shall pronounce him clean, and shall let the living bird loose in the field.' Otherwise there is obviously a risk of contagion. These matters are best left to the priesthood.

With respect to the vision of the Grail, the matter is no better. For the Grail is a sinister mystery and it was an accursed moment when the sun was darkened and Christ on the Cross beheld the vessel that was to catch His blood. Thereafter the Grail, that was the curse of Palestine, became the curse of England, for its manifestation in our country was the beginning of the breaking up of the Fellowship of the Round Table. Some that went on the quest died, some went mad, some renounced their knightly vocation and others disappeared without any report of what became of them and all of this foreshadowed the end of Arthur's rule. The Grail, a ghostly vessel, waited upon by phantoms, is a damnable mystery. The Abbot demands of Lord Scales to know of what use is a vision of the Grail if it is vouchsafed only to one knight, or at most a handful of knights. Were not salvation potentially open to all, it would be a damnable thing—a thing reserved for an aristocracy of the perfect and denied to the common ruck of men, not to mention fallible womankind. The Grail is a lure, for it is like the device that falconers use when they wish to trap a hawk—a lump of meat attached to a mass of weighted leather decorated with feathers. 'Beware the lure of the Grail, my Lord Scales.'

Elizabeth's letter to Anthony arrives a few weeks after

her father's. It too is very short, for she writes that she is too excited to compose her thoughts. She describes Edward's looks and vigour, as if Anthony were unacquainted with the man. Then she goes on at length about her new wardrobe which Jacquetta is purchasing for her in London. But the real burden of her letter comes at the end. She wants Anthony to know that all the Woodvilles are going to become very rich and that both Rivers and Anthony may expect to be appointed to high office very soon.

Anthony reflects that much of Elizabeth's allure stems from her belief in her own worth and beauty, her certainty that she deserves wealth and good fortune and her pure delight in the things of this world. She is used to being gazed at and likes to be admired, for she knows that she is beautiful and surely beauty is nothing but the outward expression of goodness?

CHAPTER EIGHT

Tiltyard

Though Anthony is now in London, letters from his father keep him abreast of events. Sundays apart, Anthony spends every day at the tiltyard close by Charing Cross. The place is increasingly rundown. Half the staircase to the upper gallery has now collapsed and Sergeant Raker cannot find the funds to repair the steps. Tattered and faded banners hang from the gallery. The armoury, just inside the yard, is stocked with weapons and armour for hire, but most of the pieces are from bygone times. There are conical helmets without visors, partial suits of plate steel, flat-topped great helms, falchions, broadswords and even a few complete hauberks of mail left over from the previous century. When not at work, Raker sits in the armoury brooding over old wars. Anthony of course has no need for hired pieces. His own suit of light steel plate has been made to measure in the latest Italianate fashion with winged poleyns, fluted cuisses and massive pauldrons.

He continues his exercises with the sword, but he now also trains to become a champion jouster. Under the close supervision of Raker, he starts by practising on foot, first hefting a light lance and then steadily taking up heavier lances. It requires extraordinary strength to manage a real tournament lance of pinewood, keeping it erect and then slowly and evenly lowering it, until he can hold it braced by his hand and arm, pressed against his chest and pointing slightly to the right. The weight of the lance must rest on the palm, not the fingers. Then he must learn to repeat this operation more swiftly. Weeks pass before he is able to perform the same feat on horseback. Now things become more difficult, for, once on horse and facing a mounted antagonist, he has to wear full armour with the helm laced to his chest and back. The problem that every would-be jouster faces is that he can see very well through the slit of the helm as long as he leans slightly forward and inclines the head, but the urge to raise one's head and even close one's eyes just before the moment of impact is instinctive and hard to fight. The whispering voice conjures up pictures of the opponent's lance breaking on the helm and piercing the slit of the helm, so that the splinters run deep into his eyeballs, and from that moment on he will be a blind man, no longer a warrior but instead an object of pity, to be led from place to place by servants and children. Scoggin will mercilessly bate his enemy. Again and again Anthony finds that, as he hurtles towards his antagonist, he looks down and, as Raker keeps yelling at him, he has no hope of becoming a champion jouster until he can see exactly where the point of his lance is going at the moment of impact.

There are other things to be mastered on horseback. He needs to ride with his stirrups short, so that he can stand on them. Black Saladin has to be trained to run close to the tilt cloth. Anthony must turn towards his opponent and lead with his right side. Now his leg must support the lance. The lance must not be lowered too soon or too late. Five lances' length from the opponent is about right. There is a lot for Anthony to master.

But the thing that is most difficult of all is the bellowing of Sergeant Raker, for Raker is an angry man. He hates Anthony's negligently arrogant manner and the way Anthony assumes that jousting is a sport that he will soon master. When at swordplay Anthony seems to strive for elegance rather than victory. Ever confident, he is careless in defence. Raker calls him a fop and tells him that he lacks the will to win, to maim and to kill and, since Raker shouts this at the top of his voice, it reaches the ears of everyone in the tiltyard. Everything enrages Raker. He cannot remember when he was born, but he thinks that he must be nearly seventy and he hates being so old. He can remember hearing of Hotspur's death at the Battle of Shrewsbury. He witnessed the execution of Archbishop Scrope and the coronation procession of Henry V. He fought under John of Bedford at Verneuil and he saw Henry VI crowned King of France in Paris. His memories bring him no comfort. He is bitter about the more recent defeats and losses in France. He hated King Henry for his feeble mind and lack of will, but he also despises Edward for his wenching, feasting, hunting and easy pleasures. Raker does not like the favour that the young King shows to other young men. Raker loathes young men, though he feels the same about old men too, despite being old himself. Raker is pickled in bile, but he knows how to go about his work.

For several months more the royal marriage remains a secret, which Edward enjoys, for he finds this to be the height of romance, but Elizabeth is impatient to be acknowledged Queen and crowned. At last, on the fourteenth of September Edward summons a meeting of his parliament in Reading. The matter could hardly be delayed any longer, for Warwick and Wenlock were about to depart for France on a mission to negotiate a marriage for the King with Bona of Savoy, a union which was intended to consecrate the political and military alliance of England and France. Now Edward tells them that their mission can have no point, for he is already married. He invites his council to rejoice in his happy marital state. Warwick is enraged to hear that his work of patient diplomacy over several years must come to nothing. Others in the council are shocked that the King has chosen to marry a woman who is older than he is and moreover of relatively low birth, though Edward retorts that the daughter of Jacquetta de St Pol and the granddaughter of the Count of St Pol is hardly a woman of low birth. But counsellors are also angry at the furtive way the King has gone about this business. But Hastings, once he has recovered from the shock of the news, sets to smoothing tempers and presenting the union in the best light he can. It is clear to him that the arrangement that he thought he had to divide the Grey estates with Elizabeth must now be null and void, but he is not such a fool as to make a fuss about a small thing like that. Moreover, as the news of the royal wedding spreads throughout Reading and then England, Edward's critics discover that the royal marriage is widely approved of, since Elizabeth is not French but English and besides she is very beautiful.

As soon as the news reaches London, Anthony finds that he seems popular with people, most of whom he does not remember having met before. A few days later when he visits Ripley in his laboratory, he finds him busy drafting the letters that will present the royal marriage in the best possible light. This Ripley does with enthusiasm. For, 'It is a marriage founded on love and it is love which exalts a man and a woman and gives them wings that will take them to heaven!'

Now he pushes his papers aside and rises to greet Anthony.

There is a flask of wine on the table and Ripley hurries to find Anthony a cup.

He proposes a toast to Elizabeth's golden destiny and Anthony can hardly refuse this.

'This was your mother's work, I am sure,' Ripley says. 'You must introduce me to Jacquetta de St Pol.'

Then he shows him a beautiful and intricate device which he says is called an astrolabe. It is capable of performing extraordinary calculations, but alas, he has been unable to discover how it works. Still it is beautiful is it not? He is babbling, but seeing that Anthony has put down his cup and is looking grim, he slows down and finally falls silent. Anthony raises his hand, before speaking, 'Brother Ripley, I have come to say farewell. I want to have no more to do with you.'

Ripley looks as though he is about to cry, but perhaps that is a pretence.

'But I am your good friend,' he says. 'I am everybody's friend and most especially yours, my beloved lord. I will only ever have your best interests at heart and I can promise you a golden future. With my help, you will become rich, win renown and triumph over all your enemies.'

But Anthony's reply is, 'I already have a golden future, for I am the King's brother-in-law.'

Ripley pours himself some more wine and drinks deeply before speaking again, 'It is exactly your prominence and your closeness to the King that puts you in grave danger, since the court is a wilderness full of wolves that slaver and paw the ground as they look on you. The old guard around Edward suspect you Woodvilles for having come over to Edward's side so recently, while those loyal to the cause of Lancaster scorn your family for having deserted Henry, and everybody hates and envies your fortune in becoming brother-in-law to the King. Edward's palaces are fair-seeming places of feasting, music, dancing and dalliance, but it is at court that men of rank rise and then fall, to be incarcerated, blinded and murdered. The court is a pit of intrigue, and dukes, lords, bullies and thieves gather from all parts of the kingdom and, drawing their swords, with gleaming teeth and sombre eyes, step down into that pit.'

Anthony snorts, for he has no fear of men with gleaming teeth and swords, since he has a sword too and knows how to use it.

Ripley continues, 'Since you and your sister have wealth, beauty and rank, you will have to learn how to be hated, for you now have powerful enemies. You must make yourselves enjoy being hated. Even so, though Edward has taken a risk in marrying Elizabeth, he needs her glamour, for glamour is a shimmering kind of enchantment and the kingdom must once more fall under enchantment, as Avalon was once enchanted...'

He has started to babble once more. Anthony turns to leave. Ripley pulls himself together.

'But my lord, stay a moment. In what possible way can I have offended you?'

Anthony speaks without troubling to turn back to Ripley, 'I do not care for these foolish and fantastical lies that you have been putting about concerning me... that I have seen the Grail, that I flagellate myself, that I remain a virgin and suchlike nonsense. People will not believe such stuff and they will think that it is I who am responsible for these vainglorious falsehoods. I see well that you believe that somehow you can use me and I do not care to be your cat's-paw. And now farewell forever.'

Ripley cries after him.

'Very good, my lord! It is good, it is very good indeed, that you should seek to make your way without me. Well done indeed! But very soon, I promise you, you will find that you will need me. Though I have heard harsh words from you just now, I will hold no grudge and I assure you that I remain your adoring friend and will ever be on hand, ready to help you. Go with God, for in His will is our peace.'

As Anthony walks out of Westminster Palace, he tries to put Ripley out of his mind. Then he remembers that, before he left for this final encounter with Ripley, a letter was put into his hand. He pauses at the postern gate and sits down on a bench to read the letter which is from the Chronicler of Crowland. The Chronicler reports that of late the Abbot has been troubled by expressions of doubt and impiety among some of his younger monks. One particular question has brought the trouble to a head. How could it be possible that Noah's Ark could have accommodated two of every species of animal, reptile and bird? Things were parlous indeed, for when the Abbot thought about it, he began to have doubts about this himself. However, his previous labours on the chronology of the world had honed his mathematical skills and so he set to performing the necessary calculations. We know from Genesis that the Ark, fashioned from gopher wood, measured three hundred cubits, by thirty cubits, by fifty cubits and the Abbot found that scholars of the Bible reckoned a cubit to be roughly equal to a foot and a half. Having completed his calculations, the Abbot found that the top deck alone would be large enough to accommodate twenty-two tilting grounds— not that Noah and his sons would have had time for jousting, since they would be too busy feeding the animals—and moreover there were three decks, giving a total deck area of over 100,000 square feet, which was more than enough for every species of creature, particularly if one considered that the birds and insects on the top deck would take up very little space and that many reptiles could swim alongside. Moreover, there was no need for all the pairs of animals to be fully grown and so one could imagine Noah welcoming cubs, fawns, kittens, puppies, ponies and other baby creatures onto his Ark. Also, there were not so many species of animals in Biblical times. For example, we know from the New Testament that there were only two types of dog in the time of Jesus (scavenging hounds and house pets), whereas in more recent times many types of dog have been bred, including greyhounds, mastiffs, alaunts harriers, spaniels, terriers, running hounds and various sorts of lapdogs. So back then there would have been plenty of space for, say 35,000 creatures together, with enough fodder for three hundred and sixty-five days and perhaps not much fodder would be needed if, by divine dispensation, the animals hibernated for the duration of the Deluge. Still the Abbot was dismayed to find that some of the young monks raised further questions regarding the Ark...

The following day Anthony is summoned to Reading to attend the formal proclamation of Elizabeth's marriage and of her future coronation. On his arrival he is brought directly to

the King who embraces him and tells him that he will shortly
have good news for him. Then a page is summoned to guide
Anthony to the Queen's private chamber. His sister hugs him
and says that she has so much to tell him. Her first meeting
with Edward in the wood and then the secret marriage did
not happen quite as Ripley's letters describe them. But first
she must show Anthony the jewels that have been purchased
for her in Flanders. Also he must look upon the two cloths of
gold purchased from Giovanni de Bardi of Florence for two
hundred and eighty pounds and the gold plate which she will
dine off on the day of her coronation. And here are the silks
for her chairs and pillions…

'We are going to become so rich!'

She is flushed with joy and Anthony must share her delight.
She tells him in confidence that Edward is going to appoint
him Governor of the Isle of Wight, which is an office of great
profit. Her happiness enhances her beauty. It is indeed a kind
of magic.

Warwick and his allies have had to accept the *fait accompli* of the wedding and on Michaelmas Day Anthony sees
Warwick, together with George Duke of Clarence, escorting Elizabeth into Reading Abbey. As Anthony looks on, he
finds himself remembering how Scoggin, by performing cartwheels in York Cathedral Close, demonstrated the way the
wheel of fortune works. At the altar Edward formally declares
that Elizabeth is his wife and that early next year she will be
crowned Queen of England.

On Anthony's return to London, he resumes his exercises
at the tiltyard, but Raker is increasingly critical and even abusive, 'You ride like a nun on her way to market. You must learn
to rouse your rage and then to master it,' he tells Anthony.
'Only rage can give you the energy that you need to win your
combats. You must feel it surging up in you like black vomit.
You are not a serious fighter unless you fight to kill. You are
not really a warrior until you have dreamt of killing a man.

Drop your lance and get off that black beast and try fencing with me. Let me see, if I cannot put some fire in your belly. Let me teach you how you can kill a man at your ease.'

Anthony dismounts, Raker produces a pair of bated swords and they set to thrusting and parrying. At first Raker is somewhat baffled by the Italianate style of swordplay that Anthony has learnt from Tiptoft, but he soon rallies and sets to provoking Anthony not only with insulting words, but also by ostentatiously adopting postures that appear to leave him vulnerable to Anthony's thrusts, but since Anthony can see that Raker seeks to provoke him, he is determined not to be so provoked.

The bout is tiring and they mutely agree to pause. They both rest and lean on the pommels of their swords as they watch their sweat drip onto the sawdust below. Without raising his head, Raker starts speaking in a low voice, 'I have heard it said that the marriage of the King to your sister was not as has been publicly proclaimed. I have heard it said that there was no priest there and so what they have been calling a Christian sacrament was no such thing and so Elizabeth is no more than the King's mistress.'

Anthony's sword flashes up, but Raker laughs mirthlessly, as he is ready for this. Now that Anthony is enraged and dangerous, it might have been expected that Raker would dance away and keep his distance while making parries. Yet he surprises Anthony by doing the opposite and moving in for close combat. The foolish and rancorous old man surely deserves to die, but since Anthony's sword is bated and Raker is so close up against him, Anthony cannot manage a proper thrust or slicing cut and instead finds himself in a combat that more closely resembles a wrestling match than it does a swordfight. Finally he attempts a lunge which at such close quarters is a feeble thing and it only results in his sword arm being trapped in an armlock. It seems that Raker is about to break his arm.

Now Raker's mouth is close to Anthony's ear, 'Drop your

sword! I have seen enough, since I know that you do indeed wish to kill me and I am well pleased with that. Yet your fight today is with the wrong man. I have mentioned this libel about the Queen to no one except you just now and that only because I wished to raise your anger, but I heard it from a man who boasts that he belongs to the Earl of Warwick's affinity. He has been haunting the taverns in Southwark where he spreads this story about your sister.'

'Very well. Then please lead me to him and I will find a way to silence him.'

Now Raker looks uncomfortable.

'I will take you to the tavern where he is most likely to be found now that the sun is setting and I will point him out to you. Yet we must go unarmed, for I guess that if you took your sword with you, then you would commit murder. I will show you this man and then we will go to the Sheriff of Southwark and have him arrested and committed to his prison which men call the Clinke.' Raker hesitates before continuing, 'You favour a fancy foreign style of handling the sword, but at least you are an Englishman and besides you give me employment. Whereas Warwick's man is called Phebus and I believe that he is a Gascon—a French dog then.'

In Raker's mouth this epithet has unusual force, for he hates dogs and Anthony has seen him spear a stray mongrel that had wandered into the tiltyard.

They set off across London Bridge towards Southwark. A one-legged beggar sits at the London end of the bridge and cries 'Alms in the name of our blessed liege lord, King Edward!' Though evening is coming on, the shops on the bridge are still doing business and they have to force their way through the crowds. At the Southwark end of the bridge there is a blind man who cries out 'Alms in the name of Henry VI, the true King of England!' As they leave the bridge, Raker explains that these two scurvy beggars work together and divide the takings equally every evening. Once across the river Raker leads the way on to the Tabard. Its sign is a sleeveless coat as might be worn by a herald and the place is the oldest of Southwark's inns. It is dark, crowded and noisy and Phebus, who seems a little tipsy, sits with other young men at a long table but Raker and Anthony manage to squeeze in on either side of him. Raker reminds Phebus that they have already met before he introduces Anthony as John Goodgroom, one of his underlings. Then Raker summons over the ale-wife and orders a jug of wine and some cakes, and he continues, 'We have come to hear stories. We like stories.'

But the expression on Raker's face does not suggest that he likes anything at all and Phebus is obviously nervous. He makes to rise, but Raker and Anthony press him down and offer him some of their wine. Surely, as long as Phebus remains in this busy tavern where he is amongst his friends, he will be safe?

'I do not tell stories,' he protests. 'I only speak of things that are true.'

'True stories are the best ones,' says Anthony. 'Think of us as collectors of true stories, of snatches of gossip and rumours that are to be verified. For example, I heard from a friend that the King's recent marriage was no such thing, as it was not celebrated according to the Christian rite and now my master here tells me that he has heard the same thing from you. I did not believe my friend and swore that he was a fool and made a bet that he was wrong, but if you can vouch for the truth of the story, then I will owe him an apology—and some money. Here, have some cake. And more wine. And a toast to the telling of stories. And here is a sovereign to hear your story.'

Now two men seated on the opposite side of the bench interrupt to say that they too would like to hear the story of the King's wedding, for they esteem Phebus as the teller of the most fantastical tales. Phebus scowls at them, but after almost emptying the wine-cup he begins, 'My story is a strange one. The first thing you should know is that the "wedding

ceremony" that was no true wedding did not take place on
the morning of May 1st, as is said, but on the night before.'

'No, the first thing we should know is how do you know
this?'

'I know this, because I was there.' Phebus pauses as those
around him signal their astonishment at this, before he continues, 'I was there because my master, the Earl of Warwick
had become worried about the safety of the King, for while
the court was residing at Stony Stratford he would frequently
ride out alone save for the company of a single squire. He said
he was going hunting and yet he took no foresters or lymerers
with him, nor did he take any dogs. The Earl became worried
lest the King be attacked by footpads or some other accident
befall him and so, after the King had ridden out thus several
times, my master asked me, whom he knew to be an expert
tracker and skilled man-at-arms, to follow the King at a distance. I was to stay at a distance because my master did not
want to embarrass the King, but I should ride close enough
behind him to be able to rush to his assistance should he meet
with any trouble. The first time I followed the King I found
that he rode to a great manor house in Grafton Regis, where
he spent some time, before returning to Stony Stratford without encountering any trouble. I reported this to my master,
who was well pleased with me and ordered me to do the same
when the King next rode out.

Less than a week later, on the morning of Wednesday
30th of April the King and his squire rode out once more
and I had no difficulty in following them to Grafton Regis.
They spent all day in the house and I was beginning to worry
about where I should find anything to eat and whether I
should end up spending the night out of doors. Then, as it
was beginning to get dark, the King emerged arm in arm
with a beautiful lady. I did not know who she was, though
I know now that she was Elizabeth Woodville. They were
followed by the lady's mother, whom I have since learnt is

called Jacquetta de St Pol. Also there was a man in a long red robe which had a cowl. The King's squire was in attendance and there was also a lady-in-waiting... Oh and there was also an old man bent double under a bundle of sticks. They all walked into the woods and, after waiting a while, I followed them. This was easy, for they carried lanterns and candles to light their way.

Soon they came to a clearing in front of a great oak tree and the old man, assisted by the King's squire set to laying out and lighting two small fires. The others stood around talking and after a while they were joined by other men and women. Some of them had the antlers of stags strapped to their heads. From the way they came tripping and running through the wood they all seemed to be young folk, but I do not know who they were, for they all wore masks, and since they came from every direction, I had great difficulty in remaining concealed and I began to be afraid. Now I could see that the man in the red robe also wore a mask and, together with the woman called Jacquetta, he seemed to be in charge of whatever was being done that night.

Now, it was very strange, the King took a run at one of the fires and jumped over it. Then it seemed that Elizabeth was urged by Jacquetta de St Pol to jump over the other fire. At first she did not want to, though it was only a little fire, but eventually she gathered up her skirts and did leap over it. Then, while the King looked, she was brought before the man in the red robe. He opened his robe... After that I do not know what happened, for at this point the old woman... Jacquetta de St Pol pointed in my direction. I do not know how she could have seen me at that distance in the dark and perhaps she had not, but I was not going to take any chances and I started running in the direction where I thought that I had left my horse. There was rustling and animal sounds all around and I was horridly afraid and I wished that I had not seen anything, for the least of it I thought would be that I should have my eyes poked out. But all was well, for I found my horse and made my escape.

The following morning I reported all that I had seen to the Earl, and when he had heard me out, he summoned his chaplain and had me repeat to him everything that I had just said. The chaplain said that it was not for me to know all that he guessed about what I had seen, for this was a danger-ous knowledge, but he would explain a little of what I had witnessed. He told me that yesterday evening had been Bel-tane. This meant nothing to me for we do not have Beltane in France, but he explained to me that, before the coming of the True Faith, the evening used to be sacred to a pagan deity called Bel. What I had seen was a blasphemous revival of an ancient form of demon worship in which the King and his woman leapt over fire in order to purify themselves accord-ing to the pagan way, before the woman I had seen could become the King's whore and the bed-slave of Satan. Later, Warwick told me to keep quiet about what I had seen, for it would be dangerous to repeat it in the presence of any of the Queen's friends. But I have heard that the Queen is arrogant and already very rich and I guess there would be none of her friends in such a tavern as this.'

'Ah well, I have lost my bet,' says Anthony and he shrugs, but he and Raker profess themselves to have been well enter-tained. Are there any more stories? But first there must be more wine. Anthony whispers to Raker who looks puzzled. The jug of wine arrives and Phebus' cup is filled and Anthony now wagers that Phebus cannot empty that cup if Raker pours it from high above directly into Phebus' mouth. Now Anthony, saying that he wants better to see the fun and make sure that the wager is fairly conducted, sits on the bench facing Phebus. As Raker begins to tip the cup Phebus looks up so that the wine falls into his mouth, but an instant later Anthony jogs Raker's hand in such a way that wine splashes into Phebus' eyes and then Anthony drives the knife edge of his hand into the man's throat. Though the windpipe is severed and Phebus dies instantly, Anthony goes through the motions of thumping him on the back, declaring loudly that a piece of cake must have gone down the wrong way. He is slow to concede that the man must be dead.

There were friends of Phebus in the tavern, yet no one challenges Anthony and Raker as they leave. Raker's reputation as a fighter is well-known and although Anthony has not been recognised, it is clear to those who were watching that he too must be a lethal fighter.

Raker is delighted to have seen his employer kill a man— and a Frenchman too! Though his smiling is like the rictus of a man in great pain. But soon his customary gloom returns. Will they not be arrested for murder? And, if not that, will not the Earl of Warwick seek bloody revenge for the killing of his man?

They are not far short of the tiltyard before Anthony replies, 'I am the King's brother-in-law. Warwick cannot touch me. Besides the man was slandering the King and his Queen and I have delivered him justice. The man got off lightly with an easy death. Edward would have dealt more harshly with him.'

Though Anthony sounds blithe, in reality he is gloomy too. For is it possible that Phebus was telling the truth and that he did see what he said he saw? Then he asks himself why Phebus was so ready with his story if Warwick had told him not to tell it? And if Warwick brings the murder of his servant before the King, will Anthony's account be believed? Then he tells himself that he is not afraid of Warwick.

The following morning Anthony has a meeting that is unexpected and somewhat strange. He is riding away from the Woodville townhouse, when a man in a broad-brimmed hat boldly plants himself in front of Black Saladin and seizes the horse's bridle. Looking down, Anthony sees that under the shadow of the hat the man is Sir Thomas Malory.

'So! They have let you out of prison again, have they?'

Then he bends to hear what Malory has to say for himself.

'My lord, I am come with a message from the Earl of Warwick. I must speak privately with you.'

Anthony is doubtful, fearing a trap, but eventually they settle upon the deserted graveyard of the Church of St John Zachary where they can walk and talk without being overheard.

'My lord, the Earl's message is simple,' says Malory. 'It is only this, that he wishes that there was peace between you and him.'

Anthony shrugs dismissively, but Malory continues, 'He will stay his hand against you and your sister, if you will swear to do him and those who serve him no injury.'

'Why should I believe you or trust the Earl?' asks Anthony.

Now it is Malory's turn to shrug.

'Well, I have delivered my message,' he says. 'The Earl is an honourable man. As for me...' Malory pauses and reflects and then he grins broadly. (It is a horrible grin.) 'As for me, it strikes me that now we two are brothers of a kind.'

Anthony protests, 'I am no brother of yours!'

Malory's response is cheerful, yet malevolent, 'Oh, but you are, for we are both murderers. I am sure that you think of yourself as the hero of your story, and perhaps you are, but you are also its villain. Now that you have murdered a man just for gossiping, you are certainly a villain and I think that you may become like me, a writer of romances. Or perhaps a poet. Stories are full of grief, danger and evil. In order for a man to write a good story or poem he must have experienced evil. He must know evil intimately. My hero is François Villon.'

And now Malory recites:

Dites moi où, en quel pays
Est Flora la belle Romaine,

Archipiades, ne Thaïs,
Qui fut sa cousine germaine,
Echo, parlant quant bruit on maine
Dessus riviere ou sus estan,
Qui beauté eut trop plus qu'humaine
Mais où sont les neiges d'antan?

Then Malory translates and abridges, 'Tell me where, or in what country is Flora, the beautiful Roman girl, or Archipiades, or Thais, or Echo who had more than human beauty. But where are the snows of yesteryear?' Malory looks sad. 'That is one of Villon's verses. I heard they captured him at Uzès a few years' back and hung him in the town square. But before that he was in prison many times. He started out by stabbing a priest to death. A little later, he masterminded the theft of 500 crowns from the Chapel of the Collège de Navarre and thereafter he went on to commit many assaults and robberies and write much beautiful poetry. He has been my hero and my villain—as you are.'

At last Malory recollects what he should be doing and asks, 'What message should I take back to the Earl?'

'I am my own man. I owe the Earl nothing and will promise him nothing.'

Malory nods and walks out of the graveyard.

Two days later, Anthony is at the tiltyard running courses with his customary jousting opponent Sir John Paston. John, like Anthony, is in his twenties, and like Anthony is determined to become a champion jouster. But John is determined to be so many things, for he desires also to be a man of great learning, a favourite at court and the lover of many women. It is proving expensive to have so many ambitions. After they have run their first course, Anthony becomes aware of a stirring in the tiltyard. Two richly apparelled figures stand at its gate looking on as Anthony and John check their armour and prepare to run against each other again. Anthony briefly unstraps his helmet to see better. Their jousting is being watched by Hastings and Tiptoft. Anthony gestures to them, signalling his readiness to dismount, but Raker shakes his head.

As Lord High Constable, Tiptoft holds the life of every man in the Kingdom in his hands. Sometimes he is merciful and an offender may get off with having his hand or his ears lopped off. The less fortunate are hanged until they lose consciousness before they are cut down and while still living, castrated, disembowelled and then, after the heads have been cut off, the torsos are impaled and displayed on stakes. Londoners are used to seeing heads on spikes, but they hold that the impalement of bodies is a cruel innovation imported from Italy by this man, 'The Butcher of England.' But still, such punishments are not for the nobility and Anthony can take some little comfort from the fact that his rank would surely guarantee him a beheading. But then he checks himself. He is sure that he is safe, for he is the Queen's brother and besides he and Tiptoft have had so many friendly discussions about books and about swordplay in the Italian manner. Yet he has just seen an unsmiling Tiptoft gazing critically upon him, before turning to talk to Raker. Though it is hard to concentrate on the jousting, Anthony breaks fourteen lances and unhorses John twice before they agree to call it a day. But by then the two lords have disappeared and Raker is nowhere to be seen. John is also worried, but that is only because the great lords have seen him fall from his horse twice.

Early the following morning, the Wednesday after the Feast of the Resurrection, three of the King's gentlemen-at-arms appear at the Woodville townhouse. Anthony is given only a little time to dress, for their orders are to escort him as swiftly as possible to Sheen Palace where the King, having moved from winter quarters at Eltham, currently holds court. They are courteous, but cannot tell him why he has been summoned, only that he is urgently required to present himself. As Anthony rides with them, he mentally prepares his defence.

But then it occurs to him that perhaps it is not the death of the Gascon that is at issue. Perhaps word has got out about his nocturnal sojourns with his wife in churches. Perhaps they will be indicted as heretical adherents of the Brothers and Sisters of the Blessed Vespers. But then he tells himself that, if that were the case then his deranged wife would have been fetched out of the convent too. But perhaps that has happened. And then he thinks that perhaps he will not be accused of anything and that he is being called to be given command of one of the armies that are being sent north once more to retake the Border fortresses from the Lancastrians. Though that would be a joyless commission, at least he would still be alive.

On their arrival it is Hastings who greets him at the gateway and he is all smiles. (But then he is usually smiling.) He says that the King is away hunting and will not return till later that evening. But it is the Queen who first requires his presence and now Hastings carefully instructs Anthony in the rituals that are to follow.

So it is that when Anthony enters the presence of his sister, he doffs his cap and kneels before her. Even now he finds it hard to accustom himself to kneeling before his sister. Then one of the Queen's maids of honour comes and kneels beside him so that she may attach a jewelled collar of gold and pearls to his thigh. The maid of honour whispers to him that this is 'The Flower of Souvenance'. At the same moment his sister throws a parchment tied with thread of gold into his cap. It is a pretty ritual, but as Anthony kneels before his sister, he finds himself wondering if it is possible that he is kneeling before a slave of the heathen god, Bel.

The collar of gold and pearls is not his to keep. A little later, when the King has returned from hunting, the scroll is unrolled and it is proclaimed to the court that the Flower of Souvenance is a token of a challenge and it is to be fought for in two days of combat between Anthony and a nobleman 'of four lineages and without reproach'. The document, which has been drafted by Tiptoft in consultation with the herald Bluemantle, specifies that the first day's combat should be in saddle of war with spears and swords and the second day should be fought on foot with spears, axes and daggers. So Anthony is to be England's champion and he now learns that his adversary has also been selected. This will be the redoubtable jouster, veteran of the Crusades and Knight of the Golden Fleece, Antoine, Count de la Roche, the Bastard of Burgundy and brother of Duke Charles.

Chester Herald reads out the challenge that will be taken by him on Anthony's behalf over to Bruges, 'I send you herewith, in all affection and cordial request, Chester, herald and servant of the King of England, beseeching and requiring you that it please you to show me so much honour and friendship as to touch the said flower of my emprise, the which flower I send over the sea to you, as the most renowned Knight I can choose. And forever I bind me and mine and all that God shall ever give me of good fortune to be yours so long as honour, life and goods shall allow...'

The document is very long. This is one of the charades of the courts of Christendom at play. This challenge to combat curiously resembles a wedding proposal, since the purpose of the forthcoming fight is a sacrament of ritualised violence which will celebrate the diplomatic and military alliance of England and Burgundy against France. As the herald reads on, Anthony's mind wanders and he finds himself thinking first of 'saddles of war' and then of the slaughter at Cock River on Palm Sunday four years earlier.

Though Edward presses him to stay at Sheen, there is no tiltyard attached to this palace and consequently Anthony prefers to return to London. It is more necessary than ever that he should fashion himself into the perfect warrior. Early every morning he rides out from the Woodville townhouse to the tiltyard where he will receive more abuse and instruction from Raker. A week after his return to London, just as he is riding out to the tiltyard once more, he finds his way blocked by four young men armed with swords and daggers. A red-headed youth, who is the boldest of them and apparently their leader, uses his dagger to stab Black Saladin in the ribs before striking the horse in the shoulder. By now Anthony has his sword out. Though he is surrounded, Black Saladin is wheeling and kicking so wildly that they cannot get near. The horse's shrieks are terrible. Surely people must hear this and come to Anthony's assistance? He leans over his horse and tries to land a heavy blow on the redhead, but that is blocked by the youth's sword and dagger crossed in defence and Anthony's own blade is shattered.

He should be afraid, but since he still wears the amulet that he wore at the Battle of Palm Sunday, he is not and because his chief anxiety is then not for his life, but for his horse, he decides to dismount in the hope that this will allow the horse to escape further injury, but at that moment it bucks and Anthony falls with one foot trapped in the stirrup. 'He is mine,' says the redhead to the others. 'I have him.' He rushes upon Anthony with his sword raised high for what should be a fatal blow, but Anthony grabs for his legs and the redhead falls with his head hitting the cobbles. Now Anthony has his foot out of the stirrup and is able to stand. The other three men have retreated before the kicking horse. Anthony finds that there is blood on the shoulder of his jerkin though he had not noticed this wound before. The redhead lies on the cobbles and looks dazed. Anthony staggers over and plans to use his broken sword to finish him off. But the redhead manages to get to his feet, and tottering slightly, raises his sword and dagger to protect his head. He is a brave man, but not a professional fighter. Anthony plunges what is left of his sword into the man's chest and he falls to the ground once more. Anthony hears shouting all around him. He calls for help, for by now a crowd has gathered to watch but, though they are shouting and pointing, no one dares to intervene. Black

Saladin has fallen to the ground and lies squealing and thrashing his legs.

Though the redhead is on the ground and bleeding heavily, he is not finished. He lunges upward with his sword and Anthony uses his gloved hand to beat the sword away, but meanwhile his assailant gets to his knees and strikes at Anthony with his dagger and brings it all the way down the ribs to Anthony's hip where it remains embedded. It is his last thrust, for now Anthony, who has dropped his broken sword, uses his right elbow to trap the man's arm and forces him to drop his sword. Though Anthony can hardly see for the blood that is running down his face, he becomes aware that help has arrived. The steward of the Woodville townhouse is first on the scene and grabs the kneeling man from behind, while Anthony scrambles for his broken sword which he smashes over the man's head, beating him once more to the ground and then he throws himself on top of him and sets to using what is left of the blade in an attempt to saw the man's left hand off.

More retainers come running out of the Woodville townhouse, and seeing this, the redhead's companions rush forward and threaten Anthony and the steward with swords and knives to force them off, so that their leader can be dragged away by his head and shoulders and then his companions manage to load him on one of the horses that they have tethered at the corner of the house before making haste to get away. At last Earl Rivers arrives at the scene. It is he who pulls the dagger from Anthony's hip and, tearing his own shirt into pieces, he uses those pieces to staunch the bleeding from the hip and other places. A great deal of blood has been lost already. Anthony tells his father to send for Ripley who must bring his skull moss with him. The horse is making such a noise that Anthony has difficulty in getting himself understood. The last thing he hears is a bystander remarking on the terrible quality of the swords they make these days. Then he loses consciousness.

When he next opens his eyes, he finds that he has been brought back to his bedchamber. He can still hear the noises that Black Saladin is making and Jacquetta, who is sitting beside the bed, explains that a team of men using large leather straps have been successful in carrying the horse into the courtyard where his wounds are being attended to.

Then Anthony sees that Ripley has arrived and he, sweating heavily, is trying to explain to Jacquetta and Richard how hoplochrisma works. Ripley insists that the redheaded man's sword or dagger must be found and brought to him before the magnetic healing can begin. The sword is found and brought to the alchemist, who with shaking hands plunges its blade into a flask containing the skull moss of the Earl of Wiltshire and the other ingredients. Then he tries to roll Anthony onto his side so that he can apply the dagger to the wound on the hip, saying as he does so, 'I knew that you would have need of me.'

Anthony tries to wave him off.

'No, I am not in such a bad way. It is not I who needs you, but I want you to go to my horse. Take the skull moss to the horse and attend to its wounds.'

Ripley ignores this and shakily sets to using the blade of the redhead's sword to paste the fungus from the decayed skull of James Butler, the Earl of Wiltshire, into Anthony's wounds.

Anthony is panicking. He calls out, 'Is Black Saladin dying?'

Those are his last sensible words for several days, since he faints once more, and with wounds that are infected, he soon becomes feverish. As he starts to float in his fever, he hears Ripley and Jacquetta arguing. In his delirium he fancies that James Butler is inside his head looking out through his eye sockets and gazing hungrily round the room as he seeks out Anthony's wife, but since Anthony cannot move his head, Butler cannot see her sitting by the doorway. Even so he can hear her voice. Butler's wraith seems angry that Anthony cannot leave his bed and discontentedly starts whispering inside Anthony's head. Butler's silvery whisperings are about fear and how it cannot be resisted, for it is a physical thing, a great chilling sickness, which grabs a man in the guts, makes his legs weak and sends piss dribbling down those legs. It is a dreadful thing to die. Yet fear is a man's best friend. Fear is good, for it takes a man away from danger and keeps him alive. Now that Anthony is infected, he will know what fear really is and surely the fever will kill him. While listening to the demented whispering, he falls asleep. When he is lucid once more, he thinks that he has just woken from a dream in which Phebus had been telling him a story, another story, only he cannot remember what the story is.

Jacquetta sits beside his bed playing with her figurines.

'So that was George Ripley, the King's alchemist,' she says eventually, 'I am very sorry for him, but there is nothing I can do that will help him, the poor man. We have thanked him for his hoplochrisma, but before we paid him and sent him away, I told him not to visit again.'

But when Anthony asks her why, she is vague. She mutters something about there being nothing to the man but words, and changing the subject, she reports that Black Saladin is back in his stable and will recover. Although Ripley had taken the redhead's sword down into the courtyard and applied the residue of his flask's contents to the horse's wounds, shortly afterwards a groom, who had not been informed of this special treatment, cleaned out the wounds before stitching and cauterizing them. She adds that she has been trying to identify the men who attacked him, but so far her little men will not help her in her inquiries. Richard believes that it must have been an attempt by someone at court to prevent the joust with the Bastard of Burgundy taking place, and that would be in the hope that this will delay the proposed Anglo-Burgundian pact against France. It is even possible that Anthony's horse was the chief target, since it would take many months for Anthony to train a new horse to run in the lists and where would he find another horse like Black Saladin? Richard does not name the 'someone at court', but it is certain that he is thinking of the Earl of Warwick. Anthony has not told his parents about the killing of Phebus.

Now Anthony, laid up in bed, has recurrent dreams of a man running. The friends who might have waited for him have gone already. Or perhaps those men were not really friends. His horse has wandered off and cannot be seen. The hill is very steep. He thought that he knew this part of the land but it seems not. Importunate people try to accost him, but he brushes past them. At last he thinks that he is free, but then looking back he sees his pursuers on the horizon, dim figures in the distance, but getting closer. What do they want of him?

When Anthony is well enough to stand once more, he goes out walking through the streets of London so that he may regain the strength in his legs, but at his father's insistence, he is always followed by two armed retainers, Amyas and Hugh. It feels strange to be moving through those streets but not on a horse, for now he is on the same level as porters, rag-and-bone men, sellers of pies and suchlike folk and this is not entirely comfortable, and after the attack he walks in fear. He scents danger everywhere and he wishes that he had given Sir Thomas Malory a better answer.

Since he now regrets the rough manner in which he broke up his association with Ripley and is ashamed too at his mother's abrupt dismissal of him, one of Anthony's first visits is to the alchemist's laboratory in the Palace of Westminster. He leaves his guards at the gatehouse of the outer courtyard. Though Anthony is nervous about how he will be received, Ripley's face lights up when he sees him.

'You are on your feet again! Oh well done, Lord Scales!

You are looking so well! Let us drink to your recovery,' and he finds the flagon of wine and they drink a toast to Anthony's health and Anthony proposes a toast of thanks to the healing power of hoplochrisma.

Then, 'I told you that there are many who hate you,' says Ripley. 'You will be safer in a tournament list or on a battle-field than in any street in London.'

Ripley is alarmed that Anthony has no sword and he is not entirely reassured when Anthony tells him about his body-guards.

'You must have a sword.' Then, 'I saw that your mother does not like me. Why is that? You can tell me. I shall not be offended. I thought that we should be friends. I am not used to being disliked. I want to be everyone's friend for it takes so little to bring a smile to a person's face.'

Anthony truthfully replies that he does not know what his mother thinks of Ripley.

'But she needs me. She may not know it but she does.' Ripley is emphatic about this. 'You are not the only person who has enemies. There are certain people, evil people who go about London, frequenting pothouses, marketplaces and churches muttering stories that are not true. One of the stories that is now being spread about is that Jacquetta de St Pol is a witch. They are saying that Eleanor Cobham taught her the dark arts when she was a girl.'

There, it is out. Anthony has long known this story, yet without his acknowledging that he did know it. He was still a small boy when Eleanor Cobham was arrested and charged with sorcery. His nurse told him the horrid story. Looking back on it, Anthony thinks that the nurse was not concerned with the effect of the story on him. It was herself that she wanted to scare. Eleanor Cobham was beautiful and clever and later became very rich. The nurse used her hands to describe Eleanor's curving body and her high arched eye-brows. Eleanor was of low birth but clever and ambitious.

A maid in the service of Jacqueline of Hainault, the wife of Humphrey Duke of Gloucester, after Jacqueline's unexpectedly early death, Eleanor had gone on to marry the Duke, and since Humphrey was brother to the King, it seemed that the throne might be within her reach, for the King was sickening and it was said that mysterious watery elements were affecting his brain.

Yet it was the King's sickness that doomed her, for those around the King judged that sorcery must be the cause of the King's growing madness and since Eleanor, Duchess of Gloucester, was the most likely suspect, she and several of her associates were arrested. Among those arrested with her was an expert wizard, canon Master Roger Bolingbroke, and another clergyman, Thomas Southwell. Margaret Jourdemayne, the notorious Witch of Eye, was also seized. Since Eleanor was of high rank, she could not be tortured, but those she had employed were put to the rack and stretched until a story could be pieced together. Jourdemayne told how Eleanor first purchased philtres from her to make Duke Humphrey fall in love with her and then later she bought more potions which she hoped would cause her to give birth to a son who might one day become King of England. Bolingbroke admitted making astrological forecasts that showed that the King would die very shortly and this kind of prophecy amounted to treason.

Then the court discovered that Jourdemayne, Bolingbroke and Southwell were all present when Eleanor, Queen of Night and Darkness, presided over a Black Mass one Sunday night in St Paul's churchyard. The nurse did her best to conjure up the scene in the churchyard in which the bare branches of the trees hovered and shook over the conspirators like clawed hands and where the tombstones tilted at odd angles as if they were being forced aside by the restless dead who pushed from below and tried to rise up out of the earth. It was there that Eleanor held conference with the emissaries of Satan from whom she sought confirmation of the imminence of the King's demise. Tiny dark figures that flickered in the smoke of the tallow candles, these emissaries whispered that there would be a price to be paid. There is always a price to be paid.

The court found all four guilty of treasonable necromancy. Bolingbroke was hanged, drawn and quartered at Tyburn, Margaret Jourdemayne was burnt at the stake and Southwell died in prison presumably from the effects of torture. Just as Eleanor's rank had saved her from torture, so it also saved her from execution. She was condemned to do public penance walking in her shift through the streets of London, after which she was sentenced to perpetual imprisonment. Looking back on the nurse's story, Anthony now realises that she was talking about the beautiful and sinister Eleanor Cobham and her dismal fate, but really the nurse was thinking about his mother who was her mistress and of whom she was greatly afraid. But Anthony does not believe that his mother ever met Eleanor Cobham, for he reckons that his mother must have been still a girl in France when the Duchess was arrested.

For a long time, he is silent in reverie. Then he recalls that there are things that he must say to Ripley, 'You should keep away from my mother and it would be best if you never so much as spoke of her. Moreover you should know that if we are to be friends and allies, you must desist from telling absurd lies about me and my heroic adventures.'

'But of course! It shall be entirely as you wish. For now I have no need to invent anything. All London knows how with only a broken sword in your hand you beat off four armed men.'

Then Ripley returns to the subject of Anthony's not wearing a sword. He insists that it is dangerous for Anthony to go about without one. And besides the wearing of a sword is a badge of his rank. Anthony replies negligently that he will see about buying one tomorrow but this is not good enough for Ripley, for he says that most of the swords that are produced these days are of inferior metal and hastily forged. They are not to be compared to the great swords of the previous century. Smithcraft was once a branch of alchemy, but only a small number of the present-day artisans are truly familiar with its secrets. However, Ripley does know one who is a master at the making of weapons and he will conduct Anthony to him tomorrow. Anthony's sword must be forged and weighted in such a manner that it will perfectly suit its master.

They meet at dawn the following morning outside the Hospital of St. Katharine by the Tower. Though it is still cool, Ripley is sweating. He has a sack slung over his shoulder.

'I am going to take you into the antechamber of Hell and there you will think that you have died once more.'

So it is that Ripley leads Anthony, Amyas and Hugh out in the direction of Wapping. The great muddy expanse of Smithfield is already filling up with cattle being brought in to be slaughtered. As the sun begins to rise Anthony thinks that it will be a pleasant day. But not in Wapping. There the pale sunshine is soon obscured by the smoke of burning sea-coal. As the darkness thickens a sense of foreboding comes over Anthony. Though sea-coal smoke has a nasty smell, it perhaps has the merit of partially concealing the stink of the buckets of excrement that are being brought into the place and the carts of quicklime going out to the countryside. Yet other smells compete and these come from soap boilers, tanneries, brewhouses and dye-houses. Occasional wisps of yellow sulphur float in the smog. The ground is slippery for its mud is mixed with tar deposits. Wapping is a little hugger-mugger village of workshops, cottages and lean-tos. Where there are spaces between the buildings, fullers' cloths have been stretched out to dry on tenters, and there are tanks in which hides and oak bark are soaked in water, and there are also lime-pits. While most of the faces of those who go through the alleys are blackened with soot, those who work at the lime-pits wear white masks to protect themselves from the poisonous fumes. They all of them look like so many sullen devils from hell and they scream and shout like animals.

Anthony and his guards cover their faces with their cloaks, but Ripley spreads out his arms exultantly for he loves to be in Wapping, since here in great profusion are all the ingredients of his craft: alum, sulphur, mercury, charcoal, salts and excrement.

He waves his arms exultantly, 'Filth! Filth! Everywhere is filthy! This is life. You can scrape it off the walls. From all these carcases and this rot comes life!'

Then suddenly Ripley vanishes. Anthony and his guards halt and nervously try to make out where they are. Then Ripley calls to them to follow him and through the murk they can make out that he is standing in a doorway and behind him there are roaring flames. So it is that they enter Pykenham's smithy. Ripley and Pykenham embrace for they recognise each other as masters of their respective crafts. Then Pykenham, a swarthy great man with abundant dark curly hair, gazes at Anthony in wonder. It may be that he has never stood so close to a person of rank before. Ripley explains their business and emphasises that they are prepared to pay a high price for a sword of exceptional quality. At Ripley's request, Anthony has brought along what remains of his broken blade and, when he shows it to Pykenham, the smith roars with laughter to see its poor craftsmanship. He explains that though it has a tolerable sharp edge, the main part of the blade is brittle and that this is the product of too much cold hammering and then too little care has been taken in annealing, or slowly cooling and heating the blade many times. The forging of that sword has been rushed. Now Anthony and his companions will see how the job should be done.

This lengthy business begins with a billet, or steel bar, which Pykenham heats before he hammers it into shape on an anvil and then, as the blade takes shape, he fullers a central ridge to give it strength. The smith is also careful to weight the blade towards what will become the hilt. Now comes the difficult part as the blade is repeatedly heated and then cooled to remove the stresses arising from the first stage of its manufacture. The quenching in cold water hardens the blade, but it is then tempered to achieve flexibility and durability.

At first the smith's visitors are fascinated by what they see, but as the blade is repeatedly moved from hearth to cooling tank in order to be heated and then very slowly cooled, they become a little bored and they start to talk amongst themselves. The bodyguards inspect the weaponry stacked in a corner waiting for collection by other customers.

'This will be a sword fit for a hero,' says Ripley to Anthony and he produces a flask from his bag and takes a swig from it before continuing, 'I am going to make you the most famous knight in Christendom.'

Anthony scowls. 'I am my own man.'

But Ripley smiles, 'I tell you no. I tell you that you are in my power and the King wants it so. But be of good cheer for I have nothing but your success at heart.' Then, it seems he recalls something, for he looks worried. He asks Anthony, 'After your recovery from your wounds, have you noticed anything strange?'

Now it is Anthony's turn to worry.

'No. What strange thing should I have noticed?'

'Ah, nothing. If you are not aware of anything different, then all is well. It is a marvel how you have recovered. I say to you again, well done, Lord Scales!' And then Ripley diverts the conversation to the preparations that must be made for the Queen's coronation in London and the welcome that should be given to noble guests coming from Burgundy and Luxemburg. Ripley chatters away and takes frequent swigs from a flask he has produced from out of his sack. Anthony, however is eager to be away. The smithy seems to him like a dark and fiery chamber of Hell and the great mass of smelly humanity that crowds through the alleys of Wapping has filled him with fear. What if the denizens of this region, barely human in appearance and behaviour, should rebel against their stinking and impoverished lot and rise up to kill their masters?

Some fifteen years ago there was such an uprising, though it began not in Wapping but among a filthy horde of rustics, discharged soldiers, mutinous retainers from Kent under the leadership of a man calling himself Jack Cade. This riffraff raged through the streets of London, looting and burning. They forced the imprisonment in the Tower of the King's Treasurer, Lord Say and then had him brought out before justices and stood over those justices while they brought the charge of treason against him. Then he was allowed to make confession before being beheaded. Cade had the head impaled on a spear and the noble lord's body dragged through the city. In the days that followed many more heads of the gentry and aldermen were placed on spikes. Prisons were opened, women were raped and books were burnt. Finally the people of London rose up against the anarchy. Cade fled, but was caught. He was beheaded and his body was quartered before being drawn about the streets on a hurdle with his head resting on the rest of his body, a lesson for all in the streets to see. The great lords returned to the city. Still Anthony and his kind are not loved.

It is so hot in this place. There is a whistling in his ears that almost drowns out the clang of Pykenham's hammer. What is the real reason for bringing him here? Why could he not purchase a sword in the normal fashion? If only Ripley's skull moss had not placed him in the alchemist's debt. But then it occurs to Anthony that the attack on him may not have been an attempt to kill him, but only to wound him, so placing him in Ripley's debt. But such fancies are absurd and Ripley only wishes him well. He must think only sane thoughts. But this is difficult, for it now seems to him that he has two brains residing in his head, each of them engaged in its own thinking.

The one brain is bold, the other is cowardly. But no sooner has he thought this than he thinks that this cannot be so. Yet why should it not be so? Ripley had asked him if, since his recovery, he had noticed anything strange. What strange thing should he be afraid to see?

At last Pykenham is ready to weld the hilt, cross-guard and pommel onto the blade. The cross-guard has hook-shaped quillons, so that Anthony may reverse his sword and use one of those hooks to trip his enemy. Then, after getting Anthony to heft the sword and feel its weight, Pykenham passes it to an apprentice who has to grind the blade with abrasives, polish it and give it a final sharpening. But all is not yet over, for Ripley insists that certain runes must be etched onto the hilt. When Anthony asks what is the meaning of the runes, Ripley laughs and says that it does not matter at all what they mean. Who knows? It is only important that there should be runes on this sword. He thinks that the sword should have a name and suggests Galatine.

So now Anthony has a sword, but on their way back to London, his hands are shaking so much that he cannot carry it and indeed he finds it difficult to walk and he clings to Ripley for support. Anthony's dread is like a cloud all around which mingles with the filthy air of the kilns and dye-houses. Surely the runes on the sword blade carry some evil omen. He fears that Ripley's management of his life will end in nothing good. He is afraid of the labouring poor with their blackened faces. Surely his party will be set upon and killed before they are out of the village of Wapping? And even if they do come out of this hideous place alive, will not the redhead and his gang make another attempt on his life? And, even if this does not happen, he still dreads the combat that is to come with the Bastard of Burgundy, for the Bastard has a mighty reputation as a warrior. Anthony fears to die once more.

He is unable to suppress his trembling after he has returned to what should be the safety of the Woodville townhouse. His mother feels his brow and spends a long time looking at his face.

Finally she says, 'Though the fever has left your body, it still lingers in your head. I can see that some frightened thing is sitting in your brain and looking out at me through your eyes.'

'Do you have a medicine for this?' Anthony wants to know.

'It may be that a story will drive out the sickness. Certain stories are known to have curative powers, but it is difficult... It will take me some time to fashion the story and when it is done and I am ready to tell it, you will have to enter the story I am telling and that will not be pleasant for you. My poor boy, exorcisms are always painful.'

It was a long time before the story was ready and indeed it was not told until the eve of Elizabeth's coronation. In the meantime, the true story of the making of Galatine was one thing. But Ripley's agents and intelligencers put about quite a different story which Anthony only learns of a few weeks later. According to the fiction, Anthony, in need of a new and better sword, a sword fit for a hero, did not have one forged for him. Instead he rode down to Guildford where he had heard that there was a professional treasure hunter called James Garnet. Anthony had learned from the famous cleric and alchemist, George Ripley that this man once had a map marked where the ten lost treasures of England were buried, though tomb robbers had reached most of these places before Garnet and left little in the way of spoils for him. Nevertheless, the map eventually led him to a place near Ravenser where he and his three accomplices dug for gold and they indeed found gold aplenty laid out beside an armed and helmeted man who lay in the rotting remains of a long wooden boat. They helped themselves to what they could carry and returned to Guild-ford drunk with the joy of their sudden wealth.

Or so they supposed, but Ripley told Anthony that their wealth brought them little joy, for soon afterwards one of them died of quartan fever. Then the other two fell out over how the first man's share of the spoils should be divided and they fought over this. One died instantly and the other died more slowly of his wounds. Garnet still lived, but he became a haunted man and a recluse, fearful lest some fever that had arisen like a vapour from the grave at Ravenser might infect him, or that thieves, knowing of the wealth he had recently acquired, might assault and torture him in order to learn where he had hidden his treasure, or perhaps the curse might strike in some other quite unexpected way. And so it did, for at dawn one morning King Henry's officers arrived at Garnet's house and demanded that all that Garnet and his associates had taken from the tomb should be surrendered to them, since it had been deemed to be treasure trove. Garnet had taken on a lawyer to contest the royal right to all this gold, for in English common law treasure trove only applies to treasures that have been hidden with animus revocandi, that is the intention to recover later what had been hidden, whereas the treasure that Garnet had found had obviously been buried with some great man in the expectation that it would comfort him in his grave for all eternity. But the lawsuit was expensive, Garnet had no influential patron and the matter was still unresolved when Edward replaced Henry on the throne.

Since Garnet still lived in fear that other nasty things might happen to him, he at first refused to allow Lord Scales to enter his house, but when he heard that Anthony was a friend of Ripley, the King's well-beloved alchemist, he did timorously open the door. Garnet had some difficulty in understanding what it is that this great lord desired, for Anthony did not want any treasure—that is, he did not want any gold or silver. The noble and pious Anthony had no interest at all in the perishable vanity of wealth. No, he wanted something that would outlive him, which is fame, and to become a famous knight he needed a sword that would be worthy of him, a sword which had been forged by Weland the Smith or one of the other great artificers of old, for the swords of nowadays are hardly more than cutlery compared to the swords wielded by the heroes of antiquity. Anthony wanted to give Garnet money so that he might guide him to the grave of some dead hero whose sword Anthony would then possess.

Of course, Garnet was in bad need of money. Even so he was reluctant. He did know of a place not far from Guildford where there was a little mound which might be an ancient grave. He could lead Anthony there, but then he would leave him and he could lend Anthony a spade and other tools but his lordship would have to do the digging, and this would have to be at night since the local people do not like to see such places disturbed, for they are afraid that the old graves are guarded by draugs as Garnet himself was, even though he did not actually know what a draug might be.

So they rode towards a stretch of woodland a few miles outside Pyrford and Garnet guided Anthony to a barrow on the edge of the trees and left him with equipment hired out to him: two lanterns, a spade, a pickaxe and a trowel. Then, as the sun was setting, Garnet hurried away. Anthony waited until it was properly dark before he began to dig. Happily his military exercises, and in particular his practice at the repeated plunging of a sword into a mound of wet clay and pulling it out again, had given him the right kind of muscles for this labour. Apart from the light of his lanterns, he noticed that a half circle of rotting tree trunks was covered in a sort of fungus that glowed with a luminous green light. He could hear Black Saladin shifting restlessly. Otherwise at first he had only owls and nightjars for company. Then, after little more than an hour of digging, he turned round and saw that he was being watched by a skinny boy who was sitting propped up against one of the decayed tree trunks.

'I saw the light from your lantern and I thought that I would come over to see who you might be and what your business is,' said the boy.

Anthony explained that he was digging there in the hope of finding a sword buried somewhere in this mound of earth and he offered to pay the boy well, if only he would assist in the digging.

But the boy replied, 'Begging your honour's pardon, I will not. It is a fearful labour and, if I were you, I would be afraid of the draug.'

'Then be off with you,' said Anthony impatiently.

But the boy did not move and he asked, 'Are you not afraid of the draug?'

Anthony, who now needed to rest a while, sat down but kept his distance from the boy as he became aware that there was a faint smell about him.

'What is a draug that I should be afraid of it?' he asked and this was the answer, 'Draugs are servants of the dead. They watch over them and guard the things which rightfully belong to them. You ask what is a draug, whereas what you should be asking is what is a man? I will tell you. A man is not just his body, for who he is also encompasses those things that are closest to him, his shirt, his helmet, his sword, his drinking cup and, it may be, his horse. All these things may be part of his body and therefore infused with his soul and that is why your ancestors were buried with their arms and armour. It is well known that draugs do not like to see a dead man dismembered. And now I will tell you why you should be afraid of a draug. A draug sleeps in the mouldy grave bed with his appointed corpse, but if anyone comes to disturb the grave, then the draug awakes and issues out to defend it. Once he is out in the open then he can swell to an enormous size and he becomes so heavy that his usual way of defending his corpse is to lie down upon the grave's attacker. He rests on the man's chest like a heavy nightmare that cannot be dispelled and so the man's ribs crack and he is crushed to death.'

But Anthony replied, 'A Christian knight fears no monsters, for his faith in God is sufficient defence against such things. And, if you are sure that draugs are so frightening, why do you not run away now? I am going to continue digging, for I have no belief in the folklore of yokels.'

But the truth was that Anthony was amazed and even somewhat cautious, for he no longer believed that the boy was an ordinary yokel.

The boy did not reply directly to Anthony's boast. Instead he announced, 'I am lonely and I want to be told a story.'

So Anthony, who was not yet ready to resume digging, told the boy the story of Melusine and added that he was himself descended from this dragon lady.

When the story was finished the boy nodded thoughtfully. He was not such a starveling as Anthony had first thought.

'True stories are the best,' said the boy at last. 'But I do not believe that you are telling the truth when you say that you are here because you want a sword. A rich gentleman like you could buy a sword anywhere. I think the truth is that you are really seeking gold, more gold than you need.'

'Believe what you choose and be damned.'

And with that Anthony resumed digging. It was a hot summer night and after a while Anthony removed his surcoat, revealing his hair shirt, and continued to dig, but then, still hot, he removed this also and at this point the boy got up and came closer so that he might inspect the scars that ran crisscross over Anthony's back. There was a stench about the boy, as if he had not washed for years, if ever. Moreover, he had swollen to a vast size and his skin glowed faintly with a death-blue light. So this was no boy from the nearby village. It was a draug. Yet the creature's voice remained courteous.

'For what crime were you so flogged, Sir?'

'I bear these marks because I am a mortal and sinful man. Yet no one else flogged me. Only it is I who scourge myself in memory and re-enactment of the Passion of Christ and in so doing I also hope to whip all earthly lusts out of me and I hope to understand how others less fortunate than myself suffer in their daily lives.'

The draug sucked in his teeth. Then he said, 'You are tired. I believe that you should rest again and tell me a story.'

'Surely it is your turn to tell me a story.'

'I must have a story,' insisted the draug. 'I will tell you a story after you have told me one more. Ghost stories are the best.'

'Why must you have a story?'

'Draugs like stories and dead men tell no tales.'

But Anthony replied, 'In the last, you are certainly mistaken.'

And then Anthony proceeded to tell the tale of how he had been killed at the Battle of Palm Sunday and how he had been guided to a mysterious castle and then how he had risen on the third day. When the story was finished, the draug opened his mouth widely and the awful smell redoubled. Yet he was smiling.

'You are like me,' he said. 'You are descended from a dragon and you have come out from the grave and so you are a Christian monster. I am a Christian like you. So I will not lie upon you and so kill you. Now if you dig over there, you will find a sword in a leather scabbard. Be careful to dig close to the edge or there is a danger that your spade may sever the arm of the sword's former owner.'

So Anthony hurried to dig at the spot he has been pointed to. As he dug, the draug told him that this barrow was the resting place of Sir Yvan, a Knight of the Round Table, who fought first with Sir Tristan and later with Sir Lancelot and yet survived both combats. It was also Yvan who fought and slew the Knight of the Hedge of Mist. Then Anthony drew the sword in its scabbard out of the grave and brushed the earth off them.

'This is a close copy of the first sword with which Cain slew Abel,' said the draug. 'You have no idea what goes into the forging of such a sword as this,' he added. Then he told Anthony that the sword's name was Galatine, as the runes on the hilt indicated. Also this was the sword which smote the Dolorous Stroke and as a consequence there was a kind of spell on it which could be seen as a blessing or a curse and the nature of the spell was this; that once the sword has been withdrawn it can only be returned to the scabbard after it had killed someone.

'Now you have a sword fit for a Christian hero,' the draug concluded.

'What about the story you were going to tell me?' demanded Anthony.

'Truly, I was going to tell you a story, but now I see that the dawn approaches and I dare not linger in the light. You will hear the story of the Dolorous Stroke soon enough.'

With that the draug, now a thinning blue gas, shrank back into the grave.

That morning Anthony rode into Guildford and in one of its churches he had the sword Galatine, still in its scabbard, rechristened and consecrated to the service of God and King Edward.

CHAPTER NINE

White Tower

The story of Bran then. Bran, who was King of the Island of Britain, or the Island of the Mighty as it once was known, was staying at Harlech, which was one of his castles, when he was told that thirteen ships had been sighted on the horizon and those ships were making for the coast at great speed. Bran sent armed men down to the shore to find out what these ships were doing in British waters. Then he went down to the shore himself ready to lead his men in the fighting if that were necessary. But as he reached the beach, he saw that small boats were being launched from the big ships and they soon brought heralds ashore and these heralds saluted Bran and told him that Matholwch, King of Ireland, was with his fleet and he had come in peace. So Bran told the messengers that he was welcome to come ashore, but the heralds replied that he would not set foot in Britain unless his mission should be accomplished.

'And what is that?' asked Bran.

'He seeks to wed your sister, Branwen, daughter of Lyr,' the heralds replied, 'for that would make a bond between Ireland and the Island of the Powerful. Branwen will be his Queen.'

What is the point of the story that they have started to listen to? What has it to do with where they are? Jacquetta de St Pol is telling the story of Bran and Branwen to Elizabeth and Anthony. It is the Saturday before Pentecost and since it is the eve of Elizabeth's coronation, they are lodged in the

White Tower from which they will ride out in solemn state towards Westminster on the following morning. Elizabeth's hair has the appearance of spun gold, fit for a princess in a fairy tale. She has been brushing her hair as if she would never be done with it and as she worked with the brush she talked without ceasing about what she should wear on the morrow and all the other fine things that Edward was lavishing on her. Eventually Jacquetta lost patience and said that she would tell them a story and they should both learn something from it. Before she started the story Jacquetta spent a long time whispering to Elizabeth. Anthony is afraid of what is coming this evening, for he guesses that it is his story, though he cannot see how this can be so.

Jacquetta continues, 'Let him come to me then and we shall discuss the matter,' said Bran.

So Matholwch landed and came to court and after some talk between the two Kings it was agreed that Branwen, who was a golden-haired beauty (and greatly resembled Elizabeth), should become Matholwch's Queen. So then there was a great celebration and a feast. The feast was held in tents, for no house that could contain the giant Bran had yet been built. But Evnissyen, Bran's half-brother, had not been consulted about the wedding and that was Bran's mistake, for though Evnissyen was a man who delighted in creating surprises, he did not care to be surprised himself. Evnissyen was the man who made things happen, and it was he who created stories, so that the storytellers who came after him merely recited what he had done.'

No sooner had she uttered those last words than his mother rose from her chair and swiftly walked over to Anthony and sitting beside him on the bench, she hissed at him,

'Now, my son! It must be now! That is you, this your story. Go into it now!'

So it was that Anthony left the darkness of the Tower and became Evnissyen. He no longer heard the words of his mother, but instead he saw what she said. He found himself walking aimlessly early one sunny morning when the mist was still rising off the grass until he came to a horse park. Anthony, or Evnissyen, had no idea whose horses they were in the park. So he asked about them and he was told that they were the horses of King Matholwch and his followers and that Matholwch had just married Evnissyen's sister. All this had been kept secret from him. So then he thought that it was time to make something happen. It was like a dark dream. You know that if you dream that you are strolling about in the sunny countryside, you cannot just continue enjoying your sunlit walk all through your night asleep. Something must happen, for that is the nature of dreaming. What he does is mad, yet though the thing in his head is screaming all the time that he must not do it, the madness prevails, for Anthony has entered a world and a time where he may do as he pleases.

Anthony knew what he as Evnissyen should do and so he set upon those horses and cut off their lips back to their teeth and severed their ears and docked their manes and sliced out their eyelids. The noise of the horses was horrible and there was also screaming in his head, for the thing that was lodged there was terrified by what he was doing. The grooms ran forward to rescue their horses, but they saw that Anthony was armed and they were not. So they stepped back and put their hands over their ears. In this way Anthony took his revenge on Matholwch for the King not telling him about his sister's marriage and, since he as Evnissyen is the King's half-brother, he dares to do this. There is blood everywhere and he revels in it. Christian morality has no jurisdiction here for these are pagan times and Christ has yet to be born. Now that Anthony has become Evnissyen he can do what he likes and he is surprised by what he likes.

When Matholwch heard of the ruin of his horses which was a monstrous insult aimed at him, he and his followers returned to their ships and made ready to sail for Ireland. As soon as Bran heard that this was happening, he sent after the King of Ireland to ask why he was leaving with such ill grace. When Bran heard of the evil that had been done to Matholwch's horses and he discovered that this evil was the work of Evnissyen, he sent a message to Matholwch explaining that it would be difficult for him to punish his half-brother, but he also apologised and sent peace offerings, including replacements for all Mathowlch's horses, a silver rod and gold plate. So Matholwch relented and returned to the feasting, but Bran, seeing that there was now a certain coldness between them, decided to offer yet more. He gave him a magical cauldron. The magic of it was that if Matholwch were to lose a man in battle, then he had only to throw him in the cauldron in the evening and then in a little while he would find that warrior revived and fully recovered, save only that he would no longer be able to speak. Matholwch joyfully accepted the cauldron.

The following morning Mathowlch and Branwen set sail for Ireland where there was much rejoicing at their arrival and at first Branwen was much honoured and received many gifts from the King's subjects and she bore Mathowlch a son who was called Gwern. But slowly word spread throughout Ireland about how their King had been insulted by Evnissyen and there was a clamour among the Irish for revenge. So Branwen was sent down to the kitchen to cook for the court and each morning when the butcher came to deliver the meat he boxed her ears. The King told his men to prevent any ships passing between Ireland and Wales, lest Bran should hear what had happened to his sister, but Branwen captured a starling and taught it to speak, so that it might report to the King of the Island of Britain how she was being punished for the wrongs done by her brother, Evnissyen.

Eventually Bran hears of this and summons his troops. The troops go into ships and set sail for Ireland. Since there is no ship large enough for Bran, he walks across the Irish Sea. When Anthony contemplates the size of his half-brother, he realises what a wild, mad story he is in. Though Jacquetta had called Bran a giant, Anthony had not previously grasped the scale of him. Although Anthony finds himself to be very tall, he is of more normal stature and he has no difficulty in finding a ship that will accommodate him. There are so many ships that it is like a forest crossing the water and they follow what looks like a mountain parting the waters, though it is Bran. Anthony on his ship also marvels at the strange shapes of the arms and armour carried by Bran's men and the primitive look of the ships' rigging. Hitherto he had not understood that everything looked different in older times and that men dressed and armed themselves in quite a different fashion from his own age. He looks forward to the coming battle, even though the thing in his head is praying to God that there will be no battle, but the prayers are useless for there is no one God presiding over this story, but many warring spirits.

When Matholwch sees the size of the army that is coming to Ireland he realises that he has no choice but to submit and he sends Branwen to plead for mercy from her brother. Now Mathowlch has become Bran's liegeman, he promises to build Bran a house that is large enough to accommodate him. The vast house is soon built and it is inside this house that the feast of reconciliation is to be held. But Anthony, who would have preferred a battle, is the first to enter and gazes angrily around him and when he sees sacks hanging on every wall he asks what is in them. 'Flour' is the answer he gets. Then he sees one of the sacks move and he realises that Matholwch is as treacherous and mad as he is himself and that an ambush has been planned. So he goes up to the sack in which he had seen movement and fumbles about until he feels the head of the warrior whereupon he squeezes until his fingers enter the man's brain. So he goes from bag to bag. Every time he is told that the sack contains flour and each time he finds the warrior's skull and squeezes it until the man is dead. Anthony glories in the strength of his hands.

Is not this the moment for him to leave the story since it is going so well? By now the villainous business with the horses has been forgotten and at this point he is presented as a cunning man and a hero. 'Leave now.' That is what the timid voice in his head is whispering. The whisperer is desperate for the story to be left unfinished. The whisperer can see that bad things are coming. 'Why is your mother telling a story in which so much blood will be shed?' But Anthony cannot muster the will to drop out of her narrative, for though he senses that dark and terrible things are about to happen in this story, he has a presentiment that dark and terrible things will also happen in the reality from which he has briefly escaped and which he is trying to forget about. In reality something horrible will happen in the Tower and he will be responsible. So it seems better to stay safe inside the story, for after all it is only a story. A story is meaningless without its end, and besides, no real people die in stories. It is a decision that he will come to regret.

By now Bran and his men have entered the house. Branwen, seeing her half-brother in the house, sends little Gwern toddling towards him. Gwern is such a pretty, friendly child that Bran's heart melts. Gwern is now to become King of Ireland under Branwen's regency and that will be the end of it. But Anthony does not care for any son of Matholwch, nor does he want the story to end so smugly, after which he would have to return to London and the gloom of the White Tower. So he snatches up the pretty little child and thrusts him headfirst into the fire and then Anthony stands with his back to the fire daring anyone to try and rescue the baby, and since he has a fiercesome reputation as a fighter, no one dares. His sister Branwen wants to throw herself in after her baby, but others hold her back.

Now a battle breaks out inside and outside the house. It is at this point that James Butler, the Earl of Wiltshire, who has fled from so many battles, finds that he dare not stay for this one either and so, with smoke coming out through the nostrils, he departs from Anthony's head. But Anthony, exultant in his newfound evil and with a clear head at last, loves a battle. After a while though he realises that Bran and he are making little headway against Matholwch's forces. This is because whenever one of the enemy is killed Matholwch has the corpse put in the cauldron and in a very short time the man emerges alive again, but dumb. So Anthony decides to impersonate a dead Irishman (which is not a difficult thing to do). Whereupon he is carried over to the vast cauldron and dropped inside it. Once inside he sets to kicking the cauldron to pieces so that its magic will never work again. This labour is hard and at the very moment he succeeds his heart bursts.

Since Evnissyen is now dead, Anthony can no longer be part of the story and he finds himself back in the White Tower where he listens to Jacquetta finish the tale and that is soon done. Despite Evnissyen's heroic sacrifice the British are defeated and only seven men return with Bran to Wales. Bran, who has been wounded in the foot with a poison dart, is in such pain that he asks them to cut off his head which they do. Back in Wales, Branwen laments and dies of a broken heart. Anthony is only listening with half an ear. He feels that he has been away for years, yet this cannot be so. Also he is thinking that he, like Evnissyen, has a sister who is married to a King and he wonders what the message of the story of Bran and Branwen might be. Anthony is accustomed to regard himself as the central character in his own story. But Evnissyen was only a supporting character in the story of Bran and Branwen. So is Anthony to become merely a supporting character in the story of Edward and Elizabeth?

Before Bran offered his head to be cut off, he asked that it should be taken to London and buried at Tower Hill with his face turned towards France. Though the seven did as he had asked, they did not hurry about it for they spent seven years feasting in Harlech as the Assembly of the Wondrous

Head. The three birds of Rhiannon, that have the power to wake the dead and lull the living to sleep, sang to them from far over the sea, so that they forgot all about the bloody and ill-fated war in Ireland. The seven companions of Bran were fine as long as none of them opened a certain door. Don't open that door! But of course that door was opened by one of the feasting warriors who was bolder and more curious than the rest. Otherwise this story would still be going on today. So he opened the forbidden door and looked out on the Bristol Channel. No sooner had he done so, than all the sadness of life came flooding back and their revels were concluded. So then they went to London where they buried Bran's head under the Tower and it is one of the three fantastic concealments of Britain. And with that Jacquetta's story is concluded.

The real world is a poor thing compared with the world of stories. Anthony wishes that he could re-enter the story of Bran and Branwen, for in it he knew that Matholwch was his enemy and that man was easy to fight against, but now that he finds himself back in the chill of the White Tower's upper chamber he knows that he has other enemies to face in the coming months and years. He can only guess at some of their names. The Earl of Warwick certainly and the redheaded man and whoever sent the redheaded man. And he senses that Ripley, for all his smiles, may be dangerous and, again, though Tiptoft seems well-disposed to Anthony, God help him if that should change.

But Elizabeth seems relieved that the story is over. 'When did all this happen?' she wants to know.

'Perhaps it has yet to happen,' Jacquetta replied.

'Oh, I hope not. I am afraid of things that may yet happen.'

'None of you have anything to fear as long as I am alive,' said Jacquetta.

But Anthony slept little that night.

The Tower is a deathly place and had been ever since Julius

Caesar ordered its building. Anthony had been at the siege of Alnwick when the Lancastrian plotters Aubrey de Vere, Sir Thomas Tuddenham, Tyrrel and Montgomery had been taken on sledges to the Tower and there beheaded and then a few days later, Aubrey's father the Earl of Oxford followed his son to the same scaffold and his head joined his son's on one of the spikes above the gate of London Bridge. Tiptoft, who as Constable of England had presided over their executions, wrote to Anthony about it. He described the drum roll used to muffle the last words of the condemned men and how the headsman made two or three passing swipes over the men's necks so as to find the range and how the headsman needed a second or even a third stroke to sever the head from the body. The cleaving of a man's head from his neck is not a simple matter for there is flesh, muscle, sinew and bone to hack through. But at least the headsman who dealt with Sir Aubrey de Vere and his fellows was an expert. As Tiptoft recalled, when during the Peasants' Revolt in the previous century, the rebels forced their way into the Tower and there had Simon Sudbury, the Archbishop of Canterbury beheaded, it had taken eight strokes of the axe to do so.

A little later, when Anthony was back in London, he sat with Tiptoft at the Court of Chivalry when John de Vere came up for trial. Treasonable letters were produced and there was no question of the man's guilt. He was dragged to the scaffold where his stomach was slit open, his entrails were pulled out and he was castrated, and these bloody pieces were cast into the fire. De Vere was still breathing as he looked down on his evisceration. Then he was dragged to the block and his head cut off. As was the custom when the head was off, the headsman seized it by the hair and presented it to the severed body, so that he who had just been decapitated, even if he was still conscious, could see that he was truly finished and know that his last sight of the world was a horrible one. The headsman displayed the head to the crowd, and Anthony was astonished to see the condemned man's lips and eyes move. Afterwards a skilled butcher flayed what was left of the body which was quartered, and finally the head was taken inside to be parboiled in salt water and cumin seeds, so that its flesh would not be consumed by birds when it was impaled upon London Bridge.

De Vere's execution had attracted a good crowd, for it is natural for a man or a woman to watch someone die and by this take joy in the fact that they who watch are still alive and unharmed. Also Tiptoft piously declares that the common folk should indeed delight in seeing great ones brought low, for these executions are sermons delivered in blood from which the people may learn of the inconstancy of men's fortune as decreed by God's providence. Tiptoft has instituted a museum of severed heads within the Tower.

Anthony should not be thinking of such gory things now, for it is a bright afternoon and he is walking with Elizabeth out of the Tower to find the horses that are ready for them just beyond the Bywater Gate and from there they will ride with a stately retinue to Westminster where Elizabeth is to be crowned. Elizabeth who walks beside him is very pale and she no longer chatters about her fine robes. Instead she turns to Anthony, 'Doubtless you thought it a very foolish story that our mother told us last night. I am sure that you judged it to be the sort of nonsense that old women tell to small children.'

And without allowing Anthony to reply, she continued, 'But that was my story. I saw the things that happened for I was in the story. You only listened to a story but I found myself inside it and I saw terrible things. I was the most important part of the story, for it was me who was betrothed to Mathowlch. I stood beside Bran's throne when news came of the horrid things done in the horse park. Later, I ruled in Ireland and for a while thought myself beloved by my new subjects, though things soon changed and I was sent to the kitchen, where I washed dishes and performed other menial tasks. Every morning the butcher would come with his meat and every morning he would deliver a blow to my face that would send me reeling against the table or crashing to the floor. I felt those blows and I can exactly describe what the butcher looked like, with his blotchy face and hairy nostrils, and I knew the smell of stale food and damp cellars. Worst of all I was held to watch as Evnissyen forced my beautiful child into the fire and held him there until his screaming stopped and he was dead. And brother Anthony, it was so horrible... I thought of all the evil wrought by Evnissyen who was my brother.'

Now she looks anxiously to Anthony. Yet he is silent, for he can think of nothing good to say to her. Despite his being in the story too, he has not understood it at all, but he fears that he will not like its message when he does seize upon it.

Fortunately they have now passed through the Byward Gate and he is spared from having to reply to his sister as she is helped into her litter. This is an elaborate business as her dress of white cloth of gold has a long train which must be folded in behind her. Anthony mounts Black Saladin, now fully recovered, and he rides directly behind the litter. When Anthony was young, he used to give Elizabeth piggyback rides.

Now he senses that his sister has been carrying him to greatness on her back and he is embarassed.

They proceed through the cheering crowds that line Cheapside. There are more crowds thronging Westminster Hall and its enclosure, but the Duke of Clarence, the Earl of Arundel and the Duke of Norfolk, all three of them riding on horses trapped with cloth of gold, clear a space for Elizabeth and the Woodvilles to process. Now she walks barefoot on a long carpet of ray cloth from Westminster Hall to the Abbey. At the door of the Abbey she is robed in a purple mantle, there is a coronal on her head and she carries two sceptres, one in each hand as she advances under a canopy born by the barons of the Cinque Ports. The Archbishop of Canterbury and other clergy walk with her. The noble ladies, headed by Jacquetta, wear red velvet and ermine. Edward is not present since it is the custom that the King should not attend his wife's coronation.

Inside the Abbey Elizabeth processes to the high altar and kneels there a while, and when she rises the Archbishop crowns and anoints her before conducting her to the throne. Though the King is not present in the Abbey, his white rose and the badge of the falcon appears on pennants and shields all the way along the nave. Once more the fierce menagerie of lions, wyverns, griffins, unicorns, bulls and eagles is on display in the Abbey just as they had been at the Battle of Palm Sunday. Anthony can read the room, for there he sees the chequer of Clifford, there the portcullis and chains of Somerset, and behind those blazons he can see Montagu's chevrons and the rampant lions of William Herbert Earl of Pembroke. One beast is absent from the heraldic menagerie; the bear with its ragged staff is nowhere to be seen, for the Earl of Warwick is abroad on another diplomatic mission to France—a mission that Warwick claimed was necessary for the future security of the kingdom, though the truth is that he could not have borne to stay in England and be forced to witness the triumphal crowning of the upstart Woodville woman. Though there is no sign of the bear, yet its very absence is menacing.

Anthony gazes on a coloured riot of or, argent, gules, azure, sable, vert and purpure. Even so he perceives that the colours in the Abbey today are not as bright as they were in the days of King Bran and King Matholwch, for as the world ages, its colours fade and its outlines become less distinct. Also, as the world ages, each generation is more stupid than the one before and men, women, beasts, winds and tides move ever more slowly. Anthony sees things differently now, since in the course of the last night he has spent seven years in the Island of the Mighty as it was when Bran ruled it. In human time he is twenty-six years old, but yet he has now lived for thirty-three years. Of course, there will be a price to be paid for the gift of those years. There is always a price to be paid when one has entered those realms.

Boredom is an essential part of ceremony and ritual. If the ceremony is not boring, then it is not a ceremony. Neither laughter nor tears have any part in such an event. Royal power exerts itself and enforces on its subjects long hours of waiting and standing. The nobility of England have been commanded to stand in serried rows so as to display their wealth and rank. They pretend to themselves that they are proud to be doing so; the truth is that they are humiliated. Anthony finds himself wishing that he was Evnissyen again so that he could make something happen. The wearisomeness does not end with the crowning of Elizabeth, for it is followed by the coronation feast which consists of seventeen courses. Elizabeth dines in great state, for the Countesses of Shrewsbury and of Kent kneel on either side of her and every time Elizabeth takes a mouthful from one of the seventeen courses, she takes off her crown and the Countesses raise a veil to conceal her mouth. Then when she has finished chewing, the veil comes down and she resumes her crown.

At length it is over and the sun is setting as Anthony comes out of Westminster Palace. He finds himself walking beside Sir Thomas Malory in the direction of the Abbey. Malory looks anxiously at Anthony, but feeling in some way guilty for all this pomp that had been staged for his sister's coronation, turns to Sir Thomas and says, 'That was a wearisome business.'

'Yes. To speak truly, I found myself thinking of the white hart, the bratchet and the black running hounds, though this was not to be,' says Malory.

Then seeing the expression on Anthony's face, Malory explains and this is the story he tells:

In the early days of King Arthur's reign, he fell in love with

Guinevere, the daughter of King Leodegraunce and determined to marry her. But when he told Merlin of his decision, the aged wizard and counsellor sought to dissuade him.

'She is among the most beautiful women in the kingdom, yet I would you loved someone else, for Guinevere's very beauty will lead to the ruin of the Kingdom of Logres and bring to shame its knights.'

But Arthur could only think of her sparkling eyes and her hair which was like spun gold.

So a high feast was made ready and the King married Guinevere in the church of Saint Stephen's in Camelot. And at the feast each knight was seated according to his rank at the Round Table or at lesser boards. They thought it should have been a stately and solemn feast. Whereupon Merlin warned them all that they were about to see something strange and marvellous. Before anyone had tasted a mouthful of what was before them, a white hart came running into the hall and skittered among the tables and close behind came a bratchet and after her followed some thirty black running hounds. The bratchet caught up with the hart and bit a chunk of its flank and the white hart leapt up in a panic and knocked over a table where a knight was seated and then made its escape out of the hall. Meanwhile the knight seized the bratchet and hurried out with her, and having found his horse rode off with the dog. Everything was still in turmoil when a lady riding on a white palfrey entered the hall and demanded of Arthur that the bratchet be returned to her since the dog was hers and no sooner had she finished speaking than another knight came after her, seized her by force and carried her away.

'I was praying for something like that to happen today,' says Malory. 'Yet it seems that high adventure is difficult to find in our own time.'

'What happened next?' Anthony asks. They pace around the Abbey's cloister as Malory continues with his story.

'Since the lady had been very noisy with her weeping and

complaints, Arthur was pleased to see her gone, but Merlin said that the King could not leave the matter there, for that would bring dishonour to his Kingdom. Rather, he must send out three knights on a quest. Sir Gawain was enjoined to bring back the white hart, Sir Tor was sent after the knight with the bratchet and King Pellinore was to return with the doleful lady. Sir Gawain set out with a heavy...'

But Anthony learns nothing now about Sir Gawain's quest, for at this point he sees that his father, who is standing at the other side of the cloister, is urgently summoning him over. So Anthony makes his excuses to Malory and hurries to join Earl Rivers.

'What is the matter? What do you need me for?'

'I need you not to be seen talking to Sir Thomas,' his father replies. 'That man is dangerous. You know that.'

'I was hearing a most interesting story about a white hart, some dogs and two disorderly knights. What was the harm in that? Why should I not have been suffered to hear the end of it? There is no danger in listening to a story.'

' "Refuse profane and old wives' fables and exercise thyself rather unto godliness", so the Bible tells us,' says Rivers. 'And you get enough of such faery nonsense from your mother. Besides it is dangerous to be seen close to Sir Thomas. At present he is allowed his liberty, since the Earl of Warwick watches over him and he also has a friendly kinsman, Robert Malory who is the Lieutenant of the Tower. Besides the King and Ripley are eager to promote a revival of legends about Arthur and Camelot as serving the interest of the state. Yet Sir Thomas is known to remain loyal to the house of Lancaster and it seems to me that, though King Edward, egged on by that fraudulent alchemist of his, likes to pose as a reborn King Arthur, the same stories could just as well serve the cause of our former King, Henry.'

Though Anthony nods to his father, he tells himself that he has no reason to fear Malory, for he will be on his guard against any treachery and he will certainly not borrow any books from that man. Yet he likes to listen to the stories. He does not see Malory again until, some two months later, on the day the captive King Henry is paraded through the streets of London. It is then by chance that Anthony finds himself at Westcheap standing shoulder to shoulder with Malory in the midst of a jeering crowd.

Indeed, Henry cuts a sorry figure. He had spent months hiding in the Lake District until in July Yorkist officers caught up with him at the village of Bungerly Hippingstones. Then he was sent south and the Earl of Warwick, who was back from his French mission, rode out to meet the captive King at the little village of Islington before escorting him to London.

The Earl rides at the head of the procession and Henry follows. His feet are tied by leather thongs to the stirrups of his horse. Though it is raining his head is uncovered. His hair is straggly, his beard unkempt and his cloak is patched. Yet he is seen to be smiling peacefully as he is paraded through the mostly hostile streets. Perhaps he is glad to be done with running and hiding. The crowd thins as the King has passed on towards the Tower where he will be lodged and Anthony turns to Malory and says, 'I am pleased that we are met for I should like to hear how the adventure of the hart, the bratchet and the running hounds ended.'

But Malory replies, 'No, brother murderer, this is not the place or the moment for such a story. I have not the heart for it.' And indeed he looks tired and sad. But after a little while he continues, 'Yet, I will tell you another tale, which shall be one that is more fitting to this day and your condition. I know a tavern not far away, and if you follow me, I will tell the story there, if you are sure that you must have a story.'

Anthony would have preferred to hear the continuation of the story of the bratchet, the hind and the screeching lady. Nevertheless he is still curious to understand this sinister storyteller better. It is not as if he will be in any danger as he has his sword and his bodyguards. Thus he is content to go along with Malory. Amyas and Hugh follow them at a distance. The tavern turns out not to be so very close and they pick their way along a bewildering succession of muddy alleys under boards and banners displaying the ignoble heraldry of trade: the tailor's scissors, the farrier's horseshoe, the taverner's bush, the grocer's apple, the doctor's or apothecary's pestle, the scribe's book. Malory is not very familiar with London and they are soon lost. They might have found their destination sooner if Malory had not begun on a most curious speech. Looking hard at Anthony, this is what he says, 'I find your hunger for tales like that of the hind, the bratchet and the running dogs surprising. You are yourself at the centre of so many stories that I should not have thought that you needed to be entertained by any more of them, for people are talking about you and how you wear a hair shirt under that handsomely blazoned surcoat of yours and that you spend your nights scourging yourself. It is said that you wear a talisman that protects you from mortal injury. It is even said that you were slain at the Battle of Palm Sunday but that you rose from the dead. You fought off four assassins with only a broken sword for your defence. You are said to have conjured up the walking dead and so driven your wife mad. It is said that you are descended from a dragon. In a tavern in Southwark you killed a man with a single blow to the throat. You are said to possess a sword which, once drawn from its scabbard, infallibly finds a victim and that you parleyed with a draug to secure it. You are said to have seen the Holy Grail, something which no other man has witnessed for centuries.' During this tirade the pitch of Malory's voice has been rising and it ends with a final sneer: 'In sum, you are unbelievable. You are not a man at all and I swear I do not believe that you exist.'

At this point Anthony steps in front of Malory and punches him hard in the stomach and Malory falls gasping to the ground.

'I refute you thus,' shouts Anthony.

'You should not have done that,' wheezes Malory.

The bodyguards come running up, but Anthony waves them away.

'Think yourself lucky that I did not aim for your throat. You would have had me killed when we were at the northern sieges. But now you have felt me, have you not? And you can hear me, can you not?' Anthony is still shouting. 'And now you shall have a taste of me.' Anthony makes ready as if to piss on the fallen man.

'I cry you mercy,' gasps Malory. 'I only meant to warn you of a certain danger and I see that I have gone about it in the wrong way.' With this he hastily struggles to his feet.

'Why should I believe in anything you say? For I now know your history, and now that I know it, I do not believe that you are human, for you are really some kind of demon.'

'I am a man as you are.' Malory's voice is a whisper.

'No, I say that you are some kind of demon. I swear that I cannot think of any kind of violence, villainy or blasphemy that you have not committed: poaching, ambush, robbery with violence, adultery, extortion, theft, rape, rustling, desecration and theft from an abbey and, it is whispered, treason. And yet you have spent so much time in so many prisons that it is hard to imagine how you have found time to commit so many crimes.'

Malory shrugs.

'These things can be explained, even if not excused. But as I say, I wanted to warn you, for you are in danger.'

Now Anthony takes Malory by the arm.

'You know something of the redheaded man... Do you know who he is?'

Malory replies, 'I swear I do not know you to be in peril from any man. You are strong, rich, and connected to the King. The peril comes from elsewhere.'

'What then?'

Malory is now busy brushing mud off his jerkin.

'The danger comes from stories. They crowd around you like little devils. It is not a comfortable thing to be a creature in someone else's fictions. In some stories you appear to be sinister. You scourge yourself until your back is a mess of bloody welts. You seek to kill a former comrade in arms. You rob the dead of their treasure. In other stories you appear as a comical figure, as in your resistance to the seductive wiles of Dame Discipline de la Chevalerie. Your life and soul are being stolen from you as you become tangled in a web of falsehoods and you are clothed in other men's deeds. Who is doing this to you? Is it your mother? People say that she is steeped in faery lore. Am I right? Is it Jacquetta de St Pol?'

Finally, 'Some of the stories are true,' says Anthony.

Malory is not impressed, 'They may start as true but still end up as falsehoods and the falsehoods will possess you and you will become a wraith, the subject and victim of dark fantasy. I know about the story-devils. So I can tell you that some of the stories that are now told about you belong to other men who are long dead. The theft of their stories is a kind of grave robbery and must be punished. The story-devils will come for you and plague you. They will crawl all over you like lice. Do you really wear a hair shirt, by the way?'

Anthony shakes his head.

'I thought not. The story-devils are serfs of the Devil. The mad things will keep you awake at night as they whisper in the corners of your bedchamber. In the corners of your bedchamber they will mate and multiply. As they fight for your attention, story will kill story. In their struggles, some stories will be mutilated and lose vital parts. Some are headless and grope their way around. Others flap their wings, though they are too weak to fly and their wings are only a burden to them. Yet these misshapen stories will still come limping or crawling towards you, begging you to listen to them, and they will tempt you with mad messages, seductive promises and narratives of past horrors.'

Nothing more is said until they reach their destination, but Anthony is thinking that it is Malory who is the man for mad messages. At the Bull and Mouth in St. Martin's-Le-Grand Malory demands and gets a room where they can be alone and he has a fire lit, so that they can dry off. Amyas and Hugh have drinks brought to them in the public parlour. Once Malory has a jug of Gascon wine in front of him he looks at Anthony and asks, 'What do you know of the matter of the Dolorous Stroke?'

'I do not know what a dolorous stroke is. How should I know?' And then Anthony hesitates. 'But now I think about it, it is said that when I met and conversed with the draug of Guildford, the creature promised to tell me about the Dolorous Stroke, though he did not keep to his word.'

'It is as I thought,' said Malory. 'It is said that when you met... Well, one more story then. Now I will tell you the story of The Dolorous Stroke.'

This is the story.

Early in the reign of Arthur he fought a great battle against King Lot of Orkney in which he was victorious and Lot and twelve Kings who fought for Lot were slain. This was in the days before the coming of Gawain, Lancelot and Galahad, the doughtiest knights who fought for Arthur in that battle were Balin, who was also known as The Knight with Two Swords, and his brother Balan. Men thought that they must have been sent from heaven as angels, or devils from Hell. But when the time came to inter the twelve Kings and Arthur asked after Balin, Merlin prophesied that it would be Balin who would deliver the Dolorous Stroke and a terrible retribution would follow. I do not think that wizard ever found anything good to foretell.

A little later, Arthur fell ill and spent some days on his

sickbed. While he lay there he was visited by an unknown knight who wept at his bedside, but when Arthur asked what the matter was, the knight replied that it was beyond the King's power to amend, and so saying, he departed towards the Castle of Meliot. Then when Balin appeared before Arthur, the King ordered him to find the grieving knight and use force if necessary to bring him back before him.

So Balin galloped off and in a little while caught up with the weeping knight who was riding in the company of a damsel. Balin demanded that the knight should return with him to the King. The knight was reluctant to do so, for he knew that he was in great peril, but Balin told him that if he did not return willingly then they would have to fight. The knight was still reluctant and sought Balin's guarantee that he would protect him. Whereupon Balin swore that he would protect him at the cost of his own life if necessary. So Balin, the knight and the damsel rode back, but when they were close to Arthur's pavilion an invisible knight attacked the man whom Balin had sworn to defend and struck him a deadly blow.

'Alas,' said the knight, 'though I was under your sworn protection, Sir Garlon has slain me. So now you must follow the damsel where she will lead you and avenge my death.'

'I shall do so,' replied Balin.

And he followed the damsel into the forest where they met a knight who had been hunting and the knight asked them what they did and when Balin told him, the knight said that he would join them. Then once the knight had fetched his armour from a hostelry and armed himself, they rode on, until they came to a churchyard by a hermitage and it was there that the invisible Sir Garlon struck at the knight who was Balin's companion and struck him a lethal blow.

'Alas!' cried the knight, 'I am slain by the traitor knight who rides invisible.'

After they had buried the knight, Balin and the damsel rode away and they travelled for four days without encountering any adventures or hearing anything of the invisible knight. But on the evening of the fourth day they found lodgings with a wealthy man who told them that in less than three weeks' time King Pellam of Listeneise would hold a tournament and that Sir Garlon was certain to make his appearance there.

It took Balin and the damsel a little over two weeks to reach the castle of Listeneise. Balin was well received and provided with a comfortable room. The servants of the castle took off his armour and provided him with rich robes, though when they made to take away his sword, he refused for he said that it was not the custom of his country to be parted from one's sword.

After this he went down to dinner where he found himself honourably seated. Then he asked after Sir Garlon.

His neighbour replied, 'He is over there, the man with the black face. He is a great knight who goes about invisibly and kills other knights.'

At this, Sir Garlon, perceiving that he was being talked about walked over and struck Balin in the face with the back of his hand, saying, 'Why were you looking at me in that fashion? For shame! Eat your meat and behave as our guest should.'

Whereupon Balin rose from his place and drawing his sword, brought it down on Garlon's head and sliced almost right through. Then King Pellam arose and wrathfully shouted, 'You knight, because you have slain my brother, you shall not leave this castle alive.'

A servant handed Pellam an axe, and rushing upon Balin, he aimed to strike at Balin's head. Balin raised his sword to defend his head, but the sword shattered under the axe blow. Since he was now without a weapon, he turned and fled through room after room looking for something with which he might defend himself. At last he came to a richly decorated chamber at the centre of which was a table of silver and gold on which there was a strange-looking spear. Balin seized the spear and with it he struck at the pursuing Pellam's groin. As Pellam fell to ground unconscious, the walls of the castle shook and began to fall apart. Balin lay unconscious in the rubble for three days before recovering and finding his way out of the ruins. The damsel was dead and so were most of King Pellam's court, though King Pellam lived on for many long years despite his horrid wound. He had been a vigorous man who had loved fishing and hunting, but that was all finished with now and he lay on his sickbed and waited for succour.

Merlin found Balin unconscious amongst the rubble and provided him with a horse, for his own horse was dead in the ruins. The damsel was also dead. Merlin told Balin that the spear that he had used against Pellam was the same spear which the centurion Longius used to pierce the breast of our Lord Jesus Christ. Pellam, who had been Balin's host, was the noblest of all living Kings and because of his wound, which would not heal, a curse had fallen on the land, for when a King is sick, his Kingdom must follow him in his sickness.

Balin said to Merlin, 'In this world we shall never meet again' and he rode away. Wherever he rode he found people dying or slain. Farms were abandoned for lack of farmhands, and cattle and sheep strayed or starved. At first fruit rotted on the ground and then their trees withered and could bear no more fruit. Fertile land became barren and dead fishes choked the rivers. Hungry dogs attacked famished people. Men fought with men to gain only a little food and that fighting continues to this day. The war between York and Lancaster is only the most recent of battles that have followed on from the maiming of Pellam and the ruin of his castle and we today live in the wasteland that Balin's stroke brought about. This is the winter of history.

People cried out against Balin for having brought ruin on the land with his Dolorous Stroke and some foretold that Balin would fall victim to divine vengeance and indeed only a few months passed before he was slain by his own brother. But that is another story.'

Now Malory looks to Anthony.

'I do not like this story,' says Anthony. 'I would rather have heard about the bratchet. The story you have just told makes no sense to me, for I think that the invisible knight, Garlon was a murderer and one moreover who used sorcery to kill his victims and therefore it was Balin's duty to slay him and Pellam was a villain to harbour Garlon, even if he was his own brother, and Pellam was wrong to seek to revenge himself on Balin, and Balin was right to defend himself in any way he could. Pellam was surely not "the noblest of all living Kings". Why then should God punish Balin, and even worse, bring devastation to the land and its innocent people?'

Malory's smile is bitter.

'I thought that you would not understand it. This story is a test for the listener and that is why I told it to you. Pellam was an anointed King. A man who strikes at a King strikes at God himself and God's ways are inscrutable. To question what has been divinely ordained is a horrid blasphemy. No matter what wrongs a King may commit, he is always right and for a subject to raise his hand against his rightful ruler must always be wrong. The health and fortunes of a monarch's subjects depend on his health and fortune.'

Of course Malory is no longer speaking of Pellam, but of Henry of Lancaster.

Then Malory closes his eyes and recites, as if reading from a book, ' "Alas," said Sir Lancelot, "that ever I should live to hear that most noble King that made me knight thus to be overset with his subjects in his own realm".'

But Anthony says, 'You are a hypocrite, for you have admitted that you are a criminal many times over and yet I hear you compare yourself to Sir Lancelot! You are certainly a hypocrite, for on the way here, I heard you denounce stories as spiteful and seductive devils and yet just now you have told me another story.'

Again Malory closes his eyes and this time he recites, ' "*Odi et amo: quare id faciam, fortasse requiris, Nescio, sed fieri sentio et excrucior.*" I hate and I love. You may ask why I do so. I do not know, but I feel it and am in torment.' And, opening his eyes, Malory continues, 'No man is simple and made from one element alone. Catullus tells us that. I would do good. There is good in me. I first discovered this when I was locked up in Ludgate Prison for poaching and at the mercy of the sheriffs of London. I was in despair, for I was already familiar with the horrors of confinement and yet not hardened to them.'

'Now I will tell you how God sent me deliverance. I prayed, and as I prayed, God sent me an answer to my prayer and He showed me not only how I could walk out of this dark cell, though all the doors and gates of the prison were locked, but also how I could leave my sinful self behind. Straightaway I closed my eyes and conjured up in my imagination a golden light and lit up by that golden light, a better land in which I travelled in the company of just Kings, brave knights, wise hermits, and I met women who were as virtuous as they were beautiful. It was strange, for these good people were everything that I am not and yet I had them all within me. It as if they were the seeds of the offspring I had yet to father.

These Kings, knights and damsels were all familiar to me from stories I had heard when I was young, but many of the stories were broken and misshapen and it came to me that I should bring them peacefully together and that I should become a healer of stories and I should write down what I had brought about and I have prayed to Jesus that He might help me with his great might by day and by night, for I have dedicated myself to the composition of a noble and joyous book entitled *Le Morte d'Arthur* which will treat of the birth, life and acts of King Arthur, of his noble knights of the Round

Table, their marvellous quests and adventures, the finding of the Holy Grail, and, in the end, the dolorous death and departing out of this world of them all. It may be that in what is to come I may find myself in prison once more and yet I can never again be confined within a gaol's walls, since I walk out at will and find myself in Camelot, Sarras, Lyonesse or Broceliande.'

Now Anthony asks once more for the story of the bratchet, the hind and the screeching lady, but Malory replies that on this day he has not the heart for it.

Whereupon Anthony rises from the table and says, 'In that case, I bid you good day. I doubt if we shall meet again.'

But Malory replies, 'I have heard that next year you are to joust at Smithfield against the Great Bastard of Burgundy. In the Kingdom of Logres there used to be a great tourney held somewhere or other every two or three weeks, but it is now a long time since we have seen jousting in England. I promise that I shall be at Smithfield to see how you acquit yourself, for I need to remind myself how such encounters are conducted so that I may write a good account of them. You may find yourself turned into one of my paladins.'

Anthony shrugs and walks out. As they make their way back to the Woodville townhouse, Amyas wants to know what Malory's business was.

But all Anthony says is, 'He is a madman and a hypocrite, or, if he is not, then I am.'

And Anthony thinks that if Malory is to be confined once more, it should not be as a rapist, a poacher or a traitor, but as a lunatic. But then he asks himself is he really Malory's brother murderer. Then he thinks about Sir Garlon in the story of the Dolorous Stroke, the invisible knight who went about murdering knights and abducting women. It is only in stories that villains rub their hands and cackle with glee. It is only in stories that villains think of themselves as villains.

CHAPTER TEN

Joust

On the Sunday before his first encounter with the Bastard, Anthony accompanies his family to matins at their customary church of St Mary at Axe.

Though he hopes to find comfort and encouragement before the ordeal that is to come, in this he is disappointed. The officiating priest, the Reverend William Crosier, anticipating that the Woodvilles would attend the Sunday service as usual, has prepared a special sermon just for Anthony.

'My text today comes from Psalm 11: "Jehovah trieth the righteous one; but the wicked, and him that loveth violence his soul hateth." And my subject today is an old sin, but recently revived. Wealthy young lords and their friends in our city have taken up with tourneying, since it is once again the fashion. But tournaments are lawless extravagances which waste the land and their expense is all for vainglory. Men enter the lists only so that they may boast about what they did there and the fine armour that they wore then—that they had a helmet of gold, and pauldrons and other external insignia of the same style and even greater price; and that he has carried into the lists a huge lance, so heavy that no one else could carry it and that he arrived at the tournament with so many horses and attendants. All this is vainglory.'

'And what is all the glory and praise worth when it comes from the mouths of the impious, of wretches and of the timid? What is fine armour worth if it makes an enemy only more eager to steal it? What is the merit in unhorsing a man, an old friend perhaps, in time of peace? How should we praise a man who is brave enough in sports in the time of peace, but when a just war comes proves to be a coward?'

Anthony tries not to listen to the unwelcome message, and in a strategy to do so, he plays the alphabet game, first awarding himself a point when he hears Crosier pronounce a word that begins with a, and then another point when he hears a word beginning with b, and so on. But he cannot shut off the priest's concluding noisy peroration:

'Those who joust here on earth will joust also in Hell and there they are forced to wear armour which is nailed to them and cannot be taken off. They are forced also to take evil smelling sulphurous baths and then afterwards, instead of the embraces of wanton young women, they are obliged to endure the amorous attentions of lascivious toads. So shall the jousting knight's prowess be rewarded in Hell!'

The Woodvilles storm out of the church and Rivers promises to see to William Crosier's future. But then he says that he must walk privately with Anthony for they have something to discuss.

'That priest was a fool, even if I do admire his courage,' Rivers begins. 'He will find no preferment now. Yet I too have to warn you not to look forward to future glory in your combats with the Bastard on Thursday and Friday.'

Anthony shrugs. What is his father talking about?

His father continues, 'What will take place on those days will look like a fight, but its real burden is the opposite, for it will be the sealing of a pact of peace and the making of an alliance. We need Burgundy's assistance to help us regain our lost lands in France. The joust will be a ceremony, or a kind of mystery play. Yesterday I was with the King and Lord Hastings and we talked at length about the alliance and its benefits and all the things that must go with it... Anthony, I am sorry, but the King and Hastings are determined that you must not be the victor in the coming combats, for England needs to send the Bastard rejoicing back to his father. So you will best serve your King by failing in the lists. It is the King's command and there can be no escape from this.'

Anthony is silent for a long time. Finally he says, 'I thought when I was chosen to fight for England that I was being honoured... Yet it seems that I have been offered a cupful of poison instead. I have spent nearly two years training for this encounter, but now I learn that I might just as well have stayed in bed. It will not be an easy thing to lose a series of combats and come out of them unmaimed. I may even die in my efforts not to defeat the Bastard.'

'Do you still wear that little manikin on a chain round your neck, the amulet that your mother gave you?'

Anthony nods.

'Well,' says his father, 'I have no belief in amulets, but your mother assures me that I do not need to believe in such magical things for them to work, so you will survive.'

But Anthony protests, 'Even if I do come out of the combats alive, I shall be the object of scorn to nobles and commoners alike.'

His father smiles, though his smile is without joy, 'But the King will look on you with favour. I doubt the scorn, if there is any, will last more than a few days. Edward proposes to make you Governor of the Isle of Wight and that office carries a very large income. Also you will be made a Knight of the Garter. And I am to replace the Earl of Worcester as Constable of England. We shall be powers in the land.'

Later that day when Anthony goes to the tiltyard, he learns from Sergeant Raker that the order of combat will be lances, swords, and finally axes. Raker continues, 'The good thing is that the weapons shall be unbated. Tiptoft, as President of the Court of Chivalry, has decreed this, for he says that the people must see some blood spilt before they go back contented to their homes, though it is my belief that it is Tiptoft who needs to see blood. That man is a demon!'

Yet it is clear to Anthony that Raker too wishes to see blood. Nevertheless, despite the common ground between them, Raker hates Tiptoft, since he is not a proper English-man, having been corrupted by his long stay in Italy. Nat-urally Raker hates the French even more and he is looking forward to Anthony wounding, or better yet, killing Antoine, the Great Bastard of Burgundy, for then at last the corpse of a Frenchman will serve as evidence that Raker's careful training of Anthony has been worthwhile. Raker's happiest memory is of the day when as a young man garrisoned in Calais he had news of the burning of the witch, Joan of Arc at the stake and the despatch of her soul to Hell. Most Frenchmen walk with a limp. The French nobles are particularly despicable since they fail to defend their peasants from English attacks. Anthony keeps telling Raker that the Bastard is a Burgundian, not a Frenchman, but Raker will not listen. It has already been agreed that he will close the tiltyard for the two days of the tourney and will accompany Anthony as his armourer and counsellor.

The day comes and Anthony rides out in splendour towards Smithfield. Black Saladin is caparisoned in white cloth of gold, with a cross of St. George of crimson velvet bordered with a fringe of gold six inches deep. Raker follows riding a horse caparisoned in tawny velvet ornamented with many great bells. Then there is Amyas whose horse is covered with russet down to the hooves, powdered with Anthony's initials couched in goldsmiths' work and Hugh's horse is cov-ered with purple damask, rich with goldsmith's work and bor-dered with blue cloth of gold. Five more men-at-arms follow on horses that are similarly richly trapped. They ride through the marvelling crowds that line the orchards and gardens of Smithfield and into its lists.

Now it is Anthony's turn to be amazed, for he had not realised how much work had gone on in Smithfield in the past weeks. The royal stand is in three storeys. The King and Queen sit in the top storey flanked by the King's sword-bearer, the constable, the marshal and the marshal's guard, together with senior members of the nobility. The second storey is reserved for knights and the last is filled with royal archers. The flight of steps is gated. On the other side of the lists there is a smaller stand for the mayor, aldermen and other officials. Lesser folk are sheltered in long galleries and behind the galleries there are people in the trees. It is a bright June day, everyone is in their finest clothes, the pennants are fluttering in the breeze, brightly coloured blazons are everywhere and Anthony feels sick to his stomach at the thought of what is expected of him.

He dismounts in front of the royal stand and advances to its gate on which he knocks. Whereupon Tiptoft, in his capacity as constable shouts down, 'What is your name and purpose?'

And Anthony replies, 'My name is Scales and I am come to accomplish a deed of arms with the Bastard of Burgundy, and demand entry into the lists to do my duty.'

Having received that permission, Anthony salutes the King before walking over to his pavilion of blue satin where he is to be armed. Once inside the pavilion, Anthony casts off his blazoned surcoat and dons a thick and strongly stitched doublet whose padding will not only absorb some of the shock of impact but also stop the plate armour from chafing and pinching. Then he dons leather shoes on to which the steel sabatons will be attached with stitching. A squire sweats over this under the close supervision of Raker. And so the arming of Anthony proceeds upwards from the sabatons to the greaves, which protect the calves, and from the greaves to the cuisses which cover the thighs. At every stage the neat overlapping of the steel pieces has to be checked and confirmed. The breastplate is next followed by the vambraces and pauldrons which cover the arms. Raker has Anthony repeatedly flex his arms and legs. Then the backplate is buckled on to the breastplate and the helmet buckled on to the backplate and Anthony has to be helped to draw on the gauntlets over his calfskin gloves. It is a wearisome business and the crowd outside must be impatient.

Now Anthony steps out, and using a mounting block, settles onto the saddle of Black Saladin and Amyas hands him his lance. Anthony waits for Antoine the Bastard of Burgundy, Comte de la Roche en Ardenne and Knight of the Golden Fleece to be similarly mounted. Then the heralds check that both men are ready, and having done so, report back to the senior herald, Bluemantle, who shouts in a stentorian voice 'Laissez aller!' and a white baton is sent spinning in the air as a sign of battle's commencement. Anthony and the Bastard thunder towards one another, but at almost the last moment, Anthony uses his knee to make Black Saladin veer away and so his lance misses the Bastard entirely and the Bastard also misses his target. A great groan of disappointment comes from those watching. At this point both men drop their lances and get their horses to turn again and now they ride against one another with drawn swords. What happens next is shocking, for the impact of Black Saladin's charge against the Bastard's horse is so fierce that it and its master are thrown to the ground. The Bastard under the horse is winded, but by a miracle not seriously injured. The matter is otherwise with the horse which will have to be put down.

When the Bastard has got his breath back, he staggers over to the royal stand and makes his complaint to Tiptoft, who as the President of the Court of Chivalry will have to adjudicate. The Bastard is accusing Anthony of having a spike concealed under his horse's trapping. At this point Anthony rides up and raises Black Saladin's caparison to show that there is no such spike. Tiptoft makes vaguely apologetic noises, but the Bastard is not easily soothed.

'Today he has fought against a horse. Tomorrow he will fight against a man,' he says, before marching back to his pavilion.

The Bastard is not the only angry man. In Anthony's

pavilion Raker spits and shouts, 'How was it possible for you to miss? No, I saw how you directed your horse away from the target. You filthy, useless coward! I am ashamed to have ever seen you in my tiltyard. After all my training, you jousted like a woman—or a Frenchman! If the Bastard does not kill you tomorrow, then I think I will.'

'And I think that you should kill me,' says Anthony sadly. 'That would be a mercy.'

Now Raker looks so shocked that Anthony decides that he will have to be told the truth and so he tells him about the King's secret command.

'Ah me, if I had known sooner, I might have taught you how to lose well and with honour.' Raker sighs heavily. 'Two years training gone for nothing.'

'I thought that I was a knight, but I find that I am a pawn. It smells, but it is all high politics and must remain a secret between us.'

At this point the flap of the tent is flung violently open and the Bastard enters followed by an equerry. The Bastard's French is fast and furious, whereas Anthony's understanding of spoken French, despite the best efforts of his mother, is poor and he has great difficulty in following whatever it is that the Bastard is shouting. But Raker's French is surprisingly excellent. Anthony had not expected a commoner to speak a foreign language well, but of course Raker had spent years in France in the service of John of Bedford. Raker knows the language and the people well. The language is very good for swearing and the people are like animals, though less dependable than animals, and Raker hates animals anyway. In between hurling abuse at the Bastard and his equerry, Raker interprets. It seems that the Bastard has come to demand compensation for his slaughtered horse. He is demanding a huge sum. He is a man who is used to deference and having his way and he is startled when Raker shows him no deference at all. Instead Raker abuses him and in doing so uses a huge amount of insulting French slang. Without consulting Anthony, he refuses compensation for the horse or even an apology. Then he goes one step further and yells at the Bastard that the only reason that he is still alive today is that the King has told Lord Scales to treat the little frog gently and let him win in the lists if he can. The Bastard looks thunderous. Finally Raker turns and reports to Anthony, 'He says that the King must settle this.'

Anthony nods and together they march out. They find the King preparing to leave the royal stand and he is displeased to find his departure delayed by two angry men. The top storey of the stand is cleared of everybody except Edward, Anthony, the Bastard and Tiptoft. Raker and the equerry are refused admission to the royal stand and now it is Tiptoft who does the interpreting. It seems that the Bastard is demanding that Anthony should fight tomorrow without constraint or care for any injury he might cause. Tiptoft, who evidently had not known about the instructions that Anthony had been given, looks shocked. Then the Bastard vows before the King and Tiptoft that, if he does not find that Anthony fights fiercely, then he will kill him and after that kill his kinsfolk also, before going back to Burgundy to report to his father the grievous insult that had been offered to him.

Just for a moment Edward too looks angry. Then he remembers himself and smiling broadly tells Tiptoft to tell the Bastard that there has been a lamentable misunderstanding and that Lord Scales has received no such command from him. Surely it is that servant of Anthony's who is responsible for this absurd mistake? Edward promises that on the morrow when he meets Anthony he will encounter a doughty warrior.

The Bastard grunts and turns on his heel. As soon as the Bastard's back is turned, Edward scowls at Anthony, but embarrassed doubtless by Tiptoft's presence, he says nothing and dismisses Anthony with a wave of his hand.

When Anthony returns to the Woodville townhouse that

evening, he finds that a letter delivered from Ludgate Gaol is waiting for him. It is from Sir Thomas Malory:

'Right worshipful lord, I commend myself to you as humbly as I can and wish for your welfare and prowess in arms. Today you looked for me on the stand at Smithfield with the other knights and did not find me there.'

The truth is that Anthony, with so much else on his mind, had not thought to look for Malory.

But the letter, which is very long, continues:

'God knows, it was my heartiest desire to see such a noble combat and I am sorry to find my body was forcibly borne elsewhere, though my spirit was with you as I wish. Now I find myself constrained and once more I find that I must take up my pen in order to pass in spirit through the walls of my prison. Then I thought to myself that my great labour which I have entitled *Le Morte d'Arthur* and which is a mighty enterprise, which I can scarce dare hope to complete before it pleases God almighty to take me to Him, this great labour of mine deserves the patronage of a noble lord of chivalrous renown. Your benevolence and good lordship would mightily assist and give lustre to my enterprise which shall be a complete chronicling of the deeds of King Arthur and his knights and at the same time, I venture that the merit of my narrative and the high matters that it deals with shall give added glory to the name Scales, if of your benevolence, you allow this.'

What follows is a lengthy synopsis of what will become *Le Morte d'Arthur* and Anthony, who is both weary and fearful of what the morrow will bring, only skims it. The work that Malory has planned resembles a vast cathedral under construction, with some parts completed, but others without their roofing and even some which merely resemble the scratchings of the ground plan on the earth. It is all very confusing. Hundreds of knights make their appearance and many of them are killed and others simply forgotten about in the course of the proliferating stories. The jousts and combats are beyond enumeration. Malory presents the reign of Arthur as a golden age and yet there is fighting all the time and Camelot resembles nothing so much as a bear-pit. Then, beyond the walls of Camelot, it is all feuds, treason, cattle-rustling, extortion and abduction. It seems to Anthony as if several hundred versions of Sir Thomas Malory fight and riot throughout the ancient Kingdom of Logres.

Anthony pauses only to read about the fight that there was between Sir Tristram and Sir Lancelot:

'Then this cry was so loud that Sir Lancelot heard it. And then he took a great spear in his hand and came towards the cry. Then Sir Lancelot cried: "The Knight with the Black Shield, make you ready to joust with me." When Sir Tristram heard him say so, he took his spear in his hand, and they both lowered their heads, and came together as thunder: Sir Tristram's spear broke in pieces, and Sir Lancelot by malfortune struck Sir Tristram a wound nigh to death; but yet Sir Tristram stayed on his saddle and so the spear broke. Thereupon Sir Tristram who was wounded got out his sword, and he rushed to Sir Lancelot and gave him three great strokes upon the helm such that sparks sprang out, and Sir Lancelot lowered his head down towards his saddle-bow. And thereupon Sir Tristram departed from the field, for he felt him so wounded that he thought he should have died; and Sir Dinadan espied him and followed him into the forest. Then Sir Lancelot remained and did many marvellous deeds.'

Anthony reflects: if only it was so easy to be a hero and do 'marvellous deeds' in truth...

The letter concludes as follows:

'And I pray that all who read my stories pray for him who wrote them, that God send him good deliverance, soon and hastily. A knight prisoner, Sir Thomas Malory.'

The twilight is deepening and Anthony pushes the manuscript away. He has to admire Malory's optimism and his impudence. This is the man who only a few years ago would have had Anthony indicted and executed for treason and now this same man is seeking his good lordship. Later, he shows the letter to his father who refuses to read it and says that Malory's treason has now been made apparent. Malory had been visiting Henry in the Tower and bringing him missals, breviaries and cakes, but then was found also to be delivering messages from Lancastrian rebels in the North and that is why he is again in prison and where he should stay. Once more Rivers advises his son to have nothing to do with this dangerous man. Then his father says he will speak to the King about what happened at the Smithfield lists that day and they must hope for the best. After this, Anthony dismisses the importunate Malory from his thoughts.

The following morning, while Anthony is being armed, his father enters the pavilion.

'The King is not pleased with you, but that will pass. Now his command is that you are to fight as hard as you like today. He did not care for being shouted at by the Burgundian Bastard. Besides, if the Queen hears of how you were ordered to play the loser, Edward will never hear the end of it and Tiptoft has already remonstrated with him.'

His father claps him on the shoulder and Raker shouts after him, 'Be sure that you kill the Frenchman!' As Anthony walks out of the pavilion, he commends himself to God.

Today the fighting is on foot and with poleaxes. Anthony and the Bastard advance slowly towards each other like silvery lobsters moving under water. Anthony is shouting 'St George! St George! St George!' and the Bastard is shouting something, God knows what. They both heft and shift their poleaxes from hand to hand as they walk on. The poleaxe has a curved blade with a spike on the other side of the haft and there is another spike at the head of the haft. Since steel stripes run along the length of the haft to protect its wood, the poleaxe is heavy and difficult to manage.

As soon as Anthony is in range, he feints at the Bastard's

head, but then brings the axe down in an attempt to smash and perhaps even sever the Bastard's leg at the knee, but he is only just within range and his strike has insufficient force behind it and is easily parried. Then Anthony, determined not to let the Bastard gain the initiative, thrusts and thrusts again towards the Bastard's helmet and keeps thrusting, so that the Bastard must repeatedly parry and cannot prepare his own strike. After a while, Anthony's feints become slower, as the weight of the axe begins to tell on his arms and the Bastard does take the initiative and gets the spike of the axe behind Anthony's neck, seeking to pull him forward and wrench him onto the ground. But Anthony grabs the haft of the Bastard's axe, and ducking his own head, shoves the axe sideways. Then both men having been thwarted of an easy victory fall into a rhythm of hacking that slowly does expensive damage to their fine armour. The Bastard, who has lost his third shoulder plate, grunts and shouts a lot. Anthony finds it hard to see because of the stinging salt sweat in his eyes. Then they break apart and by unspoken agreement they draw breath for a while. When they close again the Bastard seeks to hook Anthony's knee, but Anthony skips over the haft. Perhaps the Bastard anticipated that Anthony would have had to use his axe to parry this threat, but, having stepped over his enemy's axe, Anthony's own axe is raised over his shoulder and he brings it down with such tremendous force that not only is the Bastard's visor sheared half off, but the Bastard is brought down to his knees.

Now the Bastard's situation is perilous indeed and the King, seeing this shouts 'Whoo!' and casts his baton into the lists as a signal that the combat must end. But Anthony is in a rage and he does not want to stop until he has killed the Bastard, and the Bastard, who has not seen the signal, is simultaneously getting his hands further up the haft of his axe, so that he may thrust its spike into Anthony's groin. Bluemantle has come running forward and thrust his herald's staff between the combatants. Anthony, who is aiming for the Bastard's defenceless face, heedlessly brings his axe down anyway and smashes the herald's staff into pieces. But the staff has served its purpose and saved the Bastard's face and perhaps also his life and Anthony now sees that he must stop.

Bluemantle congratulates the two on a fine fight and tells them that the day's engagement is now concluded. The Bastard, who has staggered to his feet is in a new rage and demands that they should be allowed to continue to fight it out. Bluemantle hesitates and waits until Tiptoft comes hurrying down from the royal stand. The two of them confer and then Bluemantle announces that the combat may continue, but only if the Bastard gets on his knees once more, for that is the rule. At which point, the Bastard shrugs and throws away his axe before stumbling towards Anthony and embracing and kissing him. Once again the French is too fast for Anthony, but he gets the gist of it. That was the best fight the Bastard had had in years and he loves Anthony for it and they should be blood brothers and when they next joust they should be on the same side.

The King is now on his feet with his arms raised in exultation and the crowd is cheering. The Queen descends from the stand to embrace her brother.

A select band of courtiers join the King and Queen and the two champions in a pavilion that has been erected behind the royal stand and hippocras is served. The Bastard swiftly drains two cups before loudly announcing something. Jacquetta looks dismayed and translates the Bastard's words for Anthony.

'He swears that you were aided in the combat by some magical force. It was as if there was an invisible man standing beside you and fighting on your side.'

But then the Bastard, seeing the expressions on Jacquetta's and Anthony's faces, launches into a torrent of explanation. Anthony is to understand that no insult is intended.

Quite the contrary, it is the mark of a hero to possess some magical power and the Bastard esteems him for it, since there must be a magical quality to all heroes. The Bastard himself claims to understand the language of birds. He says that he will recount to them a tale of high magic and heroism that is told of the ancient kingdom of Burgundy, but at this point Edward restrains him and asks him to tell them all this story over dinner.

Now Edward would rather talk of hunting, feasting and music, but at this point Clarence noisily breaks in. George Duke of Clarence, as second son of Richard of York, is heir apparent to Edward, at least until Elizabeth shall bear Edward a son. Clarence is handsome though a little chubby. He is young, arrogant and noisy. Yet at the same time he is nervous, for Warwick is not at court and neither are any others of the Neville clan. Clarence hopes to marry Warwick's daughter, Isabel. This marriage would seal a pact between him and Warwick. Moreover the northern estates that the marriage would bring would make Clarence a power in the land and a great lord who would be no longer solely dependent on his brother's favour. But Warwick is once again away in France where he is futilely attempting to negotiate a treaty with Louis—a treaty that Edward will never agree to. Clarence is hostile to the Burgundian Bastard, since he follows Warwick (whom he hero worships) in preferring a French alliance.

'Magic is more often the companion of villainy than it is the helpmeet of heroism,' says Clarence. 'We need no tales of magic from ancient Burgundy when all London is rife with conjurations, false libels and rumours of sorcery and conspiracy and poison plots. We hear reports of visitations of the dead, manikins that walk and fish that talk. Dark corners are filled with lurking creatures—with conspirators and their attendant demons.'

Everyone looks at Clarence. He is babbling. Edward wonders if his brother is going mad.

But Jacquetta, who senses that Clarence's words are directed at her and her family, says that most reports of magic are only stories that have been put about to entertain. Moreover she points out that magic may serve the good and she cites the case of wise Merlin who always gave good counsel to King Arthur. At this, Edward says that he wishes that he had a Merlin to advise him.

'But you keep an alchemist in your service,' says Clarence. 'What is his name?'

'George Ripley,' replies Edward. 'But he is not a magician.'

'It is all the same thing,' says Clarence. 'What is making gold from lead, if not an act of magic? I have heard that your alchemist is supposed to do marvellous things.'

Then Elizabeth says, 'I should like to see a marvel. Let him come before us at dinner and perform a conjuration so that we can be amazed.'

Edward shakes his head and tells her that her beauty is marvel enough for them all. And indeed when Anthony looks at his sister, it seems, as ever, that there is something supernatural about her beauty. Her face shimmers with a loveliness that is not entirely human, but might be a gift of Elfland.

Elizabeth is not to be denied. She will see a marvel at dinner. Now Edward, fearing her sulks, summons a courier and orders him to ride ahead and find Ripley and bring him to the royal presence at Westminster. Clarence is as keen as Elizabeth to see the alchemist do tricks and says that if they are not good ones, he should be dismissed, for what use is the man otherwise? Now Edward wants to talk about hunting. A little later, as they ride back to Westminster, he and the Bastard will talk politics.

The accursed feast is held in the Painted Chamber of the Privy Palace at Westminster and Anthony finds himself seated opposite frescoes of violent scenes from the Old Testament, the fight of Judas Maccabeus against Nicanor and the Destruction of Sennacherib. The tables are set in a horseshoe shape on three sides of the chamber. The diners look upon an incongruous circular oven in the centre of the chamber. It has been crudely constructed from bricks and metal trays. A trench filled with a dark liquid running round the top of the oven is just visible and within circumference of the trench there is a circle of little pots. Although it is a bright summer evening outside, heavy drapes shut out that light and torches held by pages standing behind the diners provide what illumination there is. Gyroscopic brass censers roll across the stone floor filling the chamber with heavy perfume.

Everyone wants to know what the oven is doing here. Edward explains that Ripley has agreed to show them a great marvel and has requested this oven, as well as a goose and the assistance of a serving man.

'A roast goose will not be such a marvel,' says Elizabeth disappointedly.

'Perhaps the alchemist will turn the goose into solid gold,' says Clarence.

Before any food is served, Scoggin makes an appearance and does his best to caper, though he is not as agile as he once was, for the beating that he received by unknown hands some years back has slowed him down.

'Why do we see cocks rather than hens serving as weathervanes on steeples?'

Since no one else has the answer, Scoggin provides it himself, 'Because, if it were a hen, she would lay eggs and they would fall upon men's heads! Oh ho ho ho ho!' But Scoggin laughs alone.

'At what time of the year does a goose bear most feathers?'

More silence.

'When she has a gander on her back!'

Only Hastings manages a smile. Scoggin attempts a few more merry trifles. Every time he laughs the diners find themselves gazing at the inside of his broken-toothed mouth. Edward mutters about how Scoggin was good in his day, but now his wit has lost its edge. A jester should use his comic barbs to make serious criticisms of the great ones in the land.

'We all need to be reminded that we are fallible and mortal. A good fool holds a mirror to our failings.'

But Rivers says that Scoggin's mirror is clouded and cracked and urges the King to dismiss him from his employment.

After only a little while Scoggin is sent out from the room. He shuffles off swatting his head with his pig's bladder. Now servants bring ewers and bowls of water, so that the diners may wash their hands. The Royal Chaplain says grace and then withdraws. Trenchers of baked swan in a spiced wine sauce are brought in and the diners serve themselves from the trenchers. Edward gives himself a royal helping and Anthony notices that he is putting on weight. The way is now clear for the Bastard to tell a tale of ancient Burgundy.

'The Kingdom of Burgundy is very old—much older than the English Kingdom. Our histories tell us that three brothers, Gunther, Gernot and Giseler ruled the Kingdom from their capital at Worms. One day a young prince, Siegfried arrives at their court and after demonstrating his prowess at feats of arms, seeks the hand of their sister Kriemhild. Gunther, for his part wishes to marry Brunhild, the Queen of Iceland. But Brunhild, an Amazon of the north, is very strong and will only consent to marry the man who can defeat her in an athletic contest. Though Gunther is too feeble and cowardly to fight with her, he proposes that Siegfried should do so for him, and then and only then he may wed Kriemhild. Siegfried has all the magical trappings of a hero, for he has acquired the sword Balmung and the cloak of darkness known as the *Tarnkappe*. These things were formerly the treasures of the Nibelung. Also he knows the language of birds. Not only that, but it is almost impossible to kill or even wound him, for he has bathed in the blood of the dragon he slew.

Siegfried agrees to Gunther's proposal and they sail to

Iceland where Brunhild tells Gunther that she will only marry him if he defeats her in three challenges. A ring is marked out for the games and Brunhild appears in full armour as if ready for war. Gunther arrives in the company of his faithful hench-man Hagen, and Siegfried (who has donned the *Tarnkappe* and is consequently invisible) follows close behind them. When Hagen sees Brunhild's great shield of gold, braced by hardest steel and which is so heavy that her retainers struggle under its weight, he says to Gunther, 'We are done for. The woman whose love you desire is a rib of the Devil himself!' Gunther's own shield is much lighter. But Siegfried whispers to Gunther that he must not be afraid.

So the contest begins and Brunhild hurls her great spear which is made from three ingots of steel at Gunther's shield which is now invisibly held by Siegfried. Such is the force of Brunhild's throw that the spear passes through the shield and should have killed Siegfried were he not protected by having bathed in dragon's blood. He picks up her spear, and not wish-ing to kill the woman whom Gunther proposes to marry, he reverses it, so the point is now at the back of it and he sends the shaft hurtling towards Brunhild. She cannot stand against the force of Siegfried's throw and when she rises from the ground, she commends Gunther for his strength. Next they competed in seeing how far they each could throw a boulder. Brunhild hurls the great rock some twenty-four yards and leaps up to it, but Siegfried's strength is supernatural and his throw not only exceeds that distance, but when he leaps towards the stone he carries Gunther with him. Seeing this Brunhild, though angry, confessed herself beaten and she called upon her vassals to do homage to King Gunther.

They all return to Worms where the weddings of Sieg-fried to Kriemhild and of Gunther to Brunhild take place, but Gunther is unable to bed Brunhild, as she wrestles with him and ends by tying him up with the cord of her gown and hang-ing him on a nail in the wall. So once again Gunther seeks the assistance of Siegfried and once again Siegfried dons the *Tarnkappe*. Though he will wrestle with Brunhild in order to subdue her, he promises Gunther on his word of honour that he will not deflower her. Invisible in the darkened chamber, he had a fierce fight with the maiden for she was horribly strong. But after he had forced her submission, he stepped aside and allowed Gunther to take possession of her and so at last the King enjoyed his bride. Thereafter all is well for ten years, but when ten years have passed Siegfried and Kriemhild visit Worms and on this visit Kriemhild and Brunhild quarrel over precedence and in the heat of the argument Kriemhild reveals to Brunhild how Gunther made use of Siegfried and his magical powers to subdue her. Then Brunhild goes to Gunther to demand revenge. The cowardly King is reluctant to do so, but his loyal henchman Hagen volunteers to kill Siegfried. He tricks Kriemhild into revealing the one spot on Siegfried's body that was not covered by the blood of the dragon. There is a hunting party and Hagen strikes. He stabs Siegfried as he drinks from a spring and then returns to Worms and continues in his evil way by stealing the treasure of the Nibelung from Kriemhild and throwing it into the Rhine. From then on Burgundy was cursed and iron entered the soul of my people for Kriemhild's revenge was terrible...'

The King gestures that the Bastard should now cease, for they may hear of Kriemhild's revenge another day. Boars' heads and frumenty are brought to the tables.

'Where is the alchemist?' says Clarence. 'I want to see the alchemist.'

No one pays him any attention. Then Jacquetta speaks, 'I knew that story would end badly,' she says.

'It ended with the destruction of the Kingdom of Burgundy,' says the Bastard sadly.

Then Edward asks round the table what they would do with the gift of invisibility. For himself he says that he would use it to find out what his subjects really thought of his rule.

Hastings says that invisible, he would watch women undressing. Pembroke swears that he would use invisibility to do good by stealth, for he would steal into people's houses and leave purses of money beside their pillows. Anthony thinks he would keep it in reserve for use against unexpected assailants.

But Jacquetta says that she would seek to become visible again as soon as possible and she continues, 'One pays to acquire the gift of invisibility and then one pays again and again. For such a treasure one never finishes paying. A man who has acquired the cap of invisibility starts out by having fun. He steals little sweetmeats from a neighbour's table, he tweaks a passer-by's nose, he carries an egg across a room to the bafflement of all who watch it, he lifts up women's skirts and suchlike japes. But after a while he will find that he cannot be satisfied by this kind of childish foolery. He will dream of doing grander things while all the time unseen and he will spend more and more time under the cap of invisibility. Then a great melancholy will fall upon him, for to be invisible is to be unnoticed, unadmired, not thought of, insignificant, not fully part of the laughing world. If you are not admired by others, you will cease to admire yourself, and invisible, you are only in this world as a brooding presence. Thoughts of suicide will follow.'

Anthony thinks once more of Sir Garlon who used the gift of invisibility to murder knights and ladies at random, but who was struck down by Sir Balin during the dinner given by Sir Garlon's brother, King Pellam.

Clarence says to Jacquetta, 'You seem to know a great deal about these matters.' His tone is admiring, though Anthony knows that the sentiment is not. Then there is an awkward silence, since Clarence has spoken the truth. Finally Jacquetta's husband speaks, 'There is not a real thing that is invisibility. How could there be? It is an absence of something. But it is perhaps a poet or a romancer's way of writing about what is much more ordinary. Peasants are commonly invisible to the nobility, for we rarely notice them and these pages that stand behind us are also all but invisible.'

Rivers had wanted to move the conversation on to something more ordinary, but Clarence was set upon talking about poisons that operate at a distance, the evil eye, the conjuring up of storms and Satanic pacts. He swears that his little brother Richard's withered arm was brought about by sorcery. Finally he interrupts himself, 'Ah here he is at last, the alchemist!'

Ripley is flushed and perhaps drunk. Certainly he is drunk. He makes obeisance to the King and then turns to Anthony, 'Well done! Well done, my beloved lord! It is as I foresaw. You have become the hero of a chivalric romance.'

Anthony nods wearily. He is bruised all over and ready to fall asleep at the table. He longs for whatever the alchemist intends to do to be done quickly.

Ripley goes over to the makeshift oven and sinks on his knees to pray. As Ripley rises unsteadily to his feet, Clarence calls over to him, 'Are you going to make gold? Can you make gold? We would like to see it. We want a marvel.'

Ripley does not reply. Instead he claps his hands and a serving man enters carrying a goose which is plucked, but still very much alive. Ripley and the serving man struggle to lard the goose all over.

'It is going to be roast goose after all,' says Elizabeth, bitterly disappointed.

Next Ripley borrows a torch from one of the pages and sets the trench full of oil alight. Then he passes his hands over the goose and intones the words, *'Hoc est corpus'*, before placing the goose inside the ring of fire. The goose is frantic to escape, but cannot. Ripley, who is smiling broadly, explains that the pots are filled with water and added salt and herbs. This will give the goose flavour and prevent its meat from being burnt. Moreover, as they can see, the goose, in an attempt to stay cool, drinks from the water in some of the pots and this will clean out its insides. Also Ripley, reaching over the flames, keeps moistening the squawking goose's head. The fascinated onlookers are silent and scarcely daring to breathe. At last, when the exhausted bird stumbles, Ripley intones the words *'Consumatum est!'* and has the ring of fire doused. Next he carries the bird, which is still alive, over to the royal table and sets it before the King. Ripley urges Edward to pull off a wing, which he will find to be well roasted. Edward, appalled, draws back and refuses. So Ripley takes the lead in tearing a leg off the goose and chewing on it, and shouting over the horrible noise that the goose is making, he informs the other diners that they may all taste of the roasted goose while the bird is yet living. After a little hesitation, Clarence follows and takes the other leg. Tiptoft takes a cut of the goose's breast. This is a meal he can relish. Thereafter, the still flapping bird is passed from diner to diner and a smiling Ripley paces behind the guests urging them each to take their cut. None of the women will touch the poor creature, but Anthony and his father, ignoring Jacquetta's protests, use their knives to help themselves to some breast. Hastings, Pembroke and others of the peerage also participate in eating this rare and extraordinary dish. There is a lot of shouting and most of the diners are, like Ripley, very drunk.

Jacquetta whispers that everyone who has participated in this blasphemous horror is accursed. Once the goose is eaten, the dinner finishes with berries, baked quinces and more hippocras. While they are still drinking a procession of squires enter carrying gifts for the Bastard. These include a complete suit of armour to replace the one that was so badly hacked about this afternoon, two falcon peregrines and a panel painting of Jason stealing the Golden Fleece. The Bastard understands that this is the signal for him to take his leave from the table. But of course more jousting and more discussions of policy are planned for the coming weeks. After the Bastard has left, Edward rises from the table and he asks Clarence,

Hastings, Tiptoft, Pembroke, Richard and Anthony to join him in a more private chamber and Ripley is also ordered to join this inner ring.

Edward says that he wants their counsel regarding certain threats to the Kingdom. Clarence wants to know why Ripley should be privy to these matters, but Edward ignores this. There are disturbing reports from the north. A certain gentleman calling himself Robin of Redesdale, though that will not be his real name, has raised a small force of gentry and peasants and is marching south with the declared aim of freeing the King from his evil counsellors. 'He means you!' says Edward looking round at his lords. There is also talk of a rebel force under a Robin of Holdernesse, though this may be the same man. Then there are reports that unknown persons have been using money to suborn the garrison at Calais. Also there has been a recent attempt to release Henry of Lancaster from the Tower. Sir Thomas Malory was one of the ringleaders in this plot. Edward is also under great pressure from the Earl of Warwick and the rest of the Neville faction to come to terms with Louis and abandon the Burgundian alliance that Edward favours.

A prolonged discussion follows in which Tiptoft and Pembroke take the lead as they set out detailed proposals for mustering men to march north and punish the rebels. There is no crisis. Still Edward remains anxious. He turns to Ripley, 'There are so many rumours and rumours of rumours and reports of plots which may themselves be plots and many of these things may come to nothing, but some surely will. Tell me, you who are learned in all the arcane arts, is there a magic art of foretelling the future?'

'If there is I would not know of it,' Ripley replies, for I am not a magician, but a natural scientist. Still, I have read of a certain procedure, known to the learned doctors of Harran, though it has never been tried in England and it will be slow and difficult.'

'How slow?'

'Once I have all that is necessary for this operation, it is said to take forty days. But after that, you may learn what you like about what is to come.'

'You shall have whatever you need,' says Edward. 'Tell me now about all that is necessary and I will have the procurement instantly set in hand.'

Ripley is silent for a few moments as he struggles to remember what his requirements are. Then, 'I will need a good solid puncheon barrel, then seventy-two gallons of sesame oil...'

'Sesame oil! Seventy-two gallons! I have never seen or heard of sesame oil,' Edward protests.

But Tiptoft, who has tasted sesame oil when he was in Palestine, assures the King that the Italians will provide the oil for a price, even though it is a remarkably large quantity.

'I have to allow for some evaporation,' says Ripley. 'Also I shall need a man and he must have red hair.'

Edward again protests, 'You cannot... you may not sacrifice one of my subjects to demons. Such a ritual would be damnable!'

Ripley is calm and replies, 'I am not going to sacrifice the man. I need him alive. Though there are dangers in the procedure, I hope that the man will not die. Only he will be tightly confined and he will never walk again. Also I will need modest quantities of fruit and nuts to feed him and about a pound of borax.'

Edward, mystified, shrugs, before instructing Tiptoft to seek out a redhead and arrest him and keep him in confinement until Ripley is ready to do whatever it is that he is going to do. Now Rivers breaks in and swiftly offers his and Anthony's assistance in finding a redhead. Tiptoft looks puzzled but grateful. Edward says that their business is now concluded and rises to leave. Clarence seeks to detain him, for he wishes to get Edward's consent for his proposed marriage to Isabel

Neville. But Edward says that this is not the time and he walks out.

A friendly fight with bated swords is arranged for the following week, but on June 17th news comes that Philip the Good, the Bastard's father, has died and the Bastard has to hurry back to Burgundy. With the death of the Duke the future of an Anglo-Burgundian alliance is in doubt.

CHAPTER ELEVEN

Manhunt

The hunt for a redhead begins with an inspection of London's prisons. Tiptoft swiftly discovers a redheaded youth in Newgate Gaol and he is pleased that the mission has been so easy, but Rivers looks at Anthony before declaring that this youth will not do. Tiptoft looks puzzled and they move on to Ludgate Gaol. Here there are two redheads. But again the Woodvilles are adamant that the two men are the wrong kind of redheads. There is no hurry, for many months will pass before Ripley will have received a sufficient quantity of sesame oil. Rivers asks Tiptoft to leave the matter with him and Anthony. Tiptoft, more puzzled than ever, shrugs and agrees, for he has weightier matters to attend to. Anthony is about to leave the gaol, when a turnkey comes running up with a message. It is from Sir Thomas Malory who begs Anthony to come visit him in his cell.

He finds Malory's cell to be large and well appointed, for Lancastrian sympathisers have paid for him to be provided with food, wine, candles and firewood. Malory even has a servant who lodges in an adjoining cell. When Anthony enters, Malory rises with difficulty from the table where he has been writing and they formally embrace. Malory does not look well. Then he points to the papers on the table behind him and says that *Le Morte d'Arthur* is far advanced. He congratulates Anthony on his recent combat at Smithfield and tells him that he must agree to be the patron of this work. That would be most fitting, since there is in England no lord more renowned for chivalry and knightly prowess than Lord Scales. He asks Anthony to sit and listen as he reads from the pages that he had just been writing. Anthony asks to hear how the story of the hind, the bratchet and the sorrowing lady was concluded, but Malory says that he has not finished writing that part yet. Instead he reads from an account of how Sir Tristram, Sir Palomides and Sir Dinadan were taken and put in prison. It ends with the following sentences:

'And, as the French book says, there came forty knights to Sir Darras that were of his own kin, and they would have slain Sir Tristram and his two fellows, but Sir Darras would not suffer that, but kept them in prison, and meat and drink they had. So Sir Tristram endured there great pain, for sickness had undertaken him, and that is the greatest pain a prisoner may have. For all the while a prisoner may have his health of body he may endure under the mercy of God and in the hope of good deliverance; but when sickness touches a prisoner's body, then may a prisoner say that he is bereft of all wealth, and then he has cause to wail and to weep. Right so did Sir Tristram when sickness had undertaken him, for then he took such sorrow that he had almost slain himself.'

'But I am far from thoughts of suicide,' says Malory. 'For as you know, my writing is my deliverance and it takes me far beyond the confines of Ludgate Gaol. Besides I am almost done with Sir Tristram and though he was a great knight, I shall write of one who was greater, who was Sir Lancelot and I shall fashion him and his feats of arms on you and your deeds.'

Anthony is used to featuring in Ripley's fictions, though he does not like them. Perhaps Malory's inventions will be better. Yet the work that Malory is planning is so vast and complex that he does not believe that it will ever be completed, for Malory does not look long for this world. Still he puts a purse of money on the table as he leaves.

After an inspection of the Fleet and Marshalsea prisons,

the hunt moves out to the streets of London and armed with the King's warrant, the Woodvilles and their retainers gallop through the streets questing for and briefly detaining red-headed men. Packmen, barrow boys, sumpter horses and drovers' flocks scatter before the mounted questers. The Woodville horsemen are followed by grooms and running men. After a few days the redheads of London come to realise that they are the intended quarry and some of them try to make a break for it, dodging into passageways that are too narrow for horses, or begging for refuge in the houses of strangers.

The hunt is exhilarating and it takes the Woodville retinue to parts of the city that Anthony has never seen before. They gallop through the squalor of the hugger-mugger tenements of Aldersgate and past the cook-shops of Thames Street. They circle the imposing mass of the Steelyard of the Easterlings and the cyclopean fortress that is Baynards Castle. They ride past the timber-yards on the edge of the Thames and the gallows tree just beyond the St Catharine's Dock which is reserved for pirates. The great steeple of St Paul's rises like a star to guide them when they are lost. They pause to rest and drink at Pountney's Inn. They cross the river to break in upon the brothels and bear gardens of Southwark. The gatekeepers at Aldgate, Moorgate, Aldersgate, Newgate, Ludgate and Black-friars have been told to detain all redheads so that they may be inspected and questioned. The noble huntsmen even ride out to the smog of Wapping where they are greeted by sullen glares and much spitting.

Usually there is mist on the Thames in the mornings and then the watermen seem to float on white smoke. But it is finer to ride out in the spring evenings when the streets are lit with the glow of the setting sun and the sky is often a dark red that the river below reflects and some guess that this presages the imminent shedding of blood. Black and ragged clouds drift over the mad skyline of gables, turrets, belfries and chimneys. The spires of a hundred churches point to heaven like the fingers of so many hands imploring God. The smoke from thousands of chimneys rises as a dark and heavy incense. It seems to Anthony that London is an inhabited ruin, for half-timbered houses tilt and lean out into the streets, their roofs sag and doors hang loose from their frames. Trees force their way up through abandoned courtyards. Heir to the ravaged cities of Babylon and Camelot, London's magic is fading, though its last enchantments still linger in certain ancient buildings

Soon it will be summer and Anthony is still young and he is rich and triumphant. When he looks back on the hunt on Vauxhall marshes where the gerfalcon was discovered some years back, he recollects how insignificant he felt and how eager he was to gain the King's favour. Now all is changed. Moreover Anthony enjoys riding beside his father, for since the Battle of Palm Sunday he has spent too little time with him.

Word of the hunt reaches the court and soon the Woodvilles are joined by other lords who are eager for this new kind of exercise, among them the Lords Hastings, Pembroke, Stafford and Audley, as well as Sir John Paston. It is quite the fashion and a few ladies, riding sidesaddle, also accompany them. (Tiptoft, who does not join the hunt, is confirmed in his opinion that baldness is an estimable thing.) The custom is to meet beside the ruin of the Savoy Palace. This was the residence of John of Gaunt and almost a century earlier the insurgent peasants used gunpowder to blow up its great hall before setting fire to the rest. There remains a great flight of stone steps going nowhere and bushes grow out of what remains of an ornamental parapet. A line of battered and defaced heraldic beasts carved in stone—the lion of England, the griffin of Edward II, the falcon of Plantagenet, the bull of Lionel, Duke of Clarence, the lion of Mortimer, and the yale of Beaufort—marks what was once the perimeter of the grounds. Stirrup-cups are brought to the riders outside this ruin, which is now the abode only of owls. London was great when John of Gaunt and his affinity feasted there, but we shall not see those days return. Then horns are blown and the hunters move off.

Stories proliferate in the city. Some said that redheads were being arrested and questioned because a number of Jews had recently smuggled themselves into England. Others said that the notorious lustfulness of redheads was the problem and the colour of their hair was a presage of the fires of the Last Judgement. But no, it was more probable that red hair was being collected to stuff a mattress for the Queen's pleasure. Then it was reported that Judas had escaped from Hell and was walking the streets of London and this was whom was being searched for. Some, much closer to the truth, believed that this hunt was at the request of the King's alchemist, for he needed the blood of a redheaded man to turn copper into gold. But most called the hunt 'the folly of Earl Rivers'. Shops and inns began to turn redheads away, for though people were sorry for them, there was no point in taking risks. There was word of a Red-Headed League formed by the unfortunate creatures for their self-defence, but others, more timid either call at the Woodville townhouse to offer themselves for inspection, or they leave the city until this strange hue-and-cry should be over.

Then some redheaded Londoners take to coming out in the streets only by night and because of this the Woodvilles institute hunts with torches and lanterns. Then shadows are seen to dance in the uncertain light of hunters' torches. Anthony thinks that the windows of those houses on Cheapside whose interiors are lit up with a dull yellow light resemble the eyes of goblins and he says as much to William Herbert, the Earl of Pembroke, who is riding beside him. The Earl's response is surprising, 'Yes,' he says. 'Did I ever tell you that I was once on a goblin hunt? It was in the marchlands of Wales. The whole area was infested with these horrid creatures and they were attacking children. So their numbers had to be brought down. Their glowing eyes used to give them away. Also the hounds found it easy to follow their peculiar smell. The little creatures resembled humans so much, particularly Welshmen, that it seemed cruel to kill them, but we did and we cut off their ears for the tally. Looking back on it, perhaps we should not have held so many meets, for I believe that there are very few goblins left in England or Wales. They may even be extinct.'

Twice in these enchanted weeks the hunting party ride past a walled garden the door of which hangs open on both occasions and as Anthony rides by, he can see a garden of vines and hanging birdcages where women dance in the moonlight and he can hear the music of the lute. He thinks that it would have been pleasant to dismount and rest and dream there, but his father is a man obsessed, for he fears that his son cannot be safe until they capture the redheaded man who attempted the murderous assault last year. Nevertheless the hunters have no success and slowly the London Hunt begins to break up as its members are called away on other business.

Now Rivers spends more time closeted with the King, since the dangers that Edward guessed at a few months ago are more obvious. Warwick and George of Clarence have met in Calais and Clarence has married Warwick's daughter Isabel in defiance of Edward. A few days after the Earl of Pembroke had talked about goblins with Anthony, he is summoned to lead an army north against Robin of Redesdale's contumacious rebellion. Then Edward, Rivers and Anthony and other loyal lords make their way north more slowly. It is only when they reach Nottingham that they learn that Pembroke and his force of Welsh cavalry have been defeated at Edgecote and that Pembroke and Stafford been beheaded by the northern rebels. When Rivers hears the news, he laughs mirthlessly and exclaims, 'The goose! The goose!' When Anthony asks his father what he means, Rivers tells him that Jacquetta believes in the curse of the living goose and that every man who ate of the meat pressed upon them by Ripley at that dinner will die violently. But Rivers tells Anthony not to worry, for he does not believe that such a stupid creature as a goose can carry a curse. Indeed he does not believe in curses at all. Nor does he believe in talismans and so he refuses to wear one of Jacquetta's little manikins round his neck.

The army that Edward has brought with him begins to desert in great numbers. They are in Neville territory and soon Edward finds himself to be the 'guest' of George Neville, the man he had so recently dismissed from the Chancellorship. Though there is no question of the King being a prisoner, nevertheless he finds that he is not allowed to leave Warwick Castle.

Anthony and his father have failed to escape in time and they are lodged in Kenilworth Castle and there they are left in no doubt that they are its prisoners. Anthony's cell is much less comfortable than Malory's one in Ludgate. When will they be tried? And where? Perhaps it will be York. Anthony, who has nothing to read, plots his defence, or rather many defences since he cannot be sure of what their enemies will accuse him and his father. He wishes that he had talked more with his father and learnt more about the world that existed before he was born. Now Anthony thinks that he would like to know about his father's boyhood in Northamptonshire; and about his service in France with John of Bedford; and the famous joust at Smithfield against the Spaniard Pedro de Vasquez; then his father's secret marriage to the widow of John of Bedford, Jacquetta de St Pol and the scandal that resulted from this mésalliance; his pardon by King Henry; also Anthony would like to know what his father remembers of his and his sister's childhood.

After a few days the warden of the castle finds Anthony something to read. It is a fragmentary manuscript containing the last part of 'The Franklin's Tale' and all of 'The Squire's Tale' from *The Canterbury Tales* by Geoffrey Chaucer.

'The Squire's Tale' is as follows:

The great King Cambuskan ruled the land of Tartary. He had two sons, the older being Algarsyf and the younger Cambalo and the youngest child was a daughter called Canace. Cambuskan held a feast to celebrate the anniversary of twenty years of his rule, but the feast was interrupted by a knight who entered the hall mounted on a mechanical steed made of brass. The knight had a mirror in his hand, a gold ring on his thumb and a sword by his side. He told Cambuskan that he was an emissary from the King of Arabia and India and that the steed was a gift to mark the feast. The steed will take the King anywhere in the world in a single day. The mirror and the ring were for Canace. The mirror would reveal any danger, as well as any deceit by a lover. When she put on the ring she would understand the language of birds. The sword would cut through any armour and if someone had been wounded by it, the wound would never heal until it was touched by the flat of the sword's blade.

The strange knight was thanked and led to his chamber and the feasting resumed. That night the revellers slept long and heavily except for Canace who went out into the royal park as the sun was rising. She heard the birds, and thanks to the ring, she eavesdropped on them. A female falcon was lamenting her abandonment by her former lover and consequently she barely escaped a fowler's net. After the bird swooned in Canace's arms, she carried it into the palace where she tenderly cared for her. But the plight of the female falcon has taught her to distrust all men.

Anthony reads on. Later that morning, the mysterious ambassador offered to demonstrate to Cambuskan how the brass steed worked. First he opened a lid on the horse's back and dropped in some lighted coals. Next he pulled a lever. Whereupon the horse stamped its feet and steam came out of its nostrils. Then the ambassador invited Canace to mount up behind him so that he could take her for a short ride. No sooner had she done so than the horse unfurled its wings and rose steeply in the air. It circled twice round Cambuskan's palace before flying off in the direction of India. The ambassador had succeeded in his mission which was to abduct Canace.

The story continues with an account of Cambuskan's raising of a mighty army which he led in the direction of India; Cambalo's taking the magic sword and setting out to rescue Canace; Argalsyf's setting out to do the same with the magic mirror; an Indian prince has fallen in love with a description of Canace; his consultation with a talking head and the commissioning of a fresco which depicts the male falcon being taken by a larger bird so that it was unable to rescue his mate... 'The Squire's Tale' is full of exotic marvels, and as Anthony reads on, his mind drifts off the page. He would like to travel to the East and watch those who pray in pagan temples. He wants to see the vegetable lamb of Tartary, the Magnetic Mountain, Klingsor's palace and perhaps the Paradise Garden of the Old Man of the Mountains. He wants to talk with Indian anchorites, dog-headed men and black sages. He imagines resting in the sunny glades of Arabia Felix and later encountering the Empress of Dreams in the dark forests of Asia. And he would like to fly to these regions. Surely the conquest of the air cannot be far off?

He would like... But now his reverie is interrupted by the arrival of a gaoler who puts him in shackles before leading him out of his cell. Now Anthony thinks he must concentrate once more on the trial and on what his defence will be.

Once he is out in the courtyard he is horrified to learn that Warwick and Clarence have determined that there is no need for a trial, since the guilt of 'the King's evil counsellors' is plain for all men to see. Besides, as Warwick is fond of saying, 'Dead men make no war.' His father is standing beside the block at the far end of the courtyard. He is unshackled and is suffered to kneel and pray. Then he is made to kneel again with his head and neck extended over the block. A few moments later the axe falls. Anthony watching is almost convinced that they are all in a dark dream.

Then it is his turn to be unshackled. But, 'You were never one of the King's evil counsellors,' says a kindly sergeant who is removing his chains. 'My lord of Warwick is a merciful man and besides he says that you are nothing but a jousting popinjay. So here is your sword and the gate is open. Hurry before the Earl changes his mind.'

As Anthony staggers out of Kenilworth Castle, an absurd thought strikes him. Now he will never know how 'The Squire's Tale' ends. Then he throws up. It is only much later that he weeps for his father. He slowly makes his way to London and on the way he learns that many others of the nobility have also met their deaths. The best men in England were being slaughtered and soon, Anthony thought, the kingdom would be at the mercy of merchants, peasants and women. And more fighting must follow, for there is a new uprising in the north. It is led by Humphrey Neville, who, though a kinsman of the Earl of Warwick, is no friend of the Kingmaker. Instead, Humphrey has raised the banner on behalf of Henry of Lancaster and Margaret of Anjou.

By the time Anthony enters London autumn is setting in. As he makes his way to the Woodville townhouse, he tries to prepare himself to console his mother in her grief. But when he reaches the house he learns from the steward that his mother is not there to be consoled, for she is lodged in the Tower and will shortly be tried as a witch. It is one of Warwick's men, a certain Thomas Wake, who has accused her. He says that 'the serpent woman' had made a finger-length leaden image of a man at arms, broken in the middle and tied with thread, and used this to make Edward fall in love with her daughter. He will bring forward a priest who will testify that he saw Jacquetta perform a conjuration with the leaden image of a man before it was left behind in his church. The charge continues: 'This was the crafty serpent nurtured on the poison of ambition which, insinuating itself into the minds of princes, poisoned them so with the malice of its virus that there was scarce a King, who inflamed by the angry venom growing therefrom, did not betake himself to the clash of arms by which he sought to appease the fever of that venom'. So his mother is also accused of practising enchantment in order to envenom the King's mind against Warwick in an attempt to compass his destruction. If found guilty, she will burn. Meanwhile she is confined in the Wakefield Tower.

Anthony is allowed a brief visit. He finds her much changed. It is awful, but since the execution, really murder, of her husband and her indictment for sorcery, she does indeed appear to incarnate what Anthony imagines a witch should look like. She has lost weight and her face is pinched. Her hair has gone grey and she has not troubled to comb it. A grey cat is curled on her lap which she says is called Malkin. Her eyes glitter as she launches a maledictory tirade against Warwick and Clarence. They will rue the day that they ever sought to cross her. If they think that they have a helpless old woman at their mercy, they are so very much mistaken. She is hardly less bitter against her son-in-law, the King, not only for failing to protect her husband from judicial murder, but also for lately giving full pardons to Warwick and Clarence for any misdeeds they may have committed in the past twelve months. Anthony even gets a sense that she bears him an unspoken grudge for having been spared when his father was not.

As they talk, Anthony comes to understand that Jacquetta's case is by no means hopeless. Edward is beginning to break free from Warwick's control. Moreover Jacquetta will appeal to the mayor and aldermen of London, for she remains popular with Londoners after she helped save the city from riot and pillage in the days when she was Duchess of Bedford. Then Jacquetta smiles craftily.

'Besides I have my little men to do me service.'

Next, and this is most strange, she shouts, 'They do not

know my strength!' and with that she grabs the cat and raises it up to her face and then forces the full length of one of its legs down her throat. When she pulls it out again she spits blood, but she is triumphant.

'They will see.'

By great good fortune, as Anthony is leaving the Tower he encounters Tiptoft coming in. Tiptoft has judged that it is now safe to return to London and the King has made him Constable once more. He promises that Jacquetta will be more comfortably lodged elsewhere in the Tower, and when Anthony explains the case against her, Tiptoft says that he will interview Thomas Wake and his tame priest, so that everybody may be clear about what the facts are. Doubtless Thomas Wake will find that he has been mistaken. Before they part, Anthony asks Tiptoft if he has a manuscript of 'The Squires Tale'. Though Tiptoft does indeed possess one, it is not complete, for it is just the opening of the story and only a few pages long. But he says that he will lend Anthony *The Book of the Lion*, for that is much more exciting and easily Chaucer's best work.

Clarence is pressing Warwick to declare Edward illegitimate, so that Clarence may succeed to his brother's throne. But Warwick's position is less powerful than it seemed at first. He knows that he must raise an army to deal with his distant kinsman, Humphrey Neville's Lancastrian revolt on the northern border. Yet the other great lords prove reluctant to recognise Warwick's pre-eminence and only pitiful numbers muster for the Kingmaker. Violent feuds erupt all over England.

But Edward remains popular, for though now plump, he is still handsome and his speeches are always pleasant. He commends Clarence and Warwick, 'My beloved brother and fair cousin, these are my best friends. All shall be forgiven and bygones shall be bygones'. Then Edward with an escort provided by his brother Richard of Gloucester and Lord

Hastings, rides north to deal with Humphrey Neville's revolt and in York Edward sets about mustering a large army.

Malory had been one of those released from prison when the Earl of Warwick had entered London in triumph and now from his manor at Newbold Revel he sends Anthony chapters from *Le Morte d'Arthur*. So it is that Anthony learns about Morgan le Fay, Arthur's half-sister, who after much studying in a convent became a great clerk of necromancy. Though she was married to King Uriens she was passionately in love with a knight called Accolon and because of this love she tried to murder her husband and stole Excalibur from Arthur leaving the King with only a replica. But though Accolon was possessed of the marvellous sword and was close to killing Arthur in mortal combat, Nimue, the Damosel of the Lake, who looked on the fight, having divined that Accolon possessed the real Excalibur, used her enchantment to make him drop the sword. Whereupon Accolon was doomed. As he lay dying, he confessed all to Arthur, 'This sword has been in my keeping this twelvemonth; and Morgan le Fay, King Urien's wife, sent it me yesterday by a dwarf, to this intent, that I should slay King Arthur, her brother. For you shall understand King Arthur is the man in this world that she most hates, because he is most of worship and of prowess of any of her blood; also she loves me out of measure as paramour, and I her again; and if she might bring about to slay Arthur by her crafts, she would slay her husband King Uriens lightly, and then had she devised me to be King in this land, and so to reign, and she to be my queen; but that is now finished,' said Accolon, 'for I am sure of my death.'

And this was true, for after four days Accolon died of his wounds and Arthur commanded that his corpse be sent to Morgan le Fay.

Morgan's message to Arthur is defiant, 'I fear him not while I can make me and those with me in the likeness of stones; and let him know I can do much more when I see my time.' But later, as if in contrition, she sends to Arthur a damsel bearing as a gift the richest mantle that was ever seen for it was studded with precious stones. Arthur is pleased and is eager to try the mantle on, but Nimue comes to him in private and warns him of its danger and so, at Nimue's urging, Arthur commands Morgan le Fay's damsel to don the robe herself and in an instant the girl is consumed in flames and the robe is no more. So this was the second time that Nimue rescued Arthur, but it was this same sorceress who beguiled Merlin, who was Arthur's wisest and most trusted counsellor and brought about his doom.

Anthony reflects that he has found no good women in Malory's book; Morgan le Fay, Nimue, Guinevere, Lynette, Elaine, they are all deceitful. They are adulteresses, sorceresses or both. When Hellawes of the Castle Nigramous was thwarted in her lust for the living Lancelot, she would then have had him dead so that she might have his corpse to caress. In the *Le Morte d'Arthur* some damsels denounce Sir Marhalt as a woman hater, but he replies, 'They name me wrongfully for it is the damsels of the turret that so name me and others such as they be. Now I shall tell you for what cause I hate them so: for they be witches and enchantresses many of them. And this is the principal cause that I hate them.'

Edward, having defeated and captured Humphrey Neville, stays to watch his beheading in York, before riding back in triumph to London. There he swiftly sets about assembling a council of lords that he can trust. Anthony finds that not only has he inherited his father's title, Earl Rivers, but he has acquired some of his father's responsibilities, for he is appointed Lord High Constable of England and as such, he is also Master of the Horse, he commands the royal armies and he administers martial justice. He takes little pleasure in this onerous honour and thinks that Warwick may be right and that he is at heart only a 'jousting popinjay'.

The case against Jacquetta is brought before the King's

Great Council. The parish clerk who was supposed to bear witness against her has refused to do so and has now vanished. As for Thomas Wake, he is eager to admit that it is possible that he may have been mistaken and Edward, after agreeing with him, declares that it is likely that she may be innocent. No one is going to argue with the King and Hastings is heard to remark that, for his part, he would never sleep easily if he knew that he incurred that woman's enmity.

Anthony consults regularly with Tiptoft concerning the Constable's duties, for Tiptoft having held that office previously, is an expert on what has to be done. It is from him that he gets news of Ripley and the scheme to discover treasonous conspiracies in advance of their happening. Since Ripley, though lowborn, was notorious enough to be designated by Warwick as one of the 'King's evil counsellors', he had taken sanctuary in Westminster Abbey during the brief ascendancy of Warwick and Clarence. Now he is back once more in his laboratory inside the palace. Ripley says that he has nearly enough sesame oil, except that the last consignment mysteriously failed to reach the palace. A further replacement delivery is expected from a ship chartered by the Peruzzi in Calais. Tiptoft proposes that he and Anthony should be at the Thames at dawn and see that it is safely escorted to the Tower where the earlier deliveries of sesame oil are being guarded.

At dawn the following morning Tiptoft and Anthony arrive at Billingsgate. This is a large water-gate harbour for ships and barges unloading fresh and salt fish, salt, oranges, onions, wheat, rye and suchlike commodities. They are met there by William Caxton, who as Governor of the Company of Merchant Adventurers of London, has also received complaint from the Italians about the recent interception of one of their cargoes. They wait with a great crowd of bargees, stevedores and porters for the tide to turn. Then suddenly, just as the sun is rising, Anthony points to a bald man at the water's edge.

'That is him! That is the redhead!' Tiptoft nods and his men advance on the bald man, who looks wildly round for assistance, but if there were any there who were minded to help him, they dare not face down the combined retinues of the two Earls and the Governor of the Merchant Adventurers. So the desperate man throws himself off the wharf. But he does not land in the water and instead breaks his leg as he falls into a wherry and there he is easily taken. On closer inspection, he is not really bald, for a light fuzz of red is beginning to grow on his shaven head.

He is taken to the Tower and later in the day when Ripley has got his barrel mostly full of sesame oil, they set about getting the redhead very drunk. Before this, Tiptoft had wanted him to be taken to one of the dungeons where he could be robustly questioned so that his identity and that of his employer would be revealed. But Ripley is insistent that the man has to be healthy in both mind and body. Indeed, he is a little worried about the broken leg. Ripley adds some tincture of opium to the last two glasses of wine that the redhead is made to drink. Thus stupefied, the man is in no state to resist being lowered feet first into the barrel.

Ripley says that they must now wait forty days. He is excited, but also anxious, for he reminds them that this experiment has never before been tried in all Christendom. Tiptoft too is anxious, since forty days is a long time and he has a hunch that things in England may soon come to a head. Edward is not yet once more secure on his throne.

Forty days pass before Ripley sends word to the King that he is ready to reveal the future. The following afternoon Edward, Tiptoft and Anthony make their way to the Byward Tower that is on the outer perimeter of the Tower of London. In an upstairs chamber there they find Ripley ready for them, standing in front of a curtain. He recites, 'Whether there be prophecies, they shall fail; whether there be tongues, they shall cease; whether there shall be knowledge, it shall vanish away. For we know in part, and we prophesy in part. But when that which is perfect is come, then that which is in part shall be done away.'

Then he pulls the curtain away and they see the barrel and the man's head poking above its rim. His red hair has grown back and there is the beginning of a beard. His eyes are closed.

'He must be very uncomfortable if he has been standing in that cask for forty days,' says Edward.

'He is not standing,' says Ripley. 'The head is floating.' And so saying, Ripley goes behind the great puncheon barrel, and getting up on a low stool, he grabs the head by its ears and raises it as far as his arms will stretch. Now they can all see a wonder, for though the head is still connected to the heart, the liver and some other vital organs, there is no flesh and there are no bones to be seen, for they have dissolved in the sesame oil. A network of veins and tendons dangle beneath the head like a giant cobweb or the ghost of a human body. As the head is raised out of the oil, its eyes open and it glares like a basilisk.

The King puts his hand in front of his mouth. He has seen enough. It is horrid Saracen sorcery. He says that he will leave the interrogation to Tiptoft and Anthony and he hurriedly leaves the Tower.

'This is a blasphemous thing!' says Tiptoft. Nevertheless, he is made of sterner stuff than the King and he begins the questioning, 'What is your name?

The head is silent.

'Who was your master before we took custody of you?'

The eyes of the head look blank and Ripley intervenes, 'The Talking Head has no memory of past things. He can only respond to questions about the future,' he says.

Tiptoft grunts and tries another question.

'Will it rain tomorrow?'

The Talking Head is silent a long while and the interrogators have almost despaired of an answer when the head replies, 'It will not rain tomorrow, though it will be cloudy all day,' says the Talking Head.

'Is there presently a great conspiracy directed against the King?'

This is apparently an easier question than the one about the weather, for after only a short while, the Talking Head replies, 'There is certainly a great conspiracy against the King. It is led by the Earl of Warwick and the Duke of Clarence. In two days' time there will be a rising in Lincolnshire headed by Lord Wells who has been suborned by Warwick and Clarence. The King's army will easily defeat Lord Wells and his following. Wells will die. Since I have revealed to you that Warwick and Clarence were behind the uprising, the King will seek to apprehend them, but they will flee west to the coast and assemble a fleet which they will use to attack Burgundian and other ships. But Earl Rivers, who I see before me, will go to Southampton and take command of the King's fleet and defeat the rebels in the channel and capture some of the ships and many men. He will bring the captives back to Southampton where at the King's command, the Earl of Worcester, who I also see before me, will sit in judgement on them and he will have them, hung drawn and quartered before they are impaled. For this cruelty, he will be greatly hated.'

Tiptoft shrugs. 'So long as I am feared,' he says. Then he wants to know, 'What will my end be?'

'You will lose your head,' is the reply.

'Now that I am forewarned, I will take care to keep it on my shoulders,' Tiptoft says, but he looks disconcerted. Then he looks to Anthony as if daring him to ask how and when he will die. But Anthony is not interested, for he has died once already and he knows how it will be. Instead he asks, 'Who will be King after Edward dies?'

'Richard the Third,' is the reply.

Anthony and Tiptoft look at one another. Richard of

Gloucester! That pious cripple! Most extraordinary! And a little unlikely, for George of Clarence is older than Richard.

'What will happen after the rebel fleet has been defeated? Will Warwick and Clarence be among the captives?'

'Warwick and Clarence will escape to France where Louis will give them welcome.'

'What will happen then?' Now Tiptoft is excited, since knowledge of the future is like a drug. At first one has only a little, then one acquires the taste and needs more and more.

But the head closes its eyes and there is no reply.

'The Talking Head needs to sleep,' says Ripley. 'He likes his sleep.'

As they walk out after the first afternoon's interrogation, Tiptoft asks Ripley how it is that the head knows what will happen in the future.

'He goes to the Secret Library and there he looks for the right book,' says Ripley.

Naturally Tiptoft, who is mad for literature, wants to know what the Secret Library is.

'I think it is a library of books that have not yet been written,' says Ripley, and hearing this, Tiptoft is excited by the idea of delving into the literature of the future.

'Where is it?'

'Who knows?' Then Ripley adds, 'Let us be satisfied with what we have. Through the Talking Head we are the lords of all knowledge. He is a great thing and he gives us power over all the Kingdom.'

Tiptoft grunts.

'But how can there be a library full of books that have yet to be written?' he wants to know.

'These words from Boethius's *Consolation of Philosophy* may answer you, *"Nunc fluens facit tempus, nunc stans facit aeternintatum"*: "The now that passes produces time; the now that remains produces eternity". Under the eye of God all time is coexistent and thus the future is here in the present. That is how it is in the *nunc stans*.'

Tiptoft nods distractedly. Now he must hurry away and acquaint the King with what he has learnt from the oracle about conspiracy. Later, he is determined that he will discover the whereabouts of the Secret Library. Back at the Woodville townhouse Anthony tells his mother about what he has seen and heard that day. Jacquetta screws up her face as she hears about the latest occult horror. Then when Anthony tells her about Tiptoft's wanting to be told how he would die, she fearfully wants to know if he asked how he, or his sister or his mother would meet their ends. When he says he did not, she is greatly relieved and adds, 'Never seek to ask after your own fortune, for there is a saying that a man's fate follows the mouth of his astrologer.'

The following morning as Anthony rides over to the Tower he notes that it is cloudy, but there is no sign of rain. He walks in on Ripley who is reading to the Talking Head.

'You are early,' says Ripley. 'The Talking Head gets bored in his barrel. So I read to him from interesting books.'

Anthony notices that the book does have an interesting title, *How a Woman Who Is So Big Penetrates the Eyes Which Are So Small*.

'And he has not been fed yet,' continues Ripley and with that he puts down the book and goes over to a box in a corner from which he fishes out some handfuls of fruit and nuts. These he feeds to the Talking Head, resembling as he does so a mother tenderly caring for her small child.

He stops when Tiptoft comes storming in.

'What and where is the Secret Library?' he demands of the Talking Head.

'I cannot take you there. There is no name for its place in our present tongue and it cannot be found on your maps.'

Tiptoft growls. Ripley begs him to desist from enquiring

further into this matter and he adds that the Talking Head can only answer a few questions each day.

'So what will happen after Louis has welcomed Warwick and Clarence to his court?' asks Tiptoft.

The response is swift, 'Louis will reconcile Warwick and Clarence with Margaret of Anjou and they will agree to support the cause of Henry of Lancaster.'

Tiptoft and Anthony cannot believe that Warwick, of all men, should ally himself with Margaret, but the Talking Head may not be argued with.

Then Tiptoft wants to know if Henry of Lancaster will die in prison. He is told that Henry will die in prison, but not before being restored to the throne once more.

Now Anthony asks a question, 'Will Edward and Elizabeth have more children?

'Yes, Elizabeth will bear him two sons and they will be called Edward and Richard.'

Anthony and Tiptoft look at one another. They are thinking the same thing. So Richard of Gloucester will not become the next King after all. The gaps between questions are lengthy, as each time he is asked something, the Talking Head closes his eyes before travelling in spirit to the Secret Library where he must find the right book.

'How will the world end?' asks Tiptoft.

'This is how it will be,' comes the reply. 'The darkness will grow apace; a cold wind will begin to blow in freshening gusts from the east, and the snow will now become heavy. The waves ripple and whisper. Beyond these lifeless sounds the world is silent. It is hard to convey the stillness of it. All the sounds of man, the bleating of sheep, the cries of birds, the hum of insects, all that is over. As the darkness thickens the flakes of snow fall more thickly and the cold is greater. One by one, swiftly one after another, the white peaks of distant hills vanish into blackness and now the sky is absolutely black. That is the end.'

Tiptoft is not pleased with this answer. Surely the Talking Head has been consulting with a lying demon? And now Tiptoft lectures the Talking Head on how the world will really end.

First the Jews will be converted to the True Faith. Then Enoch and Elijah will once more be seen among the living. The Antichrist, who will be born in Damascus, will reign in Jerusalem until he will be slain by the Last Emperor. But, who knows? Perhaps he has already been born there—a nasty little boy who now plays in the dust outside a Mohammedan temple and the horn has yet to grow out of his forehead. After the Last Battle in which he is slain, the seas will rise and then sink. The fish will be stranded and groaning. Trees and plants will be seen to bleed and buildings will collapse and rocks explode. There will be earthquakes and the valleys and mountains shall be levelled. People will lose the power of speech. Stars will fall to earth. The Four Horsemen of the Apocalypse ride backwards and forwards across the face of the earth and their leader is a pale rider on a pale horse and his name is Death and Death is followed by Hell. They are all in the service of a woman arrayed in purple and scarlet who holds a cup full of abominations and filthiness of her fornications. On her forehead a name is written: MYSTERY, BABYLON THE GREAT, THE MOTHER OF HARLOTS AND ABOMINATIONS OF THE EARTH.

And the bones of the dead are joined together once more, while those that are living die and the earth will burn. The Last Trump sounds to herald the Second Coming of Christ. Everybody shall be raised up from the dust and Tiptoft anticipates encountering Aristotle, Julius Caesar, Virgil, the Black Prince and Judas Iscariot. But soon it will be time for Judgement. God, the Eternal Magistrate presides, robed in white and imperial purple and flanked by his angelic retinue. The angels have wings coloured like peacock tails. Some of the men and women who are naked will be led upwards by the angels who will garb them in light, while others who are also naked will tumble down into the eternal fires and there shall be no clothing for their sins. All this is known from our holy books.

It is a great and glorious panoply in which the good are rewarded and the wicked punished. The End of the World as envisaged by Tiptoft is brightly coloured and peopled by crowds who shout and scream and there are even those who up to the last moment are yet lustful and eager to fornicate. So it is like a vast wild party that is out of control.

The Talking Head is not impressed, 'That is not what my book says.'

Anthony's concerns are less grand. Momentarily forgetting Jacquetta's warning, he wants to know, 'Will my wife outlive me?'

'No, she will die in four years' time.'

'Will I marry again?'

'You will.'

'Will I have children?'

'No.'

'What does the Secret Library look like?' Tiptoft is grimly set upon this subject, but the Talking Head will not give way.

'You are too stupid to understand what I would say if I were to tell you.'

Tiptoft looks amazed and he strokes his bald head. Men have called him many things, but no one has described him as stupid.

The Talking Head is tired and he looks as though he needs to sleep. The interrogators make to leave. But the eyes open again.

'You have not asked me what will happen to me tomorrow,' says the Talking Head.

Tiptoft spun round. 'What will happen to you tomorrow?'

'Nothing will happen to me tomorrow.'

'Nothing! How nothing!' The Talking Head fascinates

Tiptoft, but he hates him too. 'By God, I am tempted to pull you out of that barrel and kick you to pieces on the floor.'

'That would be a great mercy,' replies the Talking Head. 'But alas, it will not happen.' The Head looks sad. Then he resumes, 'Nothing will happen to me tomorrow, because I am giving you forewarning now. Tomorrow a group of armed men will try to storm this tower in an attempt to carry me away, or failing that, destroy me in my barrel. But because I have forewarned you, you will have tripled the guard and prepared an ambush. So I shall be saved and nothing will happen to me.'

'Who will send these men?' Tiptoft wants to know.

The Talking Head looks as though he would have shrugged his shoulders, if he had had any shoulders to shrug.

'That cannot be known, as they all died in the attempt to reach me,' is the reply.

Once he is out of the Bywater Tower, Tiptoft sets about preparing for the morrow's ambush. He gives orders that at all costs at least one of the assailants must be taken alive.

It is as foretold. The following morning eight men attempt to storm the Byward Tower, but they are surrounded and easily outnumbered by the guard that Tiptoft has posted. One by one they are cut down, until one man remains. He is unwounded and surrounded on all sides by the soldiers who are mindful of Tiptoft's command. Their sergeant calls out 'Surrender to the Earl of Worcester's mercy'. Alas, the cornered man throws the sword at the feet of his enemies, before drawing his dagger, whereupon doubtless mindful of the Earl of Worcester's notorious skill at working the rack and the bilboes, he slashes his left wrist before plunging the dagger into his throat.

When Tiptoft is told what has happened, he strokes his head. He is resigned, rather than angry. 'It is as it was with Merlin and Nimue,' he says and then he explains that Nimue, who was also known as the Lady of the Lake, studied magic with Merlin and then used that magic to imprison Merlin in a tree trunk. Of course Merlin, who had great powers of prophecy, foresaw that this was going to happen, but because he had foreseen it and knew that it was his future, he was powerless to prevent it from happening.

Then Tiptoft wonders who knew about the man in the barrel? How was this secret discovered? It is dismaying. He tells Anthony that for now there will be no more questioning of the Talking Head. He adds that he is not agreeable to having his fate decided by a disembodied head. 'I control my fate,' he says and later that day he is called away to business in the West Country.

The following day Anthony returns to the Byward Tower to tell Ripley that there shall be no more questioning of the Talking Head. He finds Ripley reading to him from another strange book, this one entitled *Hopeful Monsters*. Anthony marvels at Ripley's devotion to the creature in the barrel, for recently he has become difficult to feed and often spits food out and sometimes he shouts curses as he rotates in the sesame oil. At other times he just weeps for what he has lost, even though he cannot be sure what he has lost, since he has no memory. Still in the Secret Library he has read about green fields and blue skies and would like to see them in reality.

Anthony briefly contemplates his suffering with satisfaction. Then he tells Ripley that their interrogations are concluded for now. Ripley is drunk as usual, and it is as a garrulous drunk that he detains Anthony.

'We are all characters in a story that God, the great romancer, is narrating,' says Ripley. 'Sometimes, as we learn from the Bible, He intervenes in the stories that He has been composing. Also sometimes His creations rebel against His will. The citizens of Sodom, the worshippers of the Golden Calf and King Saul who raised the Witch of Endor are all examples of people who sought to defy the narrative of God. '

Now the particular reason Ripley is drunk today is that

he has recently discovered that he has the same problem as God, for he is now most worried that the characters in stories that he has been making up are on the point of escaping from those stories and some of them are angry with him.

'Since I am the creator of the people in my stories, I am their God and like God, I have chosen to give my creations free will and consequently they may be able to escape my control, particularly if they are bold and energetic. For the time being they are still at my command, but I do not know for how much longer.' Then something else occurs to Ripley, 'Will you keep a secret?'

Anthony nods.

'You are sure? You are sure you are sure?'

Anthony nods again.

'I think that the Bible is very badly plotted. I could do better,' whispers Ripley. 'If my fellow clergy knew that I thought that, they would burn me at the stake.'

CHAPTER TWELVE

Sea Battle

Is Ripley going mad? Should Anthony report his suspicion to the King? He means to, but there is no time, for now Anthony finds it hard to keep up with events even though he is part of them and he spurs his horse from one crisis to the next. There are placards, summons to muster, soldiers marching in all directions, rumours of battles, actual battles and affrays. The sun shoots up, races across the sky and then is gone again and there is only a little time for sleep before the sun is once again speedily climbing towards its zenith. Yet there are also meetings of the Privy Council which Anthony now has to attend and he finds that these pass more slowly. The young Richard of Gloucester is given his first command and is sent west to suppress a Welsh rebellion. Then Sir Robert Welles raises the standard of revolt in Lincolnshire. Warwick and Clarence send word to the King that they are advancing on Lincoln and that they will put a speedy end to Welles' uprising. But the King's intelligencers report that Welles has been publicly summoning men to rise up in the cause of Warwick and Clarence. So Edward sends two privy seals of summons to Warwick and Clarence so that they may acquit themselves of any suspicion of treason. They send back their agreement, but then they cross the country and take ship at Exeter.

Warwick has amassed a considerable private squadron, most of which was acquired when King Henry appointed him Keeper of the Sea, and it is certain that he will use these ships. So Anthony is sent with utmost haste to Southampton where he joins Lord John Howard, the King's Admiral. Straightaway they impound Warwick's own great ship, the *Trinity*. At Southampton Anthony gets news that Elizabeth has given birth to a son and that he will be christened Edward. Church bells ring all over England.

The sea is so big! It extends as far as the eye can see. Lord Howard congratulates Anthony on his new status as uncle. He is friendly though somewhat patronising, for he does not believe that Anthony has ever been on a ship before. Of course he could not know that Anthony has sailed over to Ireland with Bran's fleet. But Anthony gazes in wonder at the cogs and carvels in Southampton harbour. With their high decks, their forecastles and aftcastles and their foremasts, mainmasts and lateen sails, they are so very different from the oared long-ships of Bran's day. He lodges in considerable comfort with Lord Howard on the flagship carvel, the *Edward*. Here there are feather beds, tapestries, table linen, a small library and even pissing basins of silver. Thanks to his estates in the wool and cloth counties of Norfolk and Suffolk as well as his commerce with the Continent, Lord Howard is one of the richest men in England, and though the *Edward* is named after the King, the ship does not belong to Edward but to Howard, as do most of the ships in Southampton Harbour. Howard will command the ships and their crews and Anthony will command the fighting men on those ships.

'They that go down to the sea in ships, that do business in great waters; These see the works of the LORD, and His wonders in the deep.' These words from Psalms are Howard's watchwords. He is stocky, weather-beaten and in the grip of a sea fever. He says that the sea is like a wheel of fortune, for it delivers death to one man and great riches to another. It has certainly brought him great wealth. He loves the sea's beguiling glitter, its flashes of temper and its eventual and invariable return to serenity. He speculates constantly on the mysteries of the deep.

A week later, they beat off an attempt by Warwick to regain the *Trinity* and to seize some of the King's ships and indeed they capture two of his.

But in the weeks that follow Warwick's armada is successful in capturing and pillaging English, Breton, Burgundian and Hanseatic ships and consequently the numbers in that armada increase and it seems that Warwick may establish a floating Kingdom in the Narrow Sea. So the royal fleet puts out in a thick fog, though this soon clears to let the sun dance on the waves. A Breton cog that has been running ahead of Warwick's piratical fleet guides them to their enemy.

There are two breech-loading guns on the forecastle of the *Edward*. Howard says they are perfectly useless and so they prove. Howard and Anthony place their faith in the company of royal archers that they have taken on board.

Howard manoeuvres so that the wind is on the starboard quarter and the sun is behind them, and on Anthony's advice, Howard orders his ships to keep some 250 yards distance from the enemy's ships if they can. Trumpets are used to signal from ship to ship and keep the royal fleet in a ragged line. For a long time ships commanded by Howard are at roughly bowshot range from the enemy but no closer.

Anthony commands the *Edward*'s archers from his position on the forecastle. 'Draw! Loose!' After the first rank of archers has fired off a volley, they step back and a second line of archers step forward with bows drawn and ready to release. The arrows rise in high parabolas before falling as potentially deadly rain on the helmets and decks of the enemy. Just the eerie clatter of arrows on helmets and decks is enough to bring on fear. Warwick's fleet also carries archers but not nearly so many and his men-at arms are desperate to close and it is only when the royal archers' stock of arrows begins to run low that Howard allows the distance between the two fleets to narrow. As the ships move closer, the archers no longer loose off their arrows in parabolas, and instead they aim in a flat trajectory at the closing enemy. At this range their arrows can penetrate steel plate. Closer yet and the ranks of archers on the deck discard their bows and grab spears and war-hammers, though the handful of archers on the forecastle continue to rain down arrows on the enemy. Also caltraps and pots of blinding quick-lime are hurled down from the forecastle and the crow's-nest of the main mast. Then grappling irons are cast and battle is fully joined between the *Edward* and the *Falcon*.

For a moment Anthony watches the press of men rip-pling backwards and forwards, before he draws his sword and descends from the forecastle to join the hand-to-hand combat. He is serene in battle and negligently confident in command, for he has the manikin on his neck and besides the Talking Head has assured him of victory. Soon the living find themselves tumbling over the dead and the decks are slip-pery with blood. Though Anthony and those who follow him have forced their way onto the *Falcon*'s deck, the enemy still resists fiercely, since there is nowhere to flee to. At the end of it fourteen of Warwick's ships have been captured and hun-dreds of his men killed. But Warwick's own ship has made its escape and as long as he and Clarence remain at large England remains in great peril.

Having supervised the tossing of the enemy's dead into the sea, Howard and Anthony proceed to dinner in the *Edward*'s forecastle. Drummers and pipers provide a concert while the dishes are being prepared. Once the musicians are dismissed, conversation is possible. Though Howard is rarely in Lon-don, he did see Anthony joust at Smithfield and he has heard stories about Anthony's sword, the Galantine, and about the hair shirt and scourgings. But what Howard is most curious about is life at court and the gossip of courtiers, for when he is not at sea, he spends most of his time in Norfolk, where he supervises the management of his sheep farms and the trade in cloth. Though he is fascinated to hear what goes on at court, for him it is like gazing into the mouth of Hell.

'The court is crowded with men and women hungry for empty honours,' says Howard. 'A great multitude strive for the favour of one man. They elbow each other out of the way and they tread upon those who have fallen from favour. The court is a hydra-headed monster. Its rewards are arbitrarily dispensed and its penalties ruthlessly enforced. There is no solid ground to tread on and no hour that is safe, and so I think that the sea is more predictable than the King's favour. I think that the King is like a fire—if you are too close, you burn; if you are too far away you freeze. A great winnowing takes place at court in which the ears of wheat are thrown out and the chaff retained.'

Does Edward ever say what he means? Does Anthony like the madman Tiptoft? Does he trust Hastings? Is Ripley manufacturing gold for Edward? Is Clarence the fool that he seems? If Warwick were successful in landing a large army and advancing towards London, who of all his fawning courtiers would stay loyal to Edward? Clearly Howard prefers the company of sheep to that of courtiers (though he will make an exception of Anthony). England has the best wool in all Christendom and it is England's chief treasure. What Anthony does not realise is that there are many sorts of sheep, including Blackfaces, Herwicks, Wensleydales, Dartmoors, Merinos. The docking of sheeps' tails is vital if the sheep are being fed on soft fodder, for if they are not docked they will become foul and rotten. The Merchants of the Staple are the wealthiest merchants in England. And so on. He tells Anthony that the wool trade is fascinating, though Anthony does not find it so.

But when Howard has finished talking about the East Anglian wool trade, he talks about stranger things.

'How long has the struggle between York and Lancaster been going on? I think that it is almost twenty years,' he says. 'When it is over and Warwick's head rests on a spike on London Bridge, I shall take my fleet and sail westward on the

Great Sea until we come to the end of it. People think of the Great Sea as empty, but it is not so, for it is full of islands and the further one sails the stranger things become. Nobody has ventured far on the Great Sea since the days of St Brendan and that was many centuries ago. St Brendan the Navigator is the patron saint of boatmen, mariners and travellers and so he has become my personal saint and model. He was Abbot of Clonfert and very old when he decided that he wanted to see Paradise and Hell before he died. So he had a little round boat built of pinewood and he took fourteen of his monks with him. It was very crowded and like sailing in a coffin.

'They sailed westward from Ireland and the first island they came to was called Faroes, which is a Scandinavian word for the Island of Sheep, and indeed the sheep there are very large, for they grow without the interference of men. If I could find that island and make it my own, I would be assured of great profits. But I would still sail further west, for I want to see the island which swims and the sea which coagulates. Then there is the Island of the Deserted Citadel where those who set foot on its shore find no people. All was darkness and silence when Brendan and his monks landed there, but then a dog led them inside the Citadel to a laden dinner table in a recently abandoned dining hall. The dinner on the table was still hot. It was on this island that Brendan encountered the Devil in the form of a black-skinned Ethiopian. Soon after they left this island their little boat was menaced by a gigantic shark, but God shifted the sea to save Brendan and his companions.

Marvel followed marvel. They discovered a great pillar of crystal, wrapped in a net, in the deepest part of the ocean. They visited Judas who was sitting on a desolate wet rock in the middle of the Great Sea. This place is known as Rockall. He told the monks that this was his holiday, for he was allowed out of Hell on Sundays and feast days. After these short respites from torment he found himself in free fall back to Hell. Such are the limits of God's compassion. (Judas had red hair.) Almost the last island that the monks landed on was the one inhabited by the neutral angels. These were the ones who, when Satan rebelled against God, did not support him, but neither did they rally behind the Archangel Michael and take up arms against the legions of Satan. Because of this they had been transformed into birds and they sang psalms all day long.

Finally they reached the Island at the End of the World. Here Brendan disembarked and walked alone until he reached a great river on the edge of Paradise that prevented him from seeing more than he could comprehend, though he thought that he glimpsed red-skinned figures dancing and singing on the far bank. He saw, but he was unable to interpret what he had seen. At this point the seven marvellous years were over and he had to return to the ordinary and sail back to Ireland. Is this not all wonderful?'

Anthony is doubtful, for among other things, he had understood from Tiptoft that Purgatory was in the southern hemisphere and that the Earthly Paradise was located at the summit of the mountain that was Purgatory.

'It is certainly marvellous,' he says. 'But it may not all be true. Much of this may be the stuff of mariner's yarns, fantastic tales spun to pass the time during long voyages and cold winter nights.'

'Of course it is true,' Howard is suddenly irritable. 'Brendan was a saint and saints never lie, and besides, if he had lied about what he had seen and experienced during his long navigation, the monks who had travelled with him would have denounced him. Furthermore there are men in Southampton today who can vouch for some at least of the Saint's discoveries. No it must all be true. What is more, I have made a pilgrimage to Clonfert and seen St Brendan's gravestone facing the door of the Cathedral.' Then a thought strikes Howard. 'You should come with me and then you will find that St Brendan told no falsehoods. It will be a great adventure—and a profitable one. We shall make the Island of Sheep our own and become fabulously rich on the sale of the wool. I will need soldiers to garrison and colonise the Island of Sheep, the Island of the Deserted Citadel and the rest of the King Edward Islands. Is this not something to dream on? I shall see, "the works of the LORD and his wonders in the deep". I long to meet the red men. My guess is that they will speak Arabic.'

Why should they speak Arabic? Is that the language of Paradise? But Anthony is not so very interested. He yearns to take another way—to Cathay, Tartary and Serendib. The mysteries of the Great Sea are not for him and he will leave Howard to his dreams of a Yorkist Empire in the West. Howard will never be able to see the Ocean of Stories for what it is. When Anthony says that he must find his cabin and sleep, Howard wonders how he can ever get to sleep wearing that prickly shirt.

But of course there is no prickly shirt and the sea rocks Anthony to sleep. That night he dreams of a Great Sheep that eats men and leaves English villages deserted. It is a savage creature and its baa is terrifying.

On their return to Southampton they are met by Tiptoft who has been sent to dispense the King's justice to the rebels. This justice is summary and Tiptoft loses little time in finding twenty of the seamen guilty of treason. They are hung by the neck until unconscious, then taken down and revived before being disembowelled, quartered and beheaded and finally impaled. There are groans and hisses from the crowd that has come to watch. Some of the men executed were sailors from Southampton and two of them were no more than boys.

Tiptoft is defiant, 'At least they were given a trial before being executed. Warwick did not allow the same mercy to your father,' he tells Anthony. 'As long as I am as feared as much as I am hated I am well content.'

Then Tiptoft struts over to the line of impaled corpses and

turns to shout at the angry crowd, 'God has willed this and I am only his servant. The whole earth, perpetually drenched in blood, is nothing but a vast altar, upon which all that is living must be sacrificed without end, without measure, without pause, until the consummation of things, until evil is extinct and the death of death.' Red-faced, he looks up to heaven as if challenging God to contradict him.

Later in the day, Tiptoft is talking to Anthony about creating his own talking head. In a few weeks' time he says that he will set about getting a big barrel made and ordering the sesame oil. He is going to have a talking head that will deliver to him the future that he wants. Moreover he will use torture, if necessary, to discover the location of the Secret Library.

CHAPTER THIRTEEN

Exile

'It is, therefore, a source of great virtue for the practised mind to learn bit by bit, first to change about in visible and transitory things, so that afterwards it may be able to leave them behind altogether. The man who finds his homeland sweet is still a tender beginner; he to whom every soil is as his native one is already strong; but he is perfect to whom the entire world is as a foreign land. The tender soul has fixed his love on one spot in the world; the strong man has extended his love to all places; the perfect man has extinguished his.' Hugh of St Victor

As Anthony rides back to London, he decides that now is the time to seek out the enchanted garden which he had ridden past when questing for the redheaded man. But there is no time. Almost every day he is summoned to the Privy Council. The Council receives reports that Warwick and Clarence have landed at Honfleur. Then they are in Paris. Then there are reports that Louis has reconciled Warwick and Clarence with Margaret of Anjou and her son Edward, and now Warwick and Clarence have declared for Henry. Men do what the Talking Head says that they will. Then Anthony has to follow Edward to York where Edward is recruiting an army to put down an uprising by Lord Montagu. Next there are landings by Warwick's men, Lancastrians and French mercenaries at Plymouth, Dartmouth and Exeter. Warwick is marching on London and Edward decides that he is not safe in York.

As Edward makes preparations to leave for Norfolk where he may find more support, he asks Tiptoft and Anthony what will happen next and Tiptoft has to tell the King that they had not thought to ask the Talking Head before the present trouble with Warwick and the King's brother blew up so suddenly. Edward is angry and thinks of commanding that the barrel and the creature inside be sent to await them at Norfolk, but really there is no time for this. So then he sends orders that it be destroyed. Tiptoft is sent ahead with much of the royal treasury. As Edward retreats into Norfolk he finds that he is actually losing supporters. Most of his 'loyal' courtiers are either retiring to their estates or proceeding down to London to welcome the Earl of Warwick and his Lancastrian allies. At Bishop's Lynn there is no sign of Tiptoft and the treasury. Finally, when Edward decides that he has no choice but to flee the country and seek refuge in Burgundy, Anthony is the only lord, apart from Richard of Gloucester, who follows the King into exile. They commandeer a few fishing vessels in the harbour and make for the Dutch coast. Since they have no money, they pay the shipmen with some of their fine robes.

As the English coast is lost to sight, Edward begins to weep. After a stormy crossing in little boats, they land at Alkmar where they are greeted by Louis, Lord of Gruthuyse, an old friend of Edward's, who escorts Edward to his palatial mansion in The Hague. Eventually the Lords Hastings and Say also find their way there. But they have far too few men with them for an invasion of England to be contemplated and Charles, Duke of Burgundy, does not respond to Edward's appeals for assistance.

Anthony feels himself to be naked as he walks through the streets and squares of The Hague, for he has lost everything—not only his office, rank, estates and treasures, but also the fields, woods and hills that he took for granted, yet were part of who he was. Like Adam, he has been expelled from Paradise by God's inscrutable decree and now he is a beggar in a foreign land. Once more he thinks of Scoggin doing cartwheels to demonstrate the wheel of fortune. Holland is deathly flat and even its sky is different from the English one. Anthony tries to find comfort in the words of Hugh of St Victor and fails. He cannot stay in this country. He thinks that he will seek permission from Edward to go on pilgrimage. He will travel to Venice and take ship to Jaffa and from there proceed on to Jerusalem, but he thinks that should not be his journey's end, for he will travel on in search of the ruins of Babylon, the Island of Women and the Kingdom of Prester John.

Anthony usually avoids cripples. He, like many others, believes that cripples are branded by God with deformity as a warning, so that healthy men should shun them. Consequently he avoids the dwarfish strongman Chernomor and similarly he has had little to do with Richard of Gloucester until now. But in this small Dutch town it is almost inevitable that they should spend time together, even though Anthony guesses that Richard does not like him very much, while he for his part does not care for Richard. But Anthony has another reason for seeking Richard's company. Soon after their arrival in The Hague, Anthony finds him reading under a tree in Gruthuyse's orchard. Richard is sallow-faced, serious, and as ever, dressed in black. The book he is reading turns out to be *The Visions of St Matilda*.

'Everywhere I have sought peace and have not found it except in a corner with a book,' says Richard.

Whatever Richard's faults, he is passionate in his faith in God and fiercely loyal to Edward. Warwick had tried very hard to win him over, but Richard had refused to follow Clarence in his treachery. He is bitter about Clarence.

'I hate him. I hate disloyalty. I hate greed and extravagance. I hate sorcery. I hate all forms of evil. It is a fault in me, I know. I should not set myself up in judgement over evildoers, for God will give them their requital. Moreover I know that I am not perfect and there must be some who hate me. I have many faults, which others have to endure. I have a more than perfect hatred of Clarence. He has betrayed Edward in the hope of becoming King. Yet Clarence would make a terrible King and Warwick will never allow that fool to take the throne. But perhaps Warwick will take the throne for himself…'

'Clarence will never become King, nor will Warwick,' says Anthony. 'It may be that you will be the next King after Edward. The Talking Head spoke of a "Richard".'

'Ah, I did not know that. And Clarence? What will become of him?'

'We did not ask that question.'

Richard is thoughtful, but then he says, 'Why should I believe the word of a monster? It is absurd. It seems to me that prophecy is like a will-o'-the-wisp that dances brightly over a swamp with the intent to lead men to their doom. One should not seek to know what God has chosen to conceal and instead one should humbly submit to whatever He has ordained.'

Richard's description of the Talking Head makes Anthony think of the draug and how it described him as a 'Christian monster'.

A few days later, for want of anything else to do, Anthony accompanies Richard to a little village outside The Hague. Almost all the inhabitants of this village follow the way of the Brethren of the Common Life and devote themselves to good deeds and pious study. Richard conducts Anthony to the village chapel where a gloomy man called Hugo is painting a large altarpiece.

'There is no man in England who could have painted this,' says Richard. 'It shows the world as it is.'

It is a jewel-bright triptych featuring the Nativity and it is near completion. It shows a winter scene in which there are no leaves on the trees. The infant Jesus lies naked on a bed of golden rays that doubtless keep him warm. Wealthy patrons stand or kneel in the wings of the triptych. They are bland-faced and perhaps even bored. In the central panel the Virgin looks down on the miracle to which she has given birth and richly robed angels kneel in prayer before the infant, but the scene is dominated by three shepherds, dressed like beggars, who crowd over one another in order to get a better look and strain towards the baby in fervent adoration. They have calloused hands, deeply lined faces and gap-toothed mouths and they are full of passion.

Though Anthony does not say so, he finds that the painting lacks decorum. It is unseemly that poor and ugly persons should so dominate this holy scene. Jesus is, after all, of royal blood. That is not Richard's response.

'I come here often to watch Hugo at work and I like to imagine myself in the picture that he has painted, so that I may find myself kneeling shoulder to shoulder in all humility with these simple peasants. The more humble a man is, the more at peace he will be with himself and his God.' Then, looking hard at Anthony, 'Christ came for all mankind, for simple shepherds like these here depicted and even for the salvation of wicked lords like you and me. Then having entered the painting and having paid Lord Jesus proper worship, I imagine that I might go walking in the hills that you see lying beyond the stable and I might find some peace there.'

But Anthony thinks that he would not like to encounter these shepherds in a dark alley. Besides, must they not be Jews? And then he spots something that Richard seems not to have noticed. Nor have the shepherds seen what Anthony has seen. There in the darkest part of the manger, black, horned Lucifer is lurking. What is he doing there?

Edward and his miniature court in exile receive regular reports from England. Tiptoft failed to reach Norfolk, for all ways there were blocked. Near Huntingdon he and the few men who still followed him bought dirty old clothes from some shepherds and then used walnut juice on their faces and hands, so that they might also appear to be shepherds. But when Tiptoft sent one of them to buy food from a local farmer and a gold piece was offered for that food, the ruse was discovered and Tiptoft and the royal treasury were seized. He was arraigned at Westminster on the charge of treason and brought before John de Vere, the thirteenth Earl of Oxford. Since Tiptoft had overseen the death of the twelfth Earl, the outcome of the trial was never in doubt. A beautiful scaffold, hung with tapestries and carpets, was erected on Tower Hill. Tiptoft was made to walk from Westminster to the Tower. Priests surrounded him on the scaffold. One of them, a member of the Dominican Order, upbraided him, 'My Lord, you are brought here today by reason of your unheard-of cruelties, especially when, desiring to put an end to certain leaders, enemies of the state, you killed also two innocent young children, urged on by the lust for power.' But the Earl replied, 'This all was done for the good of the state.' He stroked his head one last time as if to reassure himself that it was still on his shoulders. Then he tipped the headsman generously and instructed him to carry out the beheading in three blows 'in honour of the Holy Trinity'. The day of his execution was celebrated as a holiday in London. Even so, his body and head were honourably buried at Blackfriars. Anthony wonders if Tiptoft, in asking the Talking Head about his fate, had sealed that fate. Or was it perhaps the curse of the living goose? Anthony will miss Tiptoft badly. It is a fault in him, but he much prefers interesting people like Tiptoft and Malory to virtuous people like Richard of Gloucester.

As Warwick and his allies approached London, Queen Elizabeth fled from the Palace and sought sanctuary in Westminster Abbey for herself and her new-born son. Warwick entered London and proceeded straightaway to the Tower of London. Henry was filthy and shabbily dressed in a worn blue robe, but he was King once more and he happily took the hand of the Kingmaker and allowed himself to be led wherever Warwick willed. Messages were sent to Margaret and her son, Edward of Lancaster in France, urging them to join the Lancastrian court in London. One of Ripley's agents reported that Henry seemed less a man than 'a stuffed woolsack, a shadow on the wall, a victim of a game of blindman's buff, a crowned calf'.

Then there is word about Ripley himself. Once again he had sought sanctuary in the Abbey, but George of Clarence found him there, and after some sweet talk and many promises, he persuaded Ripley to leave sanctuary and conduct him to the Talking Head (for Ripley had disregarded Edward's message and had kept the oracle secure). After Ripley had fed the Talking Head, the brief interrogation commenced. Clarence wanted to know whether he would become King. The Talking Head told him that he would not. Clarence was already angry when he asked the Talking Head how he would die. For the first and only time the Talking Head laughed.

'You will die like me,' he said. 'In a barrel!'

Ripley laughed too, but at this, Clarence in a great rage took an axe to the Talking Head's barrel. The sesame oil came gushing out and the Talking Head expired, cradled in the arms of the grieving Ripley. Then Ripley fled back to the Abbey and took the head with him. Even though he would never talk again, he has had him embalmed, in memory of the days when he was master of the future. Once he was back in his holy sanctuary, he resumed his role as director of Edward's secret agents.

One morning Anthony visits Edward in the Gruthuyse mansion and there he learns from Edward that he, Anthony, is not, as he supposed, in Holland, but in the Welsh mountains from where he and a band of zealous and bloodthirsty Yorkists are bringing death and havoc to the supporters of Henry of Lancaster and Warwick in Wales. Then, seeing the look on Anthony's face, Edward roars with laughter and explains that Ripley is up to his tricks again. From his refuge in the Abbey, Ripley, like a spider at the centre of a web, has been employing a secret army of intelligencers to put about stories that are designed to spread confusion and demoralise Edward's enemies. Anthony does not like to think of himself as being in Wales, since he understood that it was full of goblins and people who looked like goblins. But then he thinks that now perhaps he can travel to the Orient, while leaving the phantom Anthony to do what he likes in Wales.

Anthony is not the only subject of Ripley's fictions. One of the best stories is that King Henry is even madder than he looks and has come to believe that he is made of glass. That is why he takes his seat so slowly and carefully. He is frightened that his bottom may break. According to Ripley's agents, Henry is terrified of Margaret and it was her rages that drove him mad. Moreover, it seems that Henry's son Prince Edward of Lancaster, who is still in France with Margaret, has inherited a violent form of his father's madness. The Prince talks of nothing but cutting off heads or making war, as if he were the god of battle. He launches surprise attacks on his friends and tries to beat them up. Also he uses maidservants to practice his boxing on.

Another of Ripley's stories is that the Earl of Warwick is negotiating to sell England to the French King for an enormous sum of money. Of course, Ripley has made a particular set against Clarence, and has spread the story that he is about to desert Warwick, for Clarence is reported to be angry that, under the agreement of Warwick with Margaret of Anjou, Henry has been put back on the throne and moreover Henry's son, Edward, will succeed him as King, whereas, when Clarence allied with Warwick in rebellion, his understanding was that he would replace Edward on the throne and become King George the First. Now, disillusioned, he has begun secret negotiations to return to the Yorkist side. This story is close enough to the truth to be widely believed. Therefore Warwick regards Clarence with great suspicion and Clarence, for his part, senses the new coldness.

Thomas Wake has reappeared in Westminster and consequently Jacquetta has gone into hiding. There is one more piece of news. Sir Thomas Malory, as a knight of the shire, has taken his seat in Parliament. *Le Morte d'Arthur* is said to be finished, but Malory is looking for a new patron to sponsor the work since Anthony's career is finished.

Antoine, the Great Bastard of Burgundy, arrives in The Hague. Edward is briefly excited and optimistic, but though the Bastard warmly embraces Anthony, he has bad news for Edward. He has come with a message from Duke Charles that Burgundy is not prepared to finance and supply an invasion of England, nor is he prepared to welcome Edward to Bruges, for Burgundy wants peace with France and England. However, Charles will provide generous pensions to Edward and his retinue of landless lords so long as they remain quietly in Holland.

Over dinner that night, the Bastard resumes the story that he had begun in happier circumstances on the evening after his great combat with Anthony at Smithfield. So this, the story of Kriemhild's revenge, is the continuation of *The Saga of the Nibelungs*.

After the murder of Kriemhild's husband, Siegfried, by Hagen at the behest of Gunther, Attila the ruler of the Huns sought her hand in marriage and she assented and travelled to join him in Hungary. In the castle of Etzelnburg she reigned in royal splendour. She soon bore Attila a son who was called Ortlieb. As the years passed Attila came to glory in the boy's wit, courage and horsemanship. Thirteen years passed and yet Kriemhild still brooded on the murder of her husband Siegfried and the wrong done to her in Burgundy. She felt herself to be not a woman, but an instrument of fate.

Then she told Attila that she wanted to invite her beloved Burgundian kinsmen to Etzelnburg for a great feast of reconciliation and Attila agreed. When the Hun's invitation arrived at the Burgundian palace in Worms, King Gunther was charmed and flattered. Hagen, though, was not so foolish.

'Beware, my King. We must always fear Kriemhild, for I killed her husband with my own hand and at your behest.'

Gunther replied that he was not afraid of Kriemhild. Was Hagen so afraid? Thus challenged, Hagen agreed to accompany Gunther, even though he was certain that he would be riding towards his death, for he could not live with the reputation of being a coward. Three thousand knights and squires escorted Gunther towards Hungary.'

At this point Edward breaks in, 'Lord Antoine, there is no need to continue with this story, for we all know how it must end. Gunther and Hagen and everyone with them will be slaughtered. The end is right there in its beginning.'

Lord Say disagrees, 'No, in real life as in stories, we all know that we must die, but none of us knows exactly how he will die. I should like to hear how the Burgundians met their end.'

But Edward says, 'Why should you be so concerned with the fate of Gunther and Hagen and those who follow them? Gunther and Hagen were murderers and they will meet the bloody end they deserve. We know they will die and we know they should die and so the story can end straightaway.'

Now Anthony intervenes and, turning to the Bastard, asks, 'Could you not give your story a happy ending? Why not have Gunther and Hagen visit Attila and be reconciled with Kriemhild and then enjoy the feasting, music and jousting, before returning safe and sound to Burgundy? That way your story will have a happy ending that will surprise us all!'

But Edward objects that Siegfried cannot rest in his grave unavenged and the story will end happily only when Kriemhild has done what she is fated to do. Then Richard contradicts Edward and says it would be better for Kriemhild to repent, and having renounced all thought of killing Burgundians, she should retire to a convent. That would be a truly good ending.

The Bastard ignores Edward and Richard who continue

to argue about this, and he tells Anthony that it is not his personal story that he is telling, for it belongs to the whole Burgundian people and consequently it cannot be altered. Though the Bastard is annoyed by the interruptions, he is still determined to finish the story, 'When they reached the bank of the broad-flowing Danube, they could not find a ford or a ferryman. Whereupon Hagen volunteered to go and look for a ferry, even though he was sure that, if they crossed the river, they would all meet their deaths. At first there seemed to be no ferry to be found. Instead he heard splashing and the sound of laughter. Then he discovered three water fairies bathing in the great river, floating like lily pads on its surface. It was a hot day. He crept up to the bank where they were bathing and stole their clothes. They were dismayed to discover that their clothes were in this man's hands.

Then the first of the water fairies said to Hagen, 'The shadow of the future stretches into the present. We have second sight. If you will return our clothes, we will tell how your visit to Hungary will turn out for you.'

Hagen was seduced as much by their beauty as by the promise of knowledge of the future. So he agreed to this.

Then the second fairy said, 'If you cross this river and proceed on to Attila's Kingdom, you will win glory and wealth.'

Then, after he gave them back their clothes, they laughed and the third fairy said, 'My sister lied to you, because we wanted our clothes back. The truth is that you should turn back now, for if you proceed any further, you and all with you will link hands with death. Only King Gunther's chaplain will return to Burgundy to tell the tale.'

At this point Edward interrupts again, 'Why do prophecies in stories always come true? It is not so in real life. In my experience, astrologers, cunning men, wise women and weather diviners are always making predictions and they are lucky indeed if even half of what they predict comes to pass. But in a story like the one you are telling, if a water fairy tells

you that you are going to die, then that is the end of the matter. Hagen might as well lie down beside the river and ask
someone to wrap him up in a shroud. There is no point in him
going to the trouble of travelling all the way on to Etzelnburg.
Sir Antoine, forgive me, but it would be more exciting for
those who are listening to you if the water fairy turned out to
be undecided about whether or not Hagen was going to die.'

But Anthony disagrees, 'The water fairy has been waiting
for Hagen so that she may confirm his courage. We are being
told that Hagen is a hero who is undaunted in the face of certain death. The deaths of swineherds, shepherds, pie vendors
and porters are not foretold by fairies or wizards. To be the
victim of a prophecy is one of the marks of a hero.'

The Bastard nods gratefully to Anthony and continues,
'Hagen agreed that this was an evil future foretold and what
he had feared would happen, but since he is not to be deterred
from proceeding further, the water fairies guided him to a ferryman a few miles upstream and he in his turn guided Gunther
and his men to this ferry. When all the men were across Hagen
destroyed the boat so that there could be no return.

Attila was a noble and generous Hun and at first they
were royally received at his court, though it is true that some
squabbles developed between the squires and servants of both
nations. Even so, when Gunther and his senior knights sat
down to dine with Attila and his queen in the great hall on
Midsummer's Eve, all seemed well. Now Kriemhild did not
wish things to be well and therefore she summoned her son
Ortlieb to the table. The proud father Attila invited Hagen to
admire the youth who was so handsome, strong and valiant.

'He will be King one day.'

Then Attila asked Hagen to take the boy with him when
he goes back to Burgundy and supervise his growth to manhood. He would become a fine companion of arms for Hagen.

But Hagen replied, 'Were he to grow to manhood this might

be so, but the young Prince has an ill-fated look. You will never see me ride to court to wait on Ortlieb.'

Attila and his courtiers were dismayed by these words, and Kriemhild sensed that the time of her vengeance was near. She whispered to the boy, 'If you are brave, go up to Hagen and strike him a great blow on the cheek'. The innocent boy did as she suggested whereupon Hagen cut off his head, declaring as he did so, 'I have been sitting over my food too long.'

At this point, one of Hagen's comrades-in-arms came staggering into the dining hall. His sword was drawn and blood streamed over his armour.

He cried out, 'We need your strong arm, brother Hagen. I cry out injury to you, for our knights and squires have been attacked and slaughtered in their quarters.'

And so there was fighting in the great hall and throughout the castle. Attila's knights were too many for the Burgundian knights and they were all slain. Hagen and Gunther were the last to be taken. Kriemhild beheaded Gunther with Siegfried's sword and Hagen said, 'It is all exactly as I foresaw.' Then she beheaded him too. But Kriemhild did not live long to exult in her vengeance, for horrified at all the slaughter she had brought about, Attila ordered that she be executed for this atrocity. The King's high festival had ended in sorrow, as joy must ever turn to sorrow in the end.'

The Bastard has related this tale of death and doom with relish. But when he finishes his story, Edward expresses puzzlement, 'Why do most of those listening to you want Hagen to survive? He was a murderer. Kriemhild's revenge was just and yet most at this table wanted him to escape it. Personally I believe in the virtue of vengeance, as Warwick and Clarence may find out one day.'

And Richard, who does not care for romances and only reads the lives of saints, chimes in, 'Yes, why should we care what happened to Hagen? He does not exist. He never existed, except as a string of words that have issued from Sir Antoine's mouth.'

The Bastard is uncomfortable. He is sure that Hagen must have existed. He is the only famous Burgundian—apart, that is, from St Libert of Saint Trond.

But Anthony, too, has a complaint, 'A story should be more like a painting, so that we can gaze upon the people in it and the land that they inhabit. Was Kriemhild beautiful? Was Hagen ugly? What does Hungary look like? The dreadful deeds you have told us about seem to have been carried out in a great fog.'

And Richard is not going to let the matter go. He argues that not only is the story of the Nibelungs the story of people who never existed, but it is the story of imaginary, unpleasant and murderous people. The only good person in the story is Attila and he is rewarded for that by losing his wife and son. Now the argument becomes heated and Hastings, Say and Gruthuyse join in. There is widespread agreement among these lords that, despite what Richard says, Edward is right and the taking of vengeance is a virtuous act. Anthony is particularly set upon avenging the execution of his father. Let there be peace, yes, but vengeance must come first.

Then Edward says, 'Hagen wanted fame more than a long life.'

'What fame is there in killing a child like Ortlieb?' is Richard's response and he continues, 'I have heard how at Southampton the Earl of Worcester had two boys hung, drawn and quartered. Surely that was a dreadful deed and God soon punished the Earl for it.' Richard smiles briefly, before continuing. 'The Earl used to stroke my hump. He said it was for luck. Well, it seems that he did not stroke it often enough.'

'But in the end all men are punished by God, for we all die,' says Anthony. 'Tiptoft's end was, like Hagen's, a brave one. We are all here under sentence of death. Our only hope is to make a brave exit.'

'Except perhaps you, for after being killed at the Battle of Palm Sunday, you came back from death,' Edward points out and Anthony sees that now everyone is looking at him as if he is some kind of freak.

'No, we shall all die,' says Anthony. 'And since England is lost, we shall all die on a foreign shore.'

At this, Edward and Richard start to weep and Anthony and most of those at the table follow them in this. Then Edward rises and the noble lords, sad and confused, follow him out of the dining hall. As Anthony walks out, he thinks that in a day or two he will seek Edward's permission to leave him and go on a pilgrimage. He does not want to die in Holland. Jerusalem would be better.

But suddenly there is better news from England. Since Warwick has pledged himself to the service of Lancaster, he is obliged to give the Lancastrian lords back their lands and this forces him to dispossess some of his supporters, who as Yorkists had been granted Lancastrian lands and titles by Edward. And there is more. Louis has decided that time is ripe for an attack on Burgundy and Warwick is obliged to join him in the alliance against Duke Charles. The impending war with Burgundy is not popular with Londoners or those in East Anglia who are engaged in the cloth trade.

After only a few days the Great Bastard of Burgundy reappears in The Hague with a different message from Charles. Now the Duke will provide Edward with ships, money and mercenaries, and he is pressing Edward to invade England as soon as possible.

CHAPTER FOURTEEN

Barnet

They set sail from Flushing on a small fleet of boats provided by Duke Charles. Storms separate the ships and Anthony's flotilla touches the English coast at Powle. Having waded ashore, he throws himself on the pebbled beach and kisses it. Then he leads his troops south to Ravenser, at the mouth of the Humber, where Edward's ships rest in what remains of its harbour. Edward has already been reunited with the men from Richard of Gloucester's ships. Their venture is uncertain and the day feels ominous to Anthony, for Ravenser is bleak. The town was abandoned in 1362 after the Great Drowning of Men and most of it is now under water with only a spire showing above the grey rolling waves. Yet Edward standing on the narrow spit of sand, which is all that remains of Ravenser's land, seems reinvigorated. He is eager for a fight and Anthony thinks that he has lost a little weight.

But they have landed in the north where Lancastrian support is strongest, and if Edward proclaims that he has come back to reclaim his crown, he will meet with nothing but hostility in these parts. Therefore Edward puts it about that he has only come to take back the Duchy of York which is his by right of inheritance from his father. When Edward reaches Northampton he is joined by four thousand supporters of Lord Hastings. A little later, he encounters Clarence on the road. Clarence kneels before Edward and begs forgiveness. Edward raises him up and the two brothers exchange a kiss of peace. There is no sign of Warwick. Though he has instructed

London to hold out against Edward, it does not and Edward rides in triumph to give thanks in St Paul's. There is no longer any pretence that he is anything other than King of England.

Outside St Paul's, Henry is waiting under escort. Edward shakes hands with him and Henry says, 'My cousin of York, you are very welcome. I know that in your hands my life will not be in danger.'

Orders are given for Henry to be lodged once more in the Tower, before Edward rides over to Westminster Abbey to be crowned again. Elizabeth and the baby he has not seen before now are waiting for him there. Anthony encounters Ripley coming out of the Abbey. He has the embalmed Head with him, though it will talk no more.

'I am lonely without the Talking Head,' says Ripley. 'My lord, will you walk with me in the direction of the Tower? It is marvellous to see you again.'

Since Anthony is eager to learn what has been happening in England while he was in exile, he agrees. For a while Ripley talks of politics and of the strange coalition of Lancastrians and breakaway Yorkists that has been trying to govern the country until now. Then he starts to speculate about the future, as he is always prone to do. There will have to be a battle to decide things.

Then Anthony, who has been having recurrent dreams about the Great Sheep that devours all England, remembers that he dreamt last night that Edward took up arms against the Great Sheep, but then he and all his army were destroyed by the baa that flattened men, horses, trees and buildings. He fears it bodes ill for any coming encounter with Warwick. Surely the dream is warning him against going into battle?

Ripley has no time at all for this, 'My lord, a man's honour cannot depend on what he has dreamt. Dreams are fool's gold. They hold a distorting mirror to the world we must live in. The dream seeks to entertain the sleeping man with stories, but it narrates those stories very badly, for the dream is slapdash and complacent and it can afford to be both of these things as it addresses a man who is asleep, but who does not know that he is asleep and hence he is the dream's captive. The dreamer is like a man detained in a tavern by an unwelcome acquaintance who insists on telling him a story, even though the acquaintance is so drunk and incompetent that he can get neither the logic nor the details of the story right. The dream does not know how to plot a story and it is unable to fill in the background that would be essential to it. Nor does the dream know how to finish a story, for its narration may build to some great climax like a battle, a coronation, or a magical transformation, but then the dream carries on regardless, as if nothing conclusive has happened. In order to prolong its existence, the dream gabbles away and seizes on a random assortment of people and things in order to feed its gabbling. The dream cannot manage more than the briefest snatches of conversation. It harps excessively on anxiety and embarrassment. My lord, our life is no dream and thank God for that!'

While saying this Ripley has become heated, Anthony perceives that Ripley's venom against the dream is occasioned by the fact that Ripley sees the dream as a rival storyteller.

'Well perhaps the stories dreams tell us are not very good,' says Anthony. 'But is it not the case that a dream may foretell the future?'

Ripley cannot agree, 'It is only in legends and fairy stories that the predictions made by dreams invariably come true. I once dreamt that I became Sultan of Egypt and on another occasion I dreamt that I was turned by magic into a leopard. I think that neither of these dreams is ever likely to come true. Believe me, my lord, the dream has no access to the Secret Library.'

By now they are close to the Woodville townhouse and so Anthony says farewell to Ripley, who is carrying the Head on to deposit it in Tiptoft's Museum of Skulls inside the Tower. When Tiptoft first became Constable of England he gave orders that, once the heads of traitors had been embalmed and displayed for a few days on spikes over the gates of London Bridge, then they should be collected and returned to the Tower where they would find a place in his Museum. Nobody knows what the purpose of this Museum is, and now the Earl is dead, he cannot tell them. Indeed his own head occupies pride of place in the Museum which is one of the mysteries of the Tower.

There is an inscription over the entrance to the Museum:

La pluie nous a debués et laves,
Et soleil dessechiés et noircis;
Pies, corbeax, nous ont les yeux caves,
Et arraché la barbe et les sourcis.
Jamais nul temps nous ne sommes assis;
Puis ça, puis la, comme le varie,
A son plaisir sans cesser nous charie,
Plus becquetés d'oiseaux que dés à coudre,
Ne soiez donc de nostre confrerie;
Mais priez dieu que tous nous veuille absoudre.

Tiptoft had translated for Anthony: 'The rain has washed and scrubbed us; we are dried and blackened by the sun. Magpies and crows have pecked out our eyes and plucked our beards and eyebrows. We are never allowed to rest, but driven this way and that by the changing wind. The birds have pecked at us till we are more pitted than a thimble. So do not join our brotherhood, but pray to God that he will forgive us all.'

When Tiptoft had told Anthony that it was a verse from *La Ballade des Pendus* (*The Ballad of the Hanged Men*) by François Villon, Anthony replied that he knew all about Villon. Tiptoft had seemed surprised and disappointed to hear this.

Now at the townhouse Anthony is joyously reunited with Black Saladin. But his encounter with his mother is not joyous at all. She too has only just returned to the house after having hidden in a convent for the duration of Henry's Readeption. Dressed in black satin, Jacquetta seems to be shrinking into its blackness. She mutters dark things about Warwick and others who were his accomplices in the murder of her husband, but then there are other things on her mind.

'They are stealing from me,' she whispers. 'Wherever I hide my money, they find it and spirit it away.'

Who is stealing from her? She cannot say. She has drifted on to another topic.

'The magic is passing out of England,' she whispers. 'The days of the great sorceresses, Medea, Morgan le Fay, Nimue and the others whose names I now forget, are long past. Conjurations that were once possible are no longer so. Just a few cantrips can be made. We are of our time and soon our time will be over. Times change and we change in those times. When I am dead (and that is something I long for) there will be yet less magic in the world. The rule of the knights will pass too, for the autumn of chivalry has already arrived. The leaves are turning brown with the clouds.'

Then having thought of something else, she warns Anthony against Ripley, 'He is a dabbler who does not really understand what he is dabbling in. He does not realise what consequences his stories may have in the real world. You must not let him in.' She pauses for a moment and then moves onto yet another thing, 'Soon they will come for me too and spirit me away. You will seek me, but not find me.'

She waves Anthony away, but as he leaves the room he can hear that she is still talking to herself. It is not magic that is passing away, but her mind.

Two days later, Edward, having mustered his army just beyond Aldersgate, leads them north-west in search of Warwick's forces. He judges that it is vital to find and engage with Warwick before Margaret with her Lancastrian and French contingents land in England and join forces with the Earl.

Edward has brought the captive Henry of Lancaster along with him, since the deposed King is too precious a pawn to be left behind in London. Ripley is also part of Edward's retinue and he is said to be there to advise the King on the weather. Ripley is looking forward to a battle, or rather to its aftermath, where he expects to garner a plentiful harvest of eyeballs.

Two days later, as dusk is falling, Edward's scourers locate Warwick's army just beyond the little town of Barnet. Edward leads his army through the silent and darkened town. It is eerie. No drums are beaten, no trumpets blown. There is not even any talking, but only the soft clinking of harnesses and armour. Despite the silence of the Yorkist advance, Warwick knows that they have arrived, even if he cannot be sure of the exact positions they have taken in the darkness, and at first Edward, for his part, is uncertain of the exact dispositions of Warwick and his Lancastrian allies.

Eventually Edward's scourers determine where Warwick has carefully placed his men behind thick hedges and drainage ditches. Warwick has brought a huge artillery train with him and soon after the Yorkists have taken up their positions, his cannons start firing. But in the ink-black darkness Warwick and his fellow commanders have not realised how very close the Yorkist line is to the Lancastrian one and consequently the Lancastrian gunners are consistently overshooting their target. Edward gives orders to his artillerymen not to return fire for fear of revealing the Yorkists' true position. Horses are parked half a mile back, lights are doused and on the rare occasion when a stray ball from a bombard hits one of his men, that man's companions jump on him to stifle his screams and groans.

The thunder of artillery makes for a sleepless night. Anthony wishes that the dawn would hurry up. A battle is a strange business. It is as if thousands of men had gathered together outside Barnet to throw dice in order to determine whether they would live or die. So a battle is a gaming house. If Warwick wins here, he takes all. He will have the feeble shadow King Henry back once more.

Edward will probably be taken and killed, together with Richard of Gloucester, Anthony and other leading figures. Warwick's army will join up with Margaret's when finally it arrives in England. London will have to open its gates to the coalition of Lancastrian forces. The Yorkist cause will be lost beyond any redemption. The warlike, but vicious Edward of Lancaster will eventually succeed the sainted idiot that is his father. On the other hand, if King Edward wins at Barnet, he still has Margaret's army and other Lancastrian forces to deal with.

Now, as Anthony restlessly paces about, he bumps into Lord Hastings. Hastings is very cheerful. He has just been with the King and Ripley. Ripley has predicted that as soon as day breaks they will find that there is a thick mist. When Anthony objects that this might favour the Lancastrians as much as the Yorkists, Hastings replies that the Yorkists are certain to win this battle, for Ripley had consulted the Talking Head about it a year ago and got the good news then. It had not occurred to Anthony that, when he and Tiptoft ceased their questioning of the Talking Head, Ripley would have the temerity to continue investigations on his own. Anthony thanks Hastings for this information and goes in search of Ripley. The alchemist is not easy to find in the murk, but when Anthony finds him, he grabs him.

'Tell me, Ripley, what is my fate in this battle? Shall I fight well? Shall I be wounded? Shall I die?'

But Ripley, without replying, slithers out of Anthony's grasp and vanishes into the darkness.

Sometime before dawn breaks, trumpets blast out and at last Edward commands his artillery and archers to return fire, before ordering a general advance. He means to close with the Lancastrian line before its gunners can see what they should be firing at. As Edward's men advance, so does the mist. It rises from the ground and billows around the plodding knights and sergeants. It is most strange. By the time they reach the enemy's position they can hardly see more than a couple of feet in front of them. Thereafter it is all shouting and confusion. Anthony, who has no idea at all what is happening elsewhere on the field, uses the spike of his poleaxe to stab at men-at-arms who wear the badge of Warwick's brother, Lord Montagu. There is a fearful press of men around him. From far away to the left come shouts of 'Treason!' Then quite suddenly Anthony finds that he is no longer on his feet. He struggles to get up, but cannot, for it is as if one of his legs is no longer there. The frontline of battle seems to have moved on in front of him. He can hear the shouting, but the fighting is out of sight. He stretches his hand down to his left leg and, to his relief, finds that it is still there, but when he brings his hand back up to look at it, it is red with blood. Then he decides that he might as well sleep.

When he awakes, he is in a pavilion and his wound is being tightly bandaged by the King's surgeon. He has lost a lot of blood, but the wound seems to be a clean one. The surgeon had wanted him to be carried back to London on a litter, but Anthony gets men to help him mount Black Saladin and he rides back to London with the King. It is only as he rides that he learns what happened in the battle that he was in. The main thing is that the two armies were misaligned, with the result that the Lancastrian right wing under the Earl of Oxford was much stronger than the Yorkist left wing and swiftly routed them. The routed troops fled through Barnet and onwards spreading alarm and despondency as far as London. Oxford was successful in rallying his men outside Barnet and bringing them back to the battlefield. Oxford's banners displayed the heraldic emblem of a star with golden rays. It looked rather like King Edward's emblem of a sun with golden rays. And so, as Oxford's men advanced through the mist, Montagu's men mistook them for Yorkists and fired upon them. Then there were shouts of 'Treason!' and the Lancastrians started to flee in all directions. Warwick and Montagu, who had left their mounts in the horse park, were surrounded and cut down. Edward is bringing their naked corpses back to London to have them displayed in St Paul's. Oxford, Exeter and Beaumont are also dead. Ripley does not travel back with the King. He is on the battlefield with the other scavengers and he is happily putting eyeballs into flasks filled with alcohol.

Just short of London Edward is intercepted by a messenger. Margaret and her forces have landed at Weymouth. Edward's soldiers are allowed only a few days' rest in London before he has them marching west. Since Anthony is not judged fit to go into battle again, he is made Constable of the Tower of London for the duration of the crisis. This time Edward will not take Henry of Lancaster with him on campaign and Anthony's chief task is to secure Henry from any Lancastrian attempt to free him and to that end Anthony has been given an extra force of a hundred men-at-arms. Otherwise every able-bodied knight and man-at-arms is to accompany Edward as he heads west in an attempt to stop Margaret and Edward of Lancaster joining forces with Jasper Tudor.

Though Anthony's duties do not seem to be onerous, he takes them seriously.

The first thing he does is have those who are suspected of having Lancastrian sympathies rounded up and brought to the Tower to be incarcerated there. One of these is Sir Thomas Malory. He is brought under escort to Anthony. He hobbles on two sticks and he seems to have difficulty raising his head.

'You see me here, a broken old man,' he says. 'What possible danger can I be to you or your party?' Then, 'If I told you how the story of the lady and the bratchet ends, then would you set me free?'

Anthony does not reply. But perhaps Malory speaks the truth. And he would like to hear the rest of that story.

Then Malory says, 'Last night I dreamt that this would happen. I should have made my escape when I could.'

'Do you believe that dreams can foretell the future?'

Malory replies, 'Dreams are subtle spirits and I believe that sometimes they may shape the future. I am reminded of something that happened only a few years ago. A pedlar called John Chapman of Swaffham in Norfolk dreamt that, if he went to London Bridge, he would find a man who would tell him how he might become rich. So he travelled down to London and stood on the bridge for hours, but nothing happened and nobody spoke to him and he was feeling quite a fool. Finally he went into one of the shops on the bridge to buy a pie, I think, and he told the shopkeeper about his dream and how foolish it was and the shopkeeper agreed with him that dreams were indeed foolish things. For his part, he had dreamt only last night that he saw treasure being buried in the garden of a certain John Chapman in Norfolk, but the shopkeeper was not going all the way to Norfolk on a fool's errand and he said to Chapman, 'Go home and mind your business'. Then Chapman went home and started digging in his garden, and sure enough, he found two pots of gold buried beneath the roots of the tree. I have been to Swaffham and seen the house he built with this money. Also he paid for the north aisle and tower of Swaffham church.'

'It is a curious dream.' Anthony sits pondering a while before he speaks again.

'Why did the dream wish to make Chapman rich? And why did it work so crookedly? What did it need the pie merchant for? What has made the pie merchant a slave of destiny? It makes me dizzy to think about it all. I feel like a man on the edge of an abyss. Why do dreams always speak in riddles?'

'It is my opinion that it was not that the dream was so keen to make Chapman rich, but rather that it wished to make itself famous,' replies Malory. 'In any case, it is no stranger than the dream I had a week ago. Then I dreamt that I met a man who told me that if ever I was in a room full of skulls, I should find a fortune there. But where shall I ever find a catacomb in England? I know of none such. Should I travel perhaps to Rome at the behest of a dream?'

'Follow me,' says Anthony. 'Now we two shall put dreams to the test.'

Though Anthony is limping, Malory still has difficulty in keeping up with him as they make their way to the Museum of Skulls and once in there he is of little assistance, as Anthony searches behind the shelves and raps on walls in search of the treasure that Tiptoft must have hidden. Malory just gazes vacantly around him. Lit from below by a lantern, hundreds of eyes are fixed upon them, hungry for life. It is as if Anthony and Malory have interrupted a solemn conclave of the dead. Suddenly, Malory points to one of the heads and says, 'I know that man. Or rather I knew him.'

He is pointing to the Talking Head.

Anthony swivels round and grabs Malory by the jerkin.

'Who is he? Who was he? What was his name? What did you have to do with him? Speak man, or, by God, I will have you put to the rack.'

Malory's response is calm, 'We were together in Ludgate Gaol. His name was Jack Coterel. Like me he was often in and out of prison. He did terrible things, for he regularly hired himself out as an assassin, but though he was often indicted, he always escaped hanging since he had an influential friend at court.'

'What friend was this?'

'Jack was close with the royal jester. I think that the jester's name was Scoggin.'

Hearing these words, Anthony unbuckles his purse and gives it to Malory. Then, without saying a word, he leads him to an office at the foot of the Byward Tower where he sits down to write a letter. This he passes to Malory. Malory is to present this letter to the steward of the Woodville townhouse, whereupon he will be given a small chest full of gold. Anthony escorts him out of the Tower before returning to the office to write another letter. This one is to go to Westminster and it requests the arrest of Scoggin and his deliverance in shackles to the Tower.

What shall he do while he is waiting for Scoggin to be brought to him? Then he remembers that there is the matter of Tiptoft's legacy. Tiptoft has bequeathed almost all his considerable collection of books to be added to the library of Humphrey Bodley in Oxford. But in a codicil he has stipulated that Earl Rivers should be entitled to pick out ten or so books for himself. So now Anthony makes his way to the late Earl of Worcester's townhouse and after some negotiation with the porter and the steward, he is introduced to the Tiptoft's librarian who conducts him to the books. Anthony has never been in a room that is completely full of books before and he gazes round in wonder. The air is thick with the smell of leather, vellum and parchment. Who could have believed that there were so many books in the world?

Then he starts to look at the books in more detail. They are quite strange. There is a shelf full of manuscripts devoted to men who built themselves wings and attempted to fly and another shelf devoted to earth-eaters and the types of soil and clay that are deemed to be particularly edible. There is a manuscript on how to simulate the appearance of leprosy. Anthony studies a fat volume full of diagrams illustrating ways of manufacturing mechanical horses and chess players. There is an Etruscan grammar. And a manual on how to construct a revolving door. Another one on how to construct a wife from flowers. Another on cooking with testicles. Also one on sticks that feature in the Bible and in the lives of saints. There is an armorial roll displaying the heraldry of the ancient Egyptians.

Anthony is shocked that Tiptoft possesses a copy of *The Three Imposters*. This book Anthony has at least heard of, for he knows that it is a sinister book which sets out to demonstrate that Moses, Mohammed and Jesus were all charlatans. Anthony cannot bring himself even to touch it. There is a case full of treatises dealing with torture and executions. *How Boys Bathe in Finland* contains some rather odd illustrations. So does another manuscript which has no title and which is in a script unknown to Anthony. In the margins there are drawings of plants that are also unknown to him and constellations of stars that have never been seen in our sky. Also there are many images of naked women frolicking and bathing and they alternate with unfamiliar abstract structures. Anthony gazes at drawings of things which might be buildings, though they also seem to be plants. It is beyond all understanding. The Earl's own translation of a treatise on baldness, gold-tooled and bound in black leather, has its own lectern.

As Anthony gazes on all these books, he becomes increasingly uneasy. There is something that is wrong here, though he cannot put his finger on it. Then he begins to consider the way books are ordered. They are indeed ordered, but the connections between neighbouring books on a shelf are rarely the sort that any normal human being would make and he sees that Tiptoft had arranged his books in such a manner as to take the curious browser down some very strange paths of thought—his own paths of thought and he was mad and now Anthony realises that the mad Earl still lived in some manner through the ordered chaos of his library.

He shudders and hastily chooses out the most ordinary books he can find. These are Chaucer's *Book of the Lion*, Bede's *Song of Judith*, Richard Rolle's *Tower of All Towers*, William of Malmesbury's *De Antiquitate Glastoniensis Ecclesiae*, *The Saga of Earl Godwin*, Lydgate's *Siege of Thebes*, *The History of the Two Guineveres*, *The Matter of Troy* and a pretty little book in Spanish entitled *Cardenio* which Anthony picks for its miniature illustrations. Then, having arranged for a servant to come and collect these books, he hurries out.

As he walks back to the Tower, he thinks that he will saddle up Black Saladin and go riding out on a quest for what he
thinks of as the enchanted garden. This is not to be, for when
he returns to the Tower there are three messengers waiting for
him. The first messenger claims he carries important news. On
breaking the seals of this document, Anthony finds that it is a
short treatise by the Abbot of Crowland on why there are no
volcanoes in England and this he tosses aside. Next he turns
impatiently to a letter in the Queen's hand. After affectionate
greetings, Elizabeth reports that she has had enquiries made
and it appears that Scoggin left royal service over a year ago
and no one knows what has become of him. The third letter contains worse news. It is from the Bishop of Rochester
and he reports that a kinsman of the late Earl of Warwick,
Thomas Neville, better known as the Bastard of Fauconberg,
has landed in Kent. He has brought with him hundreds of
men from the Calais garrison and he has been joined by thousands of Kentish rebels. They are now marching on London,
and when they have occupied the city, their intention is to
place Henry on the throne once more. They also plan to join
forces with the Earl of Warwick whom Fauconberg claims is
not really dead.

Now Anthony has to bustle. Edward and the Yorkist army
are at Coventry. There is no hope of any help from that quarter. Anthony commands the regular garrison of the Tower, a
little over two hundred men and these are supplemented by
the extra hundred that Edward gave him. There will be a few
Yorkist knights who arrived in London after Edward's departure. There may be other Yorkists who will flee from Kent in
advance of the rebels. There is a garrison of forty at Baynard's
Castle. It is nowhere near enough to defend the city. Should
Anthony make for Coventry, taking the captive Henry with
him?

He summons the Mayor Stockton and his aldermen to
a meeting. Though they are terrified by the approach of the

Kentish army, Anthony eventually understands that this is a good thing, for what the Mayor and his friends have realised is that men of Kent have not risen because they are devoted to the memory of the Earl of Warwick, or because they need to see mad Henry on the throne once more. No, the men of Kent have joined Fauconberg because they are devoted to the prospect of sacking London. It would be as it was when London was looted and burnt during the Peasants' Revolt and then again by Jack Cade's men a little over twenty years ago. Consequently the citizens of London will defend it to the last. Also Thomas Bourchier, the Earl of Essex, arrives while the meeting is still going on and he agrees to serve as Anthony's deputy. Then the Queen arrives from Westminster with a handful of courtier knights and a troop of royal archers. London will be defended.

'But we have no experience of fighting,' says Stockton.

Nevertheless Anthony gives orders that the armoury of the Tower be opened and its store of weapons be distributed among the town bands. These weapons soon run out. Then Anthony remembers the tiltyard and leads a body of aldermen and their followers to it. Raker is first grumpily pleased to see Anthony, then furious that his stock of antique arms and armour is to be commandeered in the service of the defence of London, and finally delighted to learn that he will be paid for the weapons and for his service as a captain in charge of a town band. It is a long time since he has seen real fighting, and Kent being halfway to France, Kentish men are evil creatures. His leathery face breaks into a rare grin. It is like watching an ice floe breaking up, or so Anthony supposes, for he has never seen an ice floe. Raker immediately commences the drilling of shopkeepers, porters and apprentices in the management of war hammers and pikestaffs.

Fauconberg and his forces arrive and camp just outside Southwark from where he sends to the Mayor, aldermen and commonalty demanding to be admitted to the city. He promises that there will be no looting and that all victuals will be paid for. The Mayor sends back the message first that he was charged by King Edward to keep the city safe, secondly that he does not believe Fauconberg's promise and thirdly he adds that, contrary to Fauconberg's claims, the Earl of Warwick really is dead, for his corpse has been displayed at the church of St Paul's.

Meanwhile barrels full of sand are being placed all the way along the north shore of the Thames from Baynard's Castle to the Tower of London and artillery is moved into position.

Back at the Tower of London all is noise and confusion. Anthony ascends to the battlements of the White Tower where there is peace. He looks over the river to Fauconberg's encampment on St George's Field, where there is also confusion, and to houses on the edge of Southwark that are on fire. Then beyond the encampment there are fields and hedges, as well as trees that are late in coming into leaf. It is May and he can see some farmers, neglectful of the closeness of war, weeding what will probably turn out to be cornfields. He feels a shadow pass over him and he looks up to see a kestrel circling in widening gyres in its quest for prey. England is a ship sailing into the future and he is in its crow's nest. Then he descends.

Anthony remembers his service with Fauconberg at Alnwick. Though he thought of him as a cautious and uninspiring commander, he may have bolder officers under him. Fauconberg waits till Sunday before launching an attack on London Bridge. Though he manages to destroy the gate and some of the houses on the south end of the bridge, he is outgunned on the bridge. After this defeat he marches his men towards Kingston, where perhaps he planned to cross the Thames. Then he changes his mind and returns to St George's Field from where he organises a crossing of the river in small boats. By now his cause is desperate, for news has arrived in London that King Edward has won a great victory at Tewkesbury. Edward of Lancaster is dead and the King is bringing

Margaret back to London in a cage. So he essays one last throw
and the rabble that is his army attempts simultaneous assaults
on London Bridge, Aldgate and Bishopsgate. Bourchier leads
a sally out of Bishopsgate, while Anthony, mounted on Black
Saladin, leads an army of four hundred knights and foot out
through a postern gate of the Tower to make a flank attack
on the rebels outside Aldgate. Many of Anthony's men are
guildsmen and apprentices, but then many of those they fight
are peasants and they rout those peasants. Anthony orders
casks of wine to be rolled out to reward his following. The
wound he gained at Barnet has reopened, but he is otherwise
uninjured. He is talking with Raker about the day's events.
Raker is unwounded, but nevertheless he grumbles about the
aches and pains that the day's fighting has brought upon him.

'At least Jesus avoided the indignity of growing old,' he
says.

Then something strange happens. A bearded man comes
up to Anthony.

'My lord, do you not recognise me?'

Anthony looks carefully at the man, but no.

'I am Piers. You stayed with me in my hermitage and I
tended to your eyes when you had gone blind. When you
stayed with me, I saw that you did not approve of the hermit's
way of life and then I thought that I was beginning to weary
of it too. So now I am in London and have much business
here. But it has been good to see you so well and with no
problems with your eyes.'

And with that, the man who says that he is Piers bustles
off.

'He had the look of an old soldier,' says Raker.

Fauconberg lingers at Blackheath for a few days more, but
it is now certain that Edward's army is returning to London
and everyone knows that the Lancastrian cause is forever finished. Fauconberg flees to Kent. Eventually his head will find
its way into the Museum of Skulls.

A week later, Edward is only fifteen or so miles north of London. His triumphant army will parade through the city on the following day. But Clarence and Gloucester arrive at the Tower late on the preceding day, at the hour that is, 'between the dog and the wolf'. They tell Anthony that he must conduct them immediately to Henry of Lancaster who is in the Wakefield Tower.

'Cousins of Clarence and Gloucester and er... You are most welcome,' says Henry. His smile is trembly. 'Will you sit and have some wine?'

Gloucester looks at Clarence and nods. So they all sit and Henry, with a shaking hand, pours wine from an earthenware jug. Neither Clarence nor Gloucester seems inclined to speak, so Henry breaks the silence, 'Is it true my boy, that Edward of Lancaster is dead?'

Gloucester nods and then Henry says, 'I do not blame you, Richard. I forgive you. I swear there is no malice in me—or you, I am sure.'

Anthony notices that urine is trickling down Henry's leggings. Then Gloucester looks hard at Clarence who shakes his head vigorously before gulping down more wine. So then Gloucester says, 'Perhaps it is time for your prayers, Henry?'

'Yes, yes. I usually pray about now.'

And the former King goes to kneel in a corner. Gloucester picks up the jug, which is still half full, and smashes it against the back of Henry's head and blood and wine are sprayed all over the cell.

'A man does good business when he rids himself of a turd,' says Gloucester. 'But this was your job, George, since Edward entrusted the commission to you. I swear that you fail every test that is given to you.' Then to Anthony he says, 'You are our witness. What we have done, we have done for the good of the state.'

In the past Anthony has admired Gloucester's piety and his skill as a military commander. Now he admires his resolution.

But he also thinks that he will keep his distance from this man who is also a villain.

The following morning it is announced that Henry has died of pure displeasure and melancholy on hearing of the outcome of the Battle of Tewkesbury and the death of his son. His body is displayed in St Paul's where his head rests on a thick pillow of flowers. Now that there is peace at last, Anthony thinks that he may seek out Malory and learn more from him about Jack Coterel and in that way perhaps find some clues as to the present whereabouts of Scoggin. Also he may hunt for the enchanted garden. Also he may travel east to Scythia, Persepolis, the fiery lakes and Xanadu.

CHAPTER FIFTEEN

Coterels

For the past three weeks Anthony has garrisoned himself in the Tower. Now at last he returns to the Woodville town-house. It strikes him as he dismounts from Black Saladin that the groom is made nervous by his arrival. Then it is Ripley who opens the door to him. Ripley's welcome is effusive, and of course, he is full of praise for the charge that Anthony led against the Kentish rebels. The steward of the house, John Bromwich, hurries up behind Ripley and shrugs his shoulders at Anthony. Then his mother comes shuffling to the doorway. She looks at Anthony curiously, but it seems that she does not recognise him. Instead she takes Ripley by the arm and leads him away. Ripley looks back and smiles, as if to say, 'You see how it is.'

Anthony and Bromwich confer in the accounting room. Anthony says that he wants Ripley to be politely told to leave. Bromwich says that he has tried to close the door to him, but his mother will not allow the alchemist to go. The day Anthony left for the Tower Ripley arrived at the Woodville townhouse and sought an audience with Jacquetta. Since then she does not like to be parted from him. Instead she is his shadow who stumbles behind him everywhere in the house. Though it has become very difficult for the servants to understand what she is saying, Ripley has no difficulty in this and they spend long hours conversing and often he writes down what she says. Most nights he sleeps just outside her door where he stretches out on the floor and uses a cloak for a pillow. Often she wakes in the night and then they talk some more. He feeds her (as once he fed the Talking Head). But since Edward's return Ripley has been frequently called away on the King's business and then she wanders around the house, a lost soul.

Various documents are spread upon the table awaiting Anthony's attention and beside them is an enormous pile of manuscripts, on top of which there is a covering message. From this Anthony learns that Sir Thomas Malory has died and has bequeathed to him one of the copies of *Le Morte d'Arthur*. Anthony's first vague thought is that now he will never hear how the story of the lady and the bratchet ended. Then he wonders what happened to all the gold that he gave Malory. It is sad that he did not live to enjoy his wealth. Also, if Anthony wants to learn more about Jack Coterel, he will have to find other men to give him the information he needs. He asks Bromwich if he knows anything about a Jack Coterel and the steward replies that there are many Coterels. There is a great gang of them and from what is known as their Secret Commonwealth in Southwark, they are reputed to carry out many criminal acts. But Bromwich knows no more than that.

Then Anthony has Ripley brought before him. Before Anthony can speak, Ripley does, 'My lord, I fear that it will not be long now. I crave your hospitality and indulgence for a few days more. Soon your mother will no longer be able to stand. It is painful to see, yet I should like to be with her until the end. To be honest, though I feel pity for her, I will not conceal from you that I profit from her talk.'

Anthony gestures that he should continue. Then Ripley explains that the fairies, knowing that she will shortly die, are stripping her of everything she ever leant from them.

'She calls them fairies. I do not know what they are, but they steal things from her mind. Her head still retains some of the secret knowledge and I try to make a record of as much of it as I can, though some of it is muddled and often there are bits missing from the spells. A sorceress is nothing without her memory and Jacquetta de St Pol is losing hers.'

Anthony sternly says that his mother is not and has never been a sorceress and Ripley hastily agrees. Only he thinks that she has acquired some knowledge of what sorceresses do.

Then Ripley talks about rivalry between magicians and how when one magician enters into combat with another he attacks his enemy's memory. And then he says that we are all mostly dead before we die, for most of what we have experienced when younger has passed into oblivion. It is the ravages of forgetfulness and these many thousands of little deaths that make the final death less hard to bear. Then he starts to lecture on the subject of mnemonics…

But now Anthony raises his hand. With an ill grace he allows Ripley to stay a few days longer, even though he is quietly angry that Ripley has usurped his place with his mother. As Ripley, much relieved, is about to depart, Anthony asks what he knows about the Coterels. Ripley knows a little more than Bromwich, but not much more.

In the days that follow Anthony speaks with some of Ripley's intelligencers, with ward beadles, watchmen and one of London's sheriffs and slowly a picture is built up. The Coterels are a long-established business—though perhaps business is hardly the right word for it. They have been operating out of Southwark for almost a hundred and fifty years and so they have a longer history than the houses of Lancaster or York. The Coterels have powerful protectors. They are a large clan and other smaller clans are allied and subordinate to them. They specialise in abductions and ransoms. But they also steal lead piping, collect money from prostitutes, persuade foolish investors to take part in bogus treasure hunts and they train pickpockets. They have a schoolroom above a tavern in Southwark where lots of purses with bells attached are suspended from the ceiling and it is here that the young pickpockets are trained. The Coterels broker the sale of stolen property back to their owners. They also provide equipment for burglars.

One of the late Jack Coterel's cousins, Hugo is known as 'the trainer of tortoises'. A burglar, equipped with one of these trained tortoises, fixes a lighted candle to its shell and then slips it through the window of the house he proposes to burgle. If he then hears someone say, 'What is a tortoise with a candle on its back doing in my house?' or words like that, then the burglar will abandon his planned robbery, but if there is no sound then he may enter the house and the tortoise can serve to light him to whatever he desires to loot. The clan has its own private language, a thieves' cant. They also have an alphabet of signs they use to chalk up on houses, marking those houses as safe or dangerous places to burgle, as well as those owners who are charitable to beggars and those that are mean. Anthony is disturbed by some of what he has learnt, for he is accustomed to think of the settling of issues by violence to be an aristocratic prerogative.

Two weeks after Edward's triumphant return to London Mayor Stockton presides over a celebratory open-air banquet in a meadow beside the gardens of Holborn. Edward and Elizabeth and the King's two brothers attend, as well as many of the leading peers, the aldermen and the two sheriffs of London. Anthony receives much praise for his defence of the city. (Ripley's men have been at work magnifying Anthony's feats of arms at Aldgate.) Fish baked in pastry, swan's meat, venison in frumenty, glazed meat-apples, fritters and various subtleties are among the dishes served to the mayor's guests.

Anthony is leaning against a tree at his ease and cheerful, for he has belatedly realised that he can read what happened to the lady and the bratchet as soon as he finds the time to leaf through the pages of Malory's manuscript. Suddenly he is approached by two young men. They must be brothers, for they have the same square jaws and curly brown hair. Moreover both wear slashed doublets of black and yellow cut in the fashionable Italian style. They nod respectfully before introducing themselves, 'I am Toby Coterel.'

'And I Barnaby Coterel.'

Then Toby continues, 'My lord, we hear that you have been asking many questions about our family and we thought that we would save you further trouble by coming here today to answer any questions that you may have. We are entirely at your service.'

Anthony is pinned against the tree. The brothers have daggers at their waists. He is unarmed. He could, of course, cry out for help. But in this company that would be absurd. He would never be able to live the shame of that down. So finally he says, 'I am trying to find out what has happened to Scoggin who was formerly the King's jester and I thought that he might have had friends in Southwark who would know of his whereabouts.'

The Coterel brothers look suddenly cheerful.

'That Scoggin! What a marvel he was! He used to come to one of the schools that we have endowed in Southwark and he would entertain the apprentices with japes and merry quips. How they loved him! Tell me, my lord. What is the distance between the top of the sky and the bottom of the ocean?'

Anthony does not know.

'Why, it is but a stone's throw! Ah, ha ha!'

'And at what time of the year does a goose have most feathers on her?'

This time Anthony has the answer, 'When she has a gander on her back.'

And Toby asks, 'It is good to laugh, is it not? And it is sad that he is no longer with us. Where are we without the blessed gift of laughter?'

'What? Is Scoggin dead?' Anthony is alarmed that the Angel of Death may have cheated him of his vengeance.

'God bless you, my lord. I only meant that he is no longer in London and that he has repented his folly and forever renounced his former profession as a jester. He now holds that jokes are heinous and that for what remains of his life he will seek to purge himself of the sins he has accumulated in his former profession. He told us that from henceforth he would have nothing to do with the fellowship of we Coterels and that jokes are all either cruel or trivial. According to the new Scoggin, God wishes us all to live soberly, but we think it is a sad business. We hear that he has become a monk in a village called Pirbright.'

'Thank you for this.' Anthony is astonished by the information and the manner in which it has been delivered.

'You have become the hero of all London,' says Barnaby. 'It has been an honour to have talked with you, and we hope, to have been of assistance.'

Mayor Stockton is approaching. The brothers bow to Anthony before smartly walking away from the banqueting throng and out of the meadow.

Anthony thinks that once he has found Scoggin and dealt with him, he will travel. He will say that he is going to Portugal as a Crusader to fight against the Saracens, but after Portugal, he will travel on to the fabled deserts and jungles of the East. Edward looks very merry. Perhaps now would be a good time to approach him?

It is not the right time. Edward is furious.

'Are you quite mad, Anthony? I have only regained the throne within the last few weeks. The country still crawls with rebels. There is a huge amount to be done restoring all the damage caused by the recent strife. I need you here in London close by me. On pain of death you are forbidden to leave the country for Portugal or any place else. I will not see England's resources squandered in wars with Saracens. It is the coward's way to slink off when there is much work to be done. So many great lords have died—Tiptoft, Pembroke, Somerset, Say, Warwick, Montagu, Oxford and many others. Because of that those that are left must work harder.'

Then Hastings, who is standing close by, adds, 'And drink and wench harder.'

And Edward's customary good spirits are restored.

A week later, instead of Jerusalem or Babylon, Anthony has arrived at Pirbright. He arrives there in early afternoon. The monastery is a small place a little way out of the village and half in ruins, and thus not to be compared to the great Abbey of Crowland. There is a gatehouse, but no gate and looking through Anthony sees that half the cloister has become rubble. The Abbot, a well-built twinkly man, comes to what should have been the door. His welcome is unceremonious, 'If you have stopped here to seek accommodation, I am sorry but there is none. You will need to ride on to the great Abbey of Chertsey. It is not far.'

'Thank you, I have no need of lodgings or food. I am Earl Rivers and I carry a message from the King summoning his jester to Westminster.'

'Goodness an Earl!' The Abbot flutters his hands. 'But good sir, there is no jester here. We are all monks and our prayers and our labours are most serious.'

'I mean the man Scoggin who was formerly the King's jester.'

By now it seems that the entire population of the monastery, doubtless curious to learn what has brought a rare visitor here, has gathered behind the Abbot. There are five monks in the white robes of the Cistercian order and six boys. There is something about the boys that strikes Anthony as sinister. They are all blond and they gaze at him with cold curiosity. Scoggin is one of the monks. There is another monk whose face seems oddly familiar, though Anthony cannot think why. Perhaps he has seen him at Crowland?

The Abbot babbles away. This monastery, which once thrived, has fallen into disuse, and as can be seen, local people have stolen much of the wood and stonework. The monks' task now is to recolonise the place, though as Anthony can see there are only six of them, and so far only the two dorters, the kitchen and the brewhouse have been fully restored, though work on the roof of the church is far advanced. The orchard is horridly overgrown. The Abbot fears that he and his fellow monks spend too much time with spades or axes in their hands and too little time with their missals. (Indeed, apart from Scoggin, they look a muscular crew.) These boys, who currently serve as choristers, are oblates, for they have been offered by their parents to be educated. The Abbot wonders if the great lord might not consider making a donation to the work here.

Anthony is impatient and speaks directly to Scoggin, 'I am sent from the King to persuade you to return to his service. Since you have left the court, he has fallen into a great melancholy. You will be richly rewarded for your return.'

Anthony's thought is that, if he can persuade Scoggin to ride with him back to London, then he will kill him on the road.

But Scoggin replies, 'The King does not have it in his power to give me anything that I covet. When I danced and capered attendance at court I was like the lapdog and the harlot who used to get presents from the King, while poorer folk were turned away from his door. I have renounced my former profession, seeing that the world is made for weeping, not for joy. My trade was to mouth scandalous and shameful things. But now I, who was once the King's fool, am become God's fool. Laughter shall only be my reward in heaven. As Ecclesiasticus has it, "Let no corrupt communication proceed out of your mouth, but that which is good for the use of edifying, that it may minster grace unto the hearers". Mockery is a wicked thing.'

And now Scoggin looks sternly at the boys, before continuing, 'It is reported of Elijah: "And he went up from thence unto Bethel: and as he was going up by the way, there came forth little children out of the city, and mocked him, and said

unto him, 'Go up, thou bald head; go up, thou bald head.'
And he turned back, and looked on them, and cursed them in
the name of the Lord. And there came forth two she bears out
of the wood, and tare forty and two children of them".'

Anthony looks at the boys. They seem very solemn. They
are waiting for something.

Scoggin continues, 'Look at me. I have lost my teeth, my
hands tremble and I cannot leap about as I used to. You may
think that God cannot love such a one as me. I tell you He
can. Though I am in the winter of my years, I am once more
in love—in love with Him and the beauty of His Creation.'

He raises his arm in a preacher's gesture, 'I have heard of
a certain hermit who dwelt on the island of Patmos where he
devoted himself to prayer, fasting and all forms of pious aus-
terity, and in time, God noted this man's devotion and decided
that he should be rewarded. So He sent an emissary angel to
him and the angel spoke to the hermit and said, "Behold, the
Lord God has decreed that you should be rewarded for your
piety and I am commanded to offer you the choice between
the gift of beauty or that of stupidity." The hermit thought for
a long while and then spoke, "I choose stupidity." The angel
was astounded by his choice and said so. "Ah, but you see,"
said the hermit, "beauty fades." '

They all laugh, including Anthony. All of a sudden he is
suspicious and Scoggin, seeing this, shouts, 'Get him!' Two
men seize Anthony's arms. He manages to wrest his left arm
free and is reaching across for his sword when a member of
the Coterel family (and that is why the face seemed a little
familiar) knees him in the groin and then belts him across the
face. His left arm is seized again and pinioned against his back
and his sword is taken from him.

After the Coterel man has delivered a few more punches,
Scoggin forces some kisses on Anthony.

'The mouth of the spouse is the inspiration of Christ; the
kiss of the mouth is the love of that inspiration,' declares

Scoggin grandly. Hands on hips, he struts before Anthony and declares, 'You see how the wheel of fortune has turned. I am going to make you my wife. See boys, what a pretty wife I shall bed!'

'But not tonight,' insists the Coterel. 'Tonight we are looking at Philip.'

Scoggin shrugs and cups a hand to an ear.

'There is laughter in heaven,' he says. 'I think that I can hear the angels laughing now.' Then to Anthony, 'I shall see that you die laughing.'

Anthony's legs and arms are tightly bound with thick ropes before he is dragged to the brewhouse and locked in.

Night has fallen and it is late, when Anthony hears scuffling outside the brewhouse. He tenses himself for what may be coming. The lock turns, the door opens and a candle advances into the darkness. Five of the boys crowd into the brewhouse. Two of them have kitchen knives.

'You are our only chance,' whispers one of them. Two of the others set to cutting Anthony's bonds. Then he is handed his sword, belt and scabbard.

'We must rescue Philip.'

The boys lead Anthony to the church. Inside it is brightly lit. The boy is seated naked on the altar and clutches a rose. He is terrified. The monks sit on stools just below the altar and gaze intently at him. Anthony cuts down one of the monks before he can rise from his stool. It is not a fair fight for only Anthony and the boys are armed. The monks all try to flee. Anthony picks out Coterel and hacks him to the ground. The other monks all rush out through the door, though one of them is severely wounded by a boy with a knife. Outside Anthony gives chase. If Scoggin can no longer caper, still less can he run and he is soon caught. The others make their escape.

'They used to beat us and then cuddle us.'

'I preferred the beating to the cuddling.'

'They said they were preparing us for a special sacrament.'

'They called us girls and gave us girls' names.'

It is Scoggin's turn to spend time in the brewhouse. In the morning, he is brought out and hoisted onto the back of Black Saladin. The horse is led into the orchard and a rope brought down from one of the branches of an apple tree and a noose placed round Scoggin's neck.

Scoggin cries out, 'Spare my life, my lord, and I will tell you a story that will amaze you.'

Anthony snorts and slaps the flank of the horse to get it to move forward. He has had no practice in tying a hangman's noose and Scoggin's death is a slow one. He wheezes, chokes and spins. Finally Anthony has to step forward and pull at the legs. At last the jester's neck snaps and then his head comes off.

On an impulse Anthony finds a bag and puts the head in it. He thinks that he will find a place for it in the Museum of Skulls.

As he rides back to London, he reflects that it is right that death should be the penalty for murder, treason or false coining. But can it be right that death is the penalty that every one of us must ultimately face?

CHAPTER SIXTEEN

Compostella

Edward is a little sad to hear of Scoggin's death. 'I have missed his witty quips.'

Not only is the King sad. He also does not look well. By now he is florid and horribly overweight. And Anthony has added to his worries. Although the monastery at Pirbright was not a true Cistercian monastery at all, but an unlicensed imposture, the Archbishop of Canterbury fears that the killing of false monks may in some way set a precedent for the killing of real monks in the future. Then a more serious concern is that the Coterels will seek vengeance against Anthony. Edward proposes to send his officers into Southwark to end the reign of the gang there. But that campaign will take time to organise and in any case it is likely that a few will escape and remain at large for a while. Edward suggests that it might be better after all if Anthony went abroad until things had settled down.

Anthony's departure is delayed by his mother's funeral. He is escorted to the churchyard of St Andrew-by-the-Wardrobe at Castle Baynard by Amyas and Hugh and a dozen knights, watchful lest the Coterels should mount an ambush. There is a detachment of royal archers with Edward and Elizabeth. Gloucester and Clarence also arrive with small retinues.

Ripley, who had been with Jacquetta in her last hours, is already beside her grave. He has difficulty in standing upright and must be drunk. A white dog sits beside him. Ripley keeps glancing at it and then looking around in every direction. Who or what is he afraid of? Does he fear that Jacquetta will claw her way out of the coffin and rise from the grave to reclaim her spells? In the last few days Ripley has been diligent in spreading the story of Anthony's confrontation with the Pirbright Horror. The story is that every night Black Masses were celebrated there by unfrocked priests who substituted urine for the wine and a black turnip for the host. These devil worshippers went about the countryside kidnapping boys, and as soon as one of these boys had his throat slit on the altar, the horned demon Baphomet descended and graciously presented his arse to be kissed by the devil worshippers. But Anthony burst in on their dark conventicle and slew them all, and seeing this Baphomet soared shrieking into the air and was soon seen to shrink to the size of a gnat.

It is hard to concentrate on the funeral rites. A high wind shakes the branches of the yew trees in the churchyard and summons up dust devils in front of the church's door. Just outside the churchyard there seem to be small children hiding in the bushes and whispering. As the service proceeds, curious citizens gather to watch the interment. Though they are mostly shopkeepers and suchlike, there is one lady, dressed from head to foot in crimson, who looks as though she may be of noble birth. When Clarence notices Ripley's presence, he pleads with Edward to have the alchemist sent away, but Edward refuses. Ripley pulls a face at Clarence before staggering over to Anthony. He points at the chain round Anthony's neck on which the manikin hangs. Then he tugs hard at it, saying as he does so, 'The charm dies with its enchantress. This will no longer protect you. It is a useless piece of lead.' The chain snaps and Ripley throws the manikin into the open grave.

'He will belong to her.'

A moment later, the pallbearers bring Jacquetta's shrouded corpse to the grave's edge. They are lowering her into the grave when Ripley drunkenly stumbles against one of the pallbearers, and then as Ripley seeks to recover his balance, the dog is knocked into the grave. One of the pallbearers leaps in and pulls out the dog which is sent on its way by some hard kicks. It disappears into the crowd. The whole business is most unseemly and Elizabeth is distressed. However there will be a second, more formal interment when Jacquetta's effigy has been carved. Just before leaving the churchyard, Edward walks over to Ripley and tells him that he is dismissed from royal service.

Anthony, looking at his sister, sees that her beauty is fading fast and the lure of that beauty was only a magical semblance given to her by her mother. Only Clarence is delighted by what has happened here today and he is fool enough to show it.

So then, subject and thrall to the storms of fortune and perplexed by adversities, Anthony ships from Southampton. From Bordeaux he will travel by land to Venice and then sail to Jaffa and make his way on to Jerusalem. And he will travel further, for he thinks that there is nothing to draw him back to England. Now he should feel safe and yet he does not, for he feels that someone is watching him. Is it possible that he has been shadowed by a member of the Coterel gang? Now that he is bound at last for Jerusalem, he should feel cheerful and yet he does not, for it seems to him that death is his only regular visitor. Ever since he was a child he has thought that there is a queue for dying and that his father and mother were well ahead of him in that queue, but now that they are both dead, he feels that he has moved up among those who wait and he will not have to wait for much longer. Also, though the manikin that used to hang around his neck never spoke a word, in some odd way he was company to Anthony.

As Anthony stands on the forecastle, looking towards France, he becomes aware that he has been joined by a swarthy, bearded man. Anthony's hand slips down to his dagger, but when the man introduces himself it is plain from his accent that he has not come from Southwark. He is a Gascon, Louys de Bretaylles, and he reminds Anthony that they have met briefly when Anthony was in The Hague and Louys was in the retinue of the Great Bastard. Louys says that he will travel on from Bordeaux to Genoa and there he will find another ship that will take him on to Alexandria where he has business, trading in precious stones. Anthony becomes excited as he discovers that Louys knows the Orient well, for he has twice been as far east as Tabriz and he has talked there with merchants and ambassadors who have come from such places as Cathay and Serandib.

Yet Louys' report is discouraging. Though he has been in Jerusalem for the good of his soul, he has seen that Palestine is a wasteland, cursed by God for providing a place for the crucifixion of His Son. It is a fly-blown, sweaty, dusty land governed by corrupt Mameluke officers and plagued by marauding Bedouin. The Dead Sea is as hideous as its name suggests and on its shores are the ten accursed cities of ash, among which Chorazin is the most notable, for it is there that Satan will meet with his disciples. And there is nothing marvellous further to the east, but only deserts, beggars, snakes and taxmen who raise revenue through torture. One can travel for months across great empires where nothing happens and Cathay in particular is an empire of tedium. There is no such thing as the vegetable lamb, but in India they use women as firewood. The only sports that Orientals know are founded upon cruelty. At best the oriental landscape has a malign beauty which will sap the soul of any Christian. An Englishman or a Frenchman will soon weary of the relentless sun and endless blue skies and find himself longing for the clouds and rain of his native land. The supposed marvels of the Orient are no better than fairy stories.

'England is the true land of marvels!' says Louys. 'Take pride in what you have, my lord: the dragon of Wantley, the tomb of Arthur at Glastonbury, the Wild Hunt, Stonehenge,

Weland's forge, the miracle-working shrine of Thomas Becket, the Welsh goblins, the replica of Jesus' house in Nazareth which was built from a vision at Walsingham, the lost Kingdom of Lyonesse, Bran's head under the Tower, the invisible battle of Camberley, St Peter's candles, the phantom bulldog of the Fens, the chastity hedge of Kynisburga, the Devil's Tower of Marston Moretaine, the warlocks of Leicester. And are not the oak and the ash, and the rose and the daisy marvels too? There is no end to England's marvels and I am sorry to bid it farewell.'

Yet Anthony is not so easily dissuaded and he says that he still thinks that he will go to Jerusalem and walk where Jesus walked. Then Louys, who has noted the heaviness of Anthony's way of speaking as well as the sombreness of his garb, presses the loan of a book on him. It is called *Les dits moraux des philosophes*. Louys says that in it Anthony will find much wisdom and words that give solace from such ancient philosophers as Solon, Pythagoras, Tac, Socrates, Sedechias, Plato and Salquinus.

Anthony takes it away to read in his cabin. From it he learns that 'Plato loved to be alone in lonely rural places. One could usually detect his presence through hearing him weep. When he wept, he could be heard two miles away in deserted rural districts'. This was quite interesting. But as for the supposed wisdom of the ancients, he finds nothing but tedious injunctions to virtue by ancient wiseacres and aphorisms that manage to be both platitudes and untrue. 'When a fool prospers, he becomes all the uglier for it.' 'A sage is not obstinate and a fool is not just.' 'He who is ashamed of people, but not of himself regards himself as completely worthless.' And there is more of such stuff. Why are wisdom and virtue always so boring? Yet when he returns the book to Louys, he is polite about it and by the time they have disembarked at Bordeaux, they have decided to travel together for part of the way, since

Louys is heading for Genoa while Anthony is still set on travelling to Venice.

They purchase horses in Bordeaux. A day out of the town they stop to rest their horses and drink from a fast-running stream. As Anthony kneels to do so, he sees himself reflected in the stream twice. That is he sees himself both kneeling at the stream and standing behind his kneeling self. His first instinct is to ask, 'Who are you?' but that would be foolish, for it is obvious that he is looking on himself, only perhaps a little younger and fresher faced. His double, who is dressed from head to toe in white, smiles sadly at him.

So then Anthony asks, 'Where have you come from?'

The double gestures to Louys, who is gazing at him open-mouthed, and he signals to Louys that he should withdraw a distance so as to allow a private conversation. Only when Louys has done so does the double reply, 'I was lately in the stories of the Austin Friar, George Ripley, but I am escaped from them.' The double sits down beside Anthony and comfortably wraps his arms around his knees and he continues, 'I am come to speak with you and admonish you to virtue, for I am more virtuous than you are, since I have resisted sexual temptation, witnessed the shining of the Grail and faced down the draug. Whereas you have done none of these things, but folk think that you have and so you ride about reflected in my glory.'

Anthony is about to protest, but the double raises a hand.

'When John of Gaunt lay dying, he summoned the young King Richard to him and displayed to him his rotting and stinking genitals, as he hoped thereby to warn the King of the penalty of lust. In a similar manner I am come to you as a warner and to list your sins which are many and heinous. As Jeremiah has it, "The heart is deceitful above all things, and desperately wicked: who can know it?" Your sins are as follows. First, you betrayed King Henry whom you had sworn to serve and you went on to fight against his armies. Secondly, you defiled many churches by coupling with your wife in them. Thirdly, you led Beth to madness by attempting sex within a demonic pentacle. Fourthly, you left her neglected in a nunnery and rarely troubled to visit her in her sickness and sorrow. Fifthly, you murdered a man in Southwark. Sixthly, you partook of a goose while it was still living, which was a most cruel thing to do. Seventhly, you colluded in the murder of poor King Henry. Eighthly, when you hung Scoggin without a trial, that was murder too. Ninthly, you have regularly treated the poor and the crippled with contempt. Tenthly, you have made no attempt to curb your sister's greed and extravagance. Also you consorted with the cruel torturer John Tiptoft and the bandit Thomas Malory. And there is worse. You have mutilated many horses, created warfare between Britain and Ireland and murdered your own sister's baby boy.'

'But that was in a story!'

'And so you believe that you may behave how you like in a story? Your quibble is useless. Reflect on your crimes and sins. There is also jousting, though that may be accounted a venial sin, but as for the rest, how is it possible that you can think that you may escape the flames of Hell? As Jeremiah has it, "The harvest is past, the summer is ended, and we are not saved".'

Anthony cannot bear to look at his double.

'You are a phantom of my brain,' he says dully.

'I believe not. If I am anyone's phantom, I am that of Ripley.'

'Did Ripley send you?'

'No. I am no longer his slave, nor am I his friend. He too is in danger of eternal damnation, for he is a thief who steals from other men's stories and he has also been making away with your mother's spells. When I am returned from the East, I will deal with him.'

'You will travel to the Orient?'

'I will make our pilgrimage to Jerusalem. Now, after we have prayed together, I shall take my leave and travel on to the Holy City where I will pray again for your soul and because of this, you need not travel so far yourself. I suggest that you make your pilgrimage to some other holy shrine that is closer to reach. Santiago de Compostella is only a few weeks journey away from here. You must try to become worthy of the stories that are told about you and learn to be ashamed of what you have really done.'

By the time Anthony has finished his prayers his bright shadow has departed.

Louys is puzzled and suspicious, 'Who was that?'

'That was my brother, Robert.'

'How did he find you here?'

'Oh that was simple chance. He had business in the region.'

'That was a mighty strange chance that two English brothers should encounter one another on a lonely road in the province of Guyenne. That is a chance that runs quite contrary to nature. This meeting must have been made by witchcraft.'

But Anthony will not be drawn any further on the subject of his 'brother'. Instead, as they ride on, he tells Louys that his plans have changed and that, now he has thought about it, he sees that Louys is right after all and it would be a great waste to spend so many years travelling to Jerusalem and further eastern parts. Instead, he will turn south and cross into Spain and make his way to Santiago de Compostella.

After that he has little to say to Louys for the rest of that day, as he broods on the encounter he has just had. What a strange thing it is to discover that you are not the hero of your own story, as you thought, but its villain, just as Malory had hinted. He thinks, of course, that he should repent, but then he thinks that it might be dishonourable to repent from fear of eternal damnation. Would it not show more courage and honour to stand fast on the Devil's side? Surely God will not respect contrition that has been expressed only in the hope of

gaining Paradise and avoiding the flames of Hell? Ought there
to be room in Heaven for cowards? Now Anthony remembers
how Tiptoft described Hell to the Talking Head. There is a
great lake of fire which burns with brimstone and everywhere
a great stench. Scaly monsters with sharp-toothed mouths in
their bellies, arms and legs, are Hell's gaolers. Those who are
condemned can only shit through their mouths. What awaits
sinners is an eternity of suffering for what is by comparison
only a few years of human wickedness. Then Anthony wonders at the fact that those who are cast into Hell will be tormented by hideous monsters who delight in evil. Surely the
chastisement of sinners should be carried out by God's angels?
Then he thinks that it is likely that after a few hundred years
of torture he will forget why it is that he is being so tormented.
Or is it one of the tasks of the monsters to remind him of his
crimes as they bite and maul him? Then, is not Hell too grand
and awesome a place for the little that he has done? He is too
small to endure eternity.

As a Gascon, Louys knows the region pretty well and in
a tavern that night he gives Anthony all the details of the pil-
grim route to Santiago. Anthony must pass through Saint-
Pierre-du Mont and Saint Sever and then cross into Spain via
the pass at Roncevalles before turning west towards Santiago
de Compostella. And now Louys relates the story of Roland
and Oliver and the stand they made against the Moors at
Roncevalles.

For seven long years the Emperor Charlemagne has been
waging war against the Saracens of Spain. Then the pagan lord
of the Saracens, Marsilion offers a peace treaty. Only Charlemagne's dauntless nephew Roland is against the proposal.
After he and Ganelon, who is Roland's stepfather and leader
of the appeasers, clash in the imperial council, Roland nomi-
nates Ganelon to go on a dangerous mission to negotiate with
Marsilion and Ganelon takes this as an insult. 'This is a plot
to get rid of me!' He swears to himself that he will be avenged.

Then he goes to Marsilion and treacherously arranges for the rearguard of the French army to be ambushed as it crosses over the Pyrenees. When he returns to Charlemagne, Ganelon arranges for Roland to be in charge of that rearguard. As the rearguard makes its way through the pass at Roncevalles the Saracens attack. Roland and his deputy Oliver and the small force that they have with them are hopelessly outnumbered. Oliver urges Roland to blow upon the ivory horn known as the Olifant and so summon Charlemagne and the rest of the French army back to their rescue, but Roland refuses. 'God forbid that any living man should see me blow upon the horn from fear of the paynim.' Only when Roland is the last survivor and close to dying himself does he blow upon the horn. Charlemagne arrives too late to rescue Roland, but in time to wreak a bloody vengeance on the Saracens. Back at Aix-la-Chapelle, Ganelon is accused of treason, and after being defeated in trial by combat, he is executed. An archangel then reminds Charlemagne that he has more wars to fight against the Saracens. 'God!' says Charlemagne, 'how weary is my life!' He weeps and plucks his flowing white beard.

Naturally Louys takes pride in what is the French national epic. Anthony is not so sure what his own response should be. Should he really identify with the young, courageous and proud knight that is Roland and lament his valiant death? Or, since the double has shown Anthony to be a villain, should he not be on the side of villains in stories? In his imagination then he should stand shoulder to shoulder with Ganelon and Marsilion. After that Anthony wonders if, when he will return to England and read more from the pages of *Le Morte d'Arthur*, should he not be cheering Mordred and Morgan le Fay on. Or is it possible that, when such low and villainous folk as murderers and highwaymen listen to tales of King Arthur and the Fellowship of the Round Table, they take a perverse pleasure in the triumphs of Arthur, Lancelot and Galahad and enjoy fantasies of being virtuous paladins like them? Roland is young and heroic to the point of stupidity. Is it really heroic to allow treason to triumph? What is it that drives Roland, like Hagen in *The Saga of the Nibelungs*, to ride with all his men to his certain doom? Yet everything must happen as it does happen. While it is hard to pin down what Anthony feels about this story, in the end it is something very like foreboding.

Before Anthony retires for the night he begs Louys to be allowed to buy *Les dits moraux des philosophes* from him, but it is pressed upon him as a gift.

As he is drifting off to sleep, Anthony remembers the Abbot of Crowland's belief that the century in which Charlemagne was supposed to live never happened and Tiptoft's claim that Charlemagne was an imaginary character. So Roland, Oliver, Ganelon and Marsilion must be imaginary too. Then is it possible that he too is living in an imaginary century?

The following morning Anthony rides on alone. There is a monastery at the crest of the pass of Roncevalles and pilgrims lodge there. A few days later, Anthony passes into Galicia. Small low cottages huddle under oak and hazel trees. The meadows are studded with rocky outcrops. Now that Anthony has entered Spain, the rains begin and they hardly cease all the time he is in that region. As he gets closer to Santiago, he passes many people walking towards the city and a few are making their way there on hands and knees.

Once in Santiago he finds a hostelry, and having unsaddled his horse, he walks out into the street. His intention is to explore the city. It is of course raining. The street is crowded with Spanish and French pilgrims. But almost immediately he is stopped by someone whose native tongue is English.

'My lord do you not recognise me?'

The man is old with only a few wisps of hair on his head and he is deathly pale.

Anthony shakes his head apologetically.

'Then perhaps you will recognise my feet?'

Anthony looks down. The man is barefoot and his feet are filthy and a little bloody and some toes are missing.

He is sick with foreboding when he speaks again,

'You are the leper whose feet I am supposed to have washed.' As he says this, he thinks that it is one thing to have featured in a story in which he is described as having washed a leper's feet and quite another thing to have to wash them in reality.

'Yes, and I am grateful for that. I never did thank you.'

'I thought that you were an angel.'

'Do I look like an angel?'

'And do you now want me to wash your feet again?'

The leper thinks for a moment before replying, 'No, they would soon get dirty again in these filthy streets. But I have walked all the way here from Bilbao and I am tired. I want you to give me a ride to the Cathedral.'

Anthony starts to explain that his horse is unsaddled and stabled and needs to rest, but the leper cuts him short.

'No, you are the horse. I want to ride you piggy-back. I want you to take me to the Cathedral and then I want to see the rest of this city... I want to see the world, not just the little bit that the alchemist had determined should be my lot. You are thinking that you will not do this and that there is no reason for you to do this. But I tell you that you should accept my offer with gratitude, for your immortal soul is in peril of damnation and here I am offering you the chance to show true penitence. You may think of the weight of me on your back as the burden of your sins.'

So then Anthony submits and the leper joyfully shouts 'Gee up!' and they advance towards the Cathedral. Though they receive many curious looks, their partnership is not so very strange, for they overtake many heading the same route on hands and knees and some who support sick and paralytic pilgrims on their way to receive the blessing of Saint James and perhaps a cure for what ails them. But James is really a military sort of saint. True he led a peaceful enough life as an Apostle in Palestine until he was martyred by Herod Agrippa. But after James' death an unmanned ship brought his body to Spain and he was reverently entombed here in Santiago de Compostella. Since then the saint has made a point of turning up on a white charger at such battles as Clavijo, Coimbra and Las Navas de Tolosa in order to help the Christians to defeat the Moors—hence his name *Matamoros*, 'Moor Killer'. Anthony and his burden pass through the Gate of Glory. The interior of the Cathedral, with its sculpted scallop shells, golden columns, red hangings, together with lamps and candles in their hundreds and thousands, is magnificent. Anthony can imagine becoming a killer saint, one who gains in holiness with each battle he participates in. That would be a fine thing. Together he and the leper kneel in prayer.

Then all too soon he becomes a horse again and is driven by the leper through the narrow rain-swept streets. Sometimes in sport the leper claps his hands over Anthony's eyes. At other times, he stretches out his arms to beg from passers-by. Perhaps Anthony is in Hell. The cobbles are slippery and the mud in alleys that have not been cobbled is even worse and Anthony is often close to stumbling. Finally he does fall and in doing so pitches the leper into a stone gutter.

The leper sits howling in the rain. When at last he can bring himself to speak, he says, 'I do not like it here. I do not like the world you and your kind live in. It has too many hard edges and it is painful and it rains all the time and I keep needing to piss. I am going back to Corbenic and the story I was in. Though I wish Ripley had never thought of me. Why could he not have made me young, healthy and handsome? Why could I not be you? I hate Ripley.' And as an afterthought, he adds, 'And I hate you too.'

'But what about my penance? You were to be the burden of my sin.'

'Being the weight of your sins was less amusing than I

thought it would be. You must find your own salvation without my help. So now farewell.'

Anthony thankfully returns to the hostelry and changes into dry clothes. Then he starts to brood on this strange encounter. He thinks it possible that his double was really his guardian angel who chose to disguise himself as one of Ripley's fictions. That is much more plausible than an escapee from a story. Then the leper too could be the guardian angel in another disguise. Many people have described meeting their guardian angels. Though it is not usual, yet it is quite possible. Anthony feels comforted to have found a perfectly rational explanation for the recent strange meetings.

The following day Anthony visits the chapel which has one of the prepuces, or foreskins, of Christ as its holy relic. After Jesus was circumcised, his foreskin was carefully preserved and is guarded by the Pope in Rome, but there are other foreskins of Christ scattered all over Christendom, fourteen of them in all. Le Puy-en-Velay, Antwerp, Chartres, Stoke-on-Trent and Santiago de Compostella are among the places that display the prepuce to the devout. The multiplication of holy foreskins is a miracle and a blessing for mankind. Also, many churches have nail clippings of our Saviour among their relics, though, according to theologians of the Dominican Order, all the nail clippings of Jesus left this world and followed Him when He ascended up to Heaven and therefore the supposed holy nail clippings are no such thing. Anthony briefly wonders why the prepuces did not also follow Jesus to Heaven. But he is no theologian and he is content to kneel in devotion before the sacred relic.

Is there enough of Anthony's life left for him to work his way to salvation? Better yet, could he become a military saint and be canonised for having fought so many Saracens? Then he thinks of Henry of Lancaster. After he was discovered dead in the Tower and after he was displayed in Westminster Abbey, then his corpse was floated down to Chertsey Abbey, and even before Anthony had left England, Henry's grave had become an object of popular devotion and people said that he was a saint and one who in death had acquired healing powers. People went to Chertsey to be cured of madness, blindness, deafness, sweating sickness, plague, epilepsy, ruptures, battle wounds and heresies. The dead King also helped find lost property. Is it indeed possible that when Anthony was with Gloucester and Clarence in the Tower that he witnessed the martyrdom of a saint? But then Anthony impiously reflects that, if becoming a saint involves becoming someone like the weak and silly Henry, then the price is far too high. Anthony tries to concentrate on holiness. But then he starts to worry whether being handsome is a sin, for he has heard that Saint Bernard of Comminges used demons to punish women of excessive beauty.

As he wanders the streets of Compostella, Anthony slowly becomes aware that there are lots of Jews in the streets. Anthony had never seen a Jew before, since they are forbidden in England, and he is fascinated. Though he had thought of them as much the same as devil worshippers, now he looks on them they seem quite normal. Then just outside the walls of the city he comes across an encampment made by the Egyptians with their gaily coloured caravans. With a pang he realises that now he will never visit Cairo. His destiny is in England and after only a few days Santiago becomes wearisome to him and the rain even more so. He is sick for England. That is where he must find his salvation. He thinks that he will make penitential visits to Beth in her nunnery.

CHAPTER SEVENTEEN

Locus Amoenus

It is August when Anthony returns to the land of marvels. In these days to breathe is like drawing hot cinders into one's lungs. The sun's heat is boiling it all up—seeds, dust and butterflies are turning over and over in the sun's heat. The battle of the fields has begun. He rides past lines of men and women working to a rhythm as they take their fagging hooks and scythes to the corn. Behind them a line of stooping children and old women, the gleaners, follow. White wisps of cloud float across the blue. The land below is as if mostly painted yellow and brown. Dogs lie panting in the shade, unwilling even to pursue the hares that occasionally break from cover as the areas of upright corn shrink. It is hard to think that autumn will ever come and it is a relief when it is possible to ride through woods and find some coolness under the beech trees. How many more summers like this will he see?

When finally he arrives at the Woodville townhouse, he receives news of Beth's death in the nunnery a month and a half ago. She had turned her face to the wall and refused all food until she slipped into unconsciousness. Anthony has no time to reflect on this before he is summoned by the King to Westminster. Here there is more news. While Anthony has been in Spain Elizabeth has given birth to a second son and he has been christened Richard in honour of the Duke of Gloucester. On his way to Westminster Anthony recalls that the Talking Head had prophesied that Edward would be succeeded by a Richard. At the time Anthony had supposed that most likely this would be Richard of Gloucester. But now it seems much more probable that Richard's older brother, young Edward, will fall prey to some accident or illness and consequently the King's second son will succeed to the throne.

But of course he says none of this to the King. Edward is weary and lethargic and yet at the same time he is horribly restless.

'Last night I had a dream,' he wheezes. 'I dreamt that I was in a meadow and my crown was in front of me and I picked it up and put it on my head, but it was so heavy that it pushed me down into the ground. First, my legs sank into the soil, then the rest of me up to my chin, so that I was eyeing the grass around me, and finally the earth swallowed me up entirely. I awoke in terror, but then my wakeful days are just like that, for the business of state is heavy upon me. Now the Kingdom is at last at peace, I should be content and yet I am not. The truth is I miss the days of riding out to battle. I want adventures.' He pauses and reflects before continuing, 'And I miss Ripley. He did me good service in collecting intelligence and spreading good reports about my government, about your sister's beauty and goodness and about your own prowess in jousting and in battle. He made our lives seem more interesting than they really are.' And Edward repeats, 'I want adventures. But Westminster is all solemn rituals and London is the capital of dullness. All people do in that city is buy and sell things amongst one another.'

But then Anthony tells Edward how London had seemed to him in the days and nights when he and his father went riding through streets, hunting for the villainous redhead. Then London seemed a magical city, perhaps the capital of fairyland, and Anthony describes what he thought of as the enchanted garden that he and the huntsmen rode past several times. He recalls that he heard music and the laughter of women, but there was never time to stop. If he remembers rightly, the place was not far off Cheapside.

Edward does not reply immediately, but sits brooding. Then he brightens up.

'We shall go hunting again, you and I, and we will take along Hastings and we shall go on a quest for your garden... We shall all wear disguises! So I can throw off kingship for a while. There may be mystery and danger and perhaps I shall find out what my subjects really think of me. We will keep this secret from my wife and my wretched brothers.'

Edward finds Clarence too wild and unpredictable, while Richard, on the other hand, is somewhat solemn and pious, though he is hardworking and has taken on many of the administrative chores. Edward says that from henceforth he will rely increasingly on Anthony and Hastings (though Elizabeth has been nagging Edward, telling him that Hastings is a bad influence).

Only once the royal audience is over does Anthony have time to think again of Beth, and as he does so, it feels that there are a host of other dead who also clamour to be thought of: his father and his mother, Sir Andrew Trollope, the Earl of Wiltshire, Sir Thomas Malory, the Duke of Somerset, the Earl of Warwick, King Henry and his son, the Talking Head, the Earl of Pembroke, Scoggin, Fauconberg and countless knights and squires in a score of battles... And it is while he sits and tries to count them all that his steward brings him news that Raker has died.

Then Anthony thinks of the Museum of Skulls and how Tiptoft used to arrange the skulls and then rearrange them according to their crimes, their lineages and their dates of execution, but also according to the shapes of their skulls, their astrological death signs and the degree of their friendship with or hostility to Tiptoft. It was as if they were books that he was shelving in his mad library. He devoted himself to memorialising the dead. 'The dead long to be remembered. That is why there are ghosts.'

Tiptoft had told him the story of Simonides of Ceos, as it is related in Cicero's *De Oratore*: Simonides had been engaged to recite verses in praise of Scopas at a feast given by that man at Crannon in Thessaly. When Simonides had finished the recitation, Scopas told him that he was not satisfied with the recitation and that he was only going to give him half the stipulated sum of money. A little later, Simonides was called to the door to receive a message. Then, very shortly after he had left the hall, it collapsed crushing Scopas and all his guests to death and burying them in the ruins. When relatives and friends clawed through the ruins, they found that the remains were so mangled that identification of the corpses was impossible. But Simonides had such a precise memory of where everyone had sat that he was able to identify them all, so that each of the dead could be appropriately buried. So then he realised that in order to remember things one should set aside a section of the mind in order to provide a special location reserved for every single person or thing one wished to remember. Thus the order of spaces would preserve the order of ideas. Tiptoft said that this artificially constructed and ordered region of the mind was called a memory theatre and that it was now fashionable among Italian scholars and orators.

Anthony thinks that he may build a memory theatre where he will walk among the dead in their niches and commune with them. Black Saladin shall have a place of honour. Perhaps he should also put Ripley in one of the niches? For nobody knows what has become of him and it may be that he is dead too. There is a great store of sesame oil guarded in the Tower, since Ripley had planned to create a second Talking Head, but it now seems unlikely that the oil will ever be used for this.

Two evenings later, Anthony sits brooding, almost dozing, over the Abbot of Crowland's latest letter:

'My Lord, I do confess myself to be in some perturbation of spirit, since having spent so much of my life in questing after doubtful information concerning such marvellous and gigantic creatures as the dragons and giants of pre-Israelite times, I now wonder that I did so and presently consider even such majestic and colossal beasts as the elephant and dromedary to be vulgar curiosities and I have brought myself at last to see that the true marvels of this world are visible, under our feet and may be lifted up into our pockets and taken into our houses, for where is the man who will not be amazed after close consideration, of the Creator's ingenious fashioning of the bee, the gnat, the centipede and the ant? Consider the patient civility of the fly and that insect's tiny engine which allows it to soar freely above the ground and reach heights to which men, dromedaries and elephants may never aspire. Consider also the industrious commonwealths of the bees and ants, their amiable sociability and their perfectly conceived architecture. Truly the greatest things are hidden in little...'

Anthony is relieved to be rescued from this lecture by his steward who reports that there are two suspicious-looking men waiting for him in the courtyard. Anthony goes out and discovers that the two characters of unsavoury appearance are Edward and Hastings. They are gaudily dressed in costumes with bright patches and they carry sacks on their backs. They will not tell Anthony what they are disguised as, though they are obviously delighted with their secret identities. Anthony hastily dons his costume. He dresses as a pedlar and has a tray of ribbons suspended from his neck. Then they all set off in the direction of Cheapside where the search for the enchanted garden can begin. They try one side street after another. Anthony is sure that they are close to the place and that they must have passed it several times over, but no gate is open and he does not hear the laughter of women. Though nobody wants to buy Anthony's ribbons, the gaudy costumes of Edward and Hastings attract many curious looks from passers-by, and even if Edward was not so strangely costumed, his stature would command attention, for he is six feet three inches tall. Only slowly does Anthony become aware that Edward and Hastings are not so very interested in this particular garden. What they have set out on is a search for wenches. Anthony has unwittingly become an accomplice in the betrayal of his sister.

Of course he should withdraw from this mad enterprise. His double has already produced a long enough list of his crimes and sins. But then it occurs to him that his double was in no position to preach to him, for what did his double know of the real world? Unlike Anthony, his double had never fought in a battle, for Ripley did not have enough knowledge of warfare to invent a battle. Yet the evening is still a waste of time and Anthony does not want it to end with him sharing a whore with Edward and Hastings. He is about to make his excuses to Edward and tell him that he is going home, when he becomes aware that they have been approached by a young woman. If she is a whore, she is a very successful one, for she is richly dressed in a brocaded robe. She stands in front of Edward and Hastings and looks them up and down.

'Stop sirs. I have been sent out to look for men who have stories to tell. You two look as though you will serve. Will you come with me and spend an evening with us and tell us a story? We shall make it worth your while.'

This is just the strange sort of adventure that Edward had been hoping for and he instantly agrees, adding that he and his companion carry a story in their sacks. The three of them will follow where she leads.

'No, just you two. We do not want the pedlar. He does not look interesting.'

But Edward insists that the pedlar is his very good friend and must come with them. So then she looks at Anthony more closely and Anthony, suspicious of this woman, gazes back at her and is lost. She is a full-breasted, strawberry blonde with deep blue eyes to drown in, eyes that glow in the fading light, eyes that promise an infinity of mysterious pleasures.

Then, seeing how he gazes back at her, she laughs and says that he may come too and she gestures for them to follow her.

Suddenly Hastings has cold feet. He pulls at Edward's sleeve and whispers, 'Be careful my... This may be a trap.'

But she hears him and turns back and says, 'Of course it is a trap. It is a mantrap!' And she smiles. It is a wonderful smile.

She leads them back to Cheapside and then on to another street running northwards. She is so beautiful that Anthony does not care whether there is a trap or not. They come to a strange house. It is a tall pillared building, whose door has two ebony leaves, plated with what appears to be red gold. Anthony has never seen anything like it before. As they stand at the door, they can just hear from within the melancholy sound of a flute that seems to lament all the beauty of the world that is perishable. The young woman knocks and the door opens and Anthony looks at the woman who has opened it. She is very tall, almost as tall as Edward. She has flowing brown hair and is dressed in black satin. Anthony thinks that he has seen her before though he cannot think where. He also thinks that she seems to recognise him and Edward, though she says nothing.

Looking past her, Anthony sees that this is the place that he has dreamt of. The courtyard of the Woodville townhouse is cobbled and used for the saddling and unsaddling of horses, the reception of deliveries, the sawing and chopping of wood and suchlike useful things. But here the courtyard, which is large, has been turned into a garden and banks of flowers surround a pool on which a small boat floats. This garden is enclosed within a series of vaulted chambers and alcoves, within which are cushions and above which are birds in cages.

'Is Jane here yet?' the young woman asks of the guardian at the gate, who shakes her head.

'Then we are not ready yet and you must wait.' And she gestures that they should sit. It is a long wait and torches are brought out to supplement the light of the rising moon. After a while, the young woman, who is restless, signals to the

guardian at the gate who picks up a flute and then the young
woman begins to sing a plaintive song in an eerily high voice:

> 'Lully, lulley; lully lulley;
> The falcon has borne my love away.
>
> He bore him up, he bore him down;
> He bore him into an orchard brown.
>
> In the orchard there was a hall,
> That was hanged with purple and pall.
>
> And in that hall there was a bed;
> It was hanged with gold so red.
>
> And in that bed there was a knight,
> His wounds bleeding day and night.
>
> By that bedside there kneels a maid,
> And she weeps both night and day.
>
> And by that bedside there stands a stone,
> "Corpus Christi" written thereon.'

After that there is silence. At length another woman who must
be Jane enters the courtyard. She has a man with her. It is difficult to see much of his face under a broad-brimmed hat, but
he has long dark hair and a black beard and he is dressed like
a gentleman in a long black leather coat.

'He is the best that I could find,' she says apologetically.
Then to the men who are already there she says that she is
called Jane. The strawberry blonde says she is Mary. Finally
the lady who had been guarding the gate speaks, 'I am known
as Dame Discipline de la Chevalerie.'

Though Edward and Hastings are amused by the lady's self-description, Anthony is suddenly cold with fear.

'Oh God, now we are lost,' he mutters to himself and Edward looks puzzled.

An encounter with yet another of Ripley's inventions bodes no good. Besides, Anthony is sure that he has seen this woman quite recently, but where?

Edward claims to be 'George', Hastings is 'Hugo' and Anthony is 'Poins'. The man who came in with Jane says that he is called John. He looks puzzled to be here, as well he might. Now Jane fetches wine and when everyone is served, Mary turns to 'George' and 'Hugo' and says that she wants one of them to tell the company a story. But Edward replies that he and his associate will tell a story together, for they are puppeteers and four hands will be needed to work all the figures in the story. Then he and Hastings produce their puppets from sacks, also a cloth screen, and they set their show up in one of the alcoves.

The cow Milky White has stopped giving milk. So Jack's mother sends Jack to town with the cow to sell it for a good price if he can. Jack and the cow lollop across the front of the alcove and promptly collide with one another and then the strings get tangled up. Though Edward and Hastings have evidently been rehearsing, they are still not skilled puppeteers and besides they are a little drunk. But their incompetent fumbling produces laughter rather than scorn. When at last Hastings has got the cow to sit, Edward brings on a crafty fellow who persuades Jack to exchange his cow for a handful of beans. Jack returns home to show his mother what he has got and his mother tells him that he is a fool. But no sooner has a bean fallen to the ground than a beanstalk shoots up, hitting Jack on the nose as it ascends. Jack's climb is managed with difficulty and on the top leaf of the beanstalk the profile of a castle is unfolded. There Jack encounters a woman, who will turn out to be the giant's wife and she hides Jack. Now Hastings produces a giant puppet, over two feet high, and he intones the words:

> 'Fee, foh, fum,
> I smell the blood of an Englishman,
> Be he alive, or be he dead,
> I'll grind his bones to make my bread.'

The giant puppet crashes about, but of course fails to find Jack, who escapes with a goose that lays golden eggs. Roughly the same thing happens twice more as the giant's wife helps Jack steal a sum of money and then a magic harp. But on the third occasion the harp yells out to the giant that it is being stolen. The giant comes after Jack but he cuts down the beanstalk and beheads the giant. (Edward and Hastings are incapable of managing this last scene and it has to happen offstage.) So the story ends with Jack as lord of the giant's castle which has tumbled down to earth. Jane, who has been giggling throughout, goes to sit with Edward and Hastings and soon she is petting both of them.

John is the only one who is not at all amused.

'What was the point of this childish story?' he wants to know.

'It is a parable,' says Hastings. 'And it celebrates the triumph of youth against hoary age and it shows how a young man may climb socially to become a great lord.'

And Edward says, 'It is something to marvel at and it takes us back to our childhood, a blessed time. I could not endure a world without magic.'

Anthony says nothing, but he had been hoping that the giant would get Jack. Anthony is in his thirties and he is not inclined to support youth against age. The giant in the castle must be an aristocrat, whereas Jack is a nobody. On the other hand, it must be true that the giant who likes to eat

Englishmen would be a foreigner. But no, the giant should be supported, for besides being a jumped-up peasant, Jack is a thief and finally a murderer and Anthony guesses that he must have been an adulterer too. Otherwise the giant's wife would not have been so helpful. He has been watching a tragedy.

Now it is Anthony's turn, and since it seems appropriate for someone disguised as a pedlar, he chooses to tell the story of the Pedlar of Swaffham. When Anthony has finished, John seems once again discontented, but he says that he will bide his time. Then Edward challenges the ladies to tell a story.

So Mary tells a story from Arthurian times. She had it from her father who had it from a certain French book. So once again Anthony hears how Arthur and his knights were seated at a Pentecostal feast when a white hart pursued by hounds entered the hall and a bratchet bit the hart on the buttock, whereupon the hart leapt over a table and knocked over a knight. When the knight was on his feet again, he seized the bratchet and disappeared from the hall. Then a lady rode into the hall and demanded the return of her bratchet, but before she could receive any response an unknown knight came riding in after her and abducted her. Then on Merlin's advice Arthur sent Sir Gawain after the white hart, King Pellinore after the knight who abducted the lady and Sir Tor, who was King Pellinore's son, after the knight who stole away with the bratchet. It is the adventure of Sir Tor that Mary will tell.

So while Gawain and Pellinore took their ways, Sir Tor rode out on another track. He had not gone far before a dwarf stepped out onto the track and struck his horse such a blow on the head that it made the horse stagger.

'Why did you do that?' asked Sir Tor.

'Because all who ride this way must first joust with the knights in yonder pavilions.'

And Tor saw that there were two pavilions ahead of him, each with a shield hanging from a tree beside it and a lance leaning beside each shield.

'I have no time for this,' said Sir Tor. 'I may not tarry, for I am on a quest and I may not delay.'

'You are not going to pass,' said the dwarf and he blew upon a horn whereupon a knight emerged from one of the pavilions, leapt on his horse and grabbed his lance and shield and then bore down on Sir Tor, who scarcely had time to couch his lance. Nevertheless his lance hit the centre of the knight's shield and sent the knight flying over the horse's crupper. Then he dealt with a second knight in the same manner. He told the two knights that they must go and present themselves to Arthur as his prisoners.

Seeing how the recreant knights whom he had served had been so easily overthrown, the dwarf felt nothing but contempt for them and asked if he could become Sir Tor's servant instead. Sir Tor agreed and explained that he was on a quest for a knight who had stolen away with a white bratchet, whereupon the dwarf said that he could lead Sir Tor to that knight.

Then the dwarf led Sir Tor through the forest until they came to a Priory in front of which there were two pavilions. A red shield hung outside one of the pavilions and a white shield outside the other. Sir Tor dismounted and crept up to one of the pavilions and looked inside and saw three damsels asleep on rich couches. Then he looked in the second pavilion and saw a lady who was also asleep and beside her was the white bratchet. But the bratchet started up such a fierce barking that the lady awoke.

Sir Tor grabbed the bratchet and handed it to the dwarf. As he was remounting, the lady and the three damsels ran up to him.

'Knight, why do you take my bratchet from me?' asked the lady.

'It is not your bratchet and I have been sent from King Arthur's court to fetch it,' replied Sir Tor.

'You will be sorry for this,' said the lady.

'I shall bear quietly whatever adventure may befall me,' said Sir Tor.

He and the dwarf had not gone far before they heard the thunder of hooves behind them and they heard the voice of Sir Abelleus, the knight who had stolen away from Arthur's court with the bratchet. He was well armed at all points and demanded the dog's return, since it now belonged to his lady. Sir Tor made no reply but set his lance at rest and Sir Abelleus did the same and they rode against one another and crashed against one another so that they were both unhorsed. So then they drew their swords and rushed against one another like lions, striking so fiercely that their armour flew off them in fragments, like chips from a woodman's axe, and their hot blood ran down to the earth. Finally Sir Tor prevailed and he stood over Sir Abelleus with his sword at his throat.

'Yield now!' he cried.

'Never,' replied Sir Abelleus. 'Never while I live unless you return the bratchet to my lady.

'I will not, for it was my mission to bring the bratchet and a vanquished knight back to Arthur's court.'

At this moment a damsel on a palfrey appeared.

'Sir knight! Sir knight!' she cried. 'On your honour as a knight and for love of Arthur and the glory of his court grant me what I shall request.'

When Sir Abelleus saw the lady he started to tremble and rolled over on his side and started to crawl away.

'Well fair damsel, ask away and I shall give you whatever you request,' said Sir Tor.

'Gramercy,' said the damsel. 'What I want is the head of the false knight Sir Abelleus, for he is a vile murderer.'

'Now I am sorry for my promise and loath to do as I have promised,' said Sir Tor. 'Will you not settle for anything less from him?'

'No,' said the lady. 'For he slew my brother in front of me, even though I was on my knees in the mire for half an hour praying that he might spare my brother. He did not, but struck off his head.'

Now Sir Abelleus begged for mercy, but Sir Tor told him that he had missed his chance, and besides, the promise Sir Tor had given to the damsel was binding. Hearing this, Sir Abelleus started to crawl and then run, but Sir Tor caught up with him and smote off his head. So at the end of it all Sir Tor returned to Arthur, bringing with him the bratchet, the dwarf and the head of Sir Abelleus.

When Mary has finished this story, Edward complains that Arthur never seems to have any adventures in his own right, but his knights always have adventures for him. John declares it to be a silly story. He does not believe that Arthur and his knights ever existed, but if they did, they were no better than robbers stealing from one another and fighting over the spoils. As he sees it, Sir Abelleus was an unsuccessful murderer and Sir Tor a successful one. Though Anthony has had similar thoughts in the past, he now defends the story (since its teller is so beautiful and she took such pleasure in telling it). Anthony is joined in this by Jane and Dame Discipline de la Chevalerie, for they are angry at John's carping and his disparagement of romances.

Now Jane wants to tell her story. It is the story of 'The Laidley Worm of Bamburgh' and although it is probably simple enough, it is hard to follow as Jane insists on acting it out and getting convulsed with laughter as she does so. First, Jane is the princess and then she becomes the wicked stepmother who transforms the princess into a worm or dragon. As Jane transforms herself into a dragon, she writhes about and flaps her arms like wings while her hair flies all over the place and she makes 'Woo! Woo!' noises and then she forgets what happens next. But eventually she paces about the courtyard pretending to ravage it, but laughing as she does so. Next she is the handsome prince who kisses the dragon and finally she acts out the return of the princess to her original shape. She goes to sit with Edward who has loved her performance, but John says he does not like stories with magic in them, since then anything can happen. Stories should have rules.

'Now, it is your turn,' says Dame Discipline de la Chevalerie to John. 'And we shall see how you fare.'

'I do not like storytelling. I think it no better than lying,' says John. 'I am a merchant and I do not care to deal in romances, for they are stuff for idle women. Truth is always more interesting than fantasies about knights, wizards, dwarfs and damsels, I think. But I will first confess that I did once make a story up. My name is John Chapman and I come from Swaffham. It was I who invented the story of "The Pedlar of Swaffham" that you have heard Poins relate.'

'Are you really John Chapman?' asks Anthony, for here is a wonder indeed. 'I thought that Sir Thomas Malory might have made you up.'

'I am quite sure that I am not made up by this Thomas Malory,' replies Chapman and he chuckles, before continuing, 'It is I who have made something up, for it is I who put about that absurd story about having a dream about treasure to be found at London Bridge and there meeting a man who had a dream about treasure in my garden. You told the story very well, but it is still nonsense, for things like that do not happen—except in stories. I think that superstitious people like to see the hand of God in the careful arrangement of chance meetings and matching events, as He seeks to move the world that He has created all in one direction. But coincidences almost never happen, and when they do, they are a matter of pure chance, and as such, without any import. What is more, no man ever got rich by dreaming. I certainly did not.'

Anthony is outraged, 'But, if you do not like stories and you do not believe in coincidences or dreams, why then did you make up "The Pedlar of Swaffham" story?'

John Chapman taps his nose.

'I am a sharp man. I was making money very fast and I needed a story to explain how I had become so rich. So I told my neighbours that ridiculous story about the two dreams and I was surprised when in quite a short time that tale was being told all over England. People are so gullible. But how did I get so rich in so few years? That is the real story and you will be interested to hear it. I was never really a pedlar, but I started off trading in sarplers in a small way. I guess that you fine ladies will not know what a sarpler is. A sarpler is a quantity of wool, roughly enough to fill a large sack. I made contacts with traders across the Channel and started to sell most of my sarplers to a Spaniard based in Bruges. According to the law of England, all the wool sent overseas by the Staple—I should explain, ladies, that the Staple is the corporation of merchants who are licensed by royal charter to trade abroad in wool—according to the regulations of the Staple, all wool has to be sold in Calais where there is a fixed levy on the money made on the sale of each sarple. But though I sent my sarples of wool to Calais, I arranged for my Spaniard to send some of the money to London, thus avoiding the tax levied in Calais. I will be damned if I will have my hard-earned money being taken from me to support the extravagance of the court and the greed of the Woodvilles. Not only was I mostly paid in London, but I always exaggerated the weight of each sarple I sent to Calais. Then, lest the officials of the Staple discovered what I was up to, I produced a doctored account book in which the carefully adjusted figures served to explain the extra sums I was receiving in London. There is an art to rigging an account book. But that is the easy part and it is only the beginning...'

'That is also the end,' says Dame Discipline de la Chevalerie. 'I order you to leave this house now.'

Having curtly thanked the women for the wine, John Chapman hurries away.

'I wish I had not heard that. I liked the story of the two dreams much better,' says Anthony sadly and Mary agrees.

'I will have my men arrest him and he will end up in prison with his ears cut off,' says Edward, who is very angry.

'For not telling a proper story?' Mary is shocked.

'For cheating me of my revenue,' says Edward.

At this point, Dame Discipline de la Chevalerie explains to Jane and Mary that they have been entertaining the King, Lord Hastings and Earl Rivers. She has recognised them from the funeral of the Dowager Lady Rivers. So that was why she seemed so familiar to Anthony! She was the lady in crimson who stood on the edge of the mourners.

No sooner has Dame Discipline de la Chevalerie finished identifying the guests than her hand flies to her mouth.

'The dog! We have forgotten about the dog!' she cries. 'Fetch it Jane.'

Jane looks reluctant, but she does as she is told and soon she emerges from the main part of the house carrying a white bratchet which is barking furiously.

The dog is tied by a cord to one of the pillars of the court-yard, and once this is done, Dame Discipline de la Chevalerie sets about whipping it. She weeps as she does so and Jane and Mary also start to cry. For a while the men look on, silent and paralysed by deep mystery. Soon bloody welts appear on the back of the howling dog. At length Dame Discipline de la Chevalerie throws the whip away in despair.

'I have failed,' she cries and she unties the bratchet and picks her up, and heedless of the blood that is staining her dress, she cuddles the animal.

Suddenly Edward comes to a decision and he stands up.

'We have seen enough,' he says. 'The evening which began with so much merriment has turned dark and sour. We thank you for your hospitality, but we cannot endure it anymore.'

Edward seems to speak for all the guests, for they all rise

and make to follow him out of the courtyard. Jane asks to accompany the King.

'You are most welcome, Mistress Jane.'

'My full name is Jane Shore,' she says.

Mary is so shocked by what she has seen that she has difficulty in speaking, but she places her hand on Anthony's arm and says, 'Come, my lord.'

Anthony wants to follow Mary, for he senses that something horrible is about to happen. There is a gathering smell of death about the place, but yet he wants the mysteries of the house to be explained. The evening is an unfinished story. So he is slow to follow the others and at the gate he is stopped by Dame Discipline de la Chevalerie.

'You must stay,' she says. 'The owner of the house is coming soon and he has a surprise for you.'

Anthony shrugs.

Seeing that he is not going to follow them, Mary turns to Anthony, 'My name is Mary Fitzlewis and I presently lodge with my uncle in Westminster in Paternoster Square.' Then she follows the rest out of the courtyard.

So now Anthony is alone with Dame Discipline de la Chevalerie. She pours them out some more wine.

'It is better that Mary is gone, for she has a soft heart and I would not like her to be a witness to a man's execution.'

Coiling snakes of cloud drift across the face of the moon. It is still hot and Anthony fancies that it is the heat of the moon that is making him sweat. How will the night end? What has she planned? Anthony dares not ask for fear that he will hear something that displeases him. Instead he says, 'Nobody liked to see that poor dog whipped,' he says. 'Chapman better deserved that punishment. I believe that a man who has no faith in coincidences, in truth has no faith in God, for coincidences are God's way of stealthily working in the world. The Bible tells us: "There are many devices in a man's heart; nevertheless the counsel of the Lord, that shall stand".'

Dame Discipline de la Chevalerie says nothing, but sits looking at Anthony as she drinks.

Anthony tries again, 'What was the purpose of the gathering this evening?'

'Jane and Mary wanted men. As for myself, I wanted to know what it would be like to be outside stories and listening to them being told. Besides, storytelling would help to pass the time of waiting until the master came.'

'But why was the dog whipped?'

'Be patient. All will be explained.'

'What are we waiting for?'

'We are waiting for the coming of the master of the house. But enough questions. Be patient.'

After a while there is a faint knocking on the gate. Dame Discipline de la Chevalerie goes to open the gate. Anthony is suddenly alert, for he thinks that the master of the house has arrived. But no, it is a skinny-looking boy with tousled hair and freckles, and after a few whispered words with Dame Discipline de la Chevalerie, he goes to sit in a corner of the courtyard. The bratchet limps over to sit with him. The waiting continues.

At last the gate swings open and Ripley enters. Can he be master of the house? But then in the next instant Anthony sees that Ripley is being forced into the courtyard at swords' points and he recognises the two men who hold the swords. One is the man, who after the siege of London by Fauconberg, introduced himself to Anthony as Piers and the other is Anthony's double. Anthony notes that the double carries a sword that is identical to his own Galantine.

The double salutes Anthony ironically and says, 'You missed nothing by not going to Jerusalem. It is no longer a Christian place—if it ever was.'

'What happens now?' asks Ripley, yet he says this in such a manner as to suggest that he neither wants nor needs to know what happens next.

'You are going to release Jacquetta de St Pol's soul from the bratchet.'

'You are mistaken. Jacquetta de St Pol's soul is no longer in this world. The dog is just a dog. It has no soul.'

'I watched you at the funeral and saw you push the dog into the grave. That was a sorcerer's trick to trap the lady's soul. You thought that you could force the bratchet to lead you to fairyland.'

But Ripley insists that he is a scientist and no magician and what happened beside the grave was a pure accident. Dame Discipline de la Chevalerie replies that he is the supreme merchant of fictions and lies and she threatens to whip the lies out of him. Ripley makes the counter-proposal that she, Piers, the double and the boy in the corner should all re-enter his stories, as the leper has done. Once they are back in the stories, he guarantees that they will be well-treated. Yet Ripley's denials and promises are delivered without force or conviction. It is as if he is pretending to debate with her. While they are arguing, Piers has produced a bundle of ropes and sets about tying Ripley up in such a way that he is forced onto his knees in a painful position with his arms tied back to his legs.

With some difficulty Ripley turns to Anthony, 'Now you have met Mary Fitzlewis. She is of good lineage. She is the daughter and the sole heiress of Henry Fitzlewis of Horndon, Essex, and on her mother's side she is a granddaughter of Edmund Beaufort, Duke of Somerset. What is more, she will soon become your loving wife and later your grieving widow.'

Then seeing the look on Anthony's face, 'Why so surprised? You did not think that you were going to live forever, did you?'

(Strangely enough this was what Anthony had thought for most of his life.)

Ripley continues, 'Now, this is my last story. A man was walking down a street in Baghdad, when he noticed Death looking at him in a most curious fashion. Thinking that Death might have just singled him out as his next victim, he decided to flee Baghdad in all haste and go and hide in Samara. But when he arrived in Samara he found Death waiting for him there and Death said, "I was surprised to see you in Baghdad, since I knew that shortly we had an appointment to meet here in Samara". End of the story. Everything that happens here will happen in order to be put in a book and that book will be found in the Secret Library. You are going to watch what will happen here and do nothing. I know that. I should ask you to save me from my creations, yet I know that you will not and cannot help me. The Talking Head told me how my end shall be. As follows. She threatens to flog me, but she cannot force me to free Jacquetta de St Pol's soul from the dog, since it is not there. So then they will kill me. Once a man knows what fate the Talking Head has decreed for him, then there is no escape from it, no matter how he may try. I asked the Talking Head what your end would be…'

At this point Anthony should have covered his ears. But he does not think fast enough and he will regret this to his dying day, for Ripley continues tonelessly, 'Very shortly the King will appoint you as governor to Prince Edward and send you both out of London. You will be Prince Edward's guardian and tutor. Then, when the King dies, you will set out with the Prince to London where he should be crowned. But at Stony Stratford you will be intercepted by men in the service of the Duke of Gloucester and Lord Hastings, and after a few days you will be summarily executed. It has been all set out in a book in the Secret Library.'

'Now that you have told me this, I will do none of these things,' says Anthony. 'I will refuse the governorship of the Prince. I will not leave London. I will be on my guard against Gloucester and Hastings. I will do none of the things that have been foretold.'

'Yes, you will,' says Ripley calmly.

Again Dame Discipline de la Chevalerie is threatening to

flog Ripley in order to force him to release Jacquetta de St
Pol's soul. When he says that she is evil, Dame Discipline de la
Chevalerie replies, 'You made me so.'

Then a new debate begins when Anthony's phantom
brother declares that it is well known that, 'The enchantment
dies with the enchanter', for then there is the argument about
which of them must kill Ripley. Dame Discipline de la Chevalerie declares that the double should use his sword to cut
the man's head off, but the double replies that he is unable to
do this, since he has been made perfectly virtuous, and Piers
in his turn asserts that there is nothing in his character that
would allow him to commit a murder. It will have to be Dame
Discipline de la Chevalerie who does the deed. Or, no, let it
be Anthony. He has so many crimes on his conscience that
one more will not matter. Besides, Jacquetta de St Pol was his
mother...

Ripley is impatient, 'Let it be done quickly is all that I ask.'

And then a loud gravelly voice breaks in, 'I must kill him.'

And turning, they all see that the boy is no longer a boy,
but more like a man, and his head, torso, arms and legs are
swelling at different speeds, so that his body seems to billow
out, his skin has turned blue and there is a stench about him.
The draug continues, 'He made me a monster and a monster
I shall be.'

He now towers over everybody in the courtyard. The
draug lumbers towards Ripley, and as he begins to lower himself onto the terrified alchemist, Anthony, who can bear no
more, runs to the gate. As he fumbles with the bolts of the
gate, he hears cracking sounds which he guesses to be from
the breaking of Ripley's ribs under the weight of the draug.
So then Anthony, having escaped from the place that he had
thought of as a garden of enchantment, runs towards Cheapside.

CHAPTER EIGHTEEN

Ludlow

Anthony and Edward Duke of York are standing at the battlements on the corner of the north tower of Ludlow Castle. They look out on the inner bailey, the chapel, kitchen and gatehouse. It has been a hard winter and it is snowing again and the drovers who are leading cattle into the castle to be slaughtered trudge with their heads down against the driving snow-laden wind. Horses are being taken out in the other direction to be exercised and though they stamp their feet and the grooms around them seem to be shouting, it is eerily peaceful above, for the snow deadens all sounds. Anthony has brought the young prince up here in the hope that this may clear their heads after a philosophical wrangle that has been going on all morning and much of the afternoon. Soon, too soon, the dark will come. Anthony points to the ravens that seem to dance around the column of smoke that rises from the great kitchen. Their gronking sound can only just be heard.

'I think that ravens are as intelligent as men are,' he says. 'I have seen them gather on the eve of the battle, for they guess that there will be food for them on the morrow. I have seen them again after the battle, when they generally go first for the eyes of the slain. Do you remember the story I told you, the story of Bran and Branwen?'

Edward nods.

'Well, Bran is Welsh for raven.'

But Edward is not to be distracted.

'If I want to drop this snowball into the courtyard, I can.

See? I have free will.' And with that he drops the snowball
into the courtyard. 'No one made me do this. I did it because
I wanted to.'

If only that were true. Anthony sighs. The morning had
begun with a tussle in the classroom over a difficult passage in
St Augustine in his reply to Simplicianus, the bishop of Milan:
'To solve the question, I had previously tried hard to uphold
the freedom of choice of the human will; but the Grace of God
had the upper hand. There was no way out but to conclude
that the Apostle Paul must be understood to have said the
most obvious truth, when he said: "Who has made you different? What have you got that you did not first receive? If you
have received all this, why glory in it as if you had not been
given it?" '

It seems to Anthony, that though this must be correct, it
contradicts our lived experience, for we believe that we are
free and act as if this is so. Also he thinks that it is much
easier for a man of years to accept the deterministic doctrine
of Augustine and Aquinas than it is for a youth to do so. The
prince has most of his life before him and it shimmers with
dizzy uncertainties and possibilities—of so many summers,
dances, hunts, fights and the first love to come. It must feel as
if fate will have no chance against the fierce energy of youth.
But his years will still slip through his hands as Anthony's
have done.

Up on the battlements, Anthony tries again, 'Let me put
it another way. In order for you to make a choice, you must
in the first place have chosen to have the sort of personality
that can make choices, but in order to have chosen that sort of
personality that can choose to make choices, you must previously have chosen for this to be so… And so we go back to the
beginning of time without ever discovering the root of your
alleged freedom. You look puzzled. Let me try again. You can
do what you will, but you cannot will what you will. In a way,
man's condition is somewhat similar to a dog's, for though a

dog can think, it cannot think that it thinks. Just so, you cannot will what you will.'

But Anthony can never persuade the Prince, for of course, the abstract philosophical debate masks a more particular clash of wills. Of late, Edward has begun to challenge the burden of the stories that Anthony tells, and in particular, the Prince rejects what he sees as Anthony's cult of doomed heroes— Merlin, Hagen, Roland, Arthur, all men who advanced knowingly towards their deaths, not to mention Jesus Christ and the legion of martyred saints who came after Him. Edward has declared that Roland deserved no fame at all, for he was determined to lose and determined that he and all the men with him should be killed by the Saracens. He ought to have blown his horn to fetch up reinforcements much sooner. When Edward is King, he will seek only victories.

And behind the Prince's rejection of heroic fatalism, or craven fatalism as he thinks of it, there is a more personal issue at stake. The boy's father is dying.

Anthony has tried to keep the news from him but everyone in Ludlow knows that the King has taken to his bed. Though he is only forty, his monstrous appetite for food and drink have taken their toll and he has an intermittent sweating sickness and he breathes with difficulty. Anthony's own physician believes that the King has quartan fever. His son, who is only twelve and yet so intelligent, studious and hitherto obedient, is ceasing to be tractable, for he is desperate to see his father. He has already attempted to run away to Westminster, but the snow made riding difficult and he was intercepted by Anthony's men before he reached Ludford Bridge. Anthony is waiting on letters from the Privy Council before escorting the Prince to Westminster. But it seems that they do not want the Prince to be present at his father's deathbed. The Prince, who looks glum, mumbles something inarticulate before descending the tower.

Now Anthony is alone, he thinks back to the day he looked

down from the White Tower on the army of Fauconberg and beyond to the farmsteads. Then he, like young Edward, thought that there were many possible roads to follow. So many years on he sees that there is only one and he wonders what will the world look like after he is gone? He has enjoyed acting as the prince's surrogate father and teaching him all that he can. If only the King could hang on for a few more years or even a few more months...

Anthony knows that he has not won the debate with the boy, for his argument about having to will to will to will to be free and so on and on in an infinite regression must have sounded like mere sophistry. He should have tried some more ordinary argument, for over the years Anthony has learnt that he is not responsible for his actions, since he is made by his sex and lineage, as well as his rank, the commands of his King, the expectations of his peers and the code of chivalric honour. Almost ten years ago, when the King had announced that he was going to make him Governor to the Prince, Anthony had tried to refuse this office of honour that yet would lead to his certain death, but the King was adamant and besides Anthony thought that it would have been one thing to defy the King, but another to seek to thwart what God has decreed.

Later that day, Anthony escapes from both Ludlow and the winter by entering the memory theatre that is lodged in his head. Tiptoft, who had instructed him in the art of constructing such a theatre, had emphasised the need for all the things or people one wanted to remember to be brightly lit. Consequently it is always a cloudless summer's day in Anthony's theatre. But though Tiptoft had sought to draw a picture for Anthony of some great circular edifice with tiers and niches in a vaguely Italianate manner and lit by a myriad of torches, this meant little to Anthony and instead he uses the Tower of London to store the people that he wishes to remember. The Tower of Memory is not like the real Tower with all that bustle and noise of guards, draymen and croaking ravens.

Instead the Tower of Memory is deathly quiet. It is peopled with frozen figures, many of them have fixed imploring gestures, as if they were begging to be given life again. Tiptoft is naturally the presiding figure in this place and he stands at the entrance to the White Tower. He looks angry, as if annoyed to be once more in the Tower. He displays a pair of skulls from his Museum, since he had instructed Anthony to be sure to attach a distinctive object or two to each person he wishes to recall. Anthony walks over to Tower Green where Black Saladin stands with his head down, as if grazing, and trapped in the cloths he wore on the day of the joust with the Bastard of Burgundy.

But where are the people from his childhood? Did he have a nurse? Who first taught him to ride and handle a sword? How was he instructed in Latin? How did his mother look when she was younger? He finds it impossible to get back to before the day of the Battle of Palm Sunday. What was England like before all the battles? He must have had a childhood, yet he can hardly remember a single incident. Anthony crosses Tower Green, as in a trance, ignoring various courtiers and servants who are standing about, to find Beth posed at the foot of the Beauchamp Tower. She is naked and holds a mirror before her and Anthony joins her in admiring the beauty of her pale and flawless flesh. It is difficult to tear himself away. Mary hates these trances of his. As she has come to know her husband better, she has become alarmed at his preoccupation with those who have died before him. More particularly, she guesses that when he enters his strange castle of the mind, he goes there to visit Beth. Though she is right about this, Beth is frozen and can only be admired as a beautiful painting and Anthony knows that he needs the human comfort and warmth of Mary.

There is a cluster of figures standing in front of the Chapel of St Peter ad Vincula including Anthony's mother holding a tray of little lead figures, Scoggin with his pig's bladder and

Malory who holds a manuscript and a shield which displays his blazon. In front of the Wakefield Tower there is Ripley, who cradles the Talking Head and has an alembic at his feet. George Duke of Clarence is beside his enemy Ripley. He leans forward and rests his weight on the barrel of malmsey that was his death. Anthony reflects briefly on Ripley's failure to control his stories and he wonders whether the characters he created will outlive their creator or not, or is it indeed the case that, 'The enchantment dies with the enchanter?'

Clarence entered the memory theatre a little over five years ago. After the downfall and death of Warwick, Clarence felt himself cheated of most of the land that he should have inherited through his marriage to Isabel, Warwick's daughter. Clarence, embittered, retired to Warwick Castle. What then brought matters to a head was the death of Isabel followed by the judicial murder of Ankarete Twyniho, a former servant of Isabel. Clarence's retainers arrested Ankarete and a hasty trial was held at which she was accused of poisoning her mistress and Clarence stood over the jury to enforce their guilty verdict, whereupon she was hanged. Angered by this, Edward had Clarence's associates investigated and soon found evidence that Dr John Stacy a fellow of Merton College had been suborned by Clarence to practice sorcery aimed at bringing about the deaths of the King and Prince Edward. Clarence's supporters had also circulated prophecies that the King would shortly die. The hope was that the prophecies would be self-fulfilling, for when the King learned that he was imminently to die, the grief would kill him. When Clarence was foolish enough to protest the innocence of these traitors, he was arrested and sent to the Tower where a fortnight later, he was drowned in a butt of Malmsey, just as the Talking Head had foretold. It seems to Anthony that it is almost as if the Talking Head, by predicting such an improbable death, had actually made it happen. Soon Anthony supposes, he will have to induct King Edward to the theatre and perhaps then he will place him beside his wild and treacherous brother.

Finally Anthony walks over to the doorway of the Lanthorn Tower. There stands the Abbot of Crowland. He carries nothing but uses his hands in what must be a vain attempt to shield his eyes from a certain horror. Three years ago he received a letter dictated by the Abbot to his faithful Chronicler. The Abbot was most insistent that Anthony should take note of his recent strange experience. In it the Abbot related how he had lain in what he believed to be his deathbed and then indeed it did seem to the monks watching that the Abbot had actually passed away peacefully in his sleep. But the Abbot found that though he was no longer in the monastery's infirmary, he was fully conscious. Then he heard a voice saying, 'Follow the light' and he found himself floating up through a tunnel of light at the end of which he was greeted by kindly figures in white robes and he thought that he understood that they were to lead him to his kinsfolk and friends who were waiting for him. But in this he was mistaken for the men in white robes then cast off their white robes to reveal black robes and they passed their skeletal white hands over their faces until both the faces and the hands were entirely black. They were so utterly black that they stood before him as cowled black spaces in the white radiance. 'I am oblivion', said one. 'I am nothingness', said another. 'I am extinction', 'I am unbeing', 'I am emptiness', and 'I am a void', followed. And the black men merged to become a great black maw which was going to swallow the Abbot up. But then all of a sudden the Abbot found himself back on his bed in the infirmary where the monks were astonished to see that he had returned to life. The Abbot's letter concluded by asking Anthony to reflect on where a candle's flame goes when it is snuffed out. A week later, Anthony received another letter, this time jointly written by the Chronicler and infirmarian, informing him that the

Abbot, who in his last moments had a look of stark terror on his face, had indeed now died.

Two weeks after this visit to the Castle of Memory Anthony is in the classroom with the Prince. They have set aside an attempt to translate a difficult passage in Seneca's letters to St Paul and have turned with relief to a book in English. This is *The History of Jason* and it has been printed by William Caxton. When Anthony was last in London for a meeting of the Privy Council, he met with Caxton, who had abandoned his office in the Guild of Merchant Adventurers and he had fled abroad as a known supporter of the Earl of Warwick. When a few years later Caxton returned to England, he returned as a master of the German art of printing and he set up a shop inside the precincts of Westminster Abbey, next to the Chapter House. Anthony visited the shop and found Caxton to be a man after his own heart.

'Where is the custom and usage of chivalry that there was in the past?' Caxton demanded. 'What do men now do but go to the baths and play at dice? Alas, they are asleep and take their ease. How many knights are there now in England who know their horse, their armour and their harness? People ought to read about the knights of the past and their noble deeds, and having read about how things were done then, they should seek to emulate the past. There must be more jousting and feats of arms performed in our own time.'

Of course, the demand for printed books will always be limited since their stubby black letters are so ugly. Nevertheless, Caxton hopes that his productions may serve to preserve older values against the corruption of the age. The printing press will be a kind of engine for holding back time. Since Anthony approved all this, he commissioned the printing of copies of his translation of *The Dicts and Sayings of the Philosophers* to be used in the education of the Prince and other noble youths. Then Anthony had funded the printing of *The History of Jason*. He has also pressed on Caxton the manuscript of Malory's *Le Morte d'Arthur*. But Caxton is reluctant to take this work on, since the manuscript is very long and badly ordered, so that it will need much editing. But he will think about it.

Back to *The History of Jason*. The story of Jason and the Argonauts and their quest for the Golden Fleece is an exciting one. The Golden Fleece, which Anthony supposes is the Holy Grail of pre-Christian times, hangs on a tree in the Grove of Ares outside Colchis on the shore of the Black Sea. Anthony visualises the coal-black waves lapping the sides of the Argo. But before Jason and his fifty handpicked paladins of ancient chivalry can reach the Black Sea and Colchis, there are many adventures and ordeals: Jason's joust with Hercules at the court of Thebes, clashing rocks, the dangerously alluring water nymphs, the pestilential harpies, the six-handed Earth-born giants, the murderous royal boxer Amycus, the flock of bronze-winged birds and many other wonders and terrors. And at Colchis the royal sorceress Medea waits for Jason.

Edward was impatient to know what happened to Jason in the end, after he had gained the Golden Fleece, and Anthony had to tell him that Jason lived on to become an old man and was finally killed when a timber from the decaying wreck of the Argo fell on his head. Edward is disappointed and rightly so. How should this story have ended? How should stories ever end? Anthony finds the end of the centaur Chiron much sadder and yet more satisfying. As a boy, Jason had been educated by the learned and kindly Chiron. The centaur was skilled in almost all the arts and sciences and besides had the gift of prophecy. Though he was born immortal, after he was wounded by a poisoned arrow during the battle of Hercules against the centaurs, Chiron was in such constant pain that he prayed to the gods for the gift of immortality to be taken from him. So immortality was passed on to Prometheus and Chiron was allowed to die.

But it was while they were discussing the boring end of

Jason that a messenger burst into the classroom and knelt in homage before the boy. His father died on April 9th and it is now April 14th. Thus for some days now, without knowing it, young Edward has been King. Now at last the Privy Council summons Anthony and his charge to hasten to Westminster. But they must hasten slowly, for many men have to be summoned and many things need to be requisitioned before the new King can set out from Ludlow with his escort of 2,000 Welsh men-at-arms.

Of course Mary, who is proud and excited, wants to accompany them to Westminster, for she wants to witness young Edward's magnificent royal entry into London and then the coronation in Westminster, but Anthony, knowing how things will be, will not allow this. So he temporises and promises that she will be sent for as soon as the date of the coronation is fixed. She is surprised that the boy is not also excited about his coming coronation. Edward is weeping. Of course he mourns his father, but Anthony judges that Edward is sharper than Mary and that the boy guesses that something bad is about to happen. During the days of preparation Anthony takes care to be always busy and seen to be smiling. He must will the end.

It is only when they are at last mounted and ready to ride to London that Mary catches some of the boy's anxiety. She begs Anthony to take care, but Anthony reassures her that with an escort of 2,000 armed men they are hardly likely to be attacked by bandits on the road. But Edward has other fears and towards the end of the first day's riding, he cries out, 'I do not want to die! I am too young!' and he tries to turn his horse back towards Ludlow, but he is too closely hemmed in by his escort to succeed. Thereupon Anthony patiently tries to explain how things will be. There will be a royal entry into London and then a few days' or weeks' later the coronation will follow. Once they arrive in London Anthony must resign his role as Governor to the Prince and Richard of Gloucester will take over as Regent and Protector of the Realm, though the regency should not be overlong. Anthony tells the boy that Gloucester and Hastings served his late father most loyally and ably. They are honourable lords and doubtless Edward V will be well guided by them. Gloucester is certainly capable. The boy will become a great King. And before all that Edward will be reunited with his mother and his little brother Richard. Anthony says that, for his part, he will be glad to be soon shed of all responsibilities.

What Anthony does not say is that he feels that they all—Gloucester, Hastings, Buckingham, Essex, Stanley and himself—are part of a generation whose time is past. There are younger men who stand and wait or are even already pushing their way forward. The older lords will soon have to make way for them.

On the fifth day's riding as they approach Northampton, Anthony finds himself recalling fragments of an old tale that he heard from his mother when he was a child. He remembers that it was a frightening story. As the dark gathers two riders are passing through a wood. Who is riding so late through the dark and the wind? It is a father and his son. 'Boy why are you scared?' asks the father and the boy replies, 'Can you not see the Erl King with his crown and robe?' The father replies, 'It is only a cloud?' But the boy persists, 'Can you not hear the whispered promises of the Erl King?' 'That is the wind in the trees. Your mother and sisters will be pleased to see you.' 'Can you not see the Erl King's sisters? They want me for their husband.' 'I can only see the alder trees waving in the wind.' 'Help, father. The Erl King has me in his grip.' And when the father turns he sees that his son on the horse beside him is dead.

Anthony is roused from a dark reverie by one of his outriders who tells him that Richard of Gloucester and Henry Stafford, Duke of Buckingham, coming from the north, are also heading for the coronation in London. A few hours later,

Anthony receives a message from Gloucester which proposes a meeting at Stony Stratford so that they may dine together. At this point Anthony plays with the idea of refusing or stalling, and then withdrawing back to Ludlow? What then? But in effect, such a hostile gesture would amount to a declaration of civil war and he is outnumbered and during his retreat his Welsh archers would be picked off by Gloucester's northern horsemen. It is even possible that the new King could be killed in the fighting. At the same time it is unlikely that Elizabeth would be able to hold London against Hastings and other enemies of the Woodvilles. Having played with such fancies and then rejected them, he replies that he will be glad to join the noble lords for dinner at Stony Stratford. Then he kisses Edward's head in farewell.

So he meets Gloucester and Buckingham at Stony Stratford and they dine on quails and after some solemn deliberations about the expense of the forthcoming coronation, he and Buckingham become very merry as they refight old battles. Buckingham ends up declaring that now England is at peace it has no need of great lords such as themselves! Only Gloucester looks wey-faced and anxious and Anthony guesses that Gloucester is more afraid about what is going to happen than he is. As Anthony bids them a goodnight before leaving the hostelry's dining room, he reminds himself that though Gloucester and Buckingham believe that they have the advantage over him, all three of them have eaten of the living goose.

The following morning he finds himself under arrest and he is taken to Pontefract Castle where he is confined until it is decided to execute him without trial. While waiting for the end he finds time to write to Mary and then to compose a poem:

> Somewhat musing
> And more mourning
> In remembering

The unsteadfastness
Of this world,
What answer
To the riddle may I guess?

Willing to die,
Methinks truly
Bound am I
To be content,
Seeing plainly
Fortune does turn
All contrary to my intent.

My life was lent,
To what intent?
It is near spent,
So welcome Fate!
Though I never thought
Low to be brought,
Since she so planned
I take her hand.

On June 25th 1483 he is brought out from his cell and led to the block. His last thought is of Evnissyen and how that man had dealt with his sister's son. The axe falls and Anthony Woodville, second Earl Rivers, vanishes into history.

About the Author

Robert Irwin (born 1946) is a novelist, historian, critic and scholar. He is a Fellow of the Royal Society of Literature.

He is the author of seven novels: *The Arabian Nightmare*, *The Limits of Vision*, *The Mysteries of Algiers*, *Exquisite Corpse*, *Prayer Cushions of the Flesh*, *Satan Wants Me* and *Wonders Will Never Cease*.

All his novels have enjoyed substantial publicity and commercial success, although he is best known for *The Arabian Nightmare* (1983), which has been translated into twenty languages and is considered by many critics to be one of the greatest literary fantasy novels of the twentieth century.